THE
SECRET BOOKS
OF
PARADYS
3 & 4

TANITH LEE

THE
SECRET BOOKS
OF
PARADYS
3 & 4

The Book of the Dead
The Book of the Mad

Published by arrangement with
The Overlook Press
Lewis Hollow Road
Woodstock, New York 12498

Printed in the United States of America

CONTENTS

CONTENTS

THE
BOOK
OF THE
DEAD

Contents

Contents

LE LIVRE BLANC ET NOIR

Paradys too has its cemeteries, its little graveyards tucked out of sight, its greater yards of death that hug the churches, the cathedral that is called a Temple. It has its places of graves, between the houses in sudden alleys. Between the paving stones, here and there you may look down and see a name that paves the way, a date of beginning and the other of surcease. Even under the house floors now and then they will raise a carpet and a board and point you a grave: *Sylvie* sleeps here, or *Marcelin*. Paradys is a city of the dead as she is a city of the live, the half-live, the undead, and perhaps the deathless.

And here, on this hill, shrouded by the pretty park they have made where once the scholars bored out their eyes (but shells have burst there since), overlooking the coils of the river, is a great necropolis of Paradys.

And here I have brought you, on this windy, colorless grave-gray afternoon. To walk about, to look and see. If you wish.

We have come at an opportune moment, too. For over there, where you note that line of carriages going up, the funeral is taking place of Baubon the clown.

Baubon was immensely popular. To him of an evening, after their fancy suppers, went the women in spangles and pointed heels and the men in their capes, and white shirt fronts, like cats.

The hearse is huge, scrolled like an urn and hung with black drapes. The black horses labor beneath the black plumes and blacker tassels. No motor cars spoil the effect. Even the mourners have had to hire chariots.

Surprisingly, there are very few mourners (and no crowds rim the ground, held off by policemen). The chief mourner is a thin and white-haired man with the face of an elderly imp, enough like the mask of Baubon, publicly always seen in garish paint, to imply a brother or close cousin.

The black coffin, ebony with silver handles, is unloaded—an

enormous wreath of flowers balances white upon it—and the service begins.

Everyone stands in silence as the priest speaks over the black (blacker even than the horses) hole in the ground. He has a pompous theatrical look, and the boy swinging the censer so adoitly, why he might even be that favorite of Baubon's among the acrobats.

A few women weep a few crystal tears. They are the ones able to cry without help in the theater. The men stand solemn. There are three eulogies spoken perfectly over the hole. We are not near enough to catch all the words—Genius, Unique, Mourned, Never-to-Be-Emulated. Then the coffin is lowered into the space. Earth and flowers rain down. A white rose . . .

The celebrants shift from the grave in an exact ring, like circling black moths.

The chief mourner shakes the priest by the hand.

"Bravo, Jacques. It couldn't have been bettered. No, not at *The Tragedy* herself."

And the old imp strokes the censer boy.

A woman laughs.

"Take off the lid, then," says the brother of Baubon the clown.

Two men scramble carelessly into the grave and haul off the coffin top, flinging away the exquisite floral tributes.

In the coffin lies Baubon, in his patchwork and all his paint. As so many have seen him, laughing then, or crying, turning enormous cartwheels, falling from high towers.

"Lid back on," cries the brother of Baubon gaily. "That's enough. No respect."

And there is much amusement, back goes the lid, and the flowers are slung on any how.

Two gravediggers approach, and start to shovel in the black, moist soil.

"Are you satisfied, Baubon?"

"*Quite* satisfied."

"When we do it in reality, will you be watching then, Baubon?"

"Who knows? That's why I had my funeral now, to be sure."

Baubon *is* the imp. The priest an actor from the Comedy Theatre. The boy is . . . the boy.

Staged, the funeral. And now the grave almost filled in. The black chariots roister away to some great restaurant where they will hold the wake of Baubon the clown and chief mourner.

In five years, or ten, or more (or less), they will come again to do this thing. Then the crowds *will* press at the fences and the police-men hold them off. Then perhaps some of the tears will be real, and the single white rose, if it falls, will not give its life for nothing, only a game. Or is it a game? Is the real funeral *not* to be a game?

And *will* Baubon watch then, as today?

Perhaps the dead are always watching, and we should tread care-fully and speak low.

There will be no skulls in the grass. Though the recent storm shifted a tomb or two from its moorings, the staff of the necropolis came out like beetles in the rain and tidied everything. Even the shell that burst here was tidied. The necropolis has stood some while, two or three centuries. Always neat, even during the days of Liberty and Revolution.

(The last carriages career down into the park. There an old gen-tleman and his lady are shocked to behold the hearse go by filled with laughing actresses.)

In places there are great houses of death, you see. And in other places tiny markers half hidden in the grass and ivy, commemora-tive plaques for those who have gone down elsewhere into the dark that lies below, if not exactly beneath, everything.

Are they truly there, under our feet? Walk softly, talk quietly.

I will show you their shadows.

Here is a grave, now. . . .

The Weasel Bride

In the long echoing street the laughing dancers throng,
The bride is carried to the bridegroom's chamber through
    torchlight and tumultuous song;
I celebrate the silent kiss that ends short life or long.

                                                        Yeats

There are stories in the country told today as though they happened only a week ago. In many ways customs have not altered very much, and every village is its own empire. It is possible to imagine such things still occur, in lonely woods, under the stare of a silver moon.

A young trapper, walking home one evening across the water meadows, stopped in startlement, seeing a girl dancing on a hill in the moonlight. She was very beautiful, with long pale hair, but as she danced she wept and lamented. Pausing to watch, he also overheard her complaint. "Alas," said she, "that I may only keep this human form in the full ray of the moon. No sooner does she set, than I must return to my loathsome other shape, from which only the true love of a man can rescue me, although that forever. But what hope is there of it, seeing he must court and wed me in my other form, before his kin, and in the church. I am lost." Fascinated, the young man continued to spy on this strange maiden until at length the moon began to go down. The sky lightened, then grew black. The stars stung bright as the lunar orb sank under the hill. It was gone. At that moment, the maiden disappeared like the moon, as if into the ground. The young man ran up the hill and searched about, and as he did so he glimpsed something that flashed away into the bushes. It was a white weasel.

Now the trapper had made up his mind that he would be the one to have this girl, no matter what the cost. Therefore he laid his most cunning trap, and baited it, and went down to his village. Here he started hasty arrangements for a wedding, telling all sorts of lies, and bribing the priest and the mayor to obtain consent. The following night, which happened to be a night of no moon, he hurried to the spot where he had left his trap. And sure enough, what should he find in it but the white weasel, caught fast and crying piteously. "Fear nothing," said the suitor, "I shall befriend you, poor creature. Come, be my sweetheart, love me a little, and I shall wed you, before my kin and in the church, tomorrow morning."

Then he carried the weasel in a cage down to the village, ignoring her cheeps and struggles, which he guessed to be a part of the spell on her.

In his father's house, he had his mother and sisters put on the weasel a veil made from a lace handkerchief, and a garland made from a baby's pearl bracelet. He was the head of his own household, his father being dead, and the three women were obliged to obey him, but they did so in terror, thinking he had gone mad. The weasel, however, was most gentle now, and bore with everything that was done. Only at her lover did she hiss and bare her sharp teeth.

At sunrise, out they went, the trapper, his mother and sisters, and the bridal weasel in her cage. The whole village was about and crowding to the church, and the priest was there in his habit, with his prayerbook, waiting. But when they all saw what went on, there was a great to-do.

"Holy father," said the trapper, "you must humor me in this. For I insist this creature shall be my wife, and nobody will gainsay me. Remember," he added in a low voice to the priest, "my father's coins which I have given you."

"God moves in His own way," said the priest, and brought the young man and the weasel into the church and up to the altar. There, in the sight of the village and of the trapper's sobbing womenfolk, the priest wed the young man to the weasel.

Thereafter they repaired home for the wedding breakfast, and about noon, the young man took his bride away to the nuptial chamber, above.

The husband removed his wife from her cage and placed her on the pillows. "Dear wife," said he, "I will be patient." And there he sat quietly, as the daylight streamed in at the casement and the weasel ran about the bed and climbed the curtains, and below the wedding guests, in fear and amazement, grew drunk on his father's wine.

At length, the afternoon waned, the dusk came, and at long last, the moon rose in the east and pointed her white finger straight through the window.

"Now let us see," said the young man, and he put his hand on the weasel and stroked her snowy back. But as soon as the moon's ray touched her, she turned and bit him, under the base of the thumb, so his blood poured.

No sooner was this done than her coat of fur peeled off her, she sprang upright on the bed, and there before him in the moonlight was the lovely girl from the hill, clad only in her long, pale hair.

"You have freed me," she exclaimed.

"But at great cost," he answered.

And this was so, for despite her tender care of him, and the equally tender care of his astounded mother and sisters, the young man sickened of the bite. Within seven days he was dead and put to rest in the churchyard. And as for the weasel widow, she slunk away in the sunrise, and none saw her again, in any shape, although in those parts it was the tradition ever after to kill any weasel that they came on, if it should be a female.

The two families, the Covilles and the Desbouchamps, had ruled together over their great sprawling village for a pair of hundred years. And as each century turned, the village grew larger, fair set on being a town. The Covilles' tailored house at least had business connections with the City. Theirs was the trade of wool. The Desbouchamps' low-beamed manor, its milk churns and dove-cotes, stables and wild orchards, drowsed comfortably in the mead-ows. The Days of Liberty had not yet swept through Paradys, changing all the world. There seemed no need to hurry, or to pro-vision for any future that did not resemble the past.

It was to be a country wedding then, between Roland Coville and Marie-Mai Desbouchamps. It started at sunup, with the banging of lucky pots and pans down the village streets, and went on with the girls and their autumn roses taken to the manor, and the silver coin given to each as she bore her flowers into the cavern of the kitchen.

Then out came the lint-haired bride, crowned with the roses, in the embroidered bodice her grandmother had worn, and the little pearly shoes that just fitted her. She was piped and drummed to the church and met her bridegroom in the gate, a dark northern youth, and who did not know or could not see how eager he was? For it was not only a marriage arranged but a marriage arranged from desires. They had played together as children, Roland and Marie. He had pretended to wed her in the pear orchard when she was ten and he thirteen years of age. Seven years had passed. He had been sent to school in the City, and was no longer pure; he had known philosophy, mathematics, Latin, and three harlots. But unscathed he still was. And the girl, she was like a ripe, sweet fruit misleading in its paleness: She was quite ready.

And how he loved her. It was obvious to all. Not only lust, as was proper, but veneration. *He will treat her too well,* they said, *she will get the upper hand.* But she was docile, was she not, Marie-Mai? Never had anyone heard of anything but her tractability, her gentleness. *She will make a good wife.*

For Roland himself, it might be said that he had always known she must be his. At first she had reminded him of the Virgin, so fresh and white, so *clean.* But then the stirrings of adult want had found in her the other virgin, the goddess of the pastoral earth that was his in the holidays, the smooth curving forms of hills and breasts, shining of pools and eyes, after the chapped walls and hands, the hard brisk hearts of Paradys. She allowed him little lapses. To kiss her fingers, then her lips, to touch fleetingly the swansdown upper swell above her bodice. When he said to his father, "I will have Marie-Mai," his father smiled and said, "Of course. We'll drink to it." So easy. And why not, why must all love be fraught and tragic, gurning and yearning, unfulfilled or snatched on the wing of the storm?

And for Marie-Mai, what could be said for her? She had answered correctly all the searching lover's questions. Her responses were perfect, and if she offered nothing unasked, that was surely her modesty, her womanly decorum. Could anyone say they knew her? Of course. They all did. She was biddable, and loving in mild, undisturbing ways. She was not complex or rebellious. There was nothing to know. Who probes the flawless lily? It is the blighted bloom that gets attention.

A country wedding, then, and in the church Roland thought his bride like an angel, except he would not have planned for an angel what he planned to do to her. And the church over, outside in the

viny afternoon, they had their feast on the square, under the sky.
These were the days once sacred to the wine god. The girls had
wreathed the clay jugs with myrtle; the great sunny roses crowded
the tables like the guests. And when the humped western clouds
banked up, and the faint daylight moon appeared in a dimming
glow, they bore the bride and groom to the smart stone house
behind the wall and the iron gate decorated with peacocks. They let
them in with laughter and rough sorties. They let them go to the
laundered bedroom whose windows were shuttered, whose candles
were lit. They closed the doors and shouted a word or two, and left
the lovers alone for their night. And in the square a band played
and Madame Coville danced with Monsieur Desbouchamps, and
Madame Desbouchamps was too shy to do more than flirt with
Monsieur Coville. The moon rose high, and owls called from the
woods. The roses bloomed in the dark over the old walls, as if
winter would never come.

In the morning, an autumn country morning that began about half
past six, Roland's manservant knocked on the bedroom door, and
the maid waited behind him with the pot of chocolate. In the old
days—not twenty years before—the elderly women of the house
would have arrived, to strip the bed and view the blood of the
maidenhead. This was no longer done in such sophisticated villages. When the first knock went unanswered, the manservant
knocked again, and grinned at the maid, and called, "Shall I return
a little later, 'sieur Roland?"

Then, and what follows now comes directly from the evidence
given later in the courtrooms of Paradys, the voice of Roland was
raised clearly behind the door. It was not an embarrassed or plea-
sured voice. It cried in terrible despair: *Oh God, what shall I do?*"
And then, very loudly and without any expression. "Come in and
see. But leave the girl outside."

The young manservant raised his brows. More sympathetic than
he, the maid was already trembling and biting her lip. The man
opened the door and went into his master's bedroom. There he
beheld at once, as he said, some vestiges of a slight tussle, but perhaps these might not have been unnatural. Then he saw that the
bride lay half out of the bed, in her ribboned nightgown. There
were bruises on her throat, her face was engorged and nearly black,
and her eyes had extruded from their sockets. She had been strangled, had been dead some while. The manservant exclaimed some-

thing like, "My God, who has done this?" To which the young husband replied quietly, "I did it. I killed her." And at this point it was noticed how two of the fingers of his right hand were very savagely bitten, doubtless by the dying girl in her struggle for life.

The subsequent commotion that next boiled through the house is easily imagined. It passed into every chamber, every cranny, like a noxious odor. There was screaming, and every sort of human outcry, male and female. Roland was led down into the lower rooms, where an interrogation took place, his mother on her knees, his aunts fainting, his father bellowing in tears. And all this was soon augmented by the frenzied arrival of the family Desbouchamps.

To each kind and type of entreaty or demand, Roland Coville would say substantially the same thing, as various testimony later showed. What he said was this: "I killed Marie. I strangled her. She's dead."

But to the eternally repeated question *Why?* he would answer, white-faced and wooden, "I have nothing to say on that."

In those parts, the unchastity of a bride might have furnished a reason. There were historic tales, to be sure, of girls slain on the wedding night, having been discovered unvirgin. The father challenged his son, but Roland shook his head. He even gave a grim and white-faced smile. No, he replied, she was intact. "What, then —what? Did she slight you?" No, he had not been slighted. Marie was a virgin and she had not insulted him. She had given no provocation. She had encouraged his advances.

"Why, then, in the name of God—"

"I won't say, Father. Nothing on this earth will induce me to do so."

It was the father of Marie, of course, who impugned the manhood of Roland. The husband had been unable to fulfill his duties, and had strangled the innocent maiden for fear she would betray him. There were a couple of girls in the city who could give the lie to this. Nevertheless, the fathers ended fighting in the cobbled yard of the Coville house, under the peacocks.

In their turn, the police came. They had little to add but the uniform and threat of the law.

The village had fallen apart like a broken garden. Stones rattled by night on the shutters of the Coville house, on the embrasures of the village jail to which Roland had been removed. They wanted his death.

He was taken to the City in the dead of night, unpublicized, in a covered carriage, like an escape. The Coville house was locked up like a box. They had gone too into the darkness, to the City. Like all cities, it reeked of Hell. This had a rightness then, the flight toward Paradys, as, not too many years in the future, others would flee away from the drums and blades of Revolution, into the outer night of the world.

The trial of Roland Coville caused no stir in Paradys, City of Damnations. It was not unusual enough. A man had killed a girl, his lover and wife. So what? It happened twice a day. That the case had been explosive enough it was removed from village to City was nothing. A cough out of season was a wonder in the provinces.

The young man stood bravely, deadly, and composed before his judges. He was courteous and exact, and he refused them nothing except what he refused all others, the motive for the murder. He was defended with great difficulty.

"It is plain to me, and to those who sit in judgment on you, that you are no murderer. Let alone of a defenseless girl at your mercy in the dark, your young wife, looking to you for love and protection, receiving death at your hands. Clearly, monsieur, there is a momentous reason. *Tell us.*"

"No," said Roland Coville. "I can tell you nothing at all."

"But it may save your life, monsieur."

Roland shook his head. He looked only sad and very young.

"But *monsieur*, for God's sake. This will end in your hanging. Don't you prefer to live?"

Roland looked surprised, as if he were unsure. "Perhaps not."

"His face," said the lawyer after, considerably shaken, "was like, I think, that of a woman I once heard of. She had been shown the mechanism of the human body, its heart, viscera, intestines, all the tubes and organs that support life. And having seen, she was so disgusted at the method whereby she lived that, when she got home, she cut her wrists and died. To be rid of it all. Just so, he looked, my Roland Coville. He isn't reluctant to die."

Once, during the examination at Paradys, Roland was asked about the lacerations on the fingers of his right hand. He answered that his wife, Marie, had indeed bitten him.

"And this was during her final moments, as she fought for her life?"

"No. It happened earlier."

"Then your wife behaved violently toward you?"

"No," said Roland.

"But you say she bit you without any act on your part that would have invited her so to do."

"No, I did not say this."

"Monsieur Coville, we must be precise. When was it that these bites occurred?"

Roland hesitated. "When I touched the lips of Marie."

"But this, then, was an extreme and unloving response."

"Perhaps."

"Did you kill her because of this? Because of her attack on you?"

Roland Coville thought for a moment, and then said, "Would it be deemed a suitable defense, to kill a woman because she had bitten me?"

"No, monsieur, of course it would not."

"I did not," said Roland, "kill Marie because of the bite."

"*Why*, then? You are bound to speak. The weight of this assembly, and of the law itself, insist."

"I can and will say nothing," said Roland Coville. "It is beyond me to say it." And then in a sudden and conclusive passion he screamed, so the room echoed and dinned, the spectators and the judges recoiled, "It would be as if you tore out my heart, to say it. It would be as if you cut out my tongue. Nothing. Nothing! I will say nothing."

And so he was judged a murderer. He was condemned. In a small gray yard at sunrise he would be hanged.

But in the cell, before that, he must confront the confessor, the priest who was to hear his final statements, and who must, of them all, get the truth from him.

"I can't tell you," said Roland Coville to the priest who angrily confronted him.

"You have forfeited your life," said the priest. "Is this not enough? You have spat upon the robe of God, and upon the gift he gave you."

"No, father," said Roland. "God knows, and understands, what I have done. And why."

And his face was then so pitifully pared, trusting, and desperate, so positive of the pity of God after all, that the angry priest was softened.

"Come, then," he said, "make what confession you can. I will absolve you, and God must do the rest."

Roland then knelt down, and unburdened himself of all his

crimes, which were none of them terrible, but for that one. And then he spoke of that too, quietly and stilly. "I strangled my young wife, she was only seventeen, and I loved her. It was on her wedding night, in our bed. She was a virgin and died so. I killed her with no compunction, and would do it again." And then, head bowed under the hands of the priest, he added softly, "For my reasons, I believe such things can't be spoken of. This would be like showing the face of the Devil. How can I be responsible for that?"

The priest was in the end very sorry for him. He was a handsome and a good young man, guilty of nothing but the one appalling and senseless act. The priest absolved Roland Coville, and went away to watch all through the night before the execution, in the little church on a slanting street of the City. And when through the narrow window a nail of light pierced in and fell on the crucifix and the white flowers, the priest knew the rope in the gray yard had performed its office, and one more benighted soul had struggled forth into the Infinite, toward long anguish or the life eternal, or toward oblivion, for he was a wise priest, faithful and doubting, a man like men.

Two days after the execution of Roland Coville, the priest was brought a letter. It was on the paper obtained in the prison, and came from the dead man, written in the last hour of his life. As such it had extraordinary weight. But on opening it anxiously, the priest read these words: "I cannot after all go into the night without passing on this burden that has consumed me. Forgive me, father, that I turn to you. Who else can I rely on? Who else can bear it?"

And after that the priest read on, and the scales fell from his eyes, the dark glass was clear before him. He did not believe, then he believed. And he locked the letter from Roland Coville away in a place where none could come at it, not even he himself. And there it stayed for seven years, burning slowly through the walls of the safe and of his mind.

One spring, when the roads were muddy, a priest came to the village by means of the coach that stopped there once a month, and he inquired for the domicile of the family Desbouchamps. On being directed, he took himself off toward the manor house in the meadows. The lanes were spare and washed with rain, the tall poplars swept the sky. The manor had lost its roselike abundance and seemed now decaying, the shutters half off, the lofts rotting. No doves flew from the cotes. A dog barked only sullenly in the court-yard.

To his inquiry at the kitchen door, the housekeeper shook her head. "Mistress sees no one." The priest indicated his habit. "What does she want with another priest? She's had enough of you, bury-ing the master."

But he won through, because he had set his mind to it. He stood with his habit and his bag and would not go. Finally a thin old woman of no more than forty years came down to the cold parlor, where drapes were on the furnishings, and she made no pretense at removing them or lighting the fire. The hearth gaped black, and cold whistled down the chimney. She leaned to it and rubbed her hands.

"We are unfortunate," said Madame Desbouchamps. "In a year, everything must be sold. Those men, those men in their holy day coats!" (She presumably meant the lawyers.)

"I'm very sorry to hear it."

"It's been a great loss. Ever since monsieur died. It was the trag-edy killed him. He always loved her so." And over her worn and discarded face there crossed a slinking jealousy, out in the open now, having no need any more to hide. Marie-Mai was dead, and her loving father was as dead as she, why dissemble?

"Your daughter, do you mean?" asked the priest with some care. "But she was very young to die."

"Murdered," said madame, "in her bridal bed."

The priest said what was inevitable.

"You will have heard," said Madame Desbouchamps. "It was the talk of the City. They made up songs about it, the filthy wretches."

The priest had never heard one, and was glad. He said, "I believe I caught a rumor of the case. The bridegroom had no motive for his action. The girl was innocent and chaste."

Madame Desbouchamps compressed her lips like withered leaves. She sat a long while in utter silence, and he intuitively al-lowed this. At length, the blossom came.

"She was a sly girl," said the mother. "She hid things, was secre-tive. She was no daughter to me. I knew no better then. But it was never affection she gave me. She saved that for her father, a clever pass. I remember, her courses came early. She wasn't nine years, she was crying and there was blood, and I said, Let me see, Marie, what's the matter with you? But she ran away. And the blood stopped, and then there was no more till the proper time. She was eleven years then. She wasn't fearful when it happened, only asked me for a napkin."

The priest might have been astonished and shocked at being awarded such information. Even in country people madame's reminiscence was forthright. But in fact he was not thinking of this. He had gone very pale. And she, she had a crafty look, as if she had meant to tell him something, and saw that she had.

"Poor young girl," said the priest after a few moments. "What a loss to you, the daughter, then the husband. Where are they buried?"

"And the house," interjected the woman brutishly. Then she said, "On the land. The Desbouchamps bury their dead close. Now what shall I do? The land's no longer mine."

"Their graves must be moved, madame," said the priest.

"I'll show you," she said. And again there was the flash of malign conspiracy. As if she knew what he was at, *liked* it, although that could hardly be.

It was a little mausoleum, like a Roman tomb, not unusual among wealthy country families. Through the grille he glimpsed the shape of coffins. He would need a pick to smash the lock, but the place was up the hill, hidden by trees and deserted. They chained the three last dogs by night, and there were only a pair of old men now on the estate.

So, at two in the morning, he duly returned, with his pickax and his lantern.

The incongruity of what he did had ceased to irk him. He was beyond that. The letter burning through the safe had gradually seared out his ethics. He struck the lock and broke it with four blows, each of which echoed away along the valley, but no light fluttered up in the manor house, no one rushed from the buildings, not even the owls hooted.

The stench and awfulness of the mausoleum did not check him either, for he had been expecting them, and once or twice he had stood over an opened grave, the stink of it worse than excrement or sewers in its omen of mortality.

Her box, the coffin of Marie-Mai, he located without difficulty, knowing what to look for. He dredged up the cobwebs and saw the tracks of a squirrel over the lid—it must have come in at the broken grille. What had attracted it to this one case alone? For it had ignored the others. Shuddering, the priest levered up the planks. He saw what he had reckoned to see, the bones of a young girl whose young girl's skin had gone to mummy and fallen away, some strands and traces of hair, the crumbled wedding garments in which she had been buried, the marriage ring rattling on the thinnest of thin fingers.

"God strengthen me. God forgive me," said the priest. And then he tore down the powdery bridal clothes. And so he saw, without any shadow of doubt, for indeed he held the lamp over the coffin, he spared himself nothing. Roland Coville had not lied.

Then, going outside, the priest threw up, tried to throw up it seemed his heart and soul. And when he was done, trembling, he went back in and shut up the coffin fast with a hammer and nails, closed it more tightly than before. This work finished, he left the place and went down the hill, and back to the village inn, where they were too respectful of a City priest to ask any questions.

The priest paced the length of three weeks, in his church on the slanting street, in his rooms, under the architraves of Paradys. There was no help for Roland, who by now was as near to dust as the thing he had killed and died for. What, then, to do with the truth, that terrible naked sword? At length, the priest made his decision, and it resembled Roland's own, for neither would he, the priest of God, tamper with the revealed face of the Devil.

He sat with papers and ink and candles, and through the night he wrote, and rewrote, what he had been privy to. And in the end, near dawn, he burned his experiments, and had it down alone on paper in a manner that at least was not hysterical, nor crude, nor yet of course entirely believable, but how could he help that? He added to it a line of Latin, by way of protection, and folded up the paper, and sealed it, and stored it, together with the letter of Roland Coville, in a new deposit that should not be opened until his death.

That, then, was how the priest dealt with what he had learned and seen. And so truth lay in the dark for another sixty years.

During that time, everything changed. The great Revolution came and went, the Days of Liberty, the Years of Blood. The paper lay in its vault, and Marie-Mai in her coffin, undisturbed, like shells of a lost sea deep in the soil, that all the turning wheels and veering scythes of the world cannot dislodge. Only the hand that knows their places, only that can find them out. Or some wild accident.

* * *

"There is a rat," said the landowner. "I tell you, I hear it, you fool."

"No rats, sir. I keep them away."

"Damn you, I tell you I hear them. I walk by this horrible spot, and I hear them, gnawing and gnashing in the vault. Look at this thing! A gargoyle of a tomb. Pull it down, I say. Scatter the bones. What were they, that family of no-goods? Rich men feeding off the poor of this region. I fought on the barricades against their sort."

He had not actually fought, he had been a clerk, but scum generally rises to the top. Now he had his farm here, and did well from it. His memories altered to fit present circumstances, and he despised the dead Desbouchamps whose land he had acquired, bloodsuckers, with their silly, half-aristocratic name—

"I watched all night. Saw not one rat."

"But did you hear the sound of their rat jaws biting together?"

"No, sir."

"Don't call me sir. You're not a serf any more. Address me as *brother*. And stop arguing with me. I gave you an order."

"Yes, brother?"

"We'll have this rotting tomb pulled down. We'll turn them *out*."

The mausoleum of the Desbouchamps was duly ripped apart, its Roman columns flung over, its piteous insides rolled forth into the blistering sunlight of that summer when the rain would fail and the crops die, and new plagues of want stalk the land, as if mere blood had not been enough. But he did not know that yet, the clerk from Paradys. Nor did he know anything of the priest's paper, which, that very year, too, had been read by a few august eyes, which had escaped the battery. A few clever eyes, that would take the paper and the letter for a symbol of the monstrous times, like the bleeding of a loaf or a frog with a tail, a portent, immaterial as to truth or lie.

The risen clerk from Paradys kicked the Desbouchamps coffins. A couple burst open and the inhabitants sprawled on the grass. He laughed at those.

"Here's one nicely nailed. More solid. Something to hide. Perhaps there are jewels in here." And thrusting off his brother workmen, to whom, to his wife, he referred as walking rubbish, the clerk prized up the lid and threw it off. "*Pough!* What an effluvia!" (He liked occasional long words.) He held his nose and attempted not to retch. Then he called one of the fellows to rummage in the bones.

There were no gems, no earrings, necklaces, only an old tarnished ring, perhaps silver, which he had away from the workman at once.

It must have been a woman. Her long hair had fallen off, her dress had been torn.

He peered at her to be sure he had missed nothing.

Then the workman gave a hoarse cry.

"What is it, you damned fool?"

The man drew away, potently terrified. He ran to one of his mates, clasped him, gabbled, and rushed off between the trees.

"Well, *he'll* be whipped."

The clerk laughed again, then he looked. And at long last he saw.

The woman was all bones, discolored as if charred, and in her skull the teeth, once young and white, had loosened and dropped out. But lower, where the dress was torn wide, he could see in at the tilted bones of her pelvis, and there, between her legs, she had another set, and these were perfect, still white and very sharp. They lay in the nest of her skeleton like a little wreath of snowy flowers. In life they would not have been visible, for plainly they had been tucked neatly away behind the smooth lips and taut maidenhead, secure in the second mouth of her vagina. There they had waited, as if any man had dared. What a bite they could have given him!

The clerk leaned back and laughed heartily. Then he got up, gray and shaking, and told his men to close the coffin. He did not want a sideshow on his property. It must go to the City. Perhaps a grave could be found for it there, in some corner of the overflowing cemeteries of Paradys.

It was about this time, that day or another, that the august and clever eyes of the priesthood also turned from the paper they had been reading. And it was then, while the one decided on a sideshow, a joke, that the others decided on a portent, the apocalypse.

Dominus illuminatio mea, et salus mea, quem timebo? said the Latin, put there on his paper by the priest.

While the clerk was telling his drunken cronies, and his drunken wife, at dinner, what he had seen, and the rafters of the old Desbouchamps manor rocked with the laughter of the jest, the wise men who had also looked on the face of the Devil crept to their hiding places, courageously repeating their affirmation, *The Lord is my light and my safety, whom shall I fear?*

So the years of Revolution swept over Paradys and her landscape, in a primordial sea.

The mysterious poet André St. Jean, who saw their beginning, apparently barely mentions anything of them, being taken up with his own affairs of the heart.

Enough is known of the bloodshed. The graveyard here bears its witness.

One anecdote is perhaps worth repeating, the curious tale of Monsieur Raccoon.

He escaped from the zoological gardens before the hungry and threatening mob could make a meal of him, and thereafter devoted himself to the rescue of forlorn innocents from the gallows. The flaunting banner of his striped tail was a fearful sight to the executioner and his assistants. From the rope he whisked away countless numbers, swooning pale maidens and paler gentlemen, in his capable paws. At length, Monsieur Raccoon was captured, and imprisoned in one of the most notorious of the prisons. But here he charmed them all so well that eventually he made his own escape, leaping high above the heads of the jailers and vanishing, swinging through the beams, with a whisk of his cream-and-charcoal tail.

He was whispered of among the forests of the gallows, among the stone cages of the prisons, for months after. The aristocrat upon the scaffold had only to mention, "Ah, for the Raccoon," to cause his assailant to blanch. In the zoo you will see a commemorative plaque concerning him. But here in the long grass where an angel's broken hand has fallen, here there is another marker.

This too owes its dead-life to the Revolution, although in a roundabout way. The name reveals perhaps a sidelong descendant of André St. Jean, or perhaps not, for the name is not uncommon in Paradys. The fate, more so . . .

The story was told me one evening in a café by the river, near to the ruined bridge. The dusk was blurred by fog, and somewhere below, where the bank ended and the water began, the vague

torched eyes of barges were creeping up and down, slow and fearful, with now and then the mournful warning of a gong. In the café,
the fog had entered too, and, with the primal oil lamps and the
smoke of cigarettes, gave us the atmosphere of Venus. An old man
was brought over suddenly under the ominous announcement
"Here is a fellow can tell you a few histories."

They sat him before me and there he was, creaking in his over-
coat. I filled him a glass, and idly invited him to begin. He started to
talk of the Revolution. He looked ancient enough to have known
the participants, when a boy. Not until he was well into his third
glass, did he squint at me slyly and say, "But the strangest stories
come after the Revolution ended. When they washed the City clean
of blood, and put the axes away. It was then."

After which he launched into a narrative that had something in it
of a Shakespearian drama, and something of the nature of a myth. I
did not know if I, or he, believed it. Punctuated by the eerie flickers
from the river, dispersed through the lamplit fog, it clung inside
my head. False or real, it had its own truth. I set it down; now you
must judge for yourself.

The Nightmare's Tale

The Devil beats his drum,
Casting out his spell,
Dragging all his own
Down into Hell.

David Sylvian

1

Of the many thousands ho had died in the murderous blood tides
of Revolutionary times, there had been a young poet and his innocent wife. Their names and lives may be found elsewhere, he a dark
and clamorous man, she pale as a swan, following her husband to
the scaffold in the white dress of a bride. They left behind a child,
then only two years old. This offspring was brought up by a surviving sister of the mother's—although in those days, it was not unusual, when one member of the family was confiscated for the gallows, for the rest soon enough to be dragged in tow.

The woman, who shall be called Andromede, raised the little boy
in the best fashion she could, and at the prpoer age saw to it that he
was educated to the highest and nicest degree she could afford.
Along with the nourishment of his body, clothing of his person, and
tutoring of his mind, she also saw to it that her sister's son was fed,
garbed, and schooled in most incredible amounts of pure bitter-
ness. It may have been that she herself was once in love with Jean
de St. Jean's father, the poet, or that she had loved her sister exces-
sively. Or it may have been simply the fact of the terrible shock she
had undergone when all her familial world was swept away in the

space of two or three horrible months: Something made of Andromede a powerful and insidious instructor in the lessons of enduring
hate.

How she did it can only be guessed. One half imagines that instead of grace before a meal, some other words were spoken, rather
in the way of the antique toast "Death to my enemies." Or that over
the beds were hung samplers that read "You shall seek out the
wicked and destroy them." And "An eye for an eye."

Probably, when she knelt down like gray marble in the church at
the end of the street, and the child asked what she prayed, Andromede may well have replied; "For *justice!*" And probaly also she
indoctrinated the little Jean with anecdotes of his parents, their
vivid talents and virtues, their fairy-tale love, and their death.

For eighteen years, until the age of twenty, Jean de St. Jean grew
to manhood in that shadowy City of aftermath, the wreckage of a
revolution, going about between a grim stony school with turrets
and cobbled yards, reeking stoves, mealy books, and a maze of
crooked, crowded, dirty streets that led up into an apartment with
windows that peered across a joiners' court at a high wall, three
rooms that were thick with dust in summer and wet with cold in
winter, and whose stove smoldered and reeked worse, and if there
was generally sufficient to eat, it came at the cost of something,
some gnawing, obscure pride to do with a state pension, a recompense for the unspeakable that could never be enough. And as he
grew up, then, forcing his way toward the light like a plant in flinty
ground, Jean de St. Jean, the poet's son, breathed up, with the
damp and dust and the church bells from the street's end and the
invisible samplers of hatred, an exquisite yearning for he knew not
what. But it was not ambition or carnality or fame or happiness.
And one day, one morning, by accident, he discovered its being and
what it was. It was revenge. And like a luscious berry, God had put
it in his hand.

He rushed home to the mean apartment of his aunt, along the
knotted streets, his heart in his mouth, bounded up the stairs, and
flung wide the door.

"Anny!" he exclaimed, which was his pet name for Andromede
the hatress. "Anny, you won't credit—"

Andromede came through from her bedroom, where she had
been pinning up her hair tightly. For the first time in eighteen
years she felt the full spasm of fear. She stared into her nephew's
face and saw him for what he was, as if, until this moment, he had

been partly hidden from her. He was a man, with the hair of her sister in a sun-caught cloud around his face, and his eyes dark and clamoring.

"Whatever—" she began.

He held up his hand to silence her.

"I have seen," said Jean, in a wild cold voice awful to hear, "a *thing*, a *monster*, walking in the garden of the Martyr Church."

"I don't understand you, Jean," said Andromede. She did. She shook from head to foot and her bowels had turned to water, exactly as had happened eighteen years ago on the night the Citizen Police hammered at the door.

"It was Dargue," said Jean. "*Dargue*," he repeated.

Then he fell silent and stood looking at her. It would have been difficult to say which of them had gone the whiter.

Dargue was the man who had been directly responsible for the execution of the poet and his wife. It was he who denounced them, and later, by adding his signature to the warrant, he that ensured there would be no escape. He had supposedly been drinking wine as he wrote his name, and a spot of the drink fell beside it like a drop of thin blood. The document had since been displayed, with others of its kind, and perhaps Jean had even seen it. Of course he knew the six letters that composed the monster D.A.R.G.U.E. And, too, he knew the man by inner sight, having had his appearance and mannerisms described uncountable times over. That Dargue had, as Jean, aged eighteen years, did not prove a deterrent. He had been away all this while, like a fiend in Hell, reveling in the illicit riches the Revolution had given over to him when, in the last days of its madness, he fled.

"He has been living in the Colonies," said Jean, referring to these far-flung possessions of the City as to another planet. "An island . . . Black Haïssa. He has a house there. They jokingly say he has three wives. Negré women."

"*I don't want to hear!*" screamed Andromede abruptly, clasping her hands over her ears.

"You must, you must," pleaded Jean. And going to her, he put his arms around her and held on to her just as he had when a child. For her various reasons, Andromede had never been a caressive or physical woman. Her returns to an embrace, especially an importunate one, were awkward and labored. Now she did nothing at all, but stood there in her gray marble mode, waiting perhaps for all this to end. "Anny," said Jean, "listen carefully. I'm not a boy now.

You know, I'm well educated thanks to you, but have no prospects in this rotten, corrupt City. I've had it said to me already, my best chance . . . would be to try my luck—in the Colonies." He paused, and when she did not respond, hurried on with "There are fortunes to be made in the islands."

"Yes," she said stupidly, sounding almost asleep. Her hands had fallen back to rest on his arms as he held her.

"There's the money you put by for me. Let me have it, Anny."

"So you can take yourself to the Colonies?"

She stole a glance at him. Her eyes were stunned rather than bleak. Was he going to leave her?

"Yes, so I can go there. Don't you see. Where *he* is."

"Why?" said Andromede.

It was astonishing, after all her work upon him. After eighteen years of a single lesson perfectly repeated and learned by heart. Now, when he replied, solving the mathematical formula in its preordained and only way, now she could not make head or tail of it.

"To kill him," said Jean de St. Jean. "What else?"

Andromede had the correctness of soul at least to bow her head and not to protest again.

"He's to return to the Island shortly. Out there," said Jean, "in that *lawlessness*, it will be easy."

"Yes, it's easy to kill."

"Anny, it's what we wanted in our dreams, and here's my chance."

"Yes."

"You'll let me have the money, then?"

"Very well. I saved it for you, Jean."

"For *us*. For *them*—my father. *Her*."

"Yes."

"You mustn't grieve. In a year I could be home. We might be rich. You'll have a carriage, and beautiful clothes—velvet for church."

"Silly," she said, brokenly.

She tried to smile. Maybe she even tried to take on again her serpent's craning, the foremovement of its venomous strike, the attitude of her insatiable hunger for justice, retribution, the getting of eyes for eyes. If so, she failed in that too. The smile was meaningless and unconvincing, but she pressed it on her face from that morning to the dawn, ten days later, when Jean caught the boat from the old Quay of the Angel, and was borne out limblessly toward the jaws of the sea.

Andromede, standing on the quayside, amid the plumes of hats and tears of others come to wave someone away, was dry and upright, like a thin blasted tree. It was her pride not to weep until she was at home, alone there amid the dust and cold and shadows, listening helplessly for the sound of his footsteps on the stair, for the snatch of a song he might now and then sing, the dropped book, the rustle of his coat, his *Anny, here I am,* his *Goodnight, God bless you, Anny.* She told herself she would never see him again, and in this she was quite right.

The journey was a lifetime. It passed across seasons, geographical barriers, climates, and spatial zones. Months were consumed by it. You could not embark on such a journey, and complete it, unaltered. And yet, with all its doings and happenings, its events of seasickness, storm, calm, boredom, the visitations that were foreign ports (and progressively more and more foreign as one advanced, moving tableaux that swam up from the depths of the ocean and slid away again behind like the white wake of the moon by night), the fishes that leapt, the stars that revolved, and the whole reasonless, rocking environ of the sea itself—such things eventually classified themselves into mere living, ordinary existence. For Jean experienced them and survived them all, and to some extent they were lost on him in any case, for he was already in pursuit. His hunt had begun at the Angel Quay indeed, when he learned which boat, and which ship, were to carry Dargue a week before him.

It was, however, as though the entire passage comprised and was framed within an afterimage: that of sailing through a sort of bottle of pale skies and water holding rain, and coming gradually out of the bottleneck into a violent sunset burning in heaven like stained glass.

Although the conflagration died as quickly as it blew up, going down beneath a curious cloud.

"There," said Jean de St. Jean to one of the less disreputable of the crew, "what is that?"

"Haïssa," the man replied. He added that they had anchored eight miles out, and would not be going in until sunrise.

Jean was left to observe the cloud darken in a sheet of drained fire, and then to darken and harden on, blacker than the star-sprayed sky.

There were mountains on Haïssa. Haïssa was, in fact, it seemed, made of mountains. There was something in the Island he had not expected, the young man intent upon his quest and his vengeance. The Island itself had importance. It possessed some kind of sentience, dimly discernible across the rhinestone rollers, the reefs, and the night.

As he stood at the ship's rail, Jean became aware of another being on the deck.

It is almost impossible to describe the way in which the awareness stole over him, especially in view of what will follow. The sensation grew rather in the manner in which a man may come to feel he has some illness, amorphous at first, the faintest disinclination, ebb of the spirits. Yet presently depression is reinforced by a score of other slight intrusive signals. At last he must acknowledge the onset of the fever that will lay him low.

Jean bore the feeling, which was not exactly of being watched, more of being waited upon, for a count of five or six minutes. They would have seemed interminable, except that all the while he was trying to argue himself from his certainty. Frankly, he did not for a moment think anything human or explicable was with him on the deck. He knew, from the evening's previous sounds, and a by now general familiarity with the noises of the vessel, crew, and passengers, the position of all men and objects. Even the ship's dog had become detectable to him during the voyage, as it lightly padded its rounds. *This* presence was of one who had not, until that hour, inhabited the ship.

Finally, Jean turned, and scanned the area about him. The moon was rising, the heavy lush moon of these regions, which on its nights of waxing seems full of sweet juice. The deck glowed and was laid bare, the masts and bundled sails, the cabins and hatches, the station of the great wheel. No one was there in all that stretched instant of moonlight. The vessel was like a floating coffin on the ocean. Only Jean remained at the rail. And nearby, somewhere, invisible and untenable and nonexistent—the other.

Jean crossed himself. It was an involuntary action, a reflex of boyhood. But when he did it, he thought he heard a soft, long, low laugh go pulsing around the deck. This laugh, if it even occurred, was suddenly in all places at once, and gone as suddenly and utterly. Jean had grown very cold, but he was not afraid. He said, under his breath, "I know you. What have you come to tell me?"

But that too was only his instinct, for he did not know, either what was there with him, or what he had said to it.

Nevertheless, there came a swift flash, like a star falling or a light quenched somewhere between himself and the next item of solid material, which happened to be one of the masts. What it was he did not see, although it seemed afterward that it might have been the reflection of a face, glimpsed as if in a mirror. It was a peculiar face, too, more a mask, that was at one and the same time black and white, but whether the black was laid over the white or the white on the black, Jean could not make out.

And then he found he could move, the air had soaked back to its usual tepid warmth, and he started to hear real sounds from the ship, and to behold some sailors over by one of the hatches smoking their pipes, and the watch motionless aloft. The other thing was gone.

The young man went down to the saloon to take his supper, trying to put off a vague sense of shame, which apparently naturally replaced the supernatural sensation that preceded it. Below, he drank more than he was used to with his meal, and went to bed amused at himself and engorged by notions of his arrival at the Island in the morning, where his search would commence at once for Dargue.

The ship entered port an hour after dawn. For whatever other reason, it was likely Haïssa had earned the epithet "Black" in one way from her looks. Behind the harbor the Town straddled a vast swooping slope that expended itself abruptly, miles off, against enormous uplands cumbered in jungles or forests that showed jet black against the vibrancy of the sky. Beyond these nearer heights yet more gigantic cliffs scaled up, thick with vegetation and trees, until distance reduced the panorama to transparency. In two or three spots a solitary waterfall shone like a straight white smoke. The Town itself was by contrast pastel and tawdry, the ripe smell of it drifting out across the harbor with the stink of fish and fruit. Parrots, in cages on peeling balconies that overhung the water, screamed. Although he had seen black men as he neared the Island, Jean had never gazed on such a quantity. Their species was so different he could not fit them into any comfortable niche. It was easier to detail them as some form of higher and less tractable animal. The brilliance of their teeth shocked him, and their women, walking barefoot on the sharp stones and broken shards above the shipping, with metal necklets and colored scarves circling their waists and brows. The women of Jean's landscape had figures made of laced bone and hair like raveled silk. These had pelt or fleece upon their heads. Their breasts swayed with the rhythm of their steps as they walked like cats.

Had he not been embued by his purpose, the young man, alone and mostly penniless in this alien world, might have given way to preliminary panic. But he was armored, was Jean. And in his armor he went ashore, and carrying his bag himself, went up the first curving street from the port, between the balconies and bird cages, across a square of big-limbed trees pendulous with gourds, under the stucco and the palms and over the steps, clung with orchids, that led to the upper Town of Black Haïssa.

And the cat-women passed him in their skins of velure, and higher up he saw the ones who were half cat and half human, swarthy near-white, driving in their carriages with fans of feathers in their carved, ringed hands. And he saw the gentlemen too, lounging by the barbers and the hotels, in striped waistcoats, and some of these were black and some not quite black. But the whites had gone to the very surface-top of the Town like froth to the top of coffee, and there were to be noticed, like pieces of mosaic among the plantains and palm trees, their froth-white mansions with faded names, and colossal gardens gone to seed, passionflowers and flowers that ate flies, snakes in the dry fountains, and giant spiders hung among vines, weaving with their legs.

But the visor of his armor was down across the eyes of Jean de St. Jean the poet's son. He knew the word "Dargue." That was what he had come for. He climbed up because that was the way the streets and steps led him, and the hanging parks of Haïssa Town. Dargue was a man of substance in this place, and should be simple to find.

And Jean knew an aching urge to see him again. It was nearly poignant. As if, in looking at this man, he could perceive, lifted miraculously out of time and decay, his two parents, whose faces he knew only from some little paintings kept in Andromede's apartment.

Jean had of course conceived a plan, partly conceived it in his home City in the days after sighting Dargue. Aboard ship, during the ocean months, he shaped the plan or was shaped by it, perhaps. The fuss that some of his fellow passengers made of him—as a young hopeful setting forth to try his fortune (naturally the true purpose was not revealed to them)—and the general talk of the way of getting on in the islands, molded the plan further. It became outrageous and possible. It appealed to Jean by its audacity, its very terribleness. For what he eventually proposed to do was to approach Dargue directly, rendering him the false identity which he, Jean, had already adopted for the voyage out—it was one of the few provisions the poet's son had taken to protect himself. And having so engaged his enemy, Jean would stand before him and beg for an occupation, flaunting the good City education, making of himself a charming and valuable prospect. That Dargue should take him on, employ him, as a secretary or assistant of some sort, was so balefully ironic, Jean did not believe it could not come to be.

Installed in Dargue's very household, privy to his secrets, which rumor suggested were often dark, debauched, dangerous, Jean foresaw a hundred opportunities both to ruin and, ultimately, to commit murder.

How the murder was to be accomplished—this he did not know, and had never truly visualized. It was a shadow act performed in dream. *That valid.* He trusted that the hour and the means would be given him.

Jean made his inquiries at Haïssa town after Dargue in the manner of the young hopeful off the ship, a fellow citizen, speaking a common tongue, clever, and prepared to be industrious. Quite quickly he had his directions to a mansion out along Oleander Road. It was a two-hour ride, which to Jean, on foot and with his bag in hand, would furnish an afternoon's walk.

Oleander Road was not a road in any sense of a city street. It was a broad avenue of earth that rambled out of the edges of the Town and curled itself away for miles through the hills. It was barricaded by banana trees, and continually encroached upon by the forest, a swollen, lubricious wall of leaves and trunks that bulged inward with incredible potency, alight with sun, with bird noises, and the quiver of insects. The air was warm, it seemed to run down in rivulets, so that everything to be seen wavered. Along Oleander Road, at considerable distances from one another, the old houses lay off the track, behind spilled paths, rough-haired lawns, and plantings of cocoa and tobacco. In one place there was even a milestone, but it indicated the leagues back to Haïssa Town.

Shade was thrown all over the road, and shots of sun. The shambling route went always higher and higher, and began at length to show, through windowpane openings, sky and sea below.

Drenched in sweat, Jean walked the road. His bag came to weigh like the weight of the sins of the one he sought.

There was nothing else he could do. It was out of the question to turn back, and he never debated that he should. He went on, sometimes turning his head to catch the weird bird cries of the forest, or slapping at some bloodsucking thing that had bitten him. It was a type of hell, this walk. He had not foretold the punishment, but neither did he resist its infliction.

The shade pool on the road deepened, and spread, and a breeze started that shook the huge hammered-iron leaves of the plantains. It was evening, and abruptly, on his left hand, Jean saw the notice that indicated the estate of Monsieur Dargue.

He felt a start of the pulses, as though he had encountered a lover unexpectedly.

The garden of Dargue's house was positively enormous and dense with the coming of darkness. The overhanging shrubs and trees seemed hung with heavy coils of snakes. A scent began of strange pale-colored flowers. The stars were piercing the sky like drops of silver sweat or blood bursting out upon a thin black skin.

Jean wandered through this tangle of night, and behind the little fires of flowers the house had suddenly appeared, two stories of masonry in a cage of verandas, lighted by oil lamps that hung on it like ripe fruit.

A dog commenced to bark and howl drearily. Jean stood beside a fountain and saw the mansion of his enemy before him, and everything became for a moment unreal. It was as if he did not even know who he himself was, or his own name. As if he had forgotten the name of his father, and why he had come here. And the word "Dargue" was meaningless.

The moment was frightful to Jean. It actually frightened him, but more than that, it caused him to struggle with some faceless adversary, and to win.

After that the house was Dargue's house, and he must get to it at once.

Perhaps he became aware as he drew nearer that there was a hush on the building. The dog had left off its dirge and the crickets were very loud. One lighted window burned in the second story, nothing else. The lanterns around the veranda seemed to grin.

Beyond the house stretched the fields of the estate, but no lamp moved there—it might have been a primeval swamp.

Jean rang the bell, which was quite ordinary. He had to wait some while, and was reaching out again for the bellpull when he heard a kind of dragging step coming toward him through the house.

Jean was conscious then that something had gone wrong.

The door opened. An elderly black man was craning out, peering up at him. He had the face of a beautiful marmoset, which themselves resemble the princes of another world. But he was so old and bent, and maybe had had to bend his inner self also; he looked at Jean with a timorous indifference, saying nothing.

"Dargue. I am here—to see Monsieur Dargue," said Jean stridently, his voice too noisy, like something that escaped him.

The old man continued peering up at him.

"I've come a long way," said Jean, and suddenly realized that he had. He trembled.

"Monsieur Dargue," said the black man, softly.

"Yes. Tell him—"

"No, monsieur," said the black man, "I can't tell him. Monsieur Dargue is dead."

The whole night caved in upon Jean, shadows, trees, darkness, stars, all came rushing down, pouring in through the top of his skull. He dropped his bag somewhere in the maelstrom. Then found himself leaning against the wall.

The servant man still watched him, still indifferent, but saying now in a craven way, "He take ill on the day he come back. He take to his bed. Then the doctor come. Then the priest come. Then Monsieur Dargue, he dies. He dies last night."

In the silence that followed the servant's recital, Jean heard himself say, equally softly, "But I've come such a long way. I came to find him."

"He dead, monsieur."

Jean said, "Yes."

And then the servant seemed to try to reward him for his compliance.

"He is lying out on the bed. You want to come in, monsieur, have look at him?"

A rush of nausea. "No," Jean said. "In God's name—"

When he recovered a little, the servant had closed the door, and was audibly making his dragging progress off again through the house.

For a few seconds Jean leaned on the wall and wept. It was the ghastly disappointment of the passionate child, whose desired gift has been snatched away at the last instant, literally out of his hand.

Worst of all, he did not know in the least what to do next. He had been almost four months tending to this, more, his entire life had in some sort latched on it. But the dream act was already performed. Even as he had stood on the ship's deck, scenting the odor of Haïssa across the night, even then. Death himself had preempted the frail revenge of Jean de St. Jean. Face to face with his own mortal inconsequence, the young man turned from the house of his enemy, a shell as meaningless as if gutted by fire. He trudged away, not quite knowing what he did, through the serpentine garden.

2

On Oleander Road, near midnight, Jean beheld a strange procession.

He supposed he had sat down at the road's edge, as he might have done in some country lane of the north, above his City. Here there were snakes and poisonous toads, hairy lianas, vampire insects—but he was past considering them. He did not sleep but sank into a stupor, in which he was aware of moisture, the dew of old rains dripping down, and things that hastened over his hands. The moon crossed the road, and when it was gone, through the dark a throbbing seemed to come, like the pulse of blood along an artery.

Jean gazed with dull eyes. Presently the curtains of night were parted, and from some obscure avenue among the trees of the forest, a troop of men and women emerged onto the road. They looked themselves black as the night, and would not have been easy to see but for the fact many of them wore light-colored garments that shone in a skull-faced flicker of lanterns. Jean noticed that several of the women carried bunches of some plant. It was not unfamiliar, perhaps he had seen it growing wild here and there, an ugly shrub, stringy, like an uncombed horse's tail.

The leader of these people was a tall man dressed in white. He stalked ahead as if alone, staring directly before him. He held a whip with a bone handle. There was also a girl who lugged in a wicker cage two or three black birds that jumped and flapped, but their outcry was lost in the drums and a deep, ceaseless murmuring that went with them up the road.

Jean was aware, incoherently, that he looked on something that maybe it would have been better he had not seen. There was an overt secrecy to the procession, which seemed to make no attempt to hide itself simply because, by an inexorable law, it must not be witnessed.

When the vision had disappeared into the tunnel of the road going in the direction perhaps of Dargue's estate, Jean stayed motionless, listening after the fading drumbeat, until it mingled with the beating of his own heart in his ears.

When he moved again, it was with a stupefied caution. He was not afraid, but he suspected he should be.

He stumbled on, and with no further encounter, came eventually back to the brink of the Town. Here, earlier, he had found a possible lodging. Having climbed the wall, he slept in the garden of this place, for he would not rouse them at that hour, the prohibitions of his upbringing forbade such a thing. It was almost dawn in any case. The sky's membrane palpitated. Beneath a mango tree with savage leaves he fell, and using his bag for a pillow, began to tell himself mindlessly over and over what he must do. That all there *was* to do now was to seek labor, as a clerk, or even at a meaner occupation, earning his return passage to the City. What else could he attempt? For he was like a somnambulist roughly wakened. The dream had misled; he had lost his way.

Although he could not sleep, every now and then the image of the procession on Oleander Road went swaying through his thoughts, scattering them.

Had the procession been going to the house of Dargue? But they had told him on the ship, the black race of the islands hated the white race. The last wave of the Revolution, breaking there, had freed the slaves of Haïssa, but made them instead mostly serfs. And those that had become black masters, in their turn, hated too, in a more perilous, educated manner, anything that was pale, even where darkness ran just visibly under the skin.

This was a land of nightmares, this country he had woken up in. He must get home. Anything else was futile. He was broken.

It is probable Jean went mad that night. Of course he had been tinged by insanity for years, for all his life. But like a deadly flower it burst open in him then, in the hours on the road, going back, cheated. Beneath the mango in the garden of the lodging house.

That is not to say his madness was incurable.

When day arrived, he heard persons stirring in the house and went and claimed his room there. Next, having washed himself and shaved, he went into the Town to look for employment. He did all this very correctly, and like a man with no soul. There is a name for this condition in the islands, and he was to hear it quite soon.

In the afternoon, when a bruised light hung over the Town, the outrider of the storm that usually occurred daily at that season, Jean de St. Jean was sitting in the dusty little office of someone who might be willing to give him some work. He had been waiting an interminable time, which was in reality only a few minutes, and his nerves were urging him sluggishly but repeatedly to get up and leave, for this could be no use to him. Then the door opened, and a black man entered.

He was dressed as a laborer, and his personal scent was strong, like the musk of the panther. He looked directly at Jean and, without a word, jerked his feline head toward the street.

Jean saw this, and said, "What do you want?"

He had not achieved the proper purblind arrogance of the white in Haïssa, or the proper uneasiness either. He reacted as he would have done to something unreal yet fundamentally inimical. To a threatening and *superior* thing.

The man did not answer him, but poised there, plainly expecting Jean to get up and go out with him.

Jean was so exhausted, so demoralized and unhinged, that in a moment this was exactly what he did.

When they were on the street, Jean said, "But—"

That was all.

They went down and down, through a kind of corkscrew of streets, where vines and palms poured over walls, and the houses came to be built of planks and tin. Finally there was a space, and a rickety hut with a tin roof, and the black man pointed at its door.

"Who are you?" said Jean.

The black man laughed. He looked like a god when he did so, lawless and all-wise. Then he spat on the ground and walked off another way, and Jean was left there, at the bottom of the corkscrew, with only the door in front of him. So he pushed the door wide.

Inside was the dusk again, redolent with such stuff as cooked rice, blood, spice, tobacco, washing, and rum. He could make out no furniture, but some black beings were seated on the earth floor in an open circle, and before them was a scatter of objects lit by one window. Jean saw dried beans and cards, a shawl, a fruit, and the bones of a dog brightly painted.

"Shut our door," said a voice.

Jean drew the door in against him, and the shack became more solid and less visible, and the bones glowed, and the white eyes in the faces like ebony, like beautiful alien masks, and like nothing human.

"Sit down with us," someone said. And someone else gave a cruel laugh.

Jean remained in the shut door. They were figments of a new dream.

Finally, a man said from the circle, "M'sir Dargue is dead. Are you sorry he dead?"

Jean choked back a confused reply. He felt compelled to respond, unbearably excited, could not speak.

"Why you would want him alive?" said the voice.

There was a great attention then. They focused it upon Jean. He did not know how many of them there were, but the eyes fastened on him like claws.

"Alive—so I—" said Jean.

"He not loved, Monsieur Dargue," said the voice. The others purred in the dark. "No one is sorry."

Jean covered his face with one hand. He longed, as though to vomit, to evict the cry: *My father's murderer!* It would not come.

"You not sorry," said the voice, soothingly.

The illness flooded from Jean, the words released him. He said hoarsely, "Yes, I came to kill him. Too late."

"Not so. We give him you, for killing."

And the others purred.

They were smiling at him. In every night of a face a sickle moon. But Dargue was dead.

"We invite you to come our God-Place," said the first voice. A black hand reached out and took up one of the bones from the ground. The bone moved as if still alive, and animal. "We invite M'sir Dargue. We fetch him. You be surprised. But we give you have M'sir Dargue, because you want him so."

Jean thought they must have pursued him back along Oleander

Road on the previous night, and read his mind. They were sorcerers, so much was apparent. He had always half believed in sorcery.

But what were they saying? That Dargue was not dead, but in some way their prisoner?

"You pay the price," said the voice.

Jean said, "I haven't any money—"

They purred again. The shack reverberated. Jean thought, Not money. It isn't that. Something they want and I want, but I must pay and then they need not.

He thought, very clearly: What am I doing? Where am I? What is happening to me? And someone else said, "*This is the Religion of the Night.*"

Then he was sitting close by them on the earth floor, cooking hot as if above a volcano, with his back to the wall and the tin ceiling above, from which feathers and paper blossoms and bells hung on threads. A mirror floated in space, like a tear, a small lizard clinging to its cracked, uneven rim. A black woman was giving him drink out of a calabash gourd. It was rum with something sweet. Jean drank, and thanked the woman, and she laughed, and touched his brow with her finger. Her touch was like a star, it burned.

Rain was drilling on the tin roof. They had given him a direction, where he must go tonight, not too late. . . .

"No," said Jean.

"Good day."

Jean returned to his lodging and dozed feverishly on the bed. He dreamed his Aunt Andromede was standing over him, wringing her hands, saying, "Let me advise you, Jean, you mustn't go anywhere with such people." But there were feathers pinned into her tight hair.

The storm flew toward the sea, and the evening descended clear, as stars rose up through it.

He went out and moved toward a market at a crossroads known as Horse Tail. He had already asked the way. He received solemn looks and vague replies, until a wizened black woman had shown him the route, drawing a diagram in the dust. Still, he meant to be late. He did not guess why he was going. They might set on him, though there was surely no motive. He was destitute; he had done nothing to annoy them, except that being alive might be enough. He concluded they meant to play some trick. But he was drawn as if by a magnet. It allowed him to dawdle, but not to resist.

It was dark when he reached the crossroads. There were some carts and awnings, and fires burning on the ground, and candles in gourds strung up. Commerce of a desultory type was in progress, scrawny chickens changing hands, some barter over beans and pots of jelly.

The market ignored Jean, as if he were invisible. Then a man came walking straight between the carts, the refuse, and the market seemed to make way for him. He wore a black robe, black on black, but in his hand was a whip with a white bone handle.

When he reached Jean, there were all at once five or six other men at this man's back.

The man said to Jean, "Come, now. We invite you."

And turning away, he strode off again, toward the forest and the hills. The other men went with him and, pulled as though by tough cord, Jean walked after them.

The God-Place crouched in a somber clearing. Water ran close by, snarled in the roots of an enormous tree, making a weird tearing sound. The roof of the temple was thatched, with an open court beneath, enclosing the sanctum, and full of the night people of Haïssa. As the man with the whip had ascended the forest path among his guard, and Jean followed, he heard the subterranean notes of conch shells blowing in the woods above. When the temple came in sight, and they approached it, these shells were blown again, a dubious, threatening greeting.

The man with the whip strode to a boundary of the court, which was marked by some small heaps of meal, petals, and paper. He used the whip's bone handle to point with. "You will stand there. You say nothing. If you fear and run away, you not get what you come for." He did not look at Jean, had never really looked into Jean's face or eyes.

Jean did not protest. He went to the indicated spot at the perimeter of the court. Five women who had been grouped inside the boundary, near where he must stand, ebbed away, turning their shadow masks from him.

The man with the whip passed into the temple. They had brought a chair and set it by the entry to the inner shrine. The chair had an abnormally high and upright back resembling a coffin. The whip man seated himself, and the crowd in the court deferred to him. Evidently he was their priest, and their magician.

The skull lamps of the calabash gourds burned from the thatch, and here and there glimmered wicks in cups of oil. The light only made one with the darkness. And the smell of the God-Place was intense and disturbing.

A girl in white came flaunting over the court. She carried a lighted candle and a jar of clear rum, from which she poured a libation under the central post of the thatch roof. Another white-clad girl came after her, an echo, a smoke-ghost. She poured flour or meal on to the ground in a pattern. A third girl came with a snake's rattle in each hand, and she whirled like a top until her white and her black merged into a vortex, out of which all three girls seemed to vanish away.

Then the three drums of the spirits began, and Jean saw the Dance of the Religion of the Night, a forbidden thing, both prayer and invocation, during which power descends, along the temple's very spine, and rays out among those who call themselves the Night Beasts, the black lynxes of the hills, whose true hills are older yet and whose rites began in cities of stone and bone when white men only whimpered at their cave mouths, afraid of all things and the dark especially, with some continuing cause.

Jean saw how the people formed into a black serpent of flesh, a body of many parts linked by a communal soul. And they passed about the spine post of the temple in the ancient benign positive right-to-right motion known in the Craft of Europe as God's Flow-ing, and commemorated by artisans in the action of clocks and watches. The steps of the Dance were a rapid stamping and tossing, and the drums formed these steps out of the muscle and skeleton of every dancer, lifting them, setting them down. The names of the three drums, which were later told to Jean, were the little cat's drum, and the drum of the second, and the mother Drum, which roars like a she-bull under the ground, the earthquake birth, the summoner.

As he watched, Jean felt his own body beginning to move with the rhythm of the Dance, although, too, he was rooted to the spot. A crazy exhilaration rose with the sweat and perfume of the God-Place. Naturally, educated and refined as he had been, Jean was instinctively resistant to it. He could not and would not give himself to the surge of power. He stayed outside, his breathing rapid and shallow and his eyes on fire, steeled, aroused, dismayed, in chains.

After a while, out of the dancing serpent, a young woman broke away. She raised her arms and screamed aloud. The dancers gave her room. She was the mare-horse, and one would come to ride her.

She was the mare among the Night Beasts and the horseman would possess her, riding in her skin, a god mounting her, and she would lose herself, gaining him.

The woman who was possessed was now in an open space against the central post. Her eyes were like blind windows, yet something flashed behind them. A girl in a pale robe came to the woman and handed her a black hen. Its terrible fluttering exploded in blood and feathers as the possessed tore off its head and wings with her teeth.

The woman flung the hen down, and drawing a pin from her dress, she thrust it through her arm, once, twice, three, four, five times. Jean beheld the bright point going in and coming out of her, but there was no blood now, no pain. She danced on the carcass of the dead bird, twirling and shouting.

The magician-priest had risen from his coffin-chair. He pointed at the woman, and all at once the blood-beat of the drumming fell away, leaving behind an extraordinary absence, as though part of the very ground had dropped into space. He spoke in the patois, which Jean did not truly understand. It was evidently a welcome.

The possessed ceased her whirling. She stood before the priest, laughing with tiger's teeth. Then she cried out in a deep man's voice; Jean caught the idea that she was now a lord and would be obeyed.

The priest nodded and bowed. Clearly he said, "Lead us."

And then the woman, or whatever she had become, went springing out of the court, and bounded away through the clearing, and the dancers broke and raced after her.

Jean stood still, not knowing what to do, until fingers brushed on his arm and someone said to him, "We go to the graveyard now."

He did not see who spoke, and the hand was gone from him like the flick of a paw.

He turned and half staggered into the rear of the swirling wave. It accepted him and rolled with him away across the clearing and up into the matted forest darkness sprinkled with wild stars.

Afterward—that is, one month later—Jean conjectured that some drug might have been pressed on him. Though he ate and drank nothing throughout the ceremony of the Night, yet there were certain poisons he had heard the Night Beasts used, and these, rubbed into the skin, worked very swiftly on the blood and brain.

As he ran through the forest, Jean had only the sensation of forward motion, and that his eyes were strangely enlarged, like those of some nocturnal animal. It occurred to him he saw, in glimpses, creatures that normally a man does not easily see—birds upon branches, lizards and frogs, etched in fine silver. . . . There were other things, too, of which only the vaguest impression was left—of a huge man, naked but for a cloak, of a species of demon that grew in the trees like leaves, of a woman anointing herself in a glade. None of them were real, yet he saw, and acknowledged, each of them, as he ran by.

The graveyard must have been some way up behind Oleander Road. It was presumably respectable, but to the Beasts of Night, open as a door. They made an invocation at the gate, and again it seemed something went prancing along the wall, but it was gone before Jean could identify it.

His next formed impression—which was abnormally apparent, in fact—was of a woman he took for a priestess standing out before the others at a place where the ground was freshly dug. All around were Christian crosses and ornate monuments on which the lianas fed in a still gray moonlight. There was a headstone, too, naked and unfinished, and here the woman's snakelike shadow fell. She wore white, like the others, but it was a gown that might have come from Jean's City, ivory satin, sashed, and sewn with brilliants, leaving her shoulders bare as smooth black lacquer. She wore a plumed hat also, and a white domino with scintillants stitched about the eyes. He did not know where she had come from. He thought she carried a fan, then he saw it was a bunch of the ugly horsetail plants. She smiled as she stood over the new grave. Jean could make out no name on the headstone, but there was no need.

The priestess straddled the grave in her satin gown. She frisked the horsetail in the air and shook her head of plumes. From everywhere there came then the clacking together of rocks and stones.

Jean held his breath, could not catch it, had surrendered. He believed in anything at this moment, and accordingly, liberated night did not fail him.

"Monsieur Dargue!" cried the night, in all its voices, over and over again.

Jean found that he had called out, too.

And the stones clacked.

And something pranced along the wall, and there went the possessed woman whirling with a burning branch in her hands, and a man's face, and the black masks all turned one way and the moon that was like a quartered fruit—

And the earth on the grave shook. It shook and shattered and a piece of wood shot up out of it, and the satin priestess screamed down into the grave, "Come out, come out, come out!" And then half a wooden coffin lid burst up and stood on end and a colorless white man's hand came creeping out of the soil like a blind crab.

The priestess stayed as she was. She never moved. The strength that seared from her was hot and palpable as the smell of living bodies and decay.

Then the ground fissured, and Dargue came up out of it.

Instantly the noise of the rocks and the shouting ended in a dense ringing silence.

Dargue stood in the bell glass of it, or what had been Dargue, a sort of man, clad in a nightshirt, and a crucifix on his breast pushed sideways. His nails were torn and dirty where he had used them to thrust off the coffin, a feat of great strength, which, alive, he might have been incapable of. His face was a dead man's face. He had lost his good angel, they said, *soul-gone.*

The dead eyes did not look around, the head did not turn, having got up from his bed he did not stir.

"*Ha!*" said the priestess. And she spat a stream of something that glowed into his face; it might only have been the white rum. Then she moved aside.

Some men ran forward. They carried the horsetails in their hands, and with those they slashed Dargue across the head and body. The spiky plants made wounds in his flesh, but Dargue did not bleed. He did not attempt to protect himself, and when, quite suddenly, he fell to his knees, the gesture evoked neither pity nor satisfaction, it was plainly only that the tendons of his legs had relaxed.

Jean stared at what he was witnessing, and now he tried desperately hard to feel something in response. Perhaps he did not even know that this was what he did. He was not afraid, no longer exhilarated. If anything, he felt very tired, for he had not slept properly or eaten much, and everything was alien, and therefore somehow all strangeness had abruptly become mundane.

What he tried most to feel was his anger, hatred of Dargue. It was there within him, but he could not get hold of it. It had faded to a memory.

The priestess moved up in front of Jean. She looked as though she were laughing at him, her wonderful dreadful teeth glittering. Her hands were gloved as if for the opera, and she was balancing on them, before him, a sword.

She nodded, and the plumes in the hat fluttered, while the sword was motionless.

"What do you want me to do?" said Jean. He used the stupidity as an amulet, but of course it was ineffectual.

"Take the sword," said the black priestess. And she put it gently into his hands, which had somehow risen to grasp it.

The Beasts of the Night waited, and the moon waited, and the graveyard, and the Island, and Dargue who was dead, he waited too.

Jean went across the silent ground, toward Dargue, who kneeled there with his head sunk on his breast.

In all his least lawful, most incoherent dreams, Jean had never deployed his vengeance in this fashion.

He used both hands and all his strength to swing the sword backward and forward again, ramming it in through the wall of Dargue's chest, through the linen, and through the flesh, which crumbled like biscuit. A trickle of murky stuff oozed out. A rib snapped and came pointing from the cavity. The body of Dargue crumpled over and took the sword with it out of Jean's grip.

Jean stood there like a fool, feeling nothing except a faint disgust, until someone should tell him what to do now.

Shortly someone did come up, and murmured—was it courteously?—that he might go, his portion was finished, out of the gate, and follow the path, and he would soon come to the edges of the Town, with the moon to watch over him.

So he stepped off the grave and walked away.

He kept repeating to himself as he went, *My father's murderer.*

This did not help.

Then, when the graveyard had been left behind and he was on a rambling track through the forest, with the moon glimpsing out like a girl's face among the balconies of the trees, he saw what he had done, that he had cheated death in an odd, insulting manner, and this was why he had been allowed to perform the act with the sword, since death was probably venerated here, and to cheat him was such a bit of cheek it must require payment.

But all Jean wanted, actually, by this stage, was to find his lodging and go to sleep. He no longer cared about anything else. He shook everything off him as he went on, like dust from his coat. And like dust, some of it was already in his system, he had swallowed it, it was a part of him.

When he reached the lodging house he no longer had scruples about waking them up. He knocked and banged on the shutters. When they let him in, he crawled through the house and dropped on the mattress in his clothes, with the dust of night in his belly, mind, and spirit. And without a single dream that he knew of he slept, like the dead.

3

As it happened, at any rate as it was told, the story of Jean de St. Jean has here a break or interval. Real life, and its experiences, are seldom completely serial. Yet the space of a year may be recounted quickly, the method indeed of my informant.

Jean's recovery—or lapse—from the hour of his murder of a dead man seems to have been immediate. His impulse was to ignore what had happened, then boldly to question it. Though he kept his reasons private, by asking casually here and there in knowledgeable, biased circles, for facts concerning Haïssa's Religion of the Night—that is, among the skeptical white community—Jean learned to behold himself as a victim of drug or fantasy. Perhaps the shock of Dargue's death had unhinged him temporarily, perhaps he had the voyager's malaise, a kind of earth-sickness, induced by stepping ashore after months on the ocean. Whatever it had been, any slight fears he may have had that some further pursuit might be made of him, threats or pleas offered, based upon his participation in the ceremony, were allayed by the passage of time. No one approached him to accuse or mock or coerce. He even grew used to the black beings of the Island, and came to think of them as inferior men, or sometimes as men, so that they lost for him their appearances of shadows and panthers, lynxes, and night personified. He was even briefly tempted by their women, but some moral code he had always tried to obey precluded such adventures. He had been brought up on a diet not solely of hate but ironically of an ideal of true love.

The previous votive of working to obtain his passage home he quickly sought and achieved. His City education and person assisted Jean, and he gained the secretary's job formerly mooted. Presently, along with the accumulation of bank notes, he was absorbed into the social context of white Haïssa. Class was held, since the Revolution, to be immaterial, but was still insidiously observed. Jean's manners were of sufficient quality, however, and his looks of enough attraction, that insidiously observed class did not much hinder him. He rose, and he bloomed, and even as conditions bore the harvest of money to return him across the sea, they drew in about his roots and began to secure him to the Island earth.

It must be wondered, in this time, if he wrote at all to his Aunt Andromede, and if so, what he told her. His reports could, soon enough, be of the nicest, full of good prospects and nostalgias. How he put it to her that Dargue had perished is conjecture. He could not have made of it the grim joke it was, nor, certainly, even in the most unsolid terms, could he have hinted at the scene in the graveyard. Letters took so long, in any case, going back and forth. It is possible that they were mislaid, or unsent. One senses she did not receive any, but that may be false. One knows at least she never heard the facts in their naked form.

Presently, along with the rest, Jean became accustomed to the climate. He came to look for the seasonal afternoon rains, the thunder, the moon-drenched nights in which, by then, he would stroll or ride without glancing over his shoulder. He liked the friends he had made. Though assiduously he saved his fare, it had turned into a sham.

He did not exactly know this until one morning, going to his office along a street above the bay, a carriage slowly passed him. Looking into it inadvertently, he saw a young woman in a dove-colored frock and pearl earrings. Her name was Gentilissa Ferrier —he identified her from the carriage, which he had seen about before. Monsieur Ferrier was a little known to Jean, and had mentioned that his daughter was to come home from one of the other islands, where family connections had for months concealed her. The sight of the girl startled Jean. For some minutes, when the carriage had gone on, he did not know why. Then he recalled the features of a Madonna from a painting he had seen as a boy. The Venus of Haïssa was also a Madonna, both carnal and immaculate, having two aspects, a flower virgin and a black virgin. Jean had in his researches heard the name of this goddess, who is wedded to all men and to none. He did not, naturally, for a second associate her with Gentilissa Ferrier, but by the time he had reached his office, Jean sensed an immanence. His father and mother had fallen in love at sight. In his efforts to recreate them, possibly Jean had yearned to do the same. Now the opportunity was before him. He took it.

Once he had convinced himself of what had happened to him there came about one of those coincidences that, to a person obsessed, indicate the hand of Destiny. Jean found he had been invited to a dinner party at the Ferrier house. This had already happened twice. There had been no reason not to invite him again; he had behaved very charmingly before.

It is curious, maybe, through this sliding frame of a year, to see Jean now, earlier an incarnation of Hamlet, currently Romeo. But the passion is constant, merely the object has been changed.

With the same headlong zeal that sent him aboard the ship, that goaded him along Oleander Road toward the estate of Dargue, in just that way he prepared himself for his first meeting with the girl Gentilissa. His eyes blazed, he was excited, fiercely determined. He had been disappointed then, by those appalling words: *He is dead.* But he put all that behind him, and could not credit a disappointment now. Gentilissa was there to be won. A year of success proved that he was able to win things. He had a half vision of her in the City on his arm, when his fortune had been made. Or they were driving through the forest roads above Haïssa Town in a taper of brief dusk, and she leaned her head upon his shoulder.

The Ferrier family was quite wealthy. This pleased Jean only because it meant Gentilissa would have been elegantly reared, though she would not, he understood, be as sophisticated as a girl of his City. What impediment could there be? He had prospects, and it was up to him to make her love him. If only he could do that.

He said a prayer to the Virgin. It was not the Virgin of the two faces, but the albino Madonna in the church. But he had already noted, if he had thought of it, that the shacks of Night Beasts often had their crosses, their icons of Christ. The gods had many names and were everywhere.

When he rode up to the house, it had a certain look of some houses in the Island. He knew it, anyway. Set off the road among large mango trees, ferns, and thickets of bamboo, constructed of apparently crumbling sugar, with orchids, and a tame parrot in a cage on the veranda, that called out in the tongue of the City: "*Who goes there?*"

A black servant ran to see to Jean's horse. Jean climbed the steps and went up into the big dining room, lit like the church with candles. Once the sun set, the moths would come in droves to die, and the sun was setting now. The guests were for going down to the classical pavilion, to see it.

Jean, with his glass of white wine in his hand, was lightheaded and anxious. He had not found her yet among the women. He wondered if he had been mistaken in her, if she would look the same.

Below the veranda on the other side, screened by a towering plantain, the kitchen fumed and the two black women were poised there to be ignored as Jean had learned to ignore them.

The pavilion stood against a break in the trees, and beyond, far down, the sea was lying, with the sun going into it like a bubble into glass.

Jean wandered off a short way. He had seen the sun set before. He was instinctively searching for Gentilissa. And suddenly there she was.

It was perfect. Against a dusky, mossy wall, she was sitting on a bench, in her party gown, which was white and left bare her throat and shoulders. Her dark hair was done in ringlets, with a rose.

This he observed, and that she was lovely. But he noticed too she cast a shadow, and the shadow was a house woman, who sat with her on the bench. And by the bench there was a plant growing that Jean remembered.

It was true, he had seen it since about the forest tracks and the cemeteries of the Town. He had even garnered its title: the Queen-Mare's Tail. They said it flourished where there had been a death. A graveyard bloom. He had never quite come to like it, or be comfortable in its vicinity—that was the residue of the night he had once spent in the hills.

Now the sight of it struck him a glancing blow, that it should be growing there, against Gentilissa's skirt. And all at once the shadow figure beside her assumed an unnamed identity. For a moment Jean even thought he knew her. But she was only an old black woman, a house servant.

Just then Gentilissa got to her feet, and looking up she saw Jean gazing at her. She must have taken his apprehension for interest, for she lowered her lashes, and hid her face behind a little fan she carried, in the coquettish mannerism of young white women of the islands. It was a silly gesture, and it reassured him.

He followed her with his eyes as she went away behind the wall, the black woman slipping after.

The sun had gone down and night smoldered in the Ferrier garden and on the veranda the parrot called. There was nothing to discompose. The family and guests and Jean went in to dinner.

Gentilissa Ferrier was beautiful and adorable; she flamed like the candles, she was serene as a nun. Her moods were variable but not hectic. Jean was fascinated. She was all he had surmised. And in addition she had the power of speech, and thoughts, she could play the piano, had a thin sweet voice that sang. When they asked her about books she had read some, and she had a dream of going to the City.

When Jean attended her, she did not seem to mind it. As he turned the pages of her music, once or twice her eyes rested upon him.

When the dinner came to its end, he was sure, and going up to her candidly, with the mantle of the City she dreamed of nonchalantly over his shoulders, he asked if he might have the rose from her hair.

She was prettily flustered. For what could he want it?

"It has been close to you, Madamoiselle Ferrier," said Jean. He was a poet's son. He had the taint if not the gift.

His final sight of her that night was upon the veranda, the whole sugar house caught in a splash of stars. The lamp that twinkled upon her put the stars at her ears and in her eyes to the very last twist of the path. The black woman was her childhood companion, a sort of nurse resembling Juliet's. She dressed neatly and had a bracelet. Jean had been polite to her on the veranda, and the woman bowed. They called her Tibelle.

In the weeks that followed, Jean often found occasion to be passing the Ferrier house. They were never unwelcoming. Monsieur spoke of the City, and of business, Madame was earnest to have cards. Then Gentilissa would come and serve juices in crystal jugs. She would take Jean away to show him birds and butterflies in the garden, and Tibelle would be their chaperon, gliding some distance behind them. And sometimes they would sit in an arbor while Gentilissa coaxed tunes from a mandolin, and Tibelle would sit far off, a black shape still as the iron owl on the gate. The woman had a pipe and now and then would smoke it, and the smoke moved in rising, but not Tibelle. The jewelry birds darted through the foliage. Jean began to court Gentilissa.

It was pleasant, there was no hurry. Everything acquiesced. Time seemed to stretch forever. If he was impatient, it was only through physical desire. He had not kissed her. These things, this temperance, were inborn. The climate, which could incite, could also calm with its false assurance, Go slowly. Lazily, a man and woman drew together. No one denied.

Then one evening, as Tibelle the black volcano sat smoking on the horizon, Gentilissa leaned to Jean and brushed his cheek with her warm lips.

It was as if a barrier fell down. He turned upon her and pulled her to him, but before his hunger found any expression, she moved away.

"No, Jean," said Gentilissa, as sweetly as she sang and out of her nun's face. "You mustn't."

"But why?"

"Because Papa would be horribly angry."

Jean was reckless at last. "But he'll have to be told. I shall ask him for you. You know I will."

"No," said Gentilissa. She looked neither sad nor unnerved. She was entirely at peace.

"You feel nothing for me," said Jean. It was a boastful demand. Despite her look, he was certain by now that she loved him.

"Oh Jean," she said.

"Then I'll ask him tonight."

"He will refuse you."

Jean hesitated. He had not made his intentions obvious, but neither had they been opaque. Would Gentilissa's father not have sounded some warning previously, if he were vehemently opposed?

"Allow me the attempt," said Jean.

"I can't. How can I? Papa has no objection to my holding court . . . that I should have admirers. But he expects me to marry a man of substance. Already there is someone in view."

"That's barbarous."

"It's how it is done here."

"Nonsense. I—"

"Jean, you will grieve me."

It was so shocking, this development, he could not credit it. He sought to take her hand. Gentilissa would not permit this.

"I love you," he said. "I think you care for me."

"I may not answer."

"Your eyes answer." This was a lie. Her eyes were blank. She said nothing, either. But he had all the evidence of several weeks, when every sigh and tremor and sideways look had concocted meaning. "Gentilissa, in a year or so I might be a rich man. It's been said to me, promised."

"Dearest Jean," said Gentilissa. Her breast rose with delirious softness as she drew in her breath. "I can't go against Papa. He means me to marry a man from another island. There's nothing I can do. I never guessed the strength of your feeling. I thought you amused yourself with me."

Jean swore by God. Gentilissa averted her head. She said, very low, "You must leave me now. We must never see each other again, until after I am married."

Jean sprang to his feet, but already Gentilissa was moving lightly away, like a piece of white cotton down. And summoned uncannily without a cry, the servant woman, Tibelle, was slinking toward them.

In a rage of powerlessness and disbelief, Jean stood in the Ferrier garden until the black woman and the white had disappeared together beyond the mango trees.

There is another name for the Religion of the Night among the islands. They term it Nightmare Magic. Once you have ever been touched by it, there is no getting free. To the devotee that is no problem. To the outsider, whom the gods, however obliquely and remotely, have ridden, the Religion is fever. It may lie dormant ten years. But it is not to be escaped from, in the end. They tell you, have nothing to do with it. But sometimes wanting is enough to bring it down, like a cloud from the mountain. No sooner did Jean run into the apartment of his aunt with the branch of their hate in blossom, no sooner did he set sail, than he called the Devil, and the Devil started forth. Before he left the ship, the first night, the entity had shown itself. It was too late. Death brought Jean de St. Jean to the Island, and cheated him and bargained with him and claimed him. There is not a boulder or a leaf there without some life in it, or something of death in it. It was not only the forests or the human skin of Haïssa that earned it the adjective *Black*.

For a month, Jean dwelled in a condition of misery and fury that was almost lunatic. Initially, he did his best to go about his affairs of business and existence otherwise as before. But that was impossible. His heart had been cut out. He was in constant agony and barely alive. Sometimes he would lose himself in awful daydreams, riding to the house and confronting Monsieur Ferrier, bursting in upon her wedding and shooting down the groom. At other, worse times, he visualized his own life stretching to infinity bereft of Gentilissa. It seemed to him his pain would never cease. If he got drunk it might abate for half an hour, only to return with redoubled ferocity. Sober, he was like a man beneath a ton weight, he could hardly raise his head.

He was thought to be ill. He was treated with sympathy, next with concern, ultimately with impatience. This was not the obliging, efficient Jean they knew.

At night he would sit in his rooms and look at his money saved for the homeward voyage. It was like the coinage of oblivion. To go away was out of the question. To remain was not to be endured.

That he also thought of killing himself is conceivable, but it was a symptom rather than an intent.

Then one afternoon there came to his office, where he was sitting in rapt dejection, a letter. He knew at once that it was from her. Tearing it open he read: *I can bear our separation no longer. If you still love me and will dare the consequences, be this evening just after sunset by the statue of the slave. Tibelle will bring you to me.*

The effect upon Jean, after his unhappiness, was galvanic, almost injurious. He shook, went white, laughed aloud once or twice, and generally furthered the prevailing opinion among his colleagues that he was not long to be among them.

The letter he did not let go of, and leaving his post early, he rushed to his rooms to prepare himself for this clandestine and romantic assignation. He had not a single qualm, although he did think her a trifle foolish, and very endearing, to trust him so much. Surely she loved him, and through the blessing of that, everything else could be made to come right.

The statue of the slave, a rough and ready work attempted in the classical mode, stood near a crossroad and a market. They were unfamiliar to Jean, although he found the statue easily enough. He had arrived before time, and watched the sun go down behind the towers of a pair of churches, and then the darkness came, and he beheld the fires burning in the market, and the ragged awnings, and the chicken corpses along the carts, and smelled the overripeness of the gourds, and heard the chattering of the black men and women who idled there. An unpleasant memory wakened in Jean. Before he had satisfactorily thrust it off, he saw the woman Tibelle coming across the street. Her hair was tied up in a cream kerchief as always, and on her ebony stick of wrist the bracelet dripped like water. She walked right up to him, and scrutinized his face. *To be sure of me, for her mistress' sake,* Jean thought to himself, but he was not easy with her look for all that.

"Now you come with Tibelle."

"Where?"

"Tibelle take you."

"Where are we going?"

"You come, you see."

Jean shrugged. He no longer felt as he had done, elated, slightly drunk, a little afraid. Now there was something heavy again, something pressing down on him. As he went after the servant woman, his entrails were cold and his heart beat in hard leaden strokes. His father might have told him, these are the sensations of a man en route to the gallows.

Up behind the market the streets rose and then there began to be the wide avenues where the fine old houses had been built, the houses of broken sugar under the poured molasses of the vines.

And then they were on a stretch that could have been Oleander Road, or Mango Tree Ride, or one of those other flowery, fruiting tracks that led into the forest and the hills. And then they came over a stony slope showing the sea in a net of trees, and there was a cemetery before them, a graveyard.

Jean stopped, and in front of him his guide halted and turned to look at him again.

"Where you think she can meet with you?" said Tibelle contemptuously, "in the hotel?"

"But here—"

"Here is safe," said Tibelle. "What you got to worry?"

And she went on again, in at the gate with a sort of stumble that might have been an obeisance, and between the graves.

Jean followed her. There was perhaps no going back. The night was all around, and the hills of Haïssa. It was too late to fly.

He noticed as he got down the ridged path behind her that things were hanging out on many of the headstones, like curious washing. There were bunches of feathers, and beads, and garlands of paper flowers, with here and there a rosary, a mask on a string with staring eyeless eyes, bones and bells that clinked and rang sometimes as the night breeze twisted at them. There was a feeling of immensity and congestion, everything too close and the night outside vast as all space where hung the bells and bones and stars inaudibly clinking and fluttering in the breath of the gods.

Jean began to cough a little, something that had not happened since he was a child, it was a sign of nerves.

Tibelle said, "Hush, hush, here you are."

And there was a shack or hut before them under a stunted palm, in the middle of the death-place.

Tibelle went aside, as she had been used to before, as if to smoke her pipe, and Jean was left by the hut in the darkness. He knew quite well that all there was to do was to push the door. He knew, and it no longer mattered. The interval of a year had evaporated, and its pleasures and agonies with it. Therefore, without hesitation finally, he opened the door and walked into the hut.

He was half surprised. For Gentilissa was sitting there before him, on a small chair, with her hands folded in her lap.

"Jean," she said.

Her eyes were large and luminous. He had always been struck by some quality in them, an effect he had taken for purity or innocence. But it was a sort of vacuity really, he could see as much now, a sort of vacancy, and when she had been with him and seemed to shine, it was because her eyes reflected him, he filled up the emptiness. It had made her attractive, like a flattering mirror.

"Jean?" she said again, now in a questioning tone.

She was wearing black. That was arresting for Tibelle the black woman had worn white. Gentilissa in black was changed. Her face was like a moon, a mask.

"Oh, Jean," she said.

And outside, the drums started, as he had heard them countless times from the hills, throbbing and rattling, for some festivity or dance. The little drum and the drum of the second and the mother Drum who roared in the earth.

Gentilissa came to her feet. She stamped lightly and tossed her head and her hair flew out, the heavy ringlets. Her eyes were flat as windowpanes. Then he began to see that something moved behind them.

Gentilissa laughed and gave herself. Her face slackened and became an idiot's. Her eyes rolled. She seemed about to fall. But something caught her and held her. Her head turned on her neck and moved around again to confront him. Behind the mask of her face, another was there, that Jean recalled. It was at the same time black and white. Whether the black lay under the white or the black was fleshed out upon the white he could not be sure. But in the eyes there was no mistaking it, the night being, the lord who had come to ride his mare, and to claim the bargain price.

Gentilissa's mouth gaped open. Out of it boomed the note of a deep bass bell. "I *here*. You *know* me," she said, in the voice of a giant man taller than the treetops, older than the Island, with the sea for blood and the bones of all the Island's dead in a necklace at his throat. "Know *me*," said Death. And Jean knew him, knew him. Knew *him*.

They said he died of a fever in Haïssa Town, having been sick for some while. The Island is noted for its seasonal fevers. They said it was a shame he died so young, the same age as his father, indeed, and far from home. You may come across the grave in a shady corner of the Christian Cemetery near Oleander Road. There is no inscription beyond his name, *Jean de St. Jean*. Though sometimes flowers may be left there, by girls in colored scarves who walk like cats and smile, blackened by the sun to the darkness of night, Negré girls, who cannot, probably, have known him.

This grave is modest, here in the cemetery of Paradys.
Easy to overlook it, but we shall not.

    Weeds grow, unpruned, there are no floral tributes.
The name: Julie d'Is.

Beautiful Lady

Sugar and spice
And all things nice.

Traditional

Chorgeh said, leaning a little over the balustrade, "How does she merit the name? I wouldn't think her even somewhat stylish. Her hair scraped back under that worm of a hat, her gloves darned. Her figure is all right; her face is nothing, only sallow. Her eyes—Well, they seem a little unusual, tilted, like an Oriental's. Is that the clue?"

"Not at all," said Chorgeh's informant. The two men (Chorgeh young and dangerous-looking in his fashionable coat, the elder conservative and restrained, yet tapping a new-fangled cigarette on a silver box) stared a moment over the gallery at the woman passing underneath along the arcade. "No, it's nothing about her appearance. Put it in the Roman tongue. Have you never heard of deadly nightshade?"

"*Poison*," said Chorgeh, abruptly smiling, pleased and satisfied. "I *see*."

Below, the woman had paused to glance into one of the tiny, dainty shops. It was true, she looked poor, shabby, and neglected, by others and herself. Close to, her face would be unpowdered, her nails too short, her hair carelessly combed and stuffed into a small bun, unbecoming and resentful.

"Other than *Bella Donna*, her name is Julie d'Is."

"You know this for a fact."

"Oh, I know all about her. I make it my business to know such things."

"You romancer," said Chorgeh. The man was his uncle, inasmuch as he had once been Chorgeh's mother's lover, and remained her friend. The man was also a writer of some eminence. His stories were always interesting, and sometimes real, but Chorgeh felt free to insult him, since he was one of the few persons Chorgeh genuinely respected. The "uncle" smoked his cigarette, and Julie d'Is, the Beautiful Lady, gazed in at delicate eggs of enamel and wonderful chocolates in the shape of flowers. Her face was like a snake's now, without expression. Clearly, she regarded such items as having nothing to do with her, she only watched their strangeness, perhaps to see if they would provide prey.

"She does look," said Chorgeh, "a remarkably horrible woman."

"Be well advised. Keep far away from her. No, I'm not joking. A distance of ten feet was reckoned barely sufficient."

"Then she *is* a poisoner."

"Aside from Bella Donna, she was called the Angel of Pestilence."

"But not any longer?"

"Now she's avoided. She lives in a tiny apartment near the Temple-Church. No one visits. She calls upon no one."

"Look, she's moving on. Shall we follow her?"

"If you like," said Chorgeh's "uncle." "But I warn you, if she turns, we retreat."

They descended from the gallery, and moved after their quarry through a light, pushing, frivolous crowd. It was a bright winter day. There was hard sparkle on everything, and now and then the wind attacked from corners, the columns below libraries, and wolf-like down long steps, mutter-howling under its breath. The sunshine insisted that they be pleased by it, but it blinded them at every white wall and pane of glass. The people on the street, not knowing about the story, brushed by Julie d'Is, almost collided with her.

"There she goes," said Chorgeh, "into a pastry shop after all. Does she eat pastry?"

"I expect so," said the "uncle." He lit another cigarette, the case a plaque of cold fire. "There were times when she was invited to dinners. She ate and drank like everyone else. Rather greedily in fact."

"Were you ever present?"

"Thankfully, no. There was only one occasion . . . I had been warned, and so declined. That was when I heard the story first, four years ago. When you, dear boy, were only thirteen."

"The worst years of my life. Tell me about Julie d'Is."

The "uncle" began his tale in a manner quite unlike his means employed when writing. Chorgeh knew that the story, if it had been or were to be translated into printable prose, would gain ornament, elongation, and proper suspense. But as a raconteur, the writer was quite brisk, almost abbreviated. Mentally Chorgeh was not above adding a brushstroke here and there.

The parents of Julie d'Is had come from the colonies of the East, some place of fans and ivories, rice, camels, bazaars, and flying carpets. They had been disgraced, the family, or simply the father, in some gambling or speculating of a nature that was kept obscure in the City—the odd codes and loyalties of the returned colonists, who would cut Monsieur d'Is, yet not betray him to outsiders. The d'Is child was female, and two years old, a weak infant mewling and puking in the tradition of weakly infants. The climate had seen to her as foolish villainy had her father; both were undone. Yet she continued, weakly, to persist, like a wan plant that straggles on, refusing to die and give up its pot to a nicer specimen. And certainly there were no other children. Shortly there began to be an exotic rumor, which was that the family had fallen afoul of a sorcerer in the Eastern lands. That just so the father lost his work and his name, and so the mother produced, from the huge burden of her womb, only the one ailing weed. Since no one spoke to the family d'Is, however, no one could verify the rumor.

Monsieur d'Is toiled as a clerk in a seedy business near the docks. Madame did her best. And the miserable daughter went on with a grisly graceless tenaciousness redolent not of courage or hope but of a dripping tap.

It was when the child, Julie, was six years old, that the tide turned for them all. They were, if not forgiven, at least forgotten. That is to say, suddenly people came upon them, exclaiming that they were the persons d'Is, and what were they doing now and how did they go on? Such reversals of attitude were not uncommon in the bored City. It ws less an act of charity than a desire to see, squirming and doing tricks under the microscope, suitable microbes.

Madame d'Is began to appear in sewing circles, at afternoon teas, her husband and she played cards and dined at this house and that once or twice in a pair of months. They were hardly overwhelmed, but no longer were they excluded. Presently the child, too, perhaps perforce and in a moment of aberration, was absorbed into a children's party.

She was not, after all, such a horrid creature. She did not cringe or seek to intimidate, often the failings of the weak. No, she went along with the little-girl games, was a modest pleased recipient of favor or victory, good at losing, quiet, but with a spark. "That child," they said, "might look almost pretty, if her mother would wash her hair in softer soap, and dress her more like a child than a parcel."

Julie began to be a social success superior to her parents. She did not fawn as they did, yet was plainly genuinely impressed and grateful as they were not. She was not without animation. She could exercise tact, unusual in a child: She was not one of those to pass raw comments on a hostess's hat or wallpaper. "Poor mite. I expect she gets little enough chance to shine at home, with *those* two." "The mother keeps her like a little slave. She heaps the child with chores. Her schooling is being carried on by the father. Not right, I am sure."

"Mama," said Sandrine, the daughter of the house, "Mama, please will you not ask Julie d'Is to my party."

"*Not?* Why ever is that? Don't you want poor Julie to see your dear new doll?"

Sandrine began to cry. She was not generally a tearful girl.

After some coaxing, it was got from her.

"I don't want Scamper to die!"

Leaves of silence, oddly flavored by mystery and darkness, fell in the room. The ladies looked at each other.

"Well, you know," said one at last, "it's a very curious thing."

"Yes," said Sandrine's aunt, "I remarked on it myself to Madame Claude only the other day."

"Of course, a coincidence—"

"Or do you think the d'Is child—?"

They stared at one another now.

During the past year, Julie had attended seven parties. Thereafter two cats sickened in a week, the Claude dog had succumbed to a malady and been put down. A parrot was found dead in its cage before the guests had even left.

"Scamper," said Sandrine, the name of the kitten. "*She'll* put a spell on him like the others."

"Good heavens, is that what the child says she does?"

Sandrine looked blank. Julie had said nothing. Her peers did not question her, for fear.

It was borne in on the ladies of that circle, and all those other circles with which it connected, that while the mothers had not been badly disposed to Julie, their children did not like her. Overnight, as it were, Julie ceased to be a social success.

"But," said Chorgeh's "uncle," "regardless of that, soon enough the child was obliged to go to school."

"My God," said Chorgeh, encouragingly.

"It was thought to be an epidemic," said the "uncle." "A fever, in some instances accompanied by vomiting and a rash. There was only one death. But somehow, again generally unspoken, the unthinkable was mooted. The child was removed from the school. It was because, they said, she herself was too unsturdy to be exposed to childish ailments. She was then tutored at home, and only ventured out on errands with her mother—"

"Whereat the drawing rooms and byways were littered with sickening small animals and babies."

"Exactly," said the "uncle," unperturbed.

Julie d'Is emerged from the pastry shop before them.

"She's been in that shop a long while," said Chorgeh. "Do you think she's assaulted anyone?"

"Very likely," said the "uncle." "But if so, the assault will have gone unseen. In all the instances of those who fell ill, nothing was reported, nothing was witnessed. Rarely did Julie make contact—she was not a tactile child. She did not fondly clasp her playmates and class-fellows to her, did not strike them, pinch, or tap their hands. They had soon got in the habit of making very sure she never came near their food or drink."

"Now where is she going?" said Chorgeh. Their object had turned into a long sliding street, a funnel for the wind.

"Toward the Church, I believe, homeward."

"She looks more interesting now," said Chorgeh. "Quite attractive in fact, as should every female poisoner. Her hair, let down, would make her seem fascinating with those slanted eyes. A veritable Medea."

Years retracted. Madame d'Is had come into an unexpected fortune, sole beneficiary of an obscure relative. With the malice of the microbes they had been, monsieur and madame began to intrude themselves everywhere, riding to horse races and galas, attending balls, financing things, overbearing all before them. Julie too appeared again out of her cupboard. Her childhood aura was dismissed or suppressed. She was found to dance well, to speak little and with some wit, to listen attentively. If not a jewel, still she shone slightly, and her hair was washed in soft soap and padded becomingly, her gowns were not parcel wrapping save in the most acceptable sense.

"Who died?" asked Chorgeh, as they strolled along the sliding street, the crowd lessened, and above them the façade of the cathedral suddenly loomed masklike in the sky. They had begun to climb hills, aware unconsciously of the backbones of Paradys beneath the streets. It was appropriate that the story should shadow, even if there was less breath for it. The brightness too had clouded over; there was a flutter of rain.

"Several died, of course. At first it wasn't associated with Julie d'Is. She was a young girl with her hair dressed low, and sometimes loose as you have recommended. Not a Medea, an Ariadne. A piquance, an intelligence, a softness suggesting pliancy."

There was a particular supper. Twelve people were there, and Julie d'Is—the magical number of thirteen. The next day two of the younger girls fell ill, quite seriously.

"Like the two cats," said Chorgeh. He noticed that despite himself, his "uncle" was elaborating quite naturally now.

"The table being stocked with an uneven number, three girls had sat adjacently. One opposite Julie, and beside her the daughter of Madame Claude."

"Must the veterinarian put her away?"

"She died by herself on the fourth night, raging with fever and calling aloud."

"Perfect," said Chorgeh.

"I never cease to enjoy," said his "uncle," "the beastliness of youth."

Julie d'Is, with her small bag of cake, was now far ahead of them. She went lightly up the hill, and vanished at a turning.

"She's getting away."

"We must allow that. It is her own street."

Chorgeh said, "You're very disappointing. Is this the end?"

"To some extent," said the "uncle." "There's only this to add. The occurrences of severe illness and occasional deaths, mysterious and unsolved, attendant on Julie at various functions, led the old suspicions of her out again. She was called the Peste Virgin, the Angel of Plague, and so on. At best, she was a harbinger of extreme unluck. Of course, no one could pin a crime to her. She came to be watched very closely, and those placed next to her at table, female or male, would find all manner of amusing excuses to absent themselves. Not every episode resulted in a fatality, or even a sickness, however. At one memorable dinner twenty-one people sat down with Julie d'Is and afterward her neighbors exchanged bets on who would expire and when. But all stayed healthy. Eventually both her parents, neither of whom had ever been seriously ill, died in the mundane way. Julie inherited their dwindling wealth, and lived on it. She was left scrupulously alone."

The "uncle" extracted another cigarette. The two men stood beneath a plane tree, as the sky tried to attract their attention.

"I must be getting on, I have to meet Vincent at my club," said the "uncle."

"But you can't leave me like this—finish the story, you devil!"

"How can I? Only life can do that. And life has just gone around a corner with her pastry."

"But—how is it done? How does she poison them?"

"Who knows? Plenty have tried to learn. Some have even resorted to inquiry of the lady, holding her the while at bay the length of a cane or umbrella. She looks amazed, it seems, insulted, normal. They can obtain nothing."

"The police—"

"The police have generally not been involved, though it's true they observed Julie d'Is for a year, after an especially tiresome death, that of a minor minister who shared a carriage with her. No evidence was found. No motive, as there had never been apparent motive. She has shown in her career neither passions nor attachments, nor jealousies, in love, or otherwise. How unusual. We all give ourselves away. You yourself, my little foreigner, have your wild and untamable streak, by which we know you."

"Indeed."

"And you are young, which gives besides a great deal away at once. Julie d'Is was also young for three decades. And gave away nothing. Since she seems to pollute and kill, that must be her only vice, and her only hobby." A raven-wing cloud scuffed through the plane. Rain dashed down. "The club," said Chorgeh's "uncle" with decision.

"No, I'm not coming with you," said Chorgeh.

"For God's sake, don't go knocking on the door of Julie d'Is."

"I shan't," said Chorgeh. "That much I do credit, that she's unfriendly. Inimical."

"Do please believe it."

Chorgeh stood and watched his "uncle" hurry off downhill through the rain. The road was a tide of blackness. Something hung heavy, not thunder, but the bottomless story. It must be concluded, somehow.

The bell of the pastry shop gave a brittle sugary tinkle as he went in. On all sides were terraces of sweetness, layers and marblings, bubbles, cords, plaits, and flutes, that made the eyes if not the stomach hungry. In the middle of it all, unmoved through long acquaintance, a plump, pretty, curly girl lifted her head like a deer at a water hole.

"Can I help you, monsieur?"

"Yes. Give me some of those, please, and a couple of those," and Chorgeh, thinking of his mother, who disliked sweet things of any type, food or human, and pictured her astoundment, when he should get home. Into the masculine study, which once Chorgeh's father had occupied, kept now as a cross between a shrine and a lumber room, Chorgeh might take himself and eat each refused cake, remembering the cake shop girl, for she was very charming.

Yet, as she reached for the second batch of cakes, she looked puzzled, this charming girl. She stepped away, and turned to Chorgeh as if to ask him something, and as she stood there, seemingly at a loss, Chorgeh instead asked something of her. "Do you recall a woman who came in here, about half an hour ago?"

"I—don't know, monsieur," said the girl, looking more puzzled than before, frowning and gazing at the ground, as if she had glimpsed a mouse, perhaps.

"A drab, nasty woman. Obviously scheming. With holes in her gloves."

"I—don't know, monsieur," repeated the girl. And then she looked at, and straight through him, as if to some other place that had suddenly grown visible in the doorway. Next moment she dropped on the floor. She lay there in a compact little puddle of skirts and curls, her eyes shut, her face icing white.

Chorgeh banged on the counter and shouted, and by magic the shop was full of women.

A minute later, the girl had been lifted up and was murmuring that she was quite well, quite well, but so cold.

"There, Olizette," said the women. And one ran out to the pharmacist's along the street.

"That gentleman," said Olizette, "is waiting for his cakes. I was serving him when I was taken queer."

"Good Lord, don't worry about that," said Chorgeh, flustered for an instant. It seemed likely the women would reckon him in some way responsible for the girl's faint. Metaphysically, was he not?

Then the pharmacist came, and after a cursory examination of the girl, declared she was feverish and must go home at once.

Chorgeh stood there with his heart beating violently, in the presence of the insanely wicked and bizarre. Evil was a palpable entity in the shop, bending to the women, its tattered wings and skull face glaring intently and specifically above Olizette. It was as if Chorgeh had invoked it, by his arrival, his quest, his query concerning Julie d'Is, Angel of Pestilence.

"Oh, how am I to get to my room?" said Olizette, made childish by her weakness. "Oh dear, oh dear, what shall I do?"

And Chorgeh rushed out to fetch a cab, into which he and a woman of the shop next bore Olizette, who was now touchingly crying from embarrassment and feebleness.

Every bump of the wheels and hoofs on the journey caused the poor girl to gasp and moan.

"There, there, Olizette," reiterated the useless woman. "She's *never* ill," she added to Chorgeh over the dark, drooping, flowerlike head. "A country girl. Two years, and never a sniffle, never once a migraine or a fainting fit. And I myself, well I'm a martyr to them, monsieur."

They reached Olizette's room (set predictably in a conglomeration of chimney and flowerpots, rambling steps, skylights, and lopsided balconies, near the old corn market). Chorgeh paid off the cab. He then went to summon a doctor, taking all responsibility on himself. It was his fault.

"I don't like the look of this," the doctor said to Chorgeh, on the landing. "You are the young woman's protector?"

"If you like," said Chorgeh, disdaining the explanatory truth.

"Then someone must be got in to look after her, a nurse. She must have fresh fruit, broth; cream and eggs as she improves."

Thus it was not cakes that Chorgeh presented to his mother. It was a plea for an increment upon his allowance.

"If you must know, I have a girl. I must give her a present, mustn't I, now and then?"

"I'm not interested in the silly details. Is she clean? Does she love you? I trust that you do *not* love *her*? Very well."

During the month of Olizette's illness, Chorgeh visited her once a day, in the afternoon. He brought flowers, fruit, and later boxes of confectionery—she did not likes cakes. Her plumpness had melted from her, and the paleness and slightness of her debility made her ethereal. Although he did not in the smallest degree "love" her, Chorgeh was very taken with her, had become fond of her, as one may with a docile and pleasing invalid one has chosen. Their words were affectionate, and soon familiar, but quite decorous, and the nurse was always in the room with her tatting, or just along the way making soup.

Chorgeh's mornings were spent on quite another woman. It was not that he made any contact with Julie d'Is, of course, only that he had begun to spy on her movements, and to question, in a carefully blatant style, her neighbors, of whom she had several, all at a distance.

Both activities, the caring visits to the pastry seller, the observation of a poisoness, were united, being two halves of a whole.

He learned a great deal more of Julie than of Olizette. Olizette told him everything he wanted to know, and her entire simple life was soon before him, lacking all complexity. But Julie's life was if anything more simple, there was no information to be had solely because nothing happened to her. From the comments of those in her vicinity, who seldom any way saw or noted her, and from his own scrupulous view of her doings in the quiet and normally deserted street, Chorgeh was quickly privy to her existence. She ventured out, this viper, about twice a week, to purchase groceries and feminine articles (he followed her where he could). Sometimes after these excursions she also took a turn in a park nearby. Her face was always blank as a stone. She must surely be frustrated, maddened by this solitary limbo, her lack of volition, yet quite inarticulately and hopelessly, for she seemed to *want* to do nothing more than she did. She did not, when indoors, ever appear at her window. (He had soon located her address, her room—which had no flowerpot, no lamp, and which on the few evenings he had overseen it at dusk, turned to dusk also, and lit no light—did not alter. Even once at midnight he had passed, and there it was, a black oblong, empty. It was as though, on entering her domain, Julie d'Is ceased to be alive or actual. And perhaps this was so.)

As the "uncle" had said, to poison must represent her only passion. All she lived for, dreamed of. And yet, visiting those same places where she made her purchases quite regularly, Chorgeh found no such startling evidence of her malignity as he had in Olizette's pastry shop. Evidently Olizette had been unlucky, perhaps because she had been alone with Julie for several minutes. Possibly too the murderess did not strike on her own territory, but always outside it.

Meanwhile long leading conversations with the latest victim gave no clue as to *how* Julie had managed her work: Olizette herself was ignorant of having been practiced on, and Chorgeh naturally did not enlighten her. He was legitimately afraid of how such knowledge might effect Olizette, for even while she improved, on some afternoons there were lapses; he would find her very white, trembling, saying that she ached from head to toe, or that the mild winter light troubled her eyes. The doctor had already ceased calling, *he* was sanguine, but Chorgeh treated the girl with caution. For the doctor had not understood the case at all. In answer to Chorgeh's probing, the doctor had remarked on the foolishness of young country girls in the City, infected by its fumes, living on cakes, neglecting their well-being in favor of unsuitable romances.

Chorgeh had one image. He nurtured it. It involved the stone-faced serpent Julie d'Is leaning slightly forward to take her pastry, and scratching the fingers of Olizette with the underside of a thin silver ring. By now Chorgeh had glimpsed such a ring on Julie's finger. (Had not the Borgias used a similar device to cart off whole table-loads of enemies?) By the time he had noticed the ring, however, he could find no cut or scrape on the smooth hands of Olizette, though he examined them meticulously, telling her he would read her fortune. Obviously, so slight a wound would have healed by now. He had been lax, too late. Another black mark.

* * *

"Good gracious, Chorgeh! It isn't suitable. After all these years! Mother will think you've come to court me."

"Your mother is far too sensible, Sandrine, ever to think that."

Like a butterfly, Sandrine hovered over the ornate and over-dressed drawing room, in a tense powdery light. He had not seen her, it was true, save at a remote distance—across salons, at the end of fashionable avenues—for five years. She had improved visually, but not necessarily in any other ways.

"Well, sit down. You shouldn't be here. Mother will be out for hours."

"During which time we can get up to the most scandalous activities." Sandrine giggled. Encouraged, Chorgeh said, "Tell me everything you know about Julie d'Is."

"Who is Julie d'Is?" asked Sandrine, in such a voice that he knew she recalled perfectly.

"A dear little girl," he said, "with whom you used, once, to play. Now a woman, looking I'm afraid a great deal older than you or her years. In rather impoverished circumstances. Retiring."

"I remember . . ." said Sandrine. ". . . Julie d'Is." She went slowly very pale. Chorgeh watched, interested. "I haven't seen her since I was ten."

"But your playmate."

"*Never*," said Sandrine vehemently. She shuddered. "Even now, at the very thought." She got up, paced over the room, and back again, and standing there before him said dramatically, "That child was a beast, a hobgoblin. Ugh! We were all terrified of her. She could make you die. She's done it. She never said so. She never said anything. To the adults it was all *May I* and *Thank you*. When she was with us, she would just sit there. She *was* older. Her eyes were down. She had horrible eyes, small and sharp, cold and colorless. And long lashes, not beautiful, but like a sort of fence, as if to stop anything getting by. Then her mother would call for her, such a poor silly woman. We had a rhyme—how did it go? I can't hink— but it was about Julie d'Is whisking you down to Hell if you didn't watch out."

"How did you know she was a hobgoblin? Apart, of course, from her eyes."

"Because the kittens died. And then Alyse, and Lucie. Surely you've heard?"

"But why a hobgoblin? Wasn't she just a poisoner?"

"A *child* who poisons?"

"Why not?" said Chorgeh. As a child, he had once or twice considered the method.

"There was a story," said Sandrine, at the fireplace where the dried flowers still stood petrified, stiff on their stalks as she now was on her stalk of dress. "Julie d'Is was a *changeling*."

"Ah," said Chorgeh.

"You can laugh" (he had not), "but when they were in the East, the silly mother offended a sorcerer. He was an old man who came to the kitchen door in rags, and she had the servants chase him off. But he was powerful, it was all a test or prank. If she'd been nice to him he would have blessed her, but she wasn't, so he exuded a curse. Madame d'Is was carrying two babies, twins. But when she gave birth, one baby vanished. And the baby that was left was changed. It stopped being wholesome and like a baby. It became this awful cold-eyed stony little toad. It became Julie."

"Yes," said Chorgeh. "But what about the other twin?"

"I suppose Julie killed it," said Sandrine flatly, "and they wrapped it in a shawl and the nurse took it and threw it in a reedy swamp. They couldn't tell anyone. It was too disgusting."

"Yes," Chorgeh said again. He imagined the two little girls lying in their cradle under the mosquito net on some veranda, the one child in the stasis of death, the other in the static condition of concentrated being that Julie d'Is so oddly evidenced. And then from Sandrine's facile and foolish words he contrived the exact perfect image, the nurse-woman with eyes of slanting slate, bearing the dead bundle, casting it in like a failed Moses, for the gurgling mud to have, and the frogs chirruping and the strange orient pearl of the moon watching from the trees. Through its curiosity this last picture was made to seem true. He believed it, even though knowing how and why he was convinced.

"How is it you suppose she manages her crimes?" he said to Sandrine.

"Oh," she said, simply, "it's Julie herself, isn't it. She's poisonous. Like certain substances—if you're near them, they can kill you. Julie is like *that*."

They had little cakes, and he thought of Olizette, and that he would be late to see her today, but never mind, he would stay with her until dinnertime. He had seen some bright flowers for sale, to his townsman's eye fresh from the country, and he would take her those, and perhaps some wine. He was growing faintly bored with Olizette, in the most gentle and patient of ways. After all, she was almost well, and had yielded no clues, and what could they talk about?

When he was sufficiently bored with Sandrine, which happened fairly soon after the cakes, Chorgeh made charming excuses and left. Sandrine seemed disappointed, and he realized with surprise that she had really not believed in his mission at all, she imagined Julie d'Is to have been only an impulsive ploy to visit.

With Julie d'Is he was not bored at all. He felt for her a wild sheer loathing quite novel to him, quite energizing.

When he reached the apartment house of Olizette, among the pots and steps, the sun was on the edge of the City, hesitating for a moment. The shape-changer light of dusk already flooded the street. Chorgeh saw the doctor's carriage there in it, like a stone in a river. Somehow Chorgeh was not startled by this. He felt a sinking in his belly, but it was neither alarm nor regret.

He went up, and met the doctor again on the landing. The doctor regarded him wish dislike, resentful of an added burden. "You must prepare yourself, monsieur, for very bad news indeed."

"She's dead," said Chorgeh.

"A sudden relapse. The woman called for me as soon as she saw what went on."

"Did the girl have a priest?" Chorgeh asked anxiously, for he had learned enough of Olizette to realize she would have wanted one.

"Yes. He is there now."

Chorgeh went into the room, and when the priest glanced up Chorgeh said directly, "Please understand, father, that the young lady was befriended by me, nothing more," for now getting the facts of her chastity straight seemed imperative for her sake.

She looked shrunken and elderly as she lay in the bed. Worse, she looked like nothing at all, like discarded washing, an old dress.

Chorgeh stared at her with heartbreaking sympathy.

The priest began to try to comfort him, and Chorgeh, perturbed, went away at once. It seemed there was a brother-in-law who had been summoned, and all the arrangements now were in hand. Even the priest had known Olizette, her character and means—there had not needed to be, after all, any embarrassing explanations.

On reaching home, Chorgeh found his mother had filled the house with guests. They were everywhere, like a plague of well-dressed mice, squeaking and waving their paws. Of the writer "uncle" there

was no sign, however, and Chorgeh was consumed by the detesta-
tion of a man whose last bolt hole had been soiled and overturned.

"Good evening, dear. Do change your clothes and join us."

He wanted to seize his mother by the throat, shouting in her face
that she had ruined him, how dare she—But she had all the rights,
and he none.

"I've a terrible headache," said Chorgeh. "I must lie down. If I'm
better, I'll make my entrance later."

He went to his room and locked the door from the outside, to
mislead anyone who came to seek him. Then he removed to his
father's study and shut himself in there.

There was a faint odor of leather, tobacco from a sacred jar, the
room was protective of Chorgeh, securing him. In a closed drawer,
skillfully negotiated, Chorgeh found what he was looking for. Prior
to dying, the father had initiated the son into a number of the male
mysteries. If he had lived, possibly they would not have got on at
all, but death had flung a glamorous veil over their parting and
their relationship. Everything that Chorgeh's father had ever said
to him or taught him, Chorgeh remembered vividly.

When he had completed his transaction, he went back to his
room and locked himself *inside*. Beyond, the noises of the guests
ebbed and flowed. He visualized Julie d'Is arriving, floating among
them in a pale gown and padded hair, some of it loose on her white
snake's neck. Here she touched and here she breathed, and once or
twice she merely looked, and the mark of death was on them.
Chorgeh patted his pillow, beneath which lay something hard and
cold now. Smiling, he slipped into sleep, and dreamed of Olizette's
burial at a tiny church in the fields, a grave with a willow, mourning
doves. He did not feel sad for her, asleep. He threw the flowers on
her mound, and drank the wine from the bottle cheerfully, and
bought a cake from a tree.

The next day Chorgeh rose early and went out. His hours were
often premature, for his business in the City was that of a sightseer,
flighty and opportune. No one had remarked anything unusual.

When he reached the street of Julie d'Is, Chorgeh positioned
himself as he had grown accustomed to do, almost opposite the
apartment building where she lived. There was a portico there, into
which he could conveniently slip and be hidden. It was a morning
when, generally, she would go out, attend to her minuscule
amounts of shopping, and then perambulate the park. No one was

about, the day was lowering and rainy, and now and then a sharp report of thunder came. It was made for him, this day, and he only feared it would put *her* off; perhaps she dreaded storms. But no, the door opened, and out stepped the creature of the legend, the serpent, clad in her squalid coat and coiled, unbecoming hat, with an umbrella to ward off the scimitars of heaven.

Chorgeh followed her, without undue caution, just as before. No one had ever noted him; she herself, the demoness, had never turned on him, never even looked over her shoulder. She went into a draper's shop, into a shop that sold cold meats and cheeses. Did she eat these things? *What* did she do? He had never fathomed, no one had ever said, he had never seen her, crouched in her room, the spider in her web, grooming herself and preening, smacking her lips over her kills. He was inclined to think she went into a cupboard in her apartment, and stayed there, like a lead soldier in its box. Whatever it was, he would never know.

In the park, which he had thought she might avoid but which she entered as ever, the black trees dripped and hissed, the paths were wet. Everything was noise, flashes and rushes and the crack of the thunder. When Chorgeh shot Julie d'Is with his father's pistol, the thunder obligingly roared and the lightning sparkled. The reek of powder was crushed in rain. He had been fifteen feet from her back and the bullet had gone in under her hat. There was a painterly wash of blood on the path, but it flushed away. Her purchases lay scattered, sodden in their paper wrappings. She was a pathetic heap of old clothes, as Olizette had seemed, a scarecrow. Chorgeh did not approach, but kept to his plan. He knew she was quite dead, for presumably she could be slaughtered in the normal fashion, and the bullet must have entered her brain. He hurried away, feeling nothing, only a little bit sick, but then he had taken no breakfast, it was probably only that.

Rain fell steadily for a week, then on the first clear day, the writer came to call on Chorgeh's mother. She was taken aback, not having seen him for months. After a while, almost surreptitiously, the writer climbed the house, and knocked on the door of the study-shrine of Chorgeh's father.

"Yes, you may come in," said Chorgeh.

He sat in the leather armchair, while the writer tactfully passed about the room, examining items with the cunning reserve of a man in a museum. Presently the writer sat down also. The fire was lit. They stretched their legs to it.

"Had you heard?" said the writer.

"That the Beautiful Lady had been killed? Yes. There was a small passage in some of the journals. I was only waiting for you to come and ask."

"What did the journals say?"

"Couldn't you read them?"

"I never read them. Nasty things. I have my knowledge from another source."

"Naturally. Likely you know much more than the rest of us. All that the journals said was that a Mademoiselle Julie d'Is had been bizarrely shot in a garden near the Temple-Church. That there were no witnesses. That nothing at all was known. They did add, a pair of them, that unpleasing speculation had surrounded Mademoiselle d'Is in her youth. But that nothing had been said against her latterly, she seemed to have neither relatives nor friends, no one in fact with a reason or wish to slay her."

"We may always rely on our relatives and friends for *that*," said the writer.

"Tell me all the rest of it, then," said Chorgeh, apparently intrigued.

Under cover of his porcelain exterior he held himself tight. He knew perfectly well the "uncle" was here in his literary capacity only. He supposed that it was Chorgeh who had murdered Julie d'Is, maybe he had no doubts. Although such pistols as Chorgeh's father's were common, although Chorgeh, even Olizette, had no glaring link to Julie d'Is, and although the writer indeed knew nothing at all of the ultimate involvement of the pastry shop, yet he had deduced the obvious. Though the police would never attach Chorgeh to the killing, the writer did, and the writer was here solely as that, to observe him, to see how Chorgeh went on. And it was possible, if Chorgeh gave himself away to the writer, that the "uncle" might take over from the writer, and feel obliged to give Chorgeh up to the authorities. Chorgeh had known this moment would come, and he had prepared for it. He was a practiced deceiver, and his youngness was on his side, for with the widespread fault of the middle-aged, the writer coupled youngness with inexperience.

"I know very slightly more," said the writer to Chorgeh. "I know there was, of course, a post-mortem. I know the result of this was the news that Julie d'Is died because of the entry of a bullet into her brain, which was evident from the first. I know that a few of her erstwhile familiars were questioned. But none of them had seen her for years. It seemed to me," said the writer, uncrossing his legs, and lighting, without permission, a cigarette, "it seemed to me that you and I, say, were worthier of an interrogation. We'd been watching the woman and discussing her fairly recently."

"Oh, not so recently as all that," said Chorgeh. "I say, I'm very sorry, but you mustn't smoke in here. Mother would fly into a fit. It's awful isn't it?"

The writer cast his cigarette into the fire and smiled. Chorgeh had revealed an arch-cleverness. The writer could not last for more than ten minutes longer without a cigarette. He would have to go out, and why should Chorgeh, plainly intent on his father's books, go with him?

"You haven't, then," said the writer, "been following Julie d'Is?"

"Why would I do that?"

"Because she fascinated you."

"That's true. Then I found someone else who fascinated me even more. You recollect how skittish I can be."

"What do you think of it, though?" said the writer.

"Of what?"

"Of her death."

"I think it's ideal," said Chorgeh. "I think it's inevitable."

"Since she had no life?"

Chorgeh did not fall into the trap.

"Well, she may have done," he said, "for all we know."

When the writer "uncle" withdrew, tapping his cigarette case, seemingly quite delighted with Chorgeh's acting or innocence, not entirely sure now either way, Chorgeh relapsed, looking at the fire, himself overseeing what he had said. He had made no slip, yet he had been truthful in his pronouncement. The death of such a beast was both ideal and inevitable. He felt himself no hero, and no villain, for seeing to it. It was a shame the post-mortem had shown nothing of significance, but perhaps it had and the "uncle" merely had not learned in his prying what it was. Some things would be hushed up. Chorgeh constructed for himself something more fanciful than the spike in the ring. He saw one of Julie's bony fingers, and out from under the nail a sort of talon extruded. It pricked the plump hand of Olizette, finer than a needle. But the bullet had not been fine, it had been harsh and shattering. He had taken no

chances, aiming for the head. Her hat was so unalluring, it really
served her right. For he would have found her more difficult to kill
if she had been lovely and dressed with taste. He would not have
wanted to spoil her appearance, and perhaps must have risked going close with a stiletto. She had fallen straight over, directly down,
and her soul went deeper yet, diving into Hell. Chorgeh considered
the twin of Julie d'Is, the sister she was supposed to have had, and
to have killed in babyhood. He saw the cradle again under the
netting, and the nurse-woman throwing out the bundle into the
mud. Was that what had decided him, or was it only Olizette?

Chorgeh sat back in the chair and composed himself for a nap.
He would be sensible to avoid the writer for a month or so—until
any ideas or fresh rumors ceased after the post-mortem and the
burial. The firelight glittered, and went from under Chorgeh's eyelids, and he heard his mother's operatic laugh rill through the
house. Everything was well.

God and men pass over the battleground, prizing great gems and
silver bullets from the helms of the fallen. Then the rats come in
gray, smooth coats and find the secrets of the labyrinth.

There was nothing ratlike to the appearance or manner of Monsieur Tritte, who was tall and plump, with the large and capable
hands of a country doctor. He had a baritone voice, a balding head,
a face at once handsome and benign. The watchman of the morgue,
he was the exact antithesis of what such a man was reckoned to be
and frequently was. Tritte was abstemious and sober, without perversity or cruelness. He pitied his charges, with a dignity that became him, yet he found them on occasion interesting. He was himself capable of scientific investigation, having studied at the elbows
of eminent practitioners, unflinching, and uncareless, as they sometimes were not.

It had happened that the men laboring at the morgue had
known the name *Julie d'Is*. They had therefore had great pains over
her. Though the corpse had lain on its slab for a day and a half
before any work commenced, precautions were taken. Not an inch
of skin, other than that of the face, was presented to the cadaver,
which was then gone over minutely for a hidden armament. None
was found. Weighed, pierced, portionally dissected, the poor dead
thing offered no answers. To Tritte this was only what he would
have expected. Her method of inflicting fatality, whatever it was,
had lost its potence in the moment of her death. He had no doubt,

as did not the scientists in the chamber, that Julie d'Is had been executed by one she had wronged with the sickness or demise of a lover or family member. That the police had failed to curtail her had after all given the public some rights in this matter. It was only surprising the sentence had been so long in its enactment. The killer might be discovered through a mistake, or a confession, but there were so many potential assassins, among them even victims who had recovered, that apprehension on evidence alone would seem to be hopeless.

Solely one man of the three had scoffed at the stories of the Pestilent Angel. He was an old fellow who thought he had learned all there was to know, a casual butcher of the slab who made jokes over the severed organs and the cups of brains.

When they were all gone, and the corpse lay at peace in her white cold meat, Tritte watched through the night in his room, where many books, and a microscope worthy of the morgue's visitors, gave notice of his serious inner nature.

In the morning the City was to bury Julie d'Is, arbitrarily, shoveling her off. Tritte felt no dismay at his last, second, night alone with her, but he felt a strong sense of her nevertheless, more so now she had been cut and overhauled, as if her silent flesh cried out—not for justice or remission, not even to be heard—it was more like the low, exhausted crying Tritte's mother had once made nightly, from toothache and worry. Though he had grown, and rescued his mother and now she did not cry, Tritte *felt* the sound. There had never before been such a weeping in his morgue.

Thus, when he went on his rounds, he left the remains of Julie d'Is for the end, and then, peeling off her gauzy mantle, he stood and looked on her under the ray of his lamp, not seeing her nudity, her thinness, the remnant of thin soft hair, but gazing slowly and thoroughly after whatever it could be to make her cry.

Her face appeared, under the debris of her brow (from which the bullet had ejected), like a carved stone. The undamaged eye was closed, and the lips also. Her ears and nostrils were exquisitely shaped, the mark of beauty showing up, as so often, at an unpublicized part. Her breasts too were lovely, and he was profoundly sorry, the watchman of the morgue, that she had lost herself. She was not old, not lined or wizened. What had it been, her wickedness, and what did it mean?

It was as he was viewing her that something flickered at the rim of his eye. He glanced aside, and there on the inner curve of her arm, he saw a speck. Tritte's vision was keen, but the lamp smoked somewhat. The speck, whatever it was, had not moved but only seemed to. Then, it moved once more, the length of one of his fingernails, and so stopped and was still.

He watched it, the watchman, for several minutes, and then, when there was no further movement, he bent down and stared. But all he could see was the speck he had seen at the first, like a grain of tea, there on her arm.

Tritte went away, back to his room, and here he loitered for perhaps half an hour. And then, taking up the lamp, he returned, through the shrouded marble and the dark, to the place of Julie d'Is, and held the light over her.

The speck was still there, where he had last seen it. Suddenly Tritte, from faraway memory, knew what it was. It was a flea.

An abrupt and searing shock ran through him. A lesser man would have dropped the lamp. His emotion was made up of astonishment and horror and a violent influx of realization. Here, *here*, was the method of the murderess, the poisoner. It was a *flea*. A tiny drinker of blood, for some reason so venomous itself that when it feasted on another (for surely normally it had sustained itself by the blood of Julie herself), it was liable to cause illness, and even death. Some were immune, as happened in all cases of infection, others recovered, several perished. Julie obviously was among the initial category, and doubtless her parents, and long associates, often bitten, also. To a stranger, the flea might be always inimical. It leapt upon them—a second of vampire action—then leapt back again to the host. The bite was so minute they either did not feel it or did not know *what* they had felt.

Everything fitted to the hypothesis. Everything combined with it to form a piece of evidence as ludicrous as it was horrifying. *A flea.*

Now, it too seemed dead. Or it was very sluggish; if not dead then dying from lack of food, the ruin of the host. He must be careful . . . or did it lack the will now to feed from another? Of those who had discovered and subsequently handled the body of Julie d'Is none, so far as he understood, had fallen sick.

After he had stood over the cadaver fifteen or twenty minutes, Tritte made a decision. Fetching an instrument, Tritte separated a wafer of the white skin from the arm. The vessels came forth, like veins in marble itself. There was, naturally, no blood. The flea, secured pathetically to the surface of the skin, did not shift itself. It clung on in its death or near-death, like a desperate child to the dead arm of its mother.

A further ten minutes, and Tritte had arranged his valuable microscope, had set the inch of skin and the flea upon a slide.

In the core of night, alone, in pity and amazement, Tritte put his eye to the magical telescope of life, to see what death had been doing.

After he had looked a long while, the man drew back. He wiped his forehead and going to the cupboard, poured for himself a measure of brandy. Only then did he look again through the microscope.

The image was as before.

There was no alteration.

Death had come, and still the miniature thing clung to the skin. Its crying, too high for the human ear to hear, too loud for the human heart not to, had ended. Under the magnifying lens, it was a woman, the flea. Almost a human woman, beautiful and perfectly formed, with short luxuriantly curling hair, and deep dark eyes set fast in oblivion. The lips were parted, and there were the usual even teeth of the human female; the infinitesimal hands had no claws. There were flowerlike breasts. But the body stopped at the pelvis. There it became a tube, scaled like a scorpion, finished in a thin coiled whip, some sort of sting or sucker, it was so ugly, this finish, so unlike the rest. You saw at once how the creature had flung herself, daring space and danger, to cling onto her prey striking like a wasp, turning then maybe to apply the perfect mouth to the wound, and springing off again, back to the safety of the sibling. For it was clearly to be seen also, a likeness to Julie. They were of an age, only one plain, and the other beautiful: sisters.

Monsieur Tritte put on his gloves. He spoke to the woman on the lens. "Forgive me."

And then he crushed her, between his nails.

The sepulcher of ornate granite that stands on the hillside, over-looking the river, has the apt, odd name of Morcara's Room. Those that know the name do not necessarily know the name's reason. Behind a door of leaden metal the bones lie properly in a box; the lintel above the door has only the name: *Morcara Venka,* and two dates—which show that the occupant of the tomb died young, at the age of about twenty-five years. The date of the tomb itself, how-ever, which is also to be found, cut into one of the mossy pillars, reveals that it came into being more than a century after the death of its tenant. Inquiries may reveal that Morcara Venka's descen-dants erected the mausoleum and ordered her remains taken to it from another place. There may also be mention of some ill fortune, even a curse, that once had connection to this woman, so that even now a faint smolder rests, as you will sense, on the hill, some hint of smoke without which there is no fire. And it has been said that to enter the tomb, even on the most legitimate business, would be unwise.

The truth, perhaps more peculiar still, is as follows.

Morcara's Room

The secret of passing away,
The cost of the change of the moon,
None knows it with ear or with eye,
But all will soon.

Swinburne

One evening a young man, who shall be called Rendart, was walking in the country above the City. It had been a hot close day, and the mellow air had now a tint of thunder. Rendart had grown tired of walking, of climbing over boulders and peering into defiles where tiny rivulets flashed and shone as in oil paintings, of the forest's edges that, so invitingly redolent of becoming forever lost, would only lead him back onto some path that ended at a farm. There were no longer wolves in the woods, or Rendart might have been tempted to stay out all night. Instead he was now looking for some house where he might foist himself. His trick was, wherever possible, to avoid the convenient inn or hotel. This was not because he lacked funds ((rather the reverse, his means were private and helpful) but because of a compulsion to view the interiors of the homes of other persons. To this end he had once regularly pretended to a wish to buy property, and agents and owners had conducted him over varieties of premises, singing the praises of much and revealing almost everything but the bad points. It was their reticence here which had discouraged him eventually from the practice, since bad points are frequently so interesting. That and, maybe, the annoyance of certain agents who finally doubted Rendart's desire actually to purchase anything.

As the sky deepened and the shadow of weather bloomed along its perimeter, Rendart came on a wide, straight track, leading between poplars in the direction of a house—indeed, a mansion. The walls of the building were very tall, and the roofs that rose above them, dilapidated and picturesque. Highest of all rose a round dark tower with a cap the color of the approaching storm.

Even as he gazed, a few spaced drops of rain plumped on the track, the poplars quivered, a darkness bubbled up in the east.

Rendart ran gleefully for the mansion.

Of course, he ruminated as the echoes rang away from a clanging bell upon the gate, it was possible they would turn him off, conceivable also that the fascinating house could be empty—then, might he not break in? Almost in disappointment he saw a shuffling movement in the rank bushes that crowded the gate. An elderly man emerged, dressed in the clothes and skin of earlier decades.

"Yes, monsieur?"

The heavens obligingly opened. Thunder pealed, a curtain of rain descended.

Rendart gasped his plight. Alone, friendless, and shelterless in the wild hills and the storm.

The servant (Rendart had classed him, and was presently proved correct) stared a while, as if listening to a foreigner speaking in an unknown tongue.

Then, through the rain, from the concealed house, came a querulous call. "What is it, Pierre?" Pierre began to answer, when out of the bushes scampered a precipitate woman in a pale dress and with an umbrella extended over her head. Seeing Rendart she beckoned frantically, "Let him in. Of course you must shelter with us, monsieur. This dreadful thunder—it may strike—" Rendart kindly did not allude to the tip of her umbrella, which might attract the very catastrophe she feared. Probably Jove would aim first at the dark tower above.

The gate was breached, and the trio hastened between the bushes, into a mad garden run to seed, where everything and every metamorphosis of a thing fought for existence under the charcoal sky.

Rendart was rushed to the house so fast he barely saw it. His hostess he had already noted, sadly, was neither young nor lovely, but she might be mysterious with luck.

It did not really seem she would be.

"Pierre, go at once and fetch some dry clothes of my brother's.

You can change in the smoking room, monsieur. Poor monsieur is soaked. Then you must come directly to the salon, we always have a fire—we feel the cold, Monsieur de Venne and I."

Within half an hour, while the tempest still cascaded on the jungle outside (from which statues protruded here and there like leprous teeth), Rendart was seated in a hot and avid salon, while Monsieur and Mademoiselle de Venne regarded him. They had lapped up his advent so gladly, he half wondered if they meant him some harm. More likely they were starved of visitors. Monsieur de Venne was indicated as being rather younger than mademoiselle, which apparently set him at about ninety.

"You'll stay to dine with us, Monsieur Rendart?" said she. "What a pleasure, a young man of education. We so seldom—yet our nephew—"

"Our nephew never calls on us," interrupted the brother testily. "Except to borrow our money. Money—does he think we have it? Where do we keep it? Would we live in this lachrymose pile if we had any?" And having recourse to the brandy tumbler at his elbow he added: "How frequently I've thought to myself, send that fellow to the *room*."

"Cesar!" cried mademoiselle.

A silence thundered in the salon, to be broken in turn by the deaf clangor of the elements.

Mademoiselle was very white under her rouge. Rendart envied her, for the fire was overpowering. Getting up on the pretext of helping her to more tea (she fluttered; her brother stuck ferociously to his brandy), Rendart managed a quick half tour of the salon, which was neither boring or intriguing. He longed for a chance to go through the mansion, the commencement of whose enormous carven stairway he had already glimpsed.

"Rooms are a problem," said Rendart, idly. "There's one in my house by the coast. Simply uninhabitable."

"Yes, there you've got it. *Uninhabitable*," snarled the pickled brother.

Mademoiselle thanked Rendart so profusely for the tea that it was an obvious signal she did not want *rooms* discussed.

Rendart ate the petit fours and bided his time, for it appeared there would be plenty. Already mademoiselle had mentally transferred him past the dining table to the white bedroom. She had given guest-conscious orders to the doddering Pierre, and a brisk stoat-faced maid of two hundred.

* * *

It was a very good dinner of five courses, two of which were cold, and Rendart was delighted to suspect things had been "laid on" for his sole benefit. Monsieur de Venne progressed from the brandy through three differing bottles of pleasing wine, two-thirds of which he drank personally, before returning to the brandy with all the snug comfort of an occasional rake returning to wife, pipe, and slippers. Mademoiselle fussed and flighted about with her hands and her conversation, and now and then let slip, as if unavoidably, a reference to the absent nephew. Monsieur said no more upon this matter, merely cleared his throat in a horrible way. As for *rooms*, the only room mentioned was the white bedroom Rendart was to occupy, and the bathroom along the passage from it. Rendart formulated a dream of tiptoeing about the mansion in the night in order to see it, as evidently he was not to get a guided tour. It would not do, however, for if they apprehended him they would be sure to think him a robber after their few and rather chipped and rusty valuables. He could not bear to tell them they had nothing he fancied thieving.

Pierre and the maid served the dinner in the salon, and after it was cleared and Monsieur de Venne had re-ensconced himself with the brandy, everyone ran out of things to say. This did not deter mademoiselle, though, who merely whirled on in a repetition of all she had said before. From her catalogue Rendart had almost instantly learned that, on inheriting the house, her mama and papa had been hard put to it to manage, that soon the gardeners had left them ("And mama declared anyway she had never known such terrible soil, everything that grew there was poisonous"), while the servants absconded with the heirlooms ("A great clock that Papa saw at auction two years later, the very same, and could not afford to repossess"). Meantime the young versions of monsieur and mademoiselle grew up, were deprived, stunted, jilted, wilted, done out of this and that expectation, to arrive at last in near penury and the latter years, amazed at both, unequal to them.

Rendart said, as he had more or less said before, "But this excellent house. It must be a consolation."

"Upkeep," snorted Monsieur de Venne. "We don't use more than three or four of the apartments. To hear her talk about this white bedroom! Damp and cobwebs. You'll think yourself lucky to get out with pneumonia. Then there are the rats—"

"Oh hush, Cesar!"

"Eating away at the foundations, nibble and gnaw, squeak and gibber. It's the room. The room does it."

"Yes," interposed Rendart—Mademoiselle had been protesting again—"rooms *are* a *problem*—"

"Want to know what it is, I daresay," gargled Monsieur de Venne through his brandy glass.

"To know what is what?" inquired Rendart.

"Cesar, I must beg you. Think of poor Mama, think of poor, poor Grisvold."

"Grisvold may be damned." ("Cesar!") "He got no more than justice. His own fault. There was the warning, did he heed? No."

Silence fell again, and Rendart realized uneasily that the rain had ceased to fall as darkness fell in its place. The night was calm, and still.

"Grisvold was an innocent, poor sickly boy," cried mademoiselle. She turned to Rendart and implored him, "Who could command a poor sickly simpleton, Run to the Devil—the *Devil*—and expect the poor creature to have the wit to abstain? It was *your* fault, Cesar, and you'll carry the blame to your Maker."

"Grisvold be damned," said the brandy glass.

Mademoiselle turned to Rendart, mute with outrage.

"Something happened to Grisvold?" he asked.

Mademoiselle buried her cheeks in an inch of lace that was unable to cope with them.

"Confounded curiosity," said Monsieur de Venne. A glow burned brightly in his eyes. He wanted and yearned to speak his confession. She also, in her way. They were a haunted pair.

Rendart gazed on them with pleasure. "Is there some strange story?"

"The tower," whispered mademoiselle. "Did you notice it, to the west of the house?"

"I did," said Rendart.

"*There*," said mademoiselle.

"I'll tell him," said monsieur. He put down the brandy glass.

In the great stillness that was the night, a change had come upon the salon. The fire burned, and the candles, for the house did not seem to run to any modernity of lights. Either side the fire the two elderly people sat, like waxworks or mummies in their old quaint clothes and sewn faces and papier-mâché hands. Once they had been elastic and fresh, had played as children, wept as lovers, screamed and sung their rage and joy. Now they piped and rasped

and stamped their feet, which might so easily be shattered were the
carpet too hard. Rendart liked them very much, for the wonder-
fully weird evening they had almost given, and might now be pro-
posing to give, him. He liked them with a capacity he had for liking
strangers as he liked their houses. And now he longed to know the
worst, as he had always wanted to see the unsafe stair and the
blocked drains they tried to hide.

"In the tower," said Monsieur de Venne, "the steps lead up to a
single round chamber. It's locked tight, my father locked it. It was
locked before that, over a century ago, and not opened. Out of
fear."

"Out of terror," whispered mademoiselle.

They glanced at Rendart, to be sure he was attending, which he
was. Then they continued.

Morcara Venka was strong and beautiful and rich, and, from the
age of five, an orphan. Her guardians were on the timorous side;
they had been chosen out of her father's dying wisdom to be precisely so. He had benefitted from the horror writers of his day, and
knew that a clever and powerful guardian will either seduce, dupe,
or murder his female ward. Morcara's guardians were straw, and
before her burgeoning vitality and arrogance, they bent, snapped,
and were flattened. Nothing stayed her. She grew and flowered,
and no man stood against her, and so this was the lesson she
learned: That no one could. Her hair was black, but the type of
black that is black still when the sun shines on it. She did as she
wished. She rode astride, as a man did, which then was thought
very shocking. Indeed, she dressed as a man when it suited her,
and memories were left over of how Morcara looked flaming white
with some enthusiasm or rage, in her male britches, her waistcoat,
the ruffled linen at her wrists, the black tide of hair down her back.
And there were images too of Morcara in silver silk and diamonds,
dancing. But once she picked a live coal off the fire and threw it in
the lap of a woman who (she thought) had insulted her, and once
she challenged a man to a duel, and when he did not go to it
because, he said, he would not fight a woman, she visited him and
cut him across the forehead with her rapier.

Like a rushing river, Morcara had only her own banks to check
her, her own uneven moods to rein her in, and she was at all other
times ungovernable.

She took lovers. She cast them off. Who was strong enough to charm her became weak at her eyes, under the lash of her words, became weak simply by wanting her in return.

Morcara desired only what she did not have, and lost desire for it when she had sampled it. Her dining room, they said, here at the mansion, surrounded then by her fields and forests—her dining room was littered by just-tasted dishes, plums bitten once and thrown away.

Some believed she was in league with the Devil, had the Evil Eye. Perhaps she had not grown jaded with that.

When she was twenty-four years of age, scandalous Morcara met a man two years her junior, at a house in the City she had charmed by visiting. He was the son of a banker, permitted in society but not lauded there, and he had, perhaps because of his situation, an extraordinary offhand and controlled arrogance that matched the flamboyant, careless arrogance of Morcara Venka. He too was rich, partly an outcast, and, incidentally, he was handsome; a portrait remains to establish this, although there are none of Morcara.

Morcara saw the young banker's son, whose name was, curiously, Angelstein. She was too accustomed to her effect to make much of an advance to him. She merely, as was later reported, touched his gloved wrist with one feather of her fan, remarking, "Well, here we are, and where tomorrow?" But her eyes met his, she looked and so did he. In the minds and mouths of others he was, by the next day's sunrise, her conquest and her lover. But in fact this did not happen. No, not at all.

During the following week, Morcara took care to be at those functions, those dinners and balls wherein Angelstein had been patronizingly allowed a part. *She* had only to enter to be admitted, such was her power, financial and otherwise.

She dined beside him at tables where swordfish lay in castles of ice and champagne jetted in fountains. She danced with him in her silver silk, with diamonds in her hair that was black as black under the candles. Angelstein was polite, but nothing more. At last, in an arbor very early in the morning, just before the dawn came, when the grass was drenched with dew, she propositioned him. She is supposed to have said something along the lines that if he were the woman and she the man he would long since have felt her weight. No one was certain, of course, for no one had chanced near enough properly to overhear. But some did see Angelstein, courteous as ever, disengage her snowy glove from his breast, her lips from his own. Saw the curt bow he gave her, heard the *tone* of his voice, a hint amused now, some regret at parting.

As he walked across the lawn, Morcara called after him, "You will come to me. I'll make you. I shall wait."

"No, mademoiselle," he said dismissively. That was all, not even looking back. *No, mademoiselle.*

Then the sun came up, and Morcara Venka vanished, like the demon spirit she was said to be.

At home in her mansion amid the fields and forests, she waited for him one whole month. She had everything made beautiful for him. She was restless, always pacing, looking from the high windows to see him coming, riding a horse maybe, or in a carriage, but always coming toward her out of the distance. She climbed at last up into the highest part of the house to keep her vigils, the round chamber in the tower that once had been her father's study, and by then was a store room only, with chests about the curving walls and an old nest under a beam, for the casement had broken in a storm and the glass had not been replaced. She preferred it that way, the round room. There was no emanation of her father, she had barely known him.

But when the month was over, and Angelstein had not ridden or driven to the house, Morcara Venka sent to him one letter. Its contents are unknown—he had the prudence, being prudent in all things, to destroy it.

Seven more days she awaited a reply. When there was no reply, she came down from the tower. She went into the house, next into the gardens, and she walked about for a while, looking at things, picking them up and examining them, a book, a little vase, a leaf, a stone.

Her servants, who were afraid of Morcara with complete justification, did not feel any pity or anxiety at her state of mind. One of the maids is supposed to have said, "She'll go to the Devil now. She'll do something that'll bring the house down around our ears."

But all Morcara did was to call the men to clear the chests from the chamber in the tower and to put into it instead a high backed chair from her own apartment. When this was done she went to her bureau and, sitting down quietly, wrote something on a piece of paper. Again, one of the servants had a premonition at this that Morcara was invoking or bespelling something or someone.

But all Morcara did was light a candle in the settling dusk, put on her silver dress and comb out her hair, and go with the candle and the paper up into the tower.

There they left her well alone, and through the early portion of the night one or two beheld the wan flicker of the candle, but later it was out.

The new day began, and Morcara was not in her bed, and nowhere to be found in the house.

Then they decided she had better be sought, for after all she could only send them away again, but for lack of diligence she could chastise them. They were used to her angers and her sparkle, not to her absence.

When they came up the steps of the tower to the round room at the top, the door was shut fast, and to it was pinned a sheet of paper, with Morcara's writing on it in black ink.

Not all the men on the stair could read, but one of them could and they brought him forward. He looked, read, and went white. "She's put a curse on this room," he said. "Go back." And he started down the steps. Just at that moment the steward came in and caught the fellow below, and asked him what had been discovered. The man blurted out then, loud enough they all heard, what was written on the paper. It said: *All you who dare to enter here will die.*

After that the men scattered, and what with Morcara's half unearthly reputation, the steward could do nothing with them, and although he tried the door himself and knocked loudly, the way was secured and no one answered.

Four days later a priest was brought from the City, along with some lawyers and other officials. They approached the tower with trepidation. It was a hot and thundery afternoon, and reaching the steps, they hesitated. One of the lawyers turned faint there, and announced that he could smell, as he put it, death. Three men went up at last, the priest with them, and the strongest—since the men of the house still refused to touch the door—put his shoulder to it. After a great deal of hammering and heaving the inner lock burst, and carried by the momentum, this man stumbled a foot or so inside the room.

A most grisly sight met all their eyes, and his firstly. There in her chair sat Morcara Venka, in her silver dress and her long black hair, with diamonds at her throat and flowers in her hand, but she was a corpse, which because of the hot summer, had already begun to rot. The stench came fast on the heels of the vision of her crumbling flesh and its fish eyes and the white bone that jutted out at her cheek and brow, and the others in her fingers like the tines of a fan. The men fell back in horror, and the first one, who had stumbled into the room, he turned in mindless fright and dashed by them, and fell the length of the stair so his neck was dislocated and he died on the bottom step.

The others who witnessed Morcara's finish, survived it, but then, of course, they had not "dared" to enter Morcara's room.

Old Monsieur de Venne, Morcara's remote relative and indirect inheritor, stabbed at the fire with a poker. Sparks showered up and the wood sank, letting show two glaring hellish hearts.

"The room was locked and sealed, and the door of the tower itself was boarded up. The corpse they left to rot in the tomb it had chosen. That Morcara was the initial sacrifice to her own curse had doubtless been her design. The poor wretch who went in there by accident was its initial victim. There shouldn't be any more. No one should enter. No one."

"*All you who dare to enter here will die,*" repeated Mademoiselle de Venne, with shrinking relish; she clasped her agitated hands as if they might fly away.

Rendart sat looking at the fire with his hosts. He was savoring what he had been told, but not quite yet sprinkled with the condiment of belief. Finally he said, "But do you mean, monsieur, mademoiselle, that the remains of Morcara Venka are still up there, in the tower?"

"Just so," said monsieur to the wickedness of the fire. "*Just so.*"

"It is," said Rendart, carefully, "a marvelous and awful story. But surely by now, someone—" He paused, to choose his words with more tact. "Surely someone must have been drawn to take the risk, at *least* to undo the door and verify the tale from outside the threshold?"

"One did," said monsieur, with a grim satisfaction that Rendart, then, found extremely convincing. "But only one."

"Cesar," murmured mademoiselle, "you mustn't—"

"'Mustn't' be fiddled," said monsieur, and had another abrupt swipe of the brandy. As he raised the glass the fire caught it and his eyes and isolated teeth. He appeared wolfish, satanic. "Piddle," he said, "on 'mustn't.'"

Rendart braced himself.

"You referred earlier to a certain Grisvold. . . ."

"Yes. So I did. Bloody Grisvold— Oh, stop your noise, you senile old hen. Am I to confess to the priest? Where is he? Hasn't been near us in a twelve-month. I could die tonight. Go up the stairs and open her door and enter into the room—"

"No, no, Cesar," implored mademoiselle.

Rendart perceived it was a rite between them, that possibly they often acted it out, if infrequently with the benefit of an audience. These two, so adjacent and yet so hedged against death, she with her provisions for lightning and wet clothes, he with his preserving brandy. Unsatisfied, sere lives burned almost down, clawing at the wicks.

"Poor Grisvold," said Rendart, temptingly.

"Poor Grisvold, yes," said Monsieur de Venne.

Grisvold had been the son of their father's cook. A wonderful cook she was too, and partially for that reason she had stayed with the family despite the birth of a child, who was not merely a bastard but an idiot as well. The illegitimacy was hushed up, and the cook equipped with a husband off at some war who was presently suitably killed during the enemy advance. The idiocy of the boy, conversely, was exaggerated, for he was retarded rather then moronic, and could tackle, despite bouts of illness, feverish and unidentified, a number of perfectly useful tasks, such as blacking boots, helping with the horses, of which at first there had been several, and so on.

In age Grisvold was six or seven years the senior of the nine-year-old Cesar de Venne, but mentally Grisvold was a year or two his junior. On this Cesar, a cruel and experimental boy, had played. Cesar had been, in his own case, very unhappy at the time. He was about to be sent away to school, far from his mama, whom he loved, and his elder sister, who irritated but admired him. Cesar had realized from the treatment his papa now and then gave out, to make of him a "man," what was to be expected more regularly at the school. Nor was Cesar overjoyed at the prospects of study, which he disliked, or the ultimate goal which would be to create him a lawyer, an occupation for which he would have neither aptitude nor eagerness (and at being which he would eventually resoundingly fail).

Grisvold Cesar had always hated, but in a casual way. Cesar did not like mess, or messy things, and Grisvold's mental messiness, as Cesar saw it, abraded. So Cesar would make Grisvold commit stupid and time-wasting actions, for which sometimes Grisvold would gain a beating—and that made the worse beating Cesar might then receive bearable.

One day, Cesar managed, fairly easily, to convince Grisvold that there was a monster, a beast of some sort, in the well from which the kitchen water was drawn. Up until this hour, Grisvold had always happily obtained water there when told to. Now he flatly and hysterically refused. A row presently ensued, and gazing over the kitchen roof from the fig tree that grew behind it, Cesar was enabled to observe Grisvold dragged screaming and wetting himself in terror to the well, there to be shown no monster existed—by the expedient of lowering and withdrawing the bucket, of leaning into the well, and of Grisvold's being made to lean into the well, after which Grisvold puked, just barely not into the well, and was beaten on the bare buttocks with a switch. Soon after, however, the row progressed into the main areas of the house, and Cesar was hauled before his father, who, after a lecture, administered a beating the like of which his son had not yet undergone.

Sobbing in agony on his bed, Cesar de Venne plotted a revenge upon all mankind, but first and foremost upon the only one of its numbers he could hope to reach, hapless Grisvold.

To this end Cesar had sworn his sister to secrecy and collusion, for he was determined now that Grisvold should suffer and he, Cesar, go unscathed—although in Cesar's opinion, "If he beat me like that again, I'd die, I'd die in front of him, and serve him right."

Cesar's sister had not entreated Cesar to reconsider what he meant to do. She was flattered to have been included in the villainy, which would involve her saying that she and her brother had been together during a particular time. She did not like the idiot either, and did not, naïve as she was, truly grasp what they were about.

Neither of them knew, indeed, exactly the nature of Morcara's room in the old tower. All the firm information they had ever gleaned was that the tower was unsafe and full of rats, therefore to be avoided. But too there was a sort of rumoring among the servants, which everyone had somehow garnered, including Cesar, and including Grisvold, that a female ancestor had slain herself there and haunted it.

"I'll make him go up," said Cesar, "into the tower. Perhaps he'll meet the ghost. That'll show him."

Given some supernatural choice, Cesar would doubtless have preferred to send his father to this shock and horror, but only Grisvold was available.

"You've always wanted to know what these words say," said Cesar to Grisvold the following morning, when they met in the garden behind the kitchen. The words in question were engraved in the wall, and related to the shrubs and vegetables grown beneath, their order being strictly adhered to, since various poisonous items also willfully came up there. Grisvold had a strange kind of lust for reading, limited to things suddenly come on or seen rather than to the mystery of books. "Well, I'll tell you. I'll tell you slowly, so you learn, and then you can go in and say them to your mother, and won't she like that, won't she be proud?" Grisvold, who had been fooled this way on another occasion into saying something obscene before his mother, for which he was beaten, had already charitably forgotten that. He stared at the words in the wall. He was still pale and sweaty from his latest thrashing. He said, gently, "Tell me."

"Not yet. You've got to do something first. Something so I'll know you're brave. Because you weren't brave about the well, were you?"

"Mam says thee lied, there ain't no monster down in it," said Grisvold, doubtfully.

"Of course there is," snapped Cesar, "and she's impertinent to say I lie. Don't you know you make a monster strong by being afraid of it? We all go to the well as if it's nothing to fear, and then the monster can't do anything. But *you*—"

Grisvold was abashed. He did not protest that Cesar had not explained before this salient point.

"Now," went on Cesar, "I'll let you prove you're not a coward another way."

"How's that?" said Grisvold.

Cesar told him.

"But there's a hant in the tower, thee knows it," said Grisvold. "And the door's boarded, and the top door's locked."

"The boards are all loose on the bottom door," said Cesar; they were. "And I know where the key's to be got." He did. Prolonged observation of his father, his father's routines and concealments, a study made like the other before him at school, perforce (know your enemy) had led Cesar one day to notice an enormous key that seemed constructed from stone, which hung in the west wine cellar. As it was not the key to the cellar itself, Cesar had pondered on it and decided at last it had to do with the west tower. He might have been wrong, but he was not wrong, and therefore once Grisvold had been got to take the key, peel off the rotted boards, and enter the tower, with Cesar, someone was in a position to undo the door of Morcara's room.

Cesar's plan was to remain the far side of it, and to bolt at once, so adding to Grisvold's terror. He would then return secretly into the house, and to his sister's company, where, if questioned, they would both declare their unity in a project to do with the pressing of plants, and encyclopedias.

As for Grisvold, anything might befall him.

The chosen hour was dusk, when the area of the west tower was unfrequented, Cesar supposed at his preparatory work, and the servants busy with their supper.

That Grisvold might disobey Cesar's orders crossed no one's mind. Least of all Grisvold's.

He stole the key and had it in his grasp when Cesar approached him in the twilight under the tower.

Most of the boards had already worked away from the door. Grisvold's inopportune brawn had soon removed their vestiges. The warped outer door also gave before it.

In the gathering of the dark, as bats flitted over the yard, they stared together, these bad companions, up the stony corkscrew of the stair.

"It'll be pitch black, it will," said Grisvold.

"No, I've brought a candle."

They went in by the base of the steps, and Cesar lit the candle with a vivid splutter from the big match.

A bleak and grim place it was, the vein of the tower, all fissures and rats' nests, the steps dank and pocked with ancient stinking rains that had come through and collected there. They went up, Grisvold first as he had been told to do. The candle flung great wheeling arcs that seemed to topple the stair, so they clung to the unsafe railing. Cesar was already unnerved and had a want to fly constantly. But Grisvold's chittering fear sustained Cesar. Helpless in his own world, Cesar wished, godlike, to see to what depths his subject's fear might go down.

At the top of the spiral was the vast timbered door, girded by iron, and with the great iron lock that had been established some two hundred years before.

"Try the key," said Cesar firmly.

Grisvold hesitated, shaking and muttering, and in that instant Cesar beheld that some message had been scratched in the wood above the lock. "Wait," said Cesar, and shone his candle there.

"What do it say," gabbled Grisvold, sweating violently and shivering all over. "Thee tell me."

And Cesar, without properly thinking, read aloud the words some admonisher had inscribed there, that the warning not be lost (who that was was never learned; everyone currently in the household disclaimed it).

All you who dare to enter here will die.

Grisvold tried to turn, and Cesar struck him lightly and correctively, another lesson learned from Papa.

"*No.* Do you want everyone to think you a ninny and a coward? Open the door. Open the door and prove you're a man."

Grisvold bleated in abject terror. But he turned back to the door, got the key into it, and by dint of his strong hand and wrist, forced the door to give and so swing wide.

Cesar too had waited on this. He was half petrified, and yet his reason had not deserted him. The warning cut in the door concerned entry to the room. As for *looking*, he would allow Grisvold to do that. Cesar crept, stiff with fright, back down two or three steps, and so he never saw, never chose to see, what the room contained. Obviously, bones, for the dead woman who had laid the curse had prevented anyone's ever shifting her to hallowed ground. There she must have sat, propped in her chair, in the desiccated ruins of her gown, and with the eternal diamonds still cold and bright upon her. Worse than a ghost, very likely, the actuality of mortal death.

Above him, where the candle held high in Cesar's hand could reach, and where the dusk faintly came through the chamber's broken window, Grisvold stood quaking, and noiseless now, staring at something which was undoubtedly Morcara's skeleton. And the Devil, who but the Devil, made Cesar whisper loudly, through nausea and panic, "*Go in*, Grisvold. I dare you to. *Go into the room.*"

And Grisvold, like a stage magician's doll, took some unflexing cloddish steps, and went into the room, into the room of Morcara's curse, and was there perhaps the half of one minute, before coming out again. And standing on the top step, the doorway of the room behind him, Grisvold looked down on Cesar his tormentor, and said to him, "It's death to go in. It says so. And thee made me. Thee killed me."

Then he dropped flat with a thud that seemed to disturb the foundations of the tower, and did not move, and Cesar fled, throwing away the candle as he did so.

* * *

There was, as the brother and sister described it, a deal of fuss. For Grisvold's mother went to look for him, and then some of the grooms went, and they found him halfway down the stair of the tower, where, somewhat recovering, he had crawled. He was carried to his mother's room, and there on her bed he raved and burned, so the doctor was called from the village. But by morning Grisvold was dead.

Then all the old truths of Morcara's room were brought out shamelessly, and Cesar's father went up alone, shut the door, and locked it. And coming out, gray himself as the stone, he set about ordering bricks and cement to seal the tower's lower door for ever. A fortnight later this was done.

As for Cesar, when questioned he and his sister adhered to their pretense. They were not believed, but neither was it feasible to disbelieve them, for that must be to accept that two children, below the age of twelve years and of good birth, had perpetrated something evil.

Presently Cesar was sent away to school, where he was subjected to all he had dreaded, and worse, and might have felt, if he had thought there any need, to have expiated his sin. Mademoiselle de Venne paid in other ways for a crime she soon shifted totally to her brother. The copious diaries of her girlhood contain only one reference to Grisvold's death, as follows: *Cesar once did, in childish ignorance, a very wicked thing, and made me lie for his sake. I have no luck, nothing goes right for me. Have I too been doomed by Morcara's curse?*

When they had finished their story, the two mummified objects at the fire fixed on Rendart their glassy eyes. After a few moments, the young man sighed. That was hardly response enough.

"What do you say to it, eh?" demanded Monsieur de Venne. And reaching out almost absently, he rang the bell for the stoat-faced maid, since his brandy decanter was empty.

Rendart sat considering. He had rather astonished himself by being deeply offended. Not only at the appalling viciousness of their childhood personas—which still in some form persisted, flutter about *poor Grisvold* as mademoiselle had, and make intimate confession as had monsieur. But also at the insane stupidity that had preserved the pair of them, to this very night, in the crediting of Morcara's curse.

It was true, Rendart would have liked to punish them, but sternly he had put this idea behind him. Then he was only left with the much harder puzzle of how to bring them to their senses in a tactful and open-ended way.

At length, after several quite harsh or insistent promptings from monsieur and mademoiselle, and after the brandy had been refilled by Pierre, Rendart spoke.

"I take it, the lower door of the tower is still bricked up?"

"What else?" flared Monsieur de Venne.

"I have to tell you," said Rendart, "it could be unbricked tomorrow, and the remains of Morcara Venka removed for burial. That might allow her peace. Perhaps you might feel easier."

"God have mercy!" cried Mademoiselle de Venne. "How could it be possible?" she said. "No one can enter that room and live." .

"I've heard the words of the curse on the room," agreed Rendart. "But I wouldn't put any faith in their effectiveness."

"Haven't you had proof enough?" grated monsieur, recharged with brandy fire. "Morcara herself. The man who broke in the door. And bloody Grisvold."

"Yes, I've heard what you've said," murmured Rendart, "but it seems to me the first man who rushed into the chamber by accident rushed out again in horror, missed his footing, and fell quite naturally, if unfortunately, to his death. Poor Grisvold, from what you say, was subject to undiagnosed fevers, which may have been linked to an inflammation of the brain. He had also been recently and savagely beaten in a manner, dare I say, the awful beatings given monsieur perhaps did not approach. Add to that a superstitious and overwhelming terror, and I must suppose his latent disease erupted and carried him off. As for Morcara," added Rendart determinedly, as alcoholic waves and pale flappings threatened from the fire, "I rather think she took her own life. From what's been said of her she would brook no denials. To live her life without a man she genuinely had come to desire would have seemed to her dramatic spirit an imposition. Neither man nor God should tell her what to do. So she shut herself up and concluded her existence with poison."

"Ridiculous!" roared monsieur.

"Not at all," said Rendart. "Mademoiselle has herself assured me the garden abounded in dangerous and venomous plants; I myself spotted three or four. You picture Morcara in her ball gown, with flowers in her hand. Probably they were one of the deadlier species, and she ate them to effect a swift dispatch."

A space of wordlessness followed this statement, during which the fire and some clocks ticked away the minutes. Seeming to understand what they did, it was Mademoiselle de Venne who quickly if hoarsely broke the silence.

"But remember the words, Monsieur Rendart. They are scratched to this day on the door."

"I do indeed remember them, perfectly. *All you who dare to enter here will die.*" Rendart paused, and let his pity for them both, even his pity of their nastiness, their evil, come back to him. He would spare them, he must. "Suffice it to say, mademoiselle, if you wish me to undertake the commission, I'll see to it the tower is unbricked, the upper room entered, and the bones removed to holy ground. For myself and those I hire for the work, I haven't any fears. I guarantee their safety—and their wages—and if you like, I'll furnish proof of their survival for, say, a year after the reburial. I'll even go so far," said Rendart, with a sudden smile, "as to set up a tomb for Morcara Venka, at my own expense. Out of respect for her romance."

They sat dumbfounded, glaring at him. They loathed his interference and yes, they would like him to perish of the curse of Morcara's room; they would give their permission.

Rendart regretted his smile all night as he lay dozing in the fearful dank white bedroom. He was sorry he had lapsed, for it had been the smile of a torturer if not the executioner: He had punished them by making a gift to the dead, rather than to themselves, the living—that state and title to which they so obstinately clung.

A month later, as the heat of summer baked into a fruiting jamlike autumn, the tower of the mansion was opened, the stair ascended, the door undone, and the heap of bones placed in a box and borne away.

Rendart for his part contracted with the workmen, and the priest who had spiritually cleansed the room of any impressed miseries, that they should monthly submit to the de Vennes, for one year after the enterprise, continued proof of their life and health, which was accordingly done. All those who entered Morcara's room, including Rendart himself, are still hale and going about their deeds in the world.

For of course, as Rendart had seen, having the youth, the scope for it, it was no curse at all Morcara Venka had laid upon her room in the tower. For she told no more than the truth, the truth which the old monsieur and mademoiselle must not be made to face so bitterly, the truth at which she, Morcara, in anticipating, had thumbed her nose. Pure self-deception caused others to dance thereafter to Morcara's tune. (As she surely knew, adding a cunning flick of the wrist to her phrase.) It was only necessary to open the eye of the mind as well as the door of the chamber, in order to go in there without terror. Or at least without any terror that was not already inherent and inevitable, and that each of us must dwell with for every year we are on the earth. *All you who dare to enter here will die.* It was a fact. All who dared the room would die. What else? For death is the destiny of all, and unavoidable, be it now, tomorrow, or eight decades hence. But how often do we like to be told, how often do we not convince ourselves we are *immortal*?

You can tell the graves of the bourgeois, always so ornate and yet so cautious, as if even here they were afraid to try too far above their stations, lest they be smitten. Sometimes you see how the living attempt to make reparation. Here the neglectful parent has strewn stony flowers above his child, but none of the real sort. The story associated with this grave is very horrible and very strange. Hearsay.

The Marble Web

Daisy, Daisy, give me your answer, do!
I'm half crazy, all for the love of you!

Harry Dacre

From the glycerine water they pulled her up, first hauling on the sodden shreds of her robe, but these gave way, finally getting purchase on the bones of her corset which had not rotted. Her hair streamed back into the water, like weed, and in the pre-dawn nothing-light, she was no longer pretty, or easily to be recognized.

There were many who got their trade out of the river, that Styx of Paradys. By night suicides came down to the edge like parched deer. Others, murdered, were thrust out into the depths, surfacing days or weeks later, by this or that bridge or muddy bar, to render up, to the scavengers of the river, a pearl locket, a silver watch, or a jet in a ring of mourning.

But Jausande Marguerite, she was not quite of the usual order, for they had heard of her, perhaps been looking out, and for that reason, wrapped in an oilskin, her body was taken presently to one of the judiciary buildings behind the Scholars' Quarter. Here, under the dreadful probing of the new electric lamps, she was identified, she was given back her name, which was no longer any use to her.

And soon after that the hunt was on, but the hunt found not a thing. Thereafter all this was sensational for a brief month, then passed into the mythology of the City, that makes itself from the ragbag of everything.

* * *

"Lower the lights," said the young man in the loud coat. "He'll perform a miracle."

"What nonsense," they said generally. And then, another: "It isn't necessary to lower the gas. He'll do it without."

Across the salon, the man with whom they were spicing their conversation glanced at them, and the group fell silent.

"What eyes," said one of the women feebly, once the man had turned away.

"Oh? I thought them surprisingly poor, considering he's supposed to use them in order to entrance, and hypnotize."

"Probably uses his ring for that," said another.

The loud coat admired the ring, someone else remarked pointedly that it was very vulgar. But others had not at all observed a ring, and looked for it in vain.

Then the group began to discuss a different topic. Their flylike minds were unable to remain for long in any one spot.

The man they had spoken of, however, was now and then commented upon by all sides. His nickname was The Conjuror, for it was said of him that he had made some money in a vaudeville act to the north. He represented therefore to the bourgeois evening salons of Paradys all that was ludicrous, contemptible, quaint; a butt for jokes, and perhaps needful in a dry social season.

In appearance, certainly, The Conjuror was recognizable by his very ordinariness. Not short, decidedly not tall, thinly built, and neither well or badly dressed, his hair was combed back and his face shaven, leaving—washed up there, as it were—two normal eyes, without exceptional luster, and actually apt to turn as dull as misted spectacle lenses.

His notoriety was founded on a collection of odd stories, the facts of which came always in an altered version.

Meanwhile, he had not said, written, done, or vowed to do anything at all celebrated. There was a rumor the walls of his narrow flat near the Observatory were plastered by bills and photographs depicting him as an archmagician, raising the dead from the floorboards of a stage. But who had been to the flat to see? He was unmarried, had no servant. He went out only to those functions to which some frustrated hostess had, on a whim, summoned him. With the perversity of the City, however, his utter dreariness—he had neither wit nor charm about him—soon lifted him to a bizarre pinnacle, that of the Anticipated. There he stayed, or nearly stayed, by now fading a little, for even if lighted by others, a candle must have wax enough to burn of itself.

"My dear," said the hostess of the evening salon, as she led her niece into the room, "I should have been lost without you."

"Why?" said her niece, who dreaded finding the salon tedious, and longed to escape.

"Your youth and prettiness," said the flattering aunt, "your poise. That dress which is—oh, perfection."

Jausande Marguerite smiled. She was one of those girls who had somehow always managed to draw genuine praise from both sexes. She was attractive enough to please but not beautiful enough to pose a threat, she was kind enough to be gentle, cruel enough to amuse, and young enough to be forgiven.

"Look there, what a fearful coat," said Jausande, and avoided the eye of the loud young man swiftly, with a delicate, apparently spontaneous vagueness.

"Yes, his father has been a great help to your uncle. Vile people, but money . . . there we are . . ."

Jausande sighed, and cleverly concealed her sigh as she had learned to conceal a yawn at the opera.

Beyond the salon windows the evening, through which she had been driven, still had on it a light blush of promise. Jausande had caught the terrible sweet illness, often recurrent as malaria, and most unbearable in youth and middle age, the longing for that nameless thing given so many names—excitement, adventure, romance, love. Every dawn, each afternoon, all sunsets, aggravated the fever.

But through the promising dusk she had come, to this. Already her eyes had instinctively swept the room over, and found all the usual elements both inanimate and physical. There was nothing here for Jausande Marguerite. But she must pretend that there was.

Her aunt led the girl about, introducing her like a flower. Everyone liked Jausande at once, it was one of her gifts, and she perpetuated it by being nice to everyone, but not so nice that they felt under an obligation. Of course, Jausande's aunt did *not* introduce her to any but the most deserving. And beyond the pale, no doubt, was The Conjuror, that awful little man. No, he did not meet Jausande in the formal way.

The gas lamps were already lit, and burned up steadily as the windows went out. The long room in which the gathering mingled grew close. White wine was being drunk, and small unsatisfying foods eaten. In half an hour, the evening party would break up, unless something should happen.

"Now what about"—shouted the young man in the loud coat—"a game of some sort? Some charade—" He winked at Jausande across the crowd, and she did not notice. He added, to a ripple of encouragement, "What if we have some magical tricks?"

"Now, now," said Jausande's aunt, "Philippe, we mustn't turn my drawing room into a bear garden."

"The idea," said loud Philippe. "But surely there's someone here can give us a show?"

At that, some of the heads turned, looking for the drab figure of The Conjuror. There he was, between the windows, a shadow with a glass of wine in its bony hand, and something repellent to him, like a smell—but he smelled of nothing at all.

To become abruptly the center of the room's gaze did not seem to trouble him. Nor did he bloom. He did nothing.

"Monsieur," said Jausande's aunt, who had forgotten his name into the bargain, "you must forgive Monsieur Philippe Labonne."

It was very strange. It was as if (as with a spell) this silly outburst, drawing attention to the supposed origins of The Conjuror, which in fact had never even been verified, were all hearsay, called up some power. The creature himself was not imbued by anything apparent. He did not change, in looks or manner (which were rather those of a funeral assistant caught out at the wake). And yet the salon, so boring a moment earlier, took on a dangerous quality, like the air during a bitter quarrel when any terrible truth may be said.

"Madame," said The Conjuror, quietly, and there was nothing of note either in his voice or his accent, except that the latter had a slight tinge of the streets. And he gave a nasty graceless little bow.

"There now," said the aunt of Jausande. "But perhaps *you*, darling, will play for us on the piano?"

Jausande did not wilt or beam. She played the piano as she did all things—nicely, effectively, not brilliantly. It gave her sometimes a quiet pleasure to play in private, none in public, nor any qualms. She would do what she must.

But it was as she took a step toward the piano that she saw The Conjuror looking at her. She saw, and she could not help but see and show that she had seen. And a flush, of a sort of ghastly shame, spread over her face and neck. There was something so awful in

The Conjuror's look, for it said everything that must, by such as he, never be said, and so very openly, and so very intently. *I love you,* said the look. *I love you at first sight.*

"Whatever—?" began Jausande's aunt.

"I'm very warm," said Jausande. "Will you excuse me if I don't play for a moment?"

She had averted her eyes, but still, still, she felt the eyes of *him* clinging on to her. Here and there in the recent past indecorous outpourings had been made to her. *Never* in *that* way.

And now other people in the room became aware of it, both the intensity of The Conjuror, and its object, and tiny, barely audible sounds were breaking across the audience, the whispers of sneers and laughs.

Perhaps what made it so appalling was its mediocrity. Here, in this unimportant drawing room, the birth of an obsession. And if he had been grotesque, and she amazingly beautiful, there would have been to it the dignity of tragedy. But she was only rather pretty, and he— He was nothing on earth.

And then he spoke again. They all heard him.

"If you like, madame, I can offer my poor skills, a few of them. If the ladies won't be alarmed."

"Why—monsieur—" and Jausande's aunt actually stammered, so instinctively startled she was. Every line of her corseted form revealed she wanted to deny him. But it was absurd—why not? In hopes of something like this she had asked him here. It would be a coup. Nowhere else, that she knew of, had he "entertained."

Besides, the mechanism was already in motion. As if at a signal, her guests were drawing back, leaving a broad space at the room's far end into which The Conjuror propelled himself. He had discarded his wineglass. His hands were empty. He lifted them slightly. They were horribly bare, as if peeled.

"Look—nothing up his sleeve," loudly said the loud Philippe.

And one of the others called, "Lower the gas!"

"No," said The Conjuror, and from his position at their front, he had now taken some authority. "That won't be necessary."

And then the extraordinary did happen. He snapped his fingers (as the aunt of Jausande said afterward, for all the world like a grocer's clerk) and each of the six gas fitments in the room was reduced to a smoky sublume. Contrastingly, the light in the area of The Conjuror was heightened. Its source was invisible.

Some of the ladies shrieked. Then there was chastened laughter.

Philippe said, "Been at the lamps—planted a helper in the basement—"

"Monsieur," said The Conjuror, "please do yourself the kindness of becoming silent."

This was nearly as dramatic as the trick of the lamps. It was so audacious, so frankly rude. It carried such weight. The stance of The Conjuror had changed, his voice had done so. This must be his stage presence, and as such, it was a good one.

"Now," said The Conjuror. "Mesdames, messieurs. I must ask you all to remain as still as possible. Not to move about. To restrain your outcry. If you will do that, I can show you something, although very little. We are surrounded by wonders, kept from us only by a veil. You must understand," he said, and now there was not a sound otherwise, "that I know how to twitch aside that veil, a fraction. To reveal more would be to endanger your sanity. You must trust me in this. You must trust me utterly. From this moment, your lives and hearts hang from my grip. I will not let you go. But your obedience is essential. How else can I protect you?"

The room was quiet as death. He had frightened and awed them. They would complain after they did not know how. But he was clever, give him that, he had done it. That common and unmusical voice had become an instrument by which he gained dominion over them. And the lamps burned low.

Then his pale hands darted out and seemed to lie there, suspended as if upon the surface of a pool.

A girl appeared. She appeared out of nothing, or the brocade wall, half transparent, ghostly, and then she grew quite solid, and was entirely there before them. She was no one they knew.

The girl was dressed in a long draped tunic with a diagonal pattern. Her hair was done up in a knot, with combs. She stretched to light a metal cup that apparently floated in the atmosphere. It blossomed out like a flower, and dimly at her back they saw the columns and cistern of a Roman atrium. Then she had turned, and the atrium was gone, rolled up with her into nothingness again.

The room was as it had been. Someone dared to speak, not Philippe Labonne. "Shadow play," the man said, "images thrown up by a small projector."

"Monsieur," said The Conjuror, moving to look at him, but holding his arms still upward, the hands suspended, a position that should have been ridiculous, but was not, as if, now, he grasped gently by ropes two opposing forces, two great dogs, perhaps. "Monsieur, you must do as I asked. Or I can't be responsible."

"Devil take you," said the guest.

"No, it is you he will take, monsieur. Be quiet, be quiet at once, or leave immediately."

Jausande's aunt said, rather tremulously, "Yes, do let's all be obedient. This is so interesting."

And somehow there was silence again, awkward and unwilling for a moment, and more fraught and nearly frightened than ever.

A man walked up out of the floor. (A woman screamed and her scream was choked down.) The man, solid as the Roman girl, solid as anyone present, wore hose and tunic, and the rounded, color-slashed sleeves of an alchemic century. He climbed an unseen stair out of the floor, up across the room, and through the air, and vanished into the ceiling.

The Conjuror spoke to them. "What I show you here are only the pictures of the past, the things that have been, on this spot. But there are other things that coexist with us, in past ages as now."

He spread his arms a little wider, as if allowing the two great dogs to pull forward and away.

There in the middle of the cleared space, where the light had been, was a globe of night. Stars shone over a garden made to the formal measure of three hundred years before, and a woman in a high-waisted gown and cap of silver wire moved among the statues and the sculpted trees. She spoke words from a book, but though the watching salon heard a murmur of her voice, her words, the accent, were so alien, they could not make them out.

Perhaps it was ventriloquism, for The Conjuror too moved his lips, but not it seemed in the same rhythm as the woman.

The woman stopped, facing out into the salon and not seeing it. She closed the book together on a jeweled finger and her cold eyes glared. Then the ground cracked at her feet. It opened into a chasm. And the woman looked into it, not stepping back, nor seemingly dismayed. And something shouldered up from the chasm, pitch dark as the night, putting out all the stars. It had no proper form, yet it was there. And leaning to the woman it made a thin, sweet sound, like distant music. But she answered angrily in wild, ornamented words, what might have been a name. Then the creature from the pit flowed and lowered and compressed itself. It made itself over. And on the grass it alighted, and with a ratlike shake, it assumed the form of the woman, even to her dress and her silver cap, and to the book in her hand. Then she gave a cry of laughter or terror—it was impossible to tell which—a sort of sneezing derision or panic, and whirled into a hundred bits like a shattered vase, and these fell down into the crack, which then healed over. And the monster that had taken human form walked away between the statues.

There was something so horrible in this scene that the silence The Conjuror had induced was now augmented by a second silence, far deeper and less negotiable.

But the garden and the night went out. And The Conjuror pointed upward, and they looked, and saw a great glowing cloud hanging in the ceiling. It lay over the whole of the drawing room, sending down soft rays of light, and a sudden mild rain, which fell among them, moist and fragrant. There came a muted exclamation, another, and these were stifled at once. But the cloud brought a feeling of hope, of possibility. There was nothing fearful to it, until there began to be glimpsed in it an exquisite angelic face with pitiless eyes, looking at them as the other apparitions or demons had not.

And it was as if they thought, *I hate this, it is too beautiful, it asks too much.*

And Jausande Marguerite thought quite clearly, *These things shouldn't be shown. Make it go away.*

At which, as if The Conjuror read her mind, it did. It dissolved like a warm ember.

A third change had come on the salon of Jausande's aunt. There was a restlessness, an anger that had nothing to do with the petty anger of before. Throats began to clear themselves, women's dresses rustled. There were faint muffled inquiries. And Jausande's aunt, the hapless hostess, said, "Do you think, monsieur—?"

Then through the brocade wallpaper something burst like a bomb.

It was black, racing, lunging, roaring—there were cries and shouts—it was a carriage with six horses going full tilt. It tore into the room, into the crowd of evening guests, who fell and tumbled in front of it.

Jausande glimpsed the savage gaping mouths of horses pulled wide on reins, felt the wind of passage graze her and saw a man flung sideways from the impact. The stink of animal sweat and fear, heat and thunder. Hoofs like iron and wheels from which white sparks sprayed off. The carriage rushed headlong through the room and out, into some tunnel of the dimensions, and the walls were whole behind it.

The guests had scattered with the furniture, where they had thrown themselves or, as it seemed, been thrown. Women sobbed and men with sick faces ranted. Two of them had seized The Conjuror, that ineffectual little man.

"You must let go," he said. "Do it, before I make you."

And they let go of him, stepping back, offering him verbal violence instead. But he only shrugged.

Jausande's aunt whispered, "Someone make him leave quickly, for heaven's sake," and pressed her handkerchief to her mouth.

It seemed to Jausande she stood on an island in the jumbled, tumbled room, she was quite alone, as if deserted by midnight in a waste. And to her, over the elaborate carpet that was the sea of sand and rock, he moved. He stood about three feet from her and said, quietly, "You will come to me."

Jausande was unnerved but not afraid. She said, "How dare you? You don't know what you're saying."

But she realized that no one else had heard, and that though there were men enough to throw him out of a window, not one would lay a finger on his dingy sleeve. She looked, and saw his insignificance. She imagined his fusty, pointless life, cramped in his little rooms by the Observatory, an area fallen into disfavor, a place she would never visit.

"But you'll come to me," he said again, "when I'm ready. Then."

"You're mad," she said. She could not see his eyes. It was as if he had none. As if he had no physical shape at all.

And then he was gone, and in the distance over the desert her aunt was entreating her for sympathy, while round about, under the lonely mysterious howls of hyenas, ladies swooned and gentlemen swore vengeance.

At first from an embarrassment, presently from the reassembly of common sense, Jausande told no one what The Conjuror had said to her. Half an hour after his departure from the salon and her life, she had returned to earth and dismissed him as what he was, a fool and charlatan with a cunning line in tricks. It was his essential inferiority that drove him to attempt to distress the gathering. She was merely another intended victim. Some abrupt thought she had had of repairing to her father with the story was soon forgotten. The father of Jausande was elderly and bookish, and her mother long dead. Her uncle, meanwhile, was away on business in foreign climes.

Long after the curious and unpleasant evening, however, Jausande remained glad that no one had heard the invitation—the order—that The Conjuror had issued to her.

She did not believe in ghosts and demons. Her image even of God was that of a just, stern magistrate.

If she had turned a hair, then she plucked it out.

The year passed with a great chrysanthemum of summer, an autumnal pause, a snowy winter of festivals and feasts.

By the coming of spring, the flowers piercing the parks with their needles, the snowdrops, the showers that turned the buildings of the avenues to amazing edifices of wet newsprint, by then no rumors of The Conjuror were any longer heard. He had gone down again into his mouse hole under the boards of the City. Spring was not the time for him. It was as if he had been papered over, and the flowers grew out where he had stood.

And by then, anyway, she had truly forgotten.

Jausande Marguerite sat down before a window. It was late in the afternoon; the slanting champagne light looked sensational, as if new, as if the sun had never shone in this way, although it had in fact, since the dawning afternoon of time. . . . Jausande glanced at the light, where it invaded the stout trees of the Labonne garden. She felt middle-aged, the young girl, because she had seen through the wiles of sunfall. She had found it out: It promised nothing, neither adventure or romance. In token, she was betrothed, to—of all people—the elder brother of Philippe Labonne. She had resigned herself to life.

For here was what life was, such long, quite pleasant, tiring, and tiresome mornings and evenings; the luncheon, the game of cards, the prospect of dinner, of more cards, of the male discussion of finance and politics.

Her fiancé was a good-looking and smart young man, who worked in his wealthy father's business. It was Jausande's aunt who had introduced them. Paul was "superior" to the rest of his family. But no, his family were in themselves perfectly delightful. It had come to be said more and more often. And Jausande had told it to herself over and over. Madame Labonne was *not* irritating, ignorant and saccharine. She was a good woman, full of kindness. And Philippe . . . well, Philippe might improve as he grew older. But

Paul was elegantly mannered, and had impressed that upon Jausande from the start: his manners, financial expectations, and his looks, of which last he was a little secretly vain, but you could not tease him about it, for then he became stiff, reproachful. Jausande's future would be, as her past had always been, a method of pleasing others, which she did so easily and so well. She would make an excellent wife. She would be weightless and charming, serious when required, firm with her children, fanciful prettily and properly within the fences of decorum and finesse. She had liked Paul at first, had almost been glad, almost excited at the first prospects of their meetings. But then she could not deceive herself quite so much. Paul, provided he was never openly crossed, always subtly praised, pampered, and respected, could make the ideal husband. "And Paul likes his books laid out just so, one must never touch. You must be sure the servant burnished the glasses. How he abhors a dusty goblet!" Such helpful hints Paul's mother gave her. "Oh, he's a stickler. What a boy!" Sometimes Jausande played the piano, at Madame Labonne's request. Then Madame Labonne would doze, and minuscule snores would issue from her. Waking, she would say, as she said now, "Such a lovely piece. Such cleverness!" Today she added, "Paul should be here quite soon. And his father, I hope, but the hours that man works, why, a general on a battlefield couldn't work harder."

Jausande imagined for an idle moment saying to this woman, soon enough to be a form of mother to her, "What do you think of dreams?"

Jausande was sure that Madame Labonne had many notions on dreams, and would launch into a recital of them.

Herself, Jausande had no yardstick at all. She was one of those people who do not recall their dreams. It seemed to her all her nights had been dreamless, even in childhood. Never had she roused weeping, or crying out at a nightmare. Never had she known the extraordinary and fantastic happiness, the marvels of the slumbering consciousness, that pursues what we will not.

Last night, Jausande had dreamed. The dream had been long and complex. On waking it lay on her like a fine mist, and as she rose and went about her habitual day, the dream was remembered, grew clearer and closer, as if focused by reality.

And with the recollection there grew also the need to speak, like a pressure on heart, mind, and tongue. But speak to whom? Never this one, surely. Nor the correct, smug young man who was to marry her. Not her father, even, who only wanted her happiness, and had been relieved she came on it so modestly. There were many friends, but no confidantes. They could not understand. It would be as if she said to them, "Last night I flew to the moon."

The fussy clock ticked on the mantel. All at once Madame Labonne, refreshed by her piano snooze, went trotting off to bully her cook. Jausande found that she reached out and drew toward herself some sheets of paper. She had meant to write letters. She dipped her pen into the ink and pressed its blackness on the paper. *I had a strange dream.* Jausande gazed at this sentence, looked up guiltily. The room was empty and the westered wild light streamed over it. She would have at least half an hour, for Madame Labonne would want to taste every dish in the kitchen. Jausande wrote: *I never had a dream in all my life. But this is what I dreamed, in case I should forget, and never again—*

And then she raised her head and murmured aloud, "I may never have another dream, as long as I live." And something struck her in that, with its intimation of mortality. So she scored through the words she had written and put down, *My Dream,* like a child with an exercise.

It had been so vivid, so real, something that awed her, for she was of course unused to the persuasiveness of dreams.

She had woken from sleep into silence. It was the silence, in the dream, that woke her. She went to the window, to see.

There was a moon, in the dream. It was very large, low, white. She knew, in the dream, she had never seen a moon of such size, and yet it did not frighten her. She thought perhaps it had drawn nearer to the earth, and that this must change everything, but in what ways she did not consider. Beyond her window a flight of steps that never before existed ran down to the garden, and over the wall was the City of Paradys. She had a curious sense as she looked at it, in the dream, of the thousands who, as she did, must have regarded it by night through all the ages of its sentience. She saw towers and hills, the loops of the river, and yet it seemed to her that its architecture was not as she had remembered, some buildings more ruinous or in better repair than she had seen them, and some not in the places that she recalled, even to the mass of the cathedral-church, which, rather than dominating the heights of the City, had drawn down into a valley of the river, as if it went there to regard itself in the water. Nowhere were there any lights, the moon had canceled them.

And then she stepped out of the window and onto the stair. She descended, and went across the little garden, which suddenly in the dream was full of palm trees, the giants of an African shore, ages old, their pineapple stems firmly fixed amid the borders of wallflowers.

Outside the garden wall, the street she had known since childhood glided into the City. Jausande walked up the street. It was very wide. On either hand, the buildings, with their peaked roofs and striped railings, seemed half a mile off. The road was paved with huge white blocks. The buildings too were extremely white in the moon, and where there were shadows they made a sort of network of black.

Jausande walked up the street she had known since childhood, which went on for much longer than she remembered, between the moonlit white buildings fretted with shadow. She thought of two lines of a poem; she could not recollect who had written them. They moved in her head, again and again, as if they were a password for traveling the City by night.

The spider moon she spun with her glow
A marble web on the earth below

A password to travel was perhaps necessary, for there was no one else out on the street, nor when it ended and she turned in to another, was there anyone there. No windows were lit. There was no sound at all. She wondered if she could hear her own footsteps, and then she listened, and heard them very faintly, for her feet were bare, and she had on only her nightgown and dressing robe. She realized that none of the street lamps was burning. Or perhaps there were no street lamps anyway. Astride the second street was an arch of white stone, skeletal and strange, with slender shining tines that rayed against the moon's disk.

A marble web on the earth below

Under the moon, the City had become marble, had become another city altogether, with bone-white towers, with terraces like ice.

She passed beneath the arch, and entered a park. Tall trees of a kind she did not know clustered across the smooth gray lawns, and things moved among them, grazing, but she could not tell what they were and did not want to see them distinctly. Above the park rose a rounded hill, and on its top was an eye of crystal. This did not startle her by now, not even when it moved, scanning over the sky. The eye was beautiful, like a great clear jewel. *I am almost there now,* she thought. *But where?*

Behind the park, rising up the hill where the observing eye tilted and quested on its axis, was a dark wood. She went into its nocturnal velvet and fragrance. And in the wood, deep inside, was a light that was not the moon. And even in the dream, she pictured to herself a shape, a kind of being, there in the light. She could not be certain of anything about it, save that its hair moved and was alive, and that it was winged.

Jausande felt then the feeling that had come to her since adolescence, at dawn, or with the westering sunfall. She felt that beckoning enticement. It was now so fierce, so heady, poignant to the edge of pain. For here the promise, whatever it was, was terrifyingly at hand, here the wish could come true.

I shall have to leave everything behind, she thought, and left her robe behind her on the bushes. And in an agony of excitement and abandon, a radiance of hungry fear, she began to run toward the burning center of the wood.

And woke. *Woke.* The shock—had been horrible. Like a fall, a faint. But she fainted into consciousness. She was in her bed. And that—had been a dream. Which in a few moments more was nothing but a mist upon her, vague, not urgent, until now. Now, in the Labonne house, when it had returned with such power.

Jausande got up and looked about at the few books teetering on the Labonne shelves. Would the library of her father furnish her the poem from the dream? *The spider moon—*

Outside the window, the light ravished, darker and more lush, more blatant than before. The spider moon would not rise until eleven o'clock. . . .

The door opened, and Madame Labonne bustled through.

"My dear, how pale you are!"

"I'm unwell," said Jausande Marguerite. "I must go home."

"But Paul—" exclaimed Madame Labonne.

And being a fool, amiably misinterpreted the violent toss Jausande gave with her head, like that of a starving lioness distracted a moment from her kill.

Because she had always been amenable, Jausande had her way. She was sent home in the carriage, and Paul, arriving ten minutes later, was vexed. He hoped aloud Jausande would not turn out after all to be one of those women given to "vapours." She would not. He would never see her again. None of them would.

Those that did see her the last, they were an assorted crew.

Her own father was the first of them. He found her in his library, and was mildly surprised, thinking she had been going to dine with her fiancé. All about Jausande on the table were her father's precious books of poetry. She glanced up at him, like a stranger. And that was usual enough, for they would meet in the house rather than dwell there together.

"Papa," she said, "I can't find my poem about the moon."

"There are so many," he said. He smiled, and quoted parts of them. Jausande interrupted him. She spoke the lines from her dream. He frowned, at the interruption—which was unlike her—and at the words. "Now, let me see. No, Jausande, it isn't a poem. What you have is a peculiar doggerel . . . from Pliny, I believe, the other Pliny. *Aranea luna plena* . . . As I recall: *The full moon, like a spider, lets down her light that covers the earth, as with a web, and there we mortals helplessly struggle, we flies of fate, until the night devours each one of us—*" His daughter rose. He said, with mild disapproval, "A very poor translation. Where can you have discovered it?"

"I forget," she said. Then she bade him good night and went away.

And this was the last *he* saw of her, the pretty, unimportant girl who lodged in his home.

In the dead of the dark, that was not dark at all, for the high round moon stood over Paradys at one in the morning, Jausande had let herself from the house. None of the servants witnessed this, but on the fashionable street outside, a flower seller wandering homeward from her post by the theater beheld a young woman with her hair undone, clad in a satin robe, and under this nothing, it would seem, but her petticoats and corset. The flower seller had, in her time, been shown many things. Jausande Marguerite in her robe was not the most amazing of these. Yet, she was odd, and the flower seller did not like her looks, and hurried away toward her burrow.

The City was not empty, nor especially quiet, even at that hour. In three more the sun would rise again, and the turmoil of the markets would begin; even now wagons were passing in from the country, while at the taverns and less salubrious hotels an all-night noise went on and the lights roared.

Near the Revolutionary Monument, two whores saw Jausande Marguerite and almost took her for one of their own. But as she went by, they thought otherwise. "Why, she's had some fright," said one. They stole up after her and asked what had happened to the lady, could they help her. But Jausande apparently did not hear or see them, and they fell back.

Perhaps through sheer accident, no police of the City happened on Jausande. Or maybe she directed herself away from the areas they frequented.

In a small park, near the Observatory, once a graveyard and still stuck here and there with an awkward blackened slab, a thief, resting from his night's ingenuities, jumped up as Jausande moved by him. He assessed her fine robe and the sparkle of a gem on her finger. A somnambulist, he reckoned her, for so she looked to him. No one was near. He caught her up and walked at her side.

"Sleeping, are you?" he said. "You shouldn't be out alone in the dark. You need Pierre to see you safe. Now, where is it you're going? You can tell me," he wheedled after a moment. His knowledge of those tranced was limited to an act he had once seen performed in the street, when a fellow hypnotized a girl from the crowd, whereat she would answer all types of lewd questions with a fascinating honesty. The sleepwalker, though, did not reply. Pierre the thief dogged her. She seemed about to go up into the cluttered streets above the park, where all manner of ruffians might be lurking. "Now, now, lovely," said Pierre, "you'd be better off with me. Perhaps someone's lost you? Perhaps they'd like to give me something nice for bringing you home?" And then he took her hand gently, to see if he could ease off the ring. It obliged him most kindly. It was new, a betrothal gift, and had not adhered to her flesh. Pierre slipped it in his pocket, and at that moment they had come out of the park of graves, into a winding alley.

Pierre later told his tale to his cronies. He was not ashamed, and did not believe he had imagined what he saw. No one taunted him. The places of the night they trod were filigreed with weirdness. Each had some anecdote of a haunt, of jewelry with a curse on it, for, moving outside the law, they were exposed to lawlessness of many conditions.

The walls of the alley, which were the sides and backs of decaying houses, were hung with weeds. The girl moved between them, with her sleepwalker's eyes still fixed inward. And Pierre loitered after. And then it was as if a curtain, which all this while had hung across the alley and the sky, shivered and twitched aside. And for two or three seconds, only two or three, Pierre saw the girl was walking in a forest of gigantic trees. It was like, he said, the world of a million years before, for he had seen paintings of such scenes in a museum. A primeval landscape, great ferns that swung into the upper air, and the stars there glaring and flaming, and the moon too big, too low. And maybe there was a suggestion of buildings, also, but not any that he had ever seen, either in Paradys or in any painting. He did not care for them, or the forest. But that was only for one or two seconds. In the final second, Pierre saw a sort of bubbling and glowing up ahead.

"God knows," said Pierre, "what that was."

The girl ran toward it. And Pierre ran the other way. He ran, and somewhere he threw the ring he had stolen over his shoulder.

"It was as if there was a second curtain behind the first. The first was lifted up for me to see, but the second was being *melted* away. I had my choice, to run or to stay and look and turn into a pillar of salt."

Pierre, then, was almost the last to see Jausande Marguerite on her journey.

Her ultimate witness was a sleepless small boy in the window of a poor apartment near the Observatory. He saw a lady with loose hair mount a flight of stairs toward a narrow door along the avenue. As she approached the door it turned molten, it blazed and gaped—and the child hid his eyes but knew better than to cry, for his drunkard father would beat him, any excuse. And in the morning, the door was only a door, as it had always been.

The disappearance of Jausande made far less motion in the pond of the City than her re-emergence, later, from its river. There was no hushing that up. And the police, who had formerly tried here, there, and everywhere, gathered themselves to the narrow flat of The Conjuror. It seemed certain persons had once overheard a whispered threat offered by this man to Jausande Marguerite. He had told her that he could make her do whatever he wanted. She, and they, had laughed at this. But suppose—?

The flat was vacant. Nothing was in it but for the rats in the walls. The windows had not been ventilated for years. Clouds of dust billowed about.

The search extended itself, spreading like a ripple from Observatory Hill, beyond the rim of Paradys, out and away into the far bays of other cities. And like a ripple, growing less and less. Who had heard of him, The Conjuror? The very world seemed vacant of him, the rats busy in its walls, its shutters fastened, its dusts blowing. The curtain that encircled it closed *tight*.

There was one who searched about this graveyard, as we are doing, but more intently. He was looking for his lost love, who perished almost as a child. They had loved as children, uncarnally but surely, and she had been taken from him first by her parents, next by death. He did not know where she lay, save it was over some other's grave, for she had been buried in secret during an epidemic of typhus. So he confused the authorities with tales of a buried treasure, a jewel, dropped in some grave, and uprooted all those of which he had a suspicion.

The jewel was really in his own possession. At length he pretended to find it and gave it over. A small price. . . . It was a black diamond, or some white pearl of unusual size.

By then he had unearthed his dead love. She was gone, she was bones, but he raised the skeleton and kissed the toothy lipless smile of the skull. To him she was beautiful still, fresh and childish, unwithered, let alone rotten.

Perhaps she had stayed for him, and dreamed that he could free her with a kiss, his forgiveness of her dying. Perhaps then she was able to sleep in peace.

But this is another marker, the memory of one lost in a far-off clime. He too searched out a sort of skull, and was in love with it. We all have our dreams. May we find them, and God have mercy on us when we do.

Lost in the World

Magnanimous Despair alone
   Could show me so divine a thing,
Where feeble hope could ne'er have flown
   But vainly flapt its tinsel wing.

Marvell

1

On the last day of every month, at the same hour, the same visitor would mount the steps of the narrow house on the west edge of Clock Tower Hill. In summer it would be sunset, and all the normal phantasmagoria of dragons, galleons, and burning towers would be on display in the sky. In winter the dark was well set, the stars above the hill dimmer than the street lamps, perhaps a light snow falling. In autumn, there was the magical dusk as now, when Monsieur Mercile, immaculate and apparently stern, would stand on the top step and ring the bell. And it would be evident that the dusk's magic was quite lost on Monsieur Mercile, that he felt no pang, just as he rarely noted the stars, the dragons, and towers, of winter and summer. This was custom, his visit to the narrow house, not un-mixed with duty. He was a man of the world, understood its rules, had kept them, and prospered. But the one he visited, he was different.

In answer to the bell, a servant woman came, compact and el-derly, a being from an earlier era, where she had completely stayed in all but body.

Monsieur Mercile acknowledged her, and passed into the house.

The rooms of the visit were on the floor above. The first was a sort of pleasant alcove, lined with books, a kind of library, having padded easy chairs by the fire, and on a highly polished stand a globe in ebony. Through the open doors of the alcove was a dining room, an oval table perched with candles, and a sideboard of sparkling decanters; here too a fire burned gently, cheerfully.

The comfortable rooms showed nothing of a woman's touch: Beyond the meticulous servant and one careful girl, no woman ever had access to them. They were graced with bachelor things, and Monsieur Mercile might have felt happiness and security in them, but he was never quite able to do so, here; here there was always a demand on him. The demand was implicit in his friend, Oberand, who now stood up before the library fire.

The two men greeted each other as if they had not met for a year, and yet with the sort of offhand sidelong glances of the eye that evidence usualness. They asked each other how they went on and mentioned the weather, and a certain cognac was produced, which they both settled to like pigeons to a familiar roof.

Oberand, like Mercile, was slim and upright, and in his fifties, but where Mercile's waist had slightly thickened, Oberand was only a little stooped at the shoulders. Oberand's hair receded, where Mercile's had retreated altogether. Oberand's eyes were larger, brighter, lacking glasses, and fraught with thin lines of pain, perhaps physical, but perhaps of something older, deeper, more difficult to bear. Mercile had no mark like this. His hands had stiffened with a trace of rheumatism, but his heart was light. What of Oberand's heart?

After their brandy, and their introductory conversation, they went into the dining room, and here soon appeared an extremely tasty, ordinary dinner. There were too a trio of excellent wines. It was all very good, orderly, and pleasing, redolent of the male satisfactions and luxuries often used in literature as the preface to a ghost story.

And Monsieur Mercile warmed like wax, lost a certain hardness of contour he had had, seemed to be thinking, *Now this isn't so bad. You see, there's nothing to dread.*

Then they took their cigarettes and wine to the fire in the library, and Oberand paused to lay one finger on the ebony globe.

Here it comes! thought Mercile, and braced himself.

The stroking of the globe was an omen as constant and unfortuitous as a comet.

"I took out the small map again," said Oberand softly, as if they were conspirators, as if they had waited only for this moment to begin—and probably this was true of Oberand; Mercile thought so. "I mean Eshlo's map. I sat up over it until three this morning. After a time, I began to seem to connect a particular ridge with a description in the geographia. I took out the two other maps of Klein's. There is one distinct formation, to the south. Eshlo marks this as the Mountains of the White Moon—I love that name, so evocative, so unhelpful, and yet. . . . so alluring."

"Yes," said Mercile, "it is a marvelous name."

"It's possible to pinpoint this geography. The first of Klein's maps relates it to the Charda region, as you know. But then, I wonder with Klein if there isn't some game involved, if some of his assertions aren't meant to be misleading."

"That might be likely."

"And does he offer any reward for struggle? But my struggling attention seems to bear fruit."

Mercile could not quite bring himself to answer, but naturally Oberand did not take this gap for disapproval. Oberand trusted Mercile, had done so for more than ten years. It was incumbent upon Mercile, now, to be trusted.

As always happened, every month, the floodgate of Oberand's obsession had opened as it did before no other one, since no other *could* be trusted save only Mercile. The waters roared and poured forth, as vehement and strong as they had been a decade ago, stronger probably. And Mercile listened, as he always did, every month, with a great patience blunted even as it had been honed, threadbare even as it was perfected. Every visit to Oberand concluded in this way, in two or three hours of Oberand's obsession (until Mercile escaped)—Oberand's maps, his notions, discoveries, dismissals, the throbbing violence, only just held in, of what he believed and *knew* and could not prove, and for which he had been mocked and laughed from eminence, squashed into the gutter, discarded by everyone.

For Oberand had been reckoned a genius, at the start. He was not merely a literary figure of reckoned worth, a bright star elevated at an age supposed precociously early, but also a scholar. Among the countries of manuscript he was thought an explorer. For Oberand had translated screeds previously declared inaccessible, he had unearthed, paying terrifying prices for them, obscure treatises and scripts—of the Romans, from Egypt, and further back and farther off. He had dealt in a murky underworld of the esoteric as other men had trafficked in bodies. And by that he made of himself a creature fabulous, permitted only in the glaring light of its own cleverness. And then it happened that Oberand, thirty-eight years of age and corruscating brightly, came on the work of Eshlo, an explorer out of the countries of landscape. And, too (doubtless), a liar and romancer.

But Oberand believed the words of Eshlo; they caught his fancy and fascinated him.

There had never been in the life of Oberand anything but his work, the pen and the page. He had never, except perhaps briefly in adolescence, felt anything special for a woman, he had not itched, let alone ached through love. The pursuit, the conquest, the culmination were intellectual, and he knew them regularly.

Now, as with a mighty philanderer, for whom love had been always too easy, there must come an elusive quarry, one that did not consent, succumb. In a space of weeks Oberand left everything he had in hand to search after that which Eshlo proffered, to hunt down the clues and keys of which there were hundreds, spurious though they might be, *ridiculous* though they might be. In doing this, Oberand uncovered Klein, a scholar so obscure he was almost invisible, but Oberand lifted him up on high, to the very pedestal where he had placed Eshlo, and lit before them a flaming torch for all to see. From the hilltop Oberand bellowed. He had been given an unlicensed and uncensored voice, he had been made a darling of that most dangerous fraternity, the mature, wise, cunning, erudite, and cruel. They will worship heroes, then at a stumble tear them to pieces in their teeth. And Oberand had stumbled. What a distance he had to fall.

Eshlo had traveled widely, in the Indies, and in Africa. His accounts were exotic, combining the information of facts with flights of elaboration having a logical wildness resembling the development of inspired symphonies. Was it the logic that had misled Oberand? If so, only at a single juncture. Many of Eshlo's claims he had amusedly sloughed. But one story, the very wildest, he had defended as if he had been present at its inception.

For Eshlo claimed to have come upon a pocket of incredible land, a freak valley locked inside a mountain wall unscalable, and penetrated by him via a secret entry that, even in his documents, he had omitted to describe, referring to it only as the Hidden Door, and marking it only in this way on his maps. The valley, when reached, was of an appalling beauty. It was a land from the prehistoric dawn, a place of giant plants, carbon swamps, and a sea like sweat, and inhabited by monsters, huge beasts, and flying things that stormed and raged and *were*, in defiance of time.

Like an echo, Klein backed up this wonder, claiming himself not to have witnessed such a place but from innumerable sources to have heard legends of it. The natives of that area, which Klein posited with imaginative flirtatiousness, avoided the mountain slopes for fear accidentally of being precipitated to their doom in the valley of monsters. (Eshlo, who had refused the secret of his entry, also denied readers the means of his exit.) Several of the indigenous populace of hutments and villages had been lost in this manner, Klein avowed, stipulating a cave or hole through which they descended. A god was propitiated in the region, a god said to be white, and of abnormal size, a giant like the plants and beasts of the valley. Klein quoted many passages, both in their original language and in adequate translation, but the oddity of sections of syntax pretranslated instantly led a critic to deduce that Klein had himself invented these paragraphs of Latin, Greek, Graeco-Persian, and the Egyptian hieroglyphs with which his essays on the subject were scattered—for the Egyptians also had heard of the monsters of the valley, which they had at first named in terms of a coffin of the day's fall, a land of shadow through which Ra the sun must pass each night, overcoming what rampaged there in order to return into the world.

The maps of Klein's related to Africa as he had known it from travelers' tales and the official reports of colonial officers. Everything was second or third hand, but he too, though never having met with Eshlo, never having himself gone farther than the hills above the City of Paradys, had caught the fantasy that Eshlo exhaled, had been poisoned by it. As, in turn, was Oberand.

To make matters worse (perhaps), both Eshlo and Klein were long dead by the hour of Oberand's first discovery of the Valley of God, as Eshlo, next Klein, had called it. Oberand could not, no one could, question the perpetrators of this nightmare-dream. Alone, he impaled himself on the hook, and presently was nailed up, crucified, by those who until then had sung his paean and encouraged him in everything.

Possibly his eccentricity alone would not have alienated them. If he had kept a measure of lightness, and so of light. If he could have chuckled, smiled at his own enthrallment, if he could have said:

Well, I may be wrong. But Oberand was accustomed by then to be right. And such was his passion that he shouted, argued, insulted, twice came to blows.

No one would believe in his belief. His brilliance and innocence went bitter and rotted on the boughs of his mind.

Inside three years he had shut himself away. He reformed his life to an insistent search, a scientific chiseling and scalpeling, of the truth as he had found it. He amassed further material, he dissected and quantified that material he had.

Sometimes he wrote a little. But always, in some however subtle way, it was tainted with his obsession. He was published as a curiosity, and then he was not published. The lecture halls and palaces of books did not any more clamor for him. He was cut. He was forgotten. It was as if a solid figure of iron had faded into mist.

And yet, this stooped man, fifty-two years of age, seared with a hot-cold life, a dreadful fire that could not be put out. And it was this Mercile confronted, this intolerable and pointless, relentlessly gouging fire, howling on inside the unobliterated shell. Confronted tonight again, also, for the thousandth time, or maybe the thousandth-and-tenth. For Oberand could not keep it down. Mercile was the only one left to him, the only one who had never scorned, never ridiculed, always apparently tacitly accepting the veracity of Eshlo's valley, listening to the facts of it over and over, never quibbling, offering only sympathetic assent, the occasional partial challenge by which Oberand might fuel himself further for his burning. Mercile had never let him down, not once, not in fourteen years.

And to Oberand this had been because Mercile credited the truth of the Valley of God. But it was not that. It was only the valiant loyalty of friendship. Something as deep, and as shallow—as useless —as that.

An hour passed. Mercile knew this for he had begun to glance surreptitiously at the clock on the mantelpiece. It was terrible, the slow passage of time now, for decently he could not yet absent himself. Calm and unequivocal, Mercile felt building within him, as always, an unspecified urge to flight, or worse, to choke Oberand to silence.

The maps were now spread on the table, the geographia had been brought. Animated, like a boy, Oberand went about the display. He discoursed on the potential of Klein's frivolity, of Eshlo's secretiveness. "No one is meant to find this place. Yet we are invited to it. Irresistibly we are seduced."

He dreamed of the valley. Mercile knew this, for Oberand had told him, now and then. Oberand already had gone there, had wandered the jungle forests, stared into the pools of salt, and heard the trampling of the vast feet of things that elsewhere had left only bones under the rocks of centuries.

"I feel the moment has come to collate these disparate works, to publish my own conclusions," said Oberand suddenly. The clock ticked. Oberand said, "Don't you agree, some reorganization of the treatise is in order?"

"But," said Mercile, slowly, "your publishers—"

"No, I must approach others. Perhaps I'll need to put up the money myself. I realize perfectly the low esteem in which I'm held, as if by tongs."

"But," said Mercile, "further efforts with this work— What else can be said of it?"

"Very much," said Oberand. "I can speak volumes."

"You should not," said Mercile.

"Oh, my friend, don't worry on my behalf. What else can they do to me or say of me?"

Mercile felt the knife rise in him, its handle toward his hand. He had never understood it was a knife that had been forged by the years of patience and listening, the *boredom*. He tried to evade. He said, "But why expose yourself to more of the vicious attacks that—"

"Why?" Oberand cried, his eyes giving off a flash from the flames of the hearth and the spirit. "Because the truth must be spoken at whatever cost."

"You must face it," said Mercile abruptly, "this truth is doubtful. For God's sake, give it up."

And now the clock ticked more loudly, and the fire cracked like gunshot. Little sounds in the street, a whisper of wind, a distant song, came up and filled the room, thickening its air until it was nearly unbreathable.

"But I thought," said Oberand, "that you, of all of them—" He stopped, and Mercile hung his head. Inside him was an awesome sadness, as if Oberand had just told him he, Oberand, was near death.

"Pardon me," said Mercile humbly, at last. "I've tried very hard."

"No, I don't pardon you," said Oberand. "You should not have tried. Or you should have tried much harder. Did you only wait all these years to make a fool out of me tonight?"

"Oberand, my faith in you is unimpaired. Only I believe that your trust in this thing—is preposterous, ill-founded. I should have said so long before."

"You must leave my house," said Oberand. "You must go at once. There's nothing to say."

Mercile was shocked, yet not surprised. The knife had glittered in his hand, he had used it. What did he expect now? With an exhausted relief strongly enhanced by automatic regret, he rose, shaking his head in an effort at normalcy.

"Then I shall leave, at once. I'm very sorry."

Oberand said nothing. His face was blank, wiped of everything. He had been stabbed in the back, of course, what else?

Mercile went down, donned his greatcoat, stepped into the street. Below, he glanced at the house, wondering if he would enter it again, aware he would not, then turned into the night of lamps and leaves. He felt a satisfaction. It was terrible. He nearly laughed as he walked homeward; certainly he could not keep back a smile.

2

The great mountain range filled the sky, and was the sky. Pitted and scarred, fissured and cracked, it was not white but dark. It had earned Eshlo's name for it not through its tints, but because it seemed to belong to the surface of a dead satellite circling the earth. Anything might lie inside the wall of it. It was impenetrable.

The man who sat in the camp half a mile from the mountains' foot was tall, thinned, and sunburnt by the lion orb of summer. He was thirty-eight. So much he knew, feeling these things sit on him, the frame within which his soul balanced. He looked from his own clear eyes, scanning the dusty plain and the first clawed slopes that pushed out of it. In the etheric sky a pair of vultures dawdled. They had been there about an hour, interested by something on the middle heights, something not yet dead enough to warrant their descent. He had noticed, no bird ever flew toward the summit of the mountains. Nothing came up over them, except rounded drifts of cloud toward sunset, like steam.

He had been here, at the foot, a month, thirty-one days. Before that was the journey, a period not of time but of time's dissolution, an unraveling of dates and seasons, flowing sidelong, nearly backward. There had been sea, a crust of land, a wide river with a belching steamer, at length the long sinuous tributary of the

Charda, with its curtains of banks dropped to the water, the masks of its reflected islands. Lions passed, or lay in the sky. A herd of zebra galloped, an alligator raised its artifact of head—such images pinned themselves upon his brain. The man thought he should and must remember such things distinctly. But then he saw that visually they did not matter, that he might let them go from him if they wished; thus they stayed.

At first he had been fearful. So much so that seasickness and mal de terre had almost disabled him. Then, as he began to accept that he was quite adrift, lost and companionless, without hope of assistance, he relaxed, grew stronger, left behind the stomach cramps and blinding migraines, and emerged from his five decades into the newer younger body, which had wasted no years, which had sprung here immediately after Eshlo's song and Klein's echo. Somewhere on the river of the Charda, while the two black men rowed and the black white stared about, his rifle ready, Oberand caught up his younger self, who all that while had been there ahead of him, waiting.

They moved through the land as Eshlo had, as if nothing had altered, save in the villages they could now barter for cigarettes. It was all quite familiar to him, the people colored like coal and the beasts of the plain, and the towering sky and the river, and the mountains finally rising into view. Eshlo had been here, and told him. More, he had himself been here, often.

They made the camp under the Mountains of the White Moon. None of them had before approached the place, apart from Oberland. The man who cooked was superstitious; he had heard something of the region. He made a shrine by his improvised cook house and sank into it a collection of bones and teeth, for the god, the giant. Oberand had tried to question this man. The man then became heated, hysterical. Sweat flew off him and he gesticulated, refusing to look at the mountains or to say anything that was of use. Froth sprayed out of his mouth and André, the black white, touched Oberand's arm, glancing at him from his odd eyes, one black and one pale gray. "He knows nothing. Best to leave him, monsieur." Oberand obeyed, and André ordered the cook back to his rice with sharp staccato words.

Oberand explored the base of the mountains with André. They climbed a little, André the guide and adviser. He would never fully meet the eyes of the white man, he had been taught not to.

They found caves, and chasms where smoldering chains of water fell, they found the carcasses of things, one with hyenas feasting on it, the nests of birds abandoned, a defile with old painting on a wall, but these symbols gave no revelation. Every cave had a back. Each access ended against the gut wall of the rock. From boulders they looked down at the tiny camp, and saw the blacks lazing or quarreling over a game, and the river far away like a varnished seam in the ground.

"There is no way through," said André.

"Yes," said Oberand, "of course. There is."

André was the first man Oberand had had any prolonged conversation with since Mercile. For this reason Oberand did not trust André. André was not like Mercile. He was young, and could have been a prince if his blood had not been mixed. His white drunkard of a father had taught him books, mathematics, and two languages. André had grown up aware he had been ruined for everything, accepting, wise, and mostly silent. Of the Valley of God he had heard, distantly, now and then. It was one of the dim wandering wisps of myth that go about any continent. It was a white man's myth of the darkness, and as such he gave it a defined and cordoned pen. The white portion of André's mind suggested to him that only white men would evolve a legend of black men worshiping a white god. But the giantism was not alien. There were stone cities of the jungles, and the size of these cities did not belong with the six-foot men of present days but, like certain temples of Egypt, suggested bigger beings nearer to the sun.

Eshlo's maps, and Klein's maps, brought into the realm of the actual, were a travesty. Though the mountains had been recognizable, they were also altered by reality. Small vital geological clues, essential in locating Eshlo's Hidden Door, were changed or unrevealed, or else had only existed in the imagination of the writer.

It was the splitting off from Mercile, the betrayal by Mercile, which had brought Oberand to the Mountains of the White Moon, more than Eshlo or Klein, more than fourteen years of waste, and fermenting humiliation.

Oberand did not miss Mercile. At first there had been no time, for within a week of their dinner, Oberand had been making arrangements to travel out from Paradys into the wide world. Presently, looking back, there was only a slight disgust that such a man as Mercile had been permitted to deceive him. At last, and very soon, Mercile was a shadow. Beneath the Mountains of the White

Moon, however, it was Eshlo that Oberand began to miss, and Klein, although Klein less painfully and clearly.

The sun was setting on the rim of the plain, and the mountains flared up, then turned suddenly to ash, lit only at their tips. There came a curious half-heard whirring note, perhaps the sunset wind passing through some hole or crevice higher up, sound carrying in the glassy air. Transparently the night came to Africa, without subterfuge, bearing the bone moon from which the mountains had been transposed. If the sun was a lion, the moon was a white-faced buck. It peered, vulnerable and savage, above the plain, lighting it as bright as day. The mountains glowed. The fire of the cook house became the center of the earth, marking, like a cross on Eshlo's map, their place in things.

"I am here," Oberand said aloud. *"Here."* But that was not enough. Yet the excitement stirred in him, properly, the first occasion. It had taken so long, for he had been so long coming to it, he had kept it waiting, like his younger self.

André stood smoking, looking at the mountains, thin and still in his European clothes. The blacks squatted at the fire, where the pot hung, full of God knew what jumble.

Speak to André, Oberand thought. Why was that important? André knew nothing, less than the cook, who feared.

Oberand watched the camp from his tent, the pale dust and the moonlight, patches of sand between the mountains' claws, shining. The strange sound had died out from the mountains, and the reflection from their tops. Miles off a lion roared. The stars were liquid, like mercury, in the bulb of sky.

Here I am.

"My father taught me that men have no souls," said André, "that this life is all we can expect, and that it will probably be unpleasant."

The moon had set; it was darker, and somewhere hyenas were busy. The night was not the same, and André had begun to talk at the fire. He had started by saying he thought the two blacks might run away tonight. He said they were not so much afraid as anxious, a kind of anxiety attack that, because they did not see it as nervous in origin, they attributed to bad spirits of the plain and mountains. Oberand said that if this happened, it must be accepted, but would the two men steal very much? Only enough, said André, to support them on their journey back down river. Let them go, then, said

Oberand, they would manage, but what of André? André had said he would remain. He was not afraid, since he did not believe that anything lay over the mountains, even if a way to it were to be found. A dry crater perhaps, an extinct volcano, poisonous and dead. Oberand was not offended by André's pragmatism. His truth-fulness, coming in a straight line after Mercile's years of deception, was nearly appealing. Because he had wanted to, Oberand in-dulged himself, beginning to attempt the drawing out of André, whom he had judged as clever, and almost in his way as educated as anyone met with in the vanished metropolis. André had alarming potential that, since he was black, could never be realized—André was not strong enough, evidently, to evolve solely for himself, as so many were not.

In the background the hyenas had commenced, and then the two blacks initiated a vague annoying chanting from a stand of trees a hundred feet off. André opened a little like a crumpled paper. He spoke of the ancient cities of giants, the legends of white gods. He explained he could not believe in anything like that, although its metaphysic intrigued him.

"But why, André, is it necessary for men to have souls, in order that there be gods? Can't this be something of a different order?"

"Man tries," said André, "to find something greater than himself, promising himself he will one day become such a thing. Is that not the basis of the religion of Christ?"

"I think that the religion of Christ offers a chance that we are already such a thing, and have only lost the way."

"Without a soul," said André, "where is the need for a god?"

"But this is a god with a valley like the Garden of Eden, the Garden before the Fall. This is a god so large that he could cover the bodies of thirty men with his palm, and crush them. What are men to such a god?"

André did not reply. He smoked his cigarette. Then he said, "What would you give to find this secret valley?"

"Everything," said Oberand. He said, "Already, I've given most of it. From the first, the idea possessed me. I sacrificed all I had, and followed it."

"Be wary, perhaps something listens."

"But," said Oberand, "what could that be, if there are no gods?"

"I don't know, monsieur. But I sense it. The way a man whose hand has been cut off will feel the hand at the end of his arm, itching him. Like that. It isn't real, but it affects him. What listens may not be real either, yet it may hear."

Oberand felt a sudden emotional liking for André. Why in God's name had this man not been given him to argue with, to wrestle with, this black angel in the night, over the body of Eshlo, on the ladder of light? But it was too late now.

"Let it hear me," said Oberand, "please God."

After a while longer, André put his cigarette into the fire.

"If we go to sleep, monsieur, the men will have their chance to run away. I will take the sugar and hide it, or they may have that too, for barter."

Oberand got up, half tranced. His muscles ached as if a heavy wine were swirling through his system. He held out his hand. André shook it solemnly. They parted without further words, the black man to his shelter, Oberand to his tent.

He lay on his back for half an hour, and the chanting ceased. The night was silent as an open bowl of space upturned upon the land.

In the night's middle darkness, sound awakened Oberand. It was as if he had been expecting it, had been prepared by a lesser sound of the evening, the huge silence that had domed in the plain as he slept.

What he heard was a sort of low rumbling, and at first he took it for lion in the distance, then for the movement of a herd of animals, shaking the plain. Then, thinking of some tremor of the earth, he sat up suddenly, but although there was the faint sense of vibration, it was not that of an earthquake. Nothing moved, rattled, or fell. After a moment, Oberand got up and went out of the tent, to see what André made of this.

Outside, the night was incredible. It had changed itself yet again, the way no night of the north ever did, or so it seemed to him. The clarity of the darkness was wonderful, like crystal, the sky miles high, drawn back like a blind to reveal the world. On the horizon something vaguely shifted about, probably deer feeding. The other way, the wall of the mountains, lunar, frozen.

Nothing stirred in the camp. Perhaps the runaways were already off. But neither had André emerged. And the sound—it was real and definite—could not be ignored.

Oberand took a step, meaning to wake André, then instantly checked.

André had not woken, or had not come out. The sound was not a summons to André, who did not believe. And the men who were afraid had already run away.

Oberand's heart gave a great leap, catching him like a spear in the breast.

He ducked back into the tent, and picked up the knife and the pistol he had not yet used, some ammunition, water. It was not a careful readying for any vast expedition, it was a token. The token of the traveler. It was ritual, as if before an altar of the night.

When Oberand emerged again, he stood, staring up at the Mountains of the White Moon. They were charcoal gray now, with pale frills of silver from the stars. To climb without ropes would be impossible. Even roped, with the expert advice of André, to reach the crest had been thought out of the question.

The rumble of sound went on, becoming part of hearing. It emanated from within the mountains, borne upward on a column of stillness, opened like an umbrella into the bowl of the sky.

Oberand walked away from the camp, crossing through the shrub and boulders, to the foot of the rock. He came among the patches of sand. He began to climb diagonally, going along the base of the wall, moving south to north, circling. He did not investigate the upright slopes of the wall, as he had been doing, he climbed up and over, and down, and up again. The starlight sliced out swaths of rock, and made pits of luminous blackness between them. He got down into these, and each time, without words he thought, *It will be this one,* but it was not. He did not know what he anticipated, some crack in the rock, something so evident as an avenue with pillars of stone. . . . The camp disappeared around the curve of the mountains.

As he was climbing down, the sound stopped. He felt a moment of deafness, almost disorientation. As if the sign had been taken from him, the promise. He hesitated, and after a moment, the sand on which he stood tipped and settled, lurched and lay flat again. And then gave way completely.

There was no time for Oberand to think. He was falling as the earth caved in. He knew what this was. It was a quicksand. It sucked him under and he caught at the land, but it slipped sideways and nothing would stay put or firm, nothing would hold him. He knew instantly reasonless mad terror and cried out, but his cries hit the void of space, and the gleaming stars swallowed them. Terror and despair, without thoughts. Screaming, he was sucked into turmoil. The sand filled his nostrils and mouth, and he struggled, choked, his eyes were put out, his ears were full of miasma, and panic began to recede into a ringing emptiness. But something struck his heels a blow like a mace. His whole spasming, suffocating body was jolted and spun. In a rush of mass he seemed catapulted down into the stars. He saw them, burning and mocking him. This was death. He lay in the belly of death and vomited out the sand, and as he did so, the grains of other sand sprayed down on him in the dark. He could breathe, he heard the noise he made, but the thing which had smote his heels struck him across the skull. He slid with the darkness closing. Thought had not yet returned. He thought nothing, and nothing. Nothing.

3

"Like a pearl, softly the morning was, and rained . . ." He could not remember the line. He saw the soft pearl light and tried to recall, ". . . and rained . . . like . . ." But this did not matter. The poem was not important now. It was the light that was relevant to him. The light—Oberand pushed up from the cloud and discovered himself, bruised and sore—headed in the tunnel of darkness with the fresh light, so pearly, raining at the tunnel's end a long way off. He should go that way. And he must go on his knees for there was not the room in this cave to stand up. He was in the mountain, in the wall. He had fallen in there through a place of sand, and somehow under it was the cave and the air; he had lived, and there the light was, he had only to crawl. In the light he could see the plain. He crawled, hurting and breathing, forward. After five minutes the outline of the cave mouth grew concrete and exact, and beyond it a dripping pre-dawn mist, and out of the mist a fern cast its tendrils like a dagger, a fern so large it surprised him. But he crawled on, and drew level with it, and from there he beheld the place outside the cave, which was not the plain.

First, perfect stasis, dim reflection of water polished under smoke, tricklings and susurrous unseen, and the nets of things flung over, and the pylon of a tree where flowers clung that were the size of flowers in a dream. Next, motion: Birds lifted from the shallows, while their pale shadows sank away from them like ghosts. They were very big, with the heads of anvils, and the leather slap of their wings tore water drops from the air. Then through the mist the creature came, quite slowly, gracefully, like a vehicle of armor, wet like silk. It was a giant lizard. Reaching the water, it glided through the colossal reeds, which bent from it in the action of courtiers. It dipped its slender and enormous head, and drank. It was beautiful as a thing fashioned, with the life blown into it by magic, and at its delicate step, the ground had moved.

Oberand watched the lizard drinking. Its armor made towers upon its back. He did not know its name. Its eye was like a jewel. Ripples spread in a muscular glittering from the firm licking of its tongue that was the length of his body.

He had reached the Valley of God.

There was no exit from the valley. Inside four weeks he knew this. He had become, again, a new and different man; he did not care, he had resigned himself to death or madness, and to life. He had met Eshlo in the dark, and the *true* truth of Eshlo. Which was romancer and liar. For somehow Eshlo had guessed the existence of the valley, perhaps even found the clues to the valley, but he had never entered it. For if he had, demonstrably, he could never have come back to write his account. The genius of perceptive imagination was Eshlo's gift, what he had handed over to Klein, and to Oberand. No more.

Oberand had searched systematically along the inner rim of the mountains. He was more thorough and more experimental than in his outer searching of a way in. There was nothing, of course. There was no route from Eden, save God made it, and ushered out there with a flaming sword.

Once this problem of escape had been dealt it, all vestige of rules or ethics was sloughed from Oberand, and he was free.

Perhaps because Eshlo's dream adventure had been charted, Oberand had ceased to calendar events. On the journey to the mountains, and in the camp, he had kept a journal. But that had been left behind. He made and attended to no device for the recording of time. The season did not alter, and he had no constant but for the recurrence of day and night. Dawn was not as he had ever seen it, neither sunset. The dream had been made leaf and flesh and feather.

He lived (the mere necessity) through lessons already learned. He set traps in which small rats and lizards, once or twice a tiny type of pig, enmeshed themselves, and these he killed with the pistol, as at other times he shot things that ran before him. He rationed these meals, knowing that with the end of his ammunition he must resort to other more brutal methods. He did not like to kill, but hunger made him able. And at last he would have to do it with a stone. Among the plethora of growing stuff he found roots and pods and berries, which he ate. He had no means of judging them, and some caused him violent sickness. One species laid him up for two days with a fever. He considered if he might die, yet did not believe it. And always he recovered. The fruit of the garden was mostly to be eaten, he had not yet come on the Forbidden Tree.

At first he sheltered in the cave tunnel from which he had first emerged. Nothing troubled him there save for inquisitive rodents (food) and once a fly with wings of jewelry gauze, larger than he from shoulder to shoulder. It startled him, but did not haunt him long.

During his search around the inner base of the mountains, the valley was hidden from him by the fern forest, which began between ten and twenty feet from the rockside, with here and there a break or glade such as that where he had seen the great lizard. Swampy places and dips of silver water lined these glades, but nothing else came to drink there that he saw, except for infrequent, peculiar birds. Others he beheld in the air, birds like a sort of enormous swan, and again arrowings of the bat-winged anvil-heads, which seemed to emanate from a distant smooth height that emerged only in the clearness of midday far above the cycad forest. His search of the mountains for an exit point was instinctive and foolish and actually alien to the person he had become. While it took his days and his thoughts, he understood it was futile, unimportant. Although he saw no further lizards or mammals of the valley at that time, apart from those little ones that supplied his traps, he heard them. Their voices were various, thin and sweet, or trumpeting and terrible. They could not be compared with anything. He sensed there would be huge beasts that fluted and sang, and smaller more fearful things that roared, ate organs and muscle, and drank blood.

When he gave up the search and his freedom came, Oberand took the few items he had constructed, the pillow of rolled dried fern and the best traps, and went down into the forest. So far he had come across several shoots of pure and drinkable water splashing from the rocks, although the pools were consistently full of salts and slimes.

Initially the cycads detained and distracted him. He must cut a way with the knife. He moved by a chain of pools where the giant

spangled insects were swarming. He did not know what they were
at, perhaps mating like dragonflies above a fountain in a park of
Paradys.

The cycads harbored groves of magnolia and laurel. Conifer
trees rose in dark pagodas. The scent of these mingled through the
heavy, curious air. The sunlight began to stream in shifting smoky
shafts, between embroidered eyelets in the canopy.

Oberand watched in wonder. This world was imbuing him, its
smells, the lens of its mist where sunrise and sunset dissolved their
fires, from which mountains came and went like ships lost at sea.

Oak trees appeared, around which lianas roped and spiraled,
and flowers like faces looked at him. Water droplets, the warm dews
of the forest, sprinkled from bough to bough, so the atmosphere
was filled always by this sound and sense of gentle rain.

He went slowly, and found in the mud the footprint of a mighty
creature, perfect as if sculpted for him, although already the moss
was growing in it.

Then the forest parted. He saw across the valley.

It was rimmed by mist, was a lake of mist, from which its shapes
rose, a map of jungle forest, and silken troughs of open land. The
great mountain cone ascended from it, and today a twisted skein of
white extended from a vent. It was a volcano, sinisterly sleeping.
Even as he stared, a flight of birds went upward. Beyond, a steel-
shining water. And on the curve of the misty skyline were twenty
waterfalls (he counted), descending in pristine lines like frayed
thread.

A bird passed overhead and its shadow enveloped him. It was
enormous. He felt no fear in the presence of something so extraordinary. He was in the country of the god. And did the god live on
the volcano-mountain? A new goal now. Oberand had reached the
unreachable, was here in the unreality he had always known to
exist. The god, then, also existed. Did he walk through the Garden
in the cool of the day? Which of the cries of the valley heralded his
passage?

He had been alone for years. He had learned that each man is
alone, even in company. He missed nothing of civilization in the
valley, not even books, for his books had all *been* the valley, had
something of the valley, and here the valley had become his book at
last, open and to be read. He did not mind the random and ill-
cooked food, it interested him. His body, which had hardened and

improved on his journey, had now reached a peak of fitness and energy that delighted him. His eyes were never tired, his eyesight had sharpened. Noises he had sometimes heard in his head had vanished in the constant natural sound of the valley. Everything was better.

It took almost a week of angling descent for Oberand to reach the valley floor. There, he had only the volcanic cone for his guide. A herd of cattle, huge and black with devilish horns, burst out of the mist and over his path on the morning he came down. They were the size of elephant, and filled him with joy. One hour later he saw three lizards, upright and grazing on the trees, with long serpentine necks, tiled with plates like burnished iron. Their bodies moved very little, their heads were busy with the leafage. Once one of them spoke. Its voice was of the sweet bell-like sort he had heard from above.

That night, in his shelter of reeds and steams, Oberand dreamed of the god walking through the valley. The great lizards lifted their heads to see him pass, and he rested his hand briefly upon them in blessing. To him they were tiny, like squirrels in a shrubbery. The earth did not quiver at the footsteps of God, it was his constant movement that caused a ceaseless, now unnoticeable tremor, which turned the world.

Oberand worked toward the cone of the volcano. Cycads grew again on its slopes. The water beyond he judged for the inner landlocked sea of Eshlo's descriptions. For Eshlo, who had never entered the valley, had yet somehow been here, so much remained obvious.

Oberand was by now mad. It was a fact. Much of his freedom came from it. It was sanity that had caused unhappiness, as so often it does.

Time, then, in the valley, unspecified. The beauty of the days of traveling toward the mountain cone, the sights and wonders, the giant snakes, the feeding vegetarian towers of lizards, a fish in a lake like a fearsome sword, the snows of the birds, the cattle that roamed the valley like soft thunder. The sun coming up in tempest, going down in such colors the sky was another country, with other mountain ranges, other seas, other airs. And the nights of stars.

He missed André just a little. He would have liked André to have seen certain of the wonders. André would have respected them,

André who had not believed, would have accepted the magic instantly. But André had not fallen through the sand into the mountain wall, André was not there.

Oberand had begun to see something white, dully gleaming on
the lower slope of the volcano, where the cycads grew.

The way up the volcano was a zigzag of lush and grassy tracts.
Among the cycads, it had absurdly the charm of a wild orchard, and
miniature reptiles darted from the path like rabbits. The sea lay
beyond the body of the mountain, a sheet of light at the edges of
vision. Oberand climbed, eating the fruit of the vines, which he
recognized from below. And in a dusky grove he found a headlong
pillar. It was gigantic, and broken in many pieces lying with gaps
only of a foot or so between them, ribbed and veined, yet freshly
white. He guessed the length of the pillar covered half a mile, and
not far behind, between the cycads and the vines, were four others.

Standing at a break in the trees, Oberand saw other evidence
stretching away, parallel to the places through which he had
climbed. A tier or sloping plateau of the mountain cone ran out,
with a white line on it like the base of a toppled barricade, and
further below was something similar, hidden until now in the
patches of forest. Above, as he moved onward, a vast gate reared
up, parting the sky. Oberand did not stop, he went to the gate, and
under it, and trod across a fissured bridge that in places raised him
perhaps twenty feet from the ground, and came into a hall. Nothing remained of it but the arched struts which once had held its
masonry. Their whiteness burned and turned the sky between to
darkness. The height was limitless. That was of no consequence. He
knew what he had found. It was a temple, of colossal bigness,
erected to the god of the valley. He sat down on the grassy floor,
and gazed at the arches of pure whiteness, where the moss grew
and the lianas festooned themselves. Again, he wished that André
had seen this. Presently Oberand lay on his back and watched the
darkened sky between the arching ribs.

The temple had collapsed, and the forest moved over it like a
slowly turning wheel. Everything was eaten away but for this marvelous fretwork, its bones.

Oberand felt emotions that had no name.

After an interval, the light altered, and the sun was setting. He
made a fire there in the grass on a flat white scale of the temple. He

ate some of the meat he had cooked the night before, and drank water from the bottle.

"I have found a temple to the white god of the legends. I do not pace it out in cubits or miles. It is of exceptional size and surely that is all one needs to know. Besides, I have no one to show it to, no means of sketching it, no means even to write of it. And so I simply write this in my mind. And perhaps, by going over these phrases again and again, as doubtless I shall come to do, I will memorize them.

"There is the remains of a walled avenue leading to the temple, and about two-thirds of the way along it I found the fallen pillars. Probably other pillars have weathered or been absorbed entirely by the forest, for surely others there must have been. Everywhere are great plates and chippings, everything so white, and oddly crenellated, and often split by the ravenous plants of the region. The gateway and the bridge puzzle me. I can find no steps, and only a crumbling of the material of which the temple is made—I do not know what that is—enables me to get up and down. The hall is awe-inspiring and staggering, like a glimpse into outer space. Even if it could be measured exactly, its circumference could only baffle, it is so huge, and yet so perfectly constructed. What walls hung from those alabaster struts? What windows pierced them? And what creatures moved about here, to worship?

"Beyond the arch-vaulted hall is a white mass at some distance, over a ravine in the mountain. Here, too, there must have been a linking bridge . . . smoke from the volcano sometimes rises in the ravine. I cannot so far reach the farther building, which is very overgrown. I think it must be a shrine, some holy of holies. This is frustrating. But possibly, approaching from another direction of the cone, I may find a route over.

"I am very excited. I do not begin to grasp what may happen now. Sometimes the mountain rumbles faintly. Perhaps it will erupt. I feel so well, so fulfilled and gratified, so optimistic, I do not believe it can go on. But my traps continue to feed me, although now I have resorted to the method of the stone—my bullets are all gone. There is water from a rill just above the temple hall.

"When I remember the City I do not credit it. It does not exist for me any more. The world has gone and there is only this.

"Tomorrow I will go down to the lower slopes again and try to find a way across the ravine, to reach the shrine."

* * *

As the sun was rising, Oberand was woken by a disturbance from the forest. Something too large had entered one of the traps, and was destroying it.

Oberand went out of the temple hall and beheld a tusked pig wrenching itself out from the trap in a shower of wood and broken vines. It rolled hot eyes at him, then bolted away, the creepers unweaving over its back.

At that moment an ink black shadow fell on Oberand, covered him and all the ground, cold and depthless as sudden water.

He looked up—and saw a whirlwind.

Out of the whirlwind flashed a wing beat, the writhing and whipping of a snakelike tail, also eyes like fire, a scimitar beak open to reveal the little pointed endless teeth, and claws of steel that gripped. They had him. The pain of them was numbing and unrealistic, and even as he tried to pry himself away, to fight this demon of the upper air, it soared and bore him with it, up between the railings of the cycads, into a vortex of sky.

Oberand heard himself shouting. He flailed and beat at the demon. It was a bird from the volcanic cone, massive, and feathered as if with wire. Its talons held him more tightly than any trap. It peered at him with its soulless mechanical eyes, seeing only his meat, not caring that he fought it.

Already he was fifty feet above the earth. It was hopeless. Oberand ceased to shout. He found he had voided himself in utter terror. Tears of pain and fear ran down his face. The bird dived upward, obliterating gravity, bearing him to some nest high on the cone, where it would kill and feed on him.

The calm of death smothered Oberand. It was as if every sensation and every thought were extinguished together.

He looked down and saw the shape of the world of the valley under him. From the claws of the bird he was granted a vision of the mountain, laid sideways and flat, combered with its forest, wreathed by its smokes and steams, and there the sidelong plateau where the temple stretched downward against the sea. And Oberand, in the claws of murder, saw what the temple was. It was the skeleton of an enormous man, a giant to whom the giant beasts of the valley were small things, like fowl and squirrels. A giant fallen, the tibias and fibulas of the legs an approaching avenue, the pelvis a mighty gate, and the smashed metacarpals of one hand, five toppled pillars. The rib cage made the hall of arches, and over the smouldering ravine was the detached head of the shrine, its two eyes forever wide, its teeth choked by the reclaiming vines. The god lay on the mountain, the god of white bone. Held high in the air in the claws of murder Oberand looked and saw, and an irresistible smiling lifted his face against its bones. Carried toward his horrible death, he could not keep back a terrifying laughter.

What a tomb this one is. Visible for a mile around, from the right positions, towering between the graves. It was designed by a well-known artist, also responsible for a quite remarkable portrait of the dead actress who lies here. It is called the Tomb of the Angel—as you see, for obvious reasons. The angel is beautiful, and bears some resemblance to the actress herself. With spread wings, she offers a mirror to the sky. The glass in the mirror is real, but unfortunately fissured by the elements.

The Glass Dagger

Out flew the web and floated wide;
The mirror crack'd from side to side.

Tennyson

"But," he said, smiling a little, "I believe, in reality, you don't love me."

"Of course," she said, "I hate you very much."

He stood out on the balcony that overhung the canal. The afternoon lay in a broad sheet across the water which, once the sun moved below the western buildings, would grow sober, equally impenetrable. It was not a surface ever to be seen through, it must be taken on trust. And so too perhaps the somber cool young woman who lay in the rumple of sheets and pillows, their bed of love, looking at him sidelong as did men of his acquaintance with whom he gambled.

"No, not hate. Nothing so intent. You like me, you enjoy me, somewhat."

"And you, Michael, take me much too seriously."

She rose from the wave of sheets, shaking back her black hair that was neither luxuriant nor very long. The warm sunlight described her as she would have described a subject in one of her own illustrations. A slim body, quite strong, of course not ugly, but hardly luscious, or perfect. Her face might have passed unremarked a million times, and had done so. Her eyes were oddly shaped, very dark, but often lacking luster when she had worked too hard at her paintings or been locked up too long in the dusts of her sculpted stones. Her hands were graceful, but rough and calloused; they passed over his pampered athlete's body like sandpaper.

He was a fundamentalist; he had never fussily asked of himself why, from the instant he beheld her, in blank, unmagical daylight outside the Temple-Church, he had wanted the artist Valmé: her. He was handsome and rich, an aristocrat, a foreigner, much pursued. He had had many women. He *could* have, within temporal reason, almost anything he desired. And in this way, desiring her, he had got Valmé also.

She had arrived calmly, in cotton gloves and a washerwoman's dress, with a straw hat on her head. She entered their liaison without demur, willingly but not eagerly. Her work she continued and he would never have dreamed of attempting to prevent that. Though he did not understand it, or even especially value its results, her talent was obvious—besides, others too thought so. She was independent, and perhaps this was part of her allure. Though probably not. It seemed to Michael Zwarian that if he had found her begging in a market, able to do nothing but whore, he would yet have had to have her.

As it was she came to him a virgin. An accomplished practiced lover, and in all his physical beauty, he rode into the kingdom of her body sure that through this alone he could make her love him. He had expected her love, for love had always been given him, usually unasked. But though he was innocent of complexity he was not a fool, and by now he knew. It was established between them. And his sad joking on her balcony was not an appeal or a test of her. It was if anything to show her that she need not pretend. And she in turn was too courteous either to protest or to confirm. In her bed (hers, like this room—she had refused to leave them) he might give her pleasure, if she were patient enough to allow it.

Today she had wanted to return to her folio of work, seven ink drawings for a volume of poetry. She had been glad to please *him*, as if he deserved it for his niceness to her, his good heart. And she herself had said, "Forgive me, I haven't the energy. I'm content. Bless you," and kissed him. And now she had begun to dress, wanting him to go away, but not to hurt or offend him. So he said, "Well, I regret I must be off. Tomorrow evening, you'll dine with me?" And she, rewarding his tact, replied that she would happily be present, she anticipated it, she might relax then, her labor completed.

Outside with him he carried away the image of her ordinary

body captured in the vast tilted mirror beyond the bed. This held too the perpetual exact image of the canal, the far western bank, the sky. So he had seen her, in the glass. Had he looked at her in the flesh in that last moment?

Zwarian's carriage trundled down a cobbled alley, following the canal to its source, the river. One day soon, discounting tradition and having no one to answer to, he would want Valmé not as mistress but as wife. Would she refuse, or would her avowal be as benignly unimpassioned as her mistressdom? It was not that she used him (he would never forget the first trinkets given back, apologetically, sternly). She did her best. She had never loved anyone else—except once or twice creatures on paper or in marble. He went to supper in a tall house near the Angel, where pretty women stared at him in astonishment, blushing and fretting.

Valmé's room was L-shaped; beyond the crook of its arm, and behind a screen, lay her studio. Two or three figures always stood in it, silent attendants on all her doings—they were larger unfinished works, one of which would occasionally be completed, only to be replaced by another. At present the god Dionysos dominated the chamber, draped in a sheet as if the City sun would never be divinely warm enough. The walls were covered in sketches, and a few paintings of which Valmé was fond. A stove, now cold, and a huge worktable holding a convention of paints, brushes, pencils, papers, rags, and implements, apparently of torture, occupied the remainder of the space. There was no window, but in the ceiling a round vent brought down the light to make a blazing hole as though into another dimension.

Valmé, dressed now for her trade, did not at once go to the seventh illustration propped up on its board. Instead she moved about the studio, silently realigning herself with its inner structure, as if she had been several months away. On these returns, there were always certain objects that she touched—the Dionysos now, inevitably, a particular ink drawing of towers, an ivory elephant . . . things that held an intimate reminder. She was very private, Valmé, and even her few acquaintances, even her lover Zwarian, who had sometimes looked on the studio, knew the personal significance of scarcely anything. One item, though, which was seldom on display, Valmé had recently begun to remove from its box, holding it up into the well of daylight. This she did now. In her hand it was a shard of burning nothingness, a sort of hard-edged flame. To glimpse it in this way was to be entirely puzzled as to what it might be. And when she lowered the thing, it gave off a flash like lightning, striking the walls in a flaming cartwheel, before going out. What was this apparition? Was it some magic trick learned from her wretched beginnings in the slums of Paradys?

Her father had been a priest. That is to say, was suspected of being one. Her mother's husband, a bookseller, had caused them to exist in a strange, dim gray artery of a street, where he crouched over his wares, and drank heavily, selling virtually nothing. Into this grim life, somewhere in the intervals of boiling turnip soup from half rotted vegetables gleaned off the market floor, and applying ointment to the bruises he gave her, Valmé's mother absorbed a child. The only man she might have been said to spend time with (including her husband) was the priest. His church stood minutes away from the apartment above the bookshop in the artery. He was old, but very strong, and things had been said of him, once or twice. Valmé's mother's husband suspected some discrepancy, and unoriginally struck her, but she too was strong, and he weak. That his wife carried the bastard of another man, probably a religious one, fueled the drunken bookseller's self-pity. He was enabled to become for himself a character in one of the books upon which he crouched like a gargoyle on architecture. "You know what she has done to me," he would say to fellow drinkers in the tavern. Meanwhile the woman had instinctively gathered about herself the impoverished and tangible wives of the district, who, as they assisted her over her pregnancy, became a fortress of chignons, skirts, and aprons. Giving birth amid a thorn hedge of women, she had nothing to fear but the dangers of parturition, and these her tough body refused.

The child, Valmé, emerged then into this world where women were reality, and men soulless creatures, monsters, myths.

Of course, the drunkard hated the child that was not his, but some indefinable moral sense kept him off her in the first six months. By the moment, therefore, when, at her baby's fractious crying, he turned on her, his arm upraised, the woman had reached a momentum. "Touch her, I'll kill you," she said, and in her hand was the knife from the turnips. As he moved, however, she did not after all stab him to death, which would have sent her elsewhere, and so deprived her child, she caught him instead a blow with the side of her fist on his nose. It bled, he fell. And lying on the floor, he vowed to see to her. But Valmé's mother answered, "No, we'll have an end to that. I've had enough. What are you, you sniveling bottle? What have you ever done for us that gives you the right of violence over me, or her?" "Not given *her* to you, surely," he said, through the blood. At that she laughed. "No, squeeze *you* and only cognac would come out. Think what you like," she said, "touch her and you'll never touch another thing in your life. They'll have you out in a box." She was strong, he weak, and this, at that time, enough.

It would come about, in later years, that the drunkard, by then reduced to total sponge, would fawn on his wife in company and out of it, praising her, saying she was his rock, saying he would be dead but for her, and perhaps all this might be said to be true. He never again raised his hand to her, or the child. He ceased to curse her quickly too, for that alone did not satisfy. He dropped easily into the role of the pathetic, guilty, and useless, surviving on the kindness of his wife. For her part, she went on feeding him and securing his clothes, she took in sewing and even began to sell cheap novels in the shop (from such works he hid in fear), thereby making an income for them all to live on.

Valmé had the little schooling that the nuns could give her. She showed an interest at six or seven in the Virgin. She began to draw the Virgin, taking strange, lovely, unblasphemous liberties with her garments and symbols. The drawings were remarkable, said the proud nuns and the proud mother, in the way partial teachers and parents always do. But it happened that, in the case of Valmé, they were correct.

At twelve years, the scrimping and saving of her mother put Valmé into a school of art across the river in the old Scholars' Quarter. Among the quantity of pupils, only five were females. On this distinction, most of them rose and sank, but Valmé paid no attention to anything that did not have to do with her work. Her reading improved, that she might read books on her subject, while to her tabulated species of the male was added one other, the Tutor. Those whose tuition she found valuable became nearly real, for Valmé. The others, like the pupils, she dismissed. None of that made her popular. But in the end this did not matter. For once, the best was also the most influential. These powers protected her and, at the age of fifteen, she emerged from the cocoon with remunerative and creative work already before her.

Five years after this she was able to buy for her mother a modest house in the hills above the City. Here the dregs of the father swiftly flowed away, mopped up finally by the healthful air, the pure food, the gentle lowing of cows and white meandering of sheep. For herself, Valmé acquired her apartment at the canal, her reputation as an artist, her consolidated and pleasing life. For pleasant it was. She liked to be alone, for her solitude was never unpopulated by anything except the human race. The aspirations she had observed in other women—to be fêted, to be adored, to mate and to produce small toy replicas of themselves—Valmé lacked. She did not even deposit in her room a cat, to act as surrogate for these things, although she was fond of cats, spoke to them on the streets, and fed such strays as occasionally haunted the bank of the canal.

One morning she had gone to church, as she did three or four times a year, to absorb the embers of windows, the music, the genuine excellence and truth of the teachings of Christ—which did not affect her in any way but the intellectual, as a perfect mathematic would the mathematician. Coming out of the Temple-Church, she was met by a tall and handsome young man in exquisite clothing. He delighted her eye. She stopped and allowed him to speak to her. Economically, he apologized for his approach, expressed a desire to walk with her, and being permitted this, gradually, another desire to take her to dine. Valmé had been propositioned by one or two others, though possibly by more than she had noticed. She had fobbed them all off. Now it seemed to her that perhaps an affair might be of value to her, extending her perceptions. To his riches she was, and remained, impervious. She saw no want of them, she had what she needed. As for his looks, although they had arrested her, as a masterful painting would have done, they evoked no fleshly response: She could only, if she had to, place Michael Zwarian in the category of the Mythical Man. She did not think he would like her for long, and was surprised when he neither tired of her nor imposed upon her. For his tact in every area of their relationship she came to value him somewhat. But only for himself. If he had left her, she would not have mourned. He did not enhance her life, merely added to it elements she felt she did not properly require, and sometimes, momentarily, he cluttered her. But he deserved only good of her, like her mother, and to both she was dutiful, the one because she was real, and the other because he tried to be.

She had been—the accepted term—Zwarian's "mistress" for two years when they were strolling one day together through the long traceries of shops below the cathedral. It was his intent to buy her a present, hers to frustrate him. Already there was a basket of dark grapes, but on this they feasted together. At the bangles, silks, even at the books, she stared as if such items were incongruous. "You'd let me think you live in a cave," he said. "So I do," she said. He was subtly persuading her toward a place where artistic materials were sold. Here she might give in. He did not want to buy for her such stuff, but would consent if she would. Then, under an awning, there was a phenomenon, a glass window full of glass. It was so odd, it caught her eye. Next, the colors, clear, smoky, chemical, and ethereal at once. "Something here?" he asked her gently. "No," she said, even more gently, for he made her impatient. "But to paint such a thing."

So they stood gazing at goblets and vases sucked out of the sky and the river, from various drinks and ichors, some mingled.

It was not allowed, to go into the shop. She would be off if he suggested it.

Finally, she said, "Michael, what is that? Isn't it a knife made of glass?"

"Yes," he said.

"But what use could it be?"

"A glass dagger," he said. "I imagine one would be able to kill an enemy with it."

The dagger of glass lay on a cushion of black plush. Where the other objects of the display were made of colored, perhaps liquid, emissions, this one thing had been cut from sheer air. It was hard, not fluid. Yet, colorless, it was hardly there. She could not see any ordinariness in it, for first of all she had assessed its parable, though not to understand the meaning.

"This you'd like," said Zwarian softly. "Let me—"

"No, of course not. You're already too generous. No. But tell me about it."

"I don't know anything. Shall I find out?"

"I'm so thirsty," she said, and turned from the window.

So he must buy her crushed fruits in a common glass, not the paradox. That once, he went against her. Part of his tact maybe, to judge where he could overstep the mark, or rather what might be essential enough she must accept. . . . Luckily no price had been displayed on the dagger. It was costly. Probably she would guess, but had not seen.

His note, which accompanied his gift, relayed this:

"The proprietor was vocal on the dagger. A century ago they were, he said, in vogue at Rome and Venice, the weapons of assassins. The blade kills, much as a shard of bottle glass can. The top and hilt can then be smashed with a stick, leaving slight evidence to the undiscerning. At least two hundred skeletons, according to my informant, lie in Italianate mausoleums, with such glass blades wedged between the ribs, and lacking a handle. Dearest, be careful of the point, which really is quite sharp."

It was this, then, this dagger made of harsh and tactile air, which Valmé had taken from its box and lifted up into the light, flashing and dying, like a flame.

Why should that be so? She had never attempted to paint the dagger. She kept it close. Had it become for her a cipher of what her lover should have been? Not necessarily noble, handsome, or wealthy, but an enigma, transparent and merciless, blazing and incalculable, the instrument of sudden death, and mystery?

"You'll come to the theater?"

"Perhaps," he said, because they hemmed him in. He did not want to go. A walk along the river alone in the dull lamplight would have agreed with him better.

"Yshtar is singing in the comedy."

He had heard of Yshtar (who, as was the fashion now among artists and performers, went by one name only).

"Very pretty, I believe."

"Oh, a sensation. Not a hoyden. A woman of class. A lovely voice, and the whitest arms, palest hair. They say she's parted from Dauvin. Naturally, how could that grocer keep her?"

At the *Goddess of Comedy* they watched two acts of a play with songs. Michael Zwarian was bored and restless, but his good manners kept him by his companions. In the intervals, they drank champagne. In the third act, Yshtar appeared. She portrayed a Roman priestess in a charming, inaccurate costume, whose main function was to bare her arms, feet, ankles, and half her breasts. She was indeed beautiful, an amazement, and with a delightful voice. Zwarian was impressed by her, as most of the City had been since her advent half a year before. He had never seen her, as it were, alive, although he had read of her in the journals, most especially the flighty *Weathervane*, whose proprietor was said to be one of her patrons.

"We'll go backstage before the last act," said Delorette. He knew

Yshtar, at least had met her. She was, he said, yet more wonderful when seen close to.

If Zwarian felt anything at this moment, as he was towed behind the towering bulwarks of the sets into the warren of the hinder stage, it was curiosity. He was not considering the actress Yshtar as a woman, or even a female creature. She was a marvelous waxwork that lived.

Her dressing room was cramped and shabby, crowded with stained mirrors and fly-blown, candle-spotted velvet, but freshened by torrents of flowers sent up that very evening by admirers.

The maid admitted them, reminding Zwarian of the brothels of which he had heard but to which he had never had recourse. It amused him, and also he felt sorry for the singer. She was like a poor lily put out for insects to crawl over and try to feed on.

Then she emerged from behind a partition.

She was clad in a satin dressing gown that fulfilled the rules of decorum as the costume had not. Her hair was still pinned up in the Roman mode, and her face was garishly plastered with the cosmetics demanded by her role. Through this mask the gorgeous, flawless sculpture of her face and neck, her lips and eyes, looked out like unsullied swans from a thicket.

"Gentlemen," she said. She appeared neither pleased nor offended, in fact immune, but kind, mild. She would not hurt them if they observed the boundaries.

It was easy to be taken with the actress Yshtar. She favored none of them especially, was gracious to all. She declined to have supper with Delorette, although he was so insistent. (She allowed Gissot to joke about writing a play for her.) Only as they were leaving, just before the last act, giving her merely five minutes to don her concluding costume—she did not, either, try the trick of putting it on behind the partition in their presence—only then did she offer Zwarian the faintest and most insubstantial smile.

He stayed for the last act. As he watched her on the stage, he wondered if it would be possible to strike a bargain with her. She was, he thought, primarily a woman of business. She had no heart, only some dainty, strong silver clockwork that ticked away in its place. Her own talents would gain her whatever it was she desired. But she would presumably like money, provided it were coated with delicacy, offered via a placid etiquette, to match her own.

He grasped exactly the spirit of Valmé's past from the very little she had told him. She had had to work for everything she found valuable. She had never had to work for the attentions of Michael Zwarian.

The affair of Yshtar with Michael Zwarian was somewhat talked of, as was inevitable. (Valmé's attachment to him had scarcely been noticed.) Meanwhile, he did not see Valmé, although he sent her a very courteous letter, explaining that although he would not be intruding on her time, he was, should she want his assistance, always her servant and her friend. With the letter he sent no form of money or expensive present, which she would have disliked, only a basket of fruit and flowers. This the artist painted. In reply she sent him a letter even more courteous than his own. If he had tried to frighten her with the loud whiff of desertion, she seemed not to mind it. She thought of him most warmly, she said, and with gratitude for his many generosities. She did not think she would need to call upon his assistance, but as a friend she would always remember him, and wished him well as such.

Zwarian was not yet daunted. He had expected nothing else. Nevertheless, even expecting nothing else, perhaps he had *hoped* for something else. Would Valmé, hearing of his attentions to the actress, fastidiously brush him off the cuff of her life? He did not actually enjoy the sense of manipulating her. He became impatient, and sequentially, a few hours after, the lover of Yshtar.

There was a summer storm of great force. The sky cracked and roared and pieces of it seemed to fall dazzling in the canal. Seen through the casement wavered by the downpour, the water boiled in the rain, while on the skylight of the artist's studio a herd of crystal beasts galloped ceaselessly by.

She had lit the lamps, it grew so dark. And yet the energy of the tempest, penetrating like a germ, sizzled in the air. Restlessly she paced from the fluttering dimness of the studio to the angle of the bedroom, longing perhaps to run out into the cauldron of wet and galvanism. But some veneer of decorum did not let her now, when three years before, probably, she would have had no scruple.

How strange. Surely she had avoided convention. What had changed her? Could it be her short time with Zwarian had done this? Insidious, then, maybe to be feared. It was as well he had, after all, grown tired of her and taken up with his actress.

The rain stabbed down. It wounded the canal over and over.

Valmé conceded that she was becoming absorbed by the idea of the woman called Yshtar. She found she thought of her often, and never having seen her, formulated idle pictures, both mental and on paper, of her appearance from description. There was, it seemed to Valmé, a momentary intimacy between them. For Zwarian had known the flesh of Valmé, and now embraced the flesh of Yshtar, and this provided an infallible, if curious, link, as though indeed the two women had lain together face to face and breast to breast, naked on a bed. There was to this nothing either sensual or homosexual. Yet it was immediate, and constant. How can a man take the impress of a lover and not carry away some of it, like the mark a shell will leave in sand, which the new consort must sense stroke against her, as they couple?

Perhaps she should visit the theater, and watch Yshtar at her trade. That would be difficult, however, without an escort—and of course now she had none. Besides the vapid sugar of the plays in which Yshtar practiced did not appeal to Valmé.

The rain continued through the night. It washed the heat from Paradys, down her towers, along her roofs and walls, and through her gutters. Unseasonably cool, the morning.

Five weeks after Zwarian had left her, held in that season of cool and filmy weather, another letter was brought to Valmé. It was not vulgar, not scented, and yet a reflex in the handwriting gave it away. Before she opened it, the artist knew she had hold of something of Yshtar's.

"Mademoiselle, it has been suggested to me that it would be useful to my career at this time to have painted a portrait of myself. Your name in turn was recommended, the freshness of your work, its faithful yet unflattering likenesses, which I have myself seen and been moved by. Your fee is yours to state. My agent will attend to that. I hope most sincerely that you will be able to undertake the commission, and trust that you will not find it inconvenient if I call on you tomorrow at the hour of eleven in the morning. I am, mademoiselle, very truly yours. *Yshtar.*"

There was no question or offer of evasion. Like an empress, the actress presented herself, inescapable, and sensitively tactful as only such authority demanded.

Then again, Valmé had no wish to evade. To her slight surprise, her pulse had quickened. She was to meet, here in her "cave," her lover's lover. She was to see her, hear her voice, was to be given indeed the ultimate power over her, that of painting her picture.

Could it be Yshtar knew nothing of her connection to Valmé? Or had she too been drawn to see the ghost of the shell?

Rain was falling, and the City was a wet slate where nothing could be written, when Yshtar's carriage entered the yard below the apartment. Shielded by a manservant's white umbrella, Yshtar entered the building. Five minutes later she stood in the L-shaped room.

"It's very kind that you should allow me to call."

"You gave me little choice," said Valmé quietly.

"My God, is that how it struck you? I'm sorry. If you prefer, I'll return another day." Yshtar too was quiet and composed. Naturally, she said without a word, I must remain.

"Naturally, you must remain," said Valmé. "Do sit down. Will you take coffee or tea?"

"A small glass of kirschvasser, if you have it."

"I do," said Valmé. She kept the liqueur on her sideboard in the corner opposite the bed. Had Zwarian told?

Yshtar wore a pale-gray dress, white gloves, a hat with a smoke of feathers. In her ears were silver chains of pearls. That was all. Her skin and hair, her garments, were in accordance with the weather. *How does she garb herself in the heat of summer? In winter?*

After they had sat in silence a long while, the actress sipping her drink, Valmé coiled in her chair, studying her, Yshtar finally spoke. "Will you be able to grant my request?"

"Probably. I must discuss the fee with your agent."

"I have his card here with me." The white glove laid the small card on a table, where it might be picked up or not as the artist chose.

"Why," said Valmé, ignoring the card, "are you disposed to favor me? My name's scarcely well known."

"Perhaps," said Yshtar, with total un-bad taste, "I can make your name for you."

"Yes, that's a chance. You're very beautiful and your bones would be a challenge to anyone, and your pallor. One of the oldest exercises, mademoiselle, is to paint a still-life, lilies, and clear glass on a plain table napkin. White on white. Who," said Valmé, "is the portrait for?"

"For myself. But obviously the theatrical management is interested in it. A classical play, something in the Greek mode. Will that be possible?"

"You would make," said Valmé, as if hypnotized, "a sensational Antigone. But could there be songs in such a play?" She added to insult.

"They would be written especially," said Yshtar, implacable. "But you must be a reader of minds, mademoiselle. That's the very part."

Valmé said, "You'll hang at the end."

"Off stage," said Yshtar.

Valmé thought her a worthy opponent. She gestured to the bottle of kirschvasser, the bowl of almonds. Disappointing her, Yshtar shook her head. She said, like a princess, "I may come to you, then?"

Valmé felt a deep masculine surge. Again, it was not sexual, but it caught her, was not deniable.

"I'll look forward to it, mademoiselle. Whenever you wish."

"Tomorrow," said Yshtar.

"Tomorrow."

She sat for her portrait for two hours almost every day, between noon and two o'clock. If she was unable to attend the studio, a message was brought around at about ten. Valmé became apprehensive until this hour was passed. Then she would begin her preparations. At twelve, Yshtar would manifest in the doorway. Her clothes were never the same, but for the sitting she would put on, behind the ebony screen (while Valmé prepared coffee), the Antigone costume, with its clusters of unreal but creamy pearls, its darted pleats. Her flax hair was already in the Grecian mode.

They spoke very occasionally throughout the sessions. Yshtar might eat a candied fruit, sip coffee or water—never again the social kirschvasser.

Valmé wore always the same dark smock, striped with tines of chalk, clay, oils.

They never mentioned Zwarian.

The painting, beginning like a scatter of pastel seeds, the faint outlines of the map of a garden, gradually blossomed out in tones and contours, colors and form.

Valmé was excited by the canvas. It seemed to her the finest thing she had fashioned. She would not let her sitter see the work; Yshtar obeyed this stricture without a hint of unease. When the actress was gone, punctually always at two, Valmé would labor on at the picture, perfecting, exacting from memory every iota she had missed in present time. In the night, wakened by rain upon the skylight, she would get up, light a lamp, prowl about the picture, the brush in her hand.

She has known all along that he and I were lovers. Didn't she place before me the clue of the liqueur? And how else had she heard of me?

At three in the morning, under her lamplit parasol of roof and rain, Valmé stood considering the portrait she made of Yshtar. Soon—four more sittings?—it would be done. The task would be over. And what then?

As the artist worked, the actress sat, each woman had maintained her trance, with only those occasional movements, words. Now and then, Valmé had crossed the room to rearrange a pleat of the Antigone dress, to draw a highlight onto a coil of hair or jewel. The body of the actress she never touched. She was not afraid of the firm muscles and damask effect of Yshtar's skin. But it was as if she knew Yshtar through. It was as if Yshtar were her own self, a reflection: altered, new, the same. And Michael Zwarian the pane of glass that separated yet made each one accessible to the other.

Shall I confront her? What shall I ask?

How beautiful she was, there was no need to be beautiful oneself if such stars rose from the mass of humanity.

Valmé studied the lines of the painting. As she had studied the face. As if in a magical spell. Surely, surely she had captured the soul of Yshtar.

Standing before the conjuration of her own sorcery, Valmé felt start up in her a winding wave, emotion, thought, part unidentifiable. She had never felt it, its like, before. She clenched her fists, and in the right of these the sturdy paintbrush, pointed forward like a weapon, snapped and splintered. Valmé gazed after it, amazed.

Jealousy. It had come to her at last. The eternal beast, the creature of the shade by the glim of whose eyes all things are made freshly visible. Could it be?

Why ask her anything? I have her here.

Valmé remembered a story she had illustrated, in which a cheated lover, a great portraitist, had thrust into the painting of his mistress the knife for grating colors.

The women of Valmé's world were real. Through the truth of Yshtar, Valmé had found the way, by night, onto the shining terrible path of actual feeling.

Suddenly she let out a cry. Through the mirror of Yshtar, she saw what she had lost. The tears ran down her face, as the natural rain poured in the water of the canal.

Four, five further sittings arrived, were. And had ended.

"And may I see my painting now, mademoiselle?"

"No . . . Not yet. If you'll be patient just a little longer. Some further details that are best worked on alone. And then," said Valmé.

"But, mademoiselle," said Yshtar, the first time that Valmé had known her arch—perhaps a method kept for inferior opponents— "I shall start to wonder what you're hiding."

Valmé said, with pain, "You're too beautiful, mademoiselle, to have any qualms. The only danger would be that I'd paint only your beauty and not yourself. But I don't think I've failed you there. You'll be able to judge quite soon. Let me get all as perfect as I can before you look. If you'd be kind enough to return tomorrow, say—"

"Alas, not feasible. Rehearsals begin for the new play. You will have to send the portrait to the theater. Tomorrow? My agent can arrange the means. What hour would be suitable?"

"But then," said Valmé, "I shan't know if you're pleased with what I've done—"

"You're too modest. I have no doubts," said Yshtar, dusting off the weeks of their duality so it scattered in tiny motes about the room.

Valmé must say, "Four o'clock would suit me."

A minute more and the actress was gone. Her carriage was gone. The rain filled up the spaces.

Valmé knew a feverish tension. The last vestige of Michael had been drawn out like a thread from a needle. She had let it go, could not have held on to it. For Yshtar had long since become Michael. She had brought him to the studio tinted on her fresh skin, smoothly tangled in her hair and breath. Yshtar's lips had caressed him. Her arms had held him. Now everything was gone.

What shall I do?

Valmé stared at the painting, which needed no further work—to work further upon it would be to mar, to unmake.

Taking up paper and a crayon, she began to draw the face of Michael Zwarian, to sketch with now unsure lines his body. She blushed as she did so.

What would follow? Enormities of time, and she adrift in them. There were two commercial commissions. She glanced at them in a sort of scorn, for what could they be to her now?

Days not like any others, and nights without sleep. She saw them waiting. The vista was like that of a cathedral, a place of anguish.

She did not even doze until dawn. At midday she started up from a pit of nothingness. Remembered: Yshtar—Michael—would not be with her any more.

At four o'clock three strong men appeared in the doorway where Yshtar had gone in and out as a nymph of rain.

They took away the portrait. They were like warders, jailors.

Valmé tore the sheet from the Dionysos and began to polish its cold dead limbs. She knew the great madness that this god was able to inflict—drunkenness, hate, religious mania, or love.

There would be omens. There began to be. (She had longed for them.) A sudden shaft of sunlight through the forward window, over the canal, so clearly wrought twice, outside and in the tilted mirror. A boat passing down to the river with a shadow sail at twilight, in the glass a barque upon the Styx. And a crack in the skylight through which the rain had commenced to infiltrate, a single tear dropped over and over on the worktable. *He will be mine again. No, he never will be mine.*

Days not like any others. And nights without sleep. But the days grew slumberous, as if impregnated by opium—easy to sleep then, deathlike, and to go back in dreams. To see him. At night there were the confines of her marvelous prison cell which she might not leave, and where she could summon up no wish to labor. Waking dreams, hallucinations, omens, in every corner. He had said this to her, and that. She was full of hunger, the greed for pain, and *almost* knew it. She rubbed herself against the razor's edge. She reveled in her wounds. She had loved him. She loved him now. It was always to be so. She drew his face over and over. She depicted him as a knight, a priest, a king, as one who had died. She sketched the lines of his body, blushing.

When she must go out, how sharp as broken glass the intervals of sun. The knives of the rain entered the mirror of the canal a million times over. On the street, returning with her meager provisions, she would weep. (She had wept before the laundress, who had not known what to make of it, had asked if she was bereaved. And Valmé recalled her mother like a stranger.)

Yshtar had all of him now.

Valmé dreamed of Yshtar. She sailed on a mirror of water, dressed in white, the white sail of the boat above her and copied out below, a swan. In the dream Valmé yearned and became Yshtar. Yshtar-Valmé raised her white arms and Michael Zwarian lay down in them.

Waking, she wept her rain into the pillow.

Her clothes were all too big for her. She was growing thin, and in the darkness of her hair had come all at once a strand of white, Yshtar's hair brought on by grief.

Valmé went one night to the *Goddess of Tragedy*, where Yshtar's latest play had been put on. To her astonishment, in the foyer, an exquisite painting was displayed, Yshtar as Antigone. Valmé's portrait. *(He will have seen it, he will have understood that I painted it. He will recognize how I have captured her, a butterfly on a pin. But no, of course he will see her quite differently, imagining I have fashioned wrongly.)* The fee for the portrait had long since been sent to Valmé, who had scrupulously placed the money where it would do most good, old teachings of her thrifty mother—but without being quite aware of what she did. Yshtar's small note of praise and gratitude she had had too. She had kept the note. The hand that penned it traced the flesh of their lover.

At the theater, a woman alone, she was somewhat insulted. She watched Yshtar from a great way off. Could Yshtar, after all, act? It seemed so. She had something of the quality of a vacuum, elements and passions, powers and perhaps angels flowed in, and filled her. Her stasis expressed more than the ranting of the best of her accomplices upon the stage.

Valmé remained through the several acts of the play—in which no songs occurred. At the end, a standing ovation bore up Yshtar like a lily.

Valmé pictured Zwarian among the audience, alight with applause. Now he would go behind the scenery, up into the cliff behind the proscenium. Aloft, he would take her to him.

The artist walked through the night, twice accosted, on the northern bank, as a whore. In the gutters peelings and papers. In windows miles high the sweet dull lamps of love.

Never in her life had she known such hurt. Nor lived so, from the gut of the heart.

Those very few who had believed themselves to be intimates of Valmé discussed her briefly. She had become thin and peculiarly graceful. She had the qualities of an actress immersed in a serious and probably classical role. It must end in her death, whatever it was: She walked in the rain, ate nothing, drank too much wine or that odd liqueur of hers. She would fall prey to a consumption. She would be consumed. A pretty, a fearful death. Who would have thought her legitimate for it? She had always been so practical. And her work suffered. But there, she had *become* her work. She had become one of her own pictures, an exquisite witch bereft and languishing after some deed of terror. She was almost lovely, now.

Those who had known of Zwarian did not guess that he might be the cause. No, this was some other swift affair that had sunk its teeth in her.

And some of them mentioned the glass dagger they had located in her studio. It had recently been hidden behind a pile of books— they glimpsed the locked box. Had she not said, despite the information given her on its uses, that she still asked herself its proper purpose—for there was more to a dagger of glass than mere butchery, mere murder.

It was as if the glass dagger chiseled away at her, as her own implements had down at the stone, finding out the thing within. Whittled, pared, polished fine by an agony of crystal. Down, down, to the bone of the soul's soul.

Michael Zwarian had been away on business in the north. It was winter when he returned to the City, everything set in a pre-frost waiting whiteness. He had had letters every fifth or seventh day from Yshtar, during the weeks of his absence. She was clever, the actress. He was intrigued by the network of spies she had amalgamated—what a criminal she would have made. He had never fathomed her fully, or maybe it was only that he had not felt the driving need to sound her depths. Or again, probably she was quite straightforward, by her own lights simple nearly in her dealings, her cunning only learned through the rule of survival, put to his service with the selfless, careless largesse he had formerly associated only with saints.

The building, the stair, were adorable to Zwarian. He could not stop himself running up the steps like a boy. He was anxious too, and behind him the man was already toiling with the hamper and the wine. "Wait a moment," said Zwarian. The man halted thankfully a flight below. Zwarian knocked. His circulation was sparkling in him. He was conscious of not wanting to shock, and of wanting to shock, that she might scream or shout, slam the door at once, drop in a faint, and he would be ready to catch her. He was remorseful. He was half frightened by what he had achieved—or what Yshtar and he had achieved between them. He longed for this to be over. He desired these moments stretched to infinity. Like Valmé, although he did not consider it, he had found true feeling, its colossal rush like wild horses, winds, chariots, blood.

The door opened. The artist stood at the entry of her cave, the irritating and beloved L-shaped room. He did not see it. He saw her, haggard, demented, and voiceless before him, her eyes glazed, her hair lank and unwashed, her lips colorless and dry. Love churned in him. He was the master magician who had produced this awful wreck. He gloried in her ruin, for he could repair it. Yet he was stunned, despite all that Yshtar, through her own observation, her web of gossips, had relayed to him. Valmé was his, could not exist entire without him. It was so cruel what he had done, what he had allowed Yshtar, clever Yshtar, who had thought of the scheme of the portrait, to do. And he loathed Yshtar at that second, and himself, naturally.

"Don't speak," he said softly. "Let me come in."

"Why?" Valmé said. She was like a dumb thing given the ability to talk by accident.

"What you've thought of me—you were mistaken. I love you, Valmé. Always and only you. Let me come in."

"No," she said, but vaguely. "This is some joke."

"Don't make me offer my confession here, on the landing."

"What confession?"

"Valmé," he said, and laughed at her and guided her gently into the room, and closed the door to shut them inside. They were before the mirror. He noticed how they reflected in it, upon the misty gleam of the canal and the passing boats, the boatmen and their passengers visible, these irrelevancies superimposed backward upon the reality of the chamber and its two lovers.

There, innocently enough, he told her, he confessed what he had arranged, and why. The trap to take her. And if he did not confess that he had once possessed Yshtar, that was kindness, not cowardice. Valmé need never suffer that sting. He could now atone for it for the rest of their lives together.

"But you're saying to me," she eventually murmured, after he had repeated, in various forms, the truth of the bargain and the charade, over and over, conceivably twenty ways, "that you and she are nothing to each other?"

"I owe her my happiness, if she's brought you to a revelation of need for me. I'll be in debt to her forever. But nothing else. It was all for you. A wicked game, concocted in desperation. My darling, how I've hurt you. Can you forgive me?"

"Oh," she said, "yes."

He held her then before the mirror. He took joy in her thinness, her sad hair. He knew that he was their balm; an infallible healer, his touch could cure all.

When she pushed at him a little he let her go, and led her to a chair. She sat down and said, "This is a surprise to me," as if nothing much had happened. Truly a shock, how terribly he had shocked her—he saw it like a physician.

"Allow me," he said.

"Please," she said, so muffled it was inaudible, he thought he read her lips, "I must be alone. I must—will you go now, Michael?"

He did not know for a moment what he should do. Then he saw, beneath the flimsy wrack of wires and tatters she had become, the vestige of her strength, which he had loved and respected, and which had so discommoded him, returning. And he was glad, for now he had brought it on, was its fount, and need be averse to it no longer. Alone—yes. She would want to enhance herself as best she could for him. She would need time for her recovery, for the lessening smart of happiness burning like a warm fire after snow.

"Then, I'll leave you. Allow my man to put in some things I brought—a few savories, some good wine. I'll come back at six."

"Yes," she said. "At six."

He went down the stairs, only slightly put out. He had expected something else, but given the circumstances, anything had been likely. In seven hours he would be with her again. He was a villain. He deserved to be kept waiting.

If startled by an apparition, Yshtar did not show it. Valmé had gained access to the actress's dressing room during the late-morning rehearsal. There they had placed a chair for her—the room itself was locked in the maid's absence. Now she sat on the chair, a figment of darkness, and stared at Yshtar in a detached yet feverish way. "Did you suspect the porter is susceptible to bribery?" asked Valmé. "You'd better know he is."

"But he would understand," said Yshtar, "that you painted my portrait, and might therefore be permitted to seek me. How can I be of service, mademoiselle?"

Valmé rose. There in the corridor, at the ends of which other doors were now opening and shutting, young women darting to and fro, Valmé blurted, "He came to me with a lie. He assured me that you and he are no longer anything to each other. What do you say?"

"One moment," said Yshtar mildly. She unlocked her door, and beckoned Valmé inside. A huge vase dominated the room, bursting with flowers. Amid the paraphernalia of drama there had begun to be the symbols of wealth.

"Michael Zwarian," said Valmé.

"Yes," said Yshtar. "Do please sit down again. I'll tell you without delay. As he will doubtless have stressed, Monsieur Zwarian and I have only been allies. He was kind enough to extend to me some patronage. Our arrangement was of a business nature. In regard to you, mademoiselle, I'm afraid he was so determined to acquire you, he played the oldest trick. He made you jealous. And I was the accomplice, a piece of acting I performed for a good friend."

"I don't believe you," said Valmé.

"Of course not. You love him, mademoiselle, and suppose all women must do the same. This is the common mistake of the lover. But I'm a businesswoman, mademoiselle. I daren't let my heart rule my head. It was a naughty game. But if it's brought you to your senses—then excellent! I apologize most sincerely for any pain or anger I had to cause you. But Monsieur Zwarian is charming, virtuous, and estimable. You've been very fortunate in winning the regard of such a man. One who would go to such lengths to have you."

Valmé stood on the floor of the dressing room like a lost child.

"No," she said, "it's absurd."

"I can," said Yshtar, "offer you proof that I've no connection in the romantic way to monsieur."

Valmé looked at her. Valmé's eyelids fluttered convulsively as if she might faint or be overcome by nausea. She said thickly, "What proof?"

"Tomorrow afternoon I shall be in the company of Monsieur de Villendorf. You've heard of him, I expect, a great patron of the arts. He's at his City house for the winter. He and I . . . I needn't, I think, offer particulars."

"So you've taken another lover."

"No, mademoiselle. He and I have been intimate some while. And tomorrow there's an excursion in the delightful boat he has had built, in the classical mode, and frivolously called *Antigone*. We'll pass your very window, mademoiselle. You may see for yourself."

Valmé said, "You never loved Michael Zwarian."

"Never. And for him—though he was never so indecorous or unkind as to speak to me at length on your peerlessness, you alone are of interest to him." Yshtar smiled. "You were liberal enough to call me beautiful. But there are many other qualities that inspire passion. He has his own beauty, and doesn't need mine."

Valmé cast at her a strange, long look. It was of a hatred so deep, so static—as to be unhuman. Yshtar did not seem to recognize it.

"Thank you," said Valmé.

"If I've set your mind at rest, I'm truly pleased, mademoiselle. Some small token for the wonderful painting. Some slight recompense for any wrong I did you."

On the stairs as she went down, passed by two girls of the theater sisterhood, Valmé was noticed. They grimaced and thought her an ill sign, some unlucky fortune teller or sick prostitute come as a last resort to beg money from a relative.

In the half-light they held hands, the lovers. They had drunk a glass or two of wine. It was he, as formerly, who had been vociferous. She sat passively. She had only told him one specific thing.

"But I must go with you."

"No, no. That would fuss her. I'll go alone."

He had agreed reluctantly, seeing the sense in some of what she said, only nonsense in her refusal of his carriage, his servant to attend her on the journey. Her mother's house in the hills was easy to reach. Her mother, so unwell, must have utter quiet, no novel thing to alarm, until she had recovered.

"But you'll send for me if you've any need?"

She promised that she would.

It was with the news of her mother's illness, her own necessary departure to nurse and tend her, that Valmé had put him off from the second scene of love he had determinedly planned. His restraint, his consideration now were—as always—faultless. He did not carp or agitate. He wanted only to help. He even mentioned cash, boldly, if it should be required. For herself Valmé would accept nothing, but on behalf of her mother, no foolish qualms must interfere. Valmé vowed that if matters came to it, she would also apply to him for funds.

And so the bed lay pristine as the windless canal under the moist hushed onset of evening. And so tomorrow and for an unstipulated number of days and nights, he could not be with her. Thus, through the falsehood of her mother's malady, a kind of dreadful tempting of fate, she had kept him off, could continue to do so, for a while.

"But you'll write to me, Valmé." At first she might be too tired. He must bear with her. "Yes, how selfish I am. Then I'll write to you, my darling."

He had thanked God that he and she were reunited before this latest blow fell. He had been forestalled in mentioning marriage. She knew she had forestalled him. His eyes, his mouth, his manicured hands were brimmed by what he might have said and done.

She managed even to get rid of him before the stroke of ten sounded from the river churches.

Then, in the dark, she sat alone and drank the wine.

She was like the victim of a disaster, a hurricane or earthquake. She could not feel. All feeling had left her. She had been robbed of it.

For she believed in the plot they had laid, Zwarian and the actress. Their flamy flight had been a masque. Now she had been shown, the character of each made it plain. Yshtar had not enchanted him, he had not loved Yshtar. Tomorrow her proof would be on the canal, the curious boat, the party of perfect figures of which Michael was not one, disporting themselves in a crisp winter radiance.

All the agony was past. It need never have existed. Valmé was reprieved.

She stood under the scaffold like an orphan, knowing as only her kind could know, that the despairing moments of her ride toward death had been the climax of her experience, her triumph. For then she had *lived*. *She had lived*. Not cerebrally, not emphatically through the pen, the brush, the aching insensate stone and blind canvas. Not in her mind but in her body. She had been real. She had been one with all the generations of those, the billions, who had loved and suffered, that vast entity, that unison of exquisite, comprehending grief.

And none of it was left. No tumult of yearning, no unscalable mountain of desire. Zwarian loved Valmé, as usual. Everything was as it had been, in the days of unwoken boredom and unneed. He would marry her now. He would snatch her up—how could she refuse? And all her days would be dust.

Sunlight rained in the L-shaped room, finding every perch. It was the cold sun of winter that has no mass, a spirit. On the canal outside a few curious papers floated like swans, moving behind Valmé as she stared into the mirror.

She was waiting, stupidly, for the last act of her drama, for the passing of the silly boat named *Antigone*.

She could not have said why, or only that through this she beheld a completion, however pointless and nullified. As if, once it were done, she might retire from her stage, and cease to be.

On the bed, different from everything, lay the glass dagger.

She had taken it out of its box during the night. She had turned it in her hands. She had wanted something, some cipher for her predicament, but the dagger was not that. The sun described it as it had in the shop window, air cut sharp and bright and hard. The dagger was all she had. It resembled a memory—but of what?

Midday, and the glacial sun went over the skylight, and then the skylight faded somewhat, and the sun had slipped beyond the roof.

Valmé watched the mirror. She was there inside, and the canal, the farther bank, its buildings, bits of sky that hung between: The stage.

But Yshtar did not come, the boat did not appear, sailing out beneath the mirror's proscenium arch.

And a wild and groundless hope stirred in Valmé—that she had been deceived. And miles down, the glory of her pain, which being life to her she had loved, that stirred. And faded. For it was all so trivial. Whatever happened or did not, the facts had been established.

And it seemed to her for a moment that there never had been any great love. They were all deceptions, of the self or another. It was only this, to live, day to day, and the forcing of illusions by eye or hand, the pretense to enormities of which no mortal thing was capable.

She turned from the mirror and went to look at them, the actual unmagical world, the truth of the water, the bank, and the sky.

On the balcony, she glanced about, bitter as a soldier whose city has surrendered. And saw, drifting toward her along the canal, all that humanity was liable to, the idiotic representation of the dream.

It was the boat, modeled after some ancient dictum misunderstood and made suitable for present-day purposes only by technical jugglery. It had a type of Grecian style, a curving sickle of sail. Oars moved in the water, but they were little and out of proportion, not rowed by fairies but through some mechanical device.

At windows here and there on the farther bank people had affixed themselves, amused by the boat. The canal had just sufficient depth to bob it up.

The boat was a parody, and as such completely apt. It said everything.

As the craft wallowed nearer, Valmé made out the ten or so persons on the deck, the glitter of wine goblets, heard a chamber-music trio of musicians playing a song in spurious classical mode.

And Yshtar. The flash of white like the glass.

Seen from this slight distance drawing close, in the crowd of ordinariness and insipidity, Yshtar shone like a pearl.

Valmé remembered. The face she had portrayed. The being. Of all things, Yshtar was the reality of the dream. There she was now, encircled by the arm of a big man in furs, her de Villendorf. That was the proof she extended, but of course the proof was of another order. For Yshtar demonstrated what was possible.

So beautiful. No, Valmé had not forgotten. But she had lost her faith. Here was the miracle to open her eyes.

The actress's furs were white for the man's sable, he set her off as black plush had set off the gleaming crystal. The sun lit her hair into a cloud.

The artist saw and judged as only an artist could. If Yshtar's beauty had loved Michael Zwarian, if *it* had determined to have and possess and keep him, whatever his plan, he could not have strayed. Not from the beauty of Yshtar. But Yshtar had let him go, not exerting herself. She was a sorceress with the power of demons and other dimensions in her grasp—but she did not bother with them. She might take up a wand of fire, instead she plied a purse.

Valmé slunk back into her cave.

The warmthless sun was bright; to any who passed, her room would be a hole of darkness, a cave indeed, with the balcony hung from it like a basket.

In the dark after the bright, the artist stood beside her ashy bed, and gazed back at the mirror on the wall.

She waited, and the confectionery boat slid into it prow first. In the mirror now she watched the dummies of the extras, the unimportant, self-important rich man, and then the beauty of the dream, the reality of the magical woman.

Yshtar was drawn slowly over the surface of the water and over the pane of the mirror. Her reflection floated behind Valmé, coming out from her side like the birth of the moon.

For moments only, the mirror would contain her. There, she slipped toward the further edge—

Valmé sprang, her hand to the bed, and up into the air. Something dazzled like a lightning. She saw what she did, and what occurred, for one split and splitting second—a shard of light, a point like clear ice entering a frozen lake—and then the tilted tear of the mirror shattered. It cracked into a hundred distortions, and triangles and orbs of glass flew off into the room.

Outside, beyond the window, there were shouts. The music ruptured and ended.

Valmé turned her head a fraction. She had an impression on the tail of her eye, as the boat drew itself from the window frame, of confusion and rushing, and she heard the high voices of women crying out. She did not go to see, although all along the opposite bank the watchers were craning forth, gesturing and squeaking. Valmé did not need to verify. The first glimpse had been enough. It had turned to vitreous in her mind. That second when the propulsion of the glass dagger she had flung had pierced through the mirror, penetrating to the hilt the reflected left breast of the whiteness of Yshtar. And the ethereal face caught forever in a faint incredulity, stopped like the heart. And the ripple that spread from the dagger's plummeting, the breast, the cessation, and smashed the mirror into bits.

Every one of the journals reported the death of the actress Yshtar. It was a sensation painted black. The sudden and inexplicable destruction of the young and beautiful: the sacrifice to the gods of a matchless thing.

Perhaps it was the extreme cold of the day that had killed her, and the drinking of the chilled wine, an unforeseen flaw in blood or brain—the word apoplexy could not be used in conjunction with such a woman.

"She was standing one moment on the deck of the boat, laughing with her friends and admirers, the next, without a premonition, she fell."

"The actress made no sound," reported the judicious *Weather-*

vane. "Her companions said she gave no evidence of feeling unwell. She looked, as ever, and as this bereft City has so often seen her, unrivaled in charm and wholesomeness. The stage has lost in her perhaps a budding genius, all else aside, certainly one of its loveliest and best."

A lesser journal, of slight circulation, reported that two or three of her fellows on the boat had noted, at the instant she was struck down, a muffled sound of breaking glass, which seemed to happen in midair.

There was not a mark upon her. Nothing had been spoiled.

Not one journal remarked upon the inevitable postmortem dissolution of the human body, the breaking of its flesh so unlike the shattering of glass or an image in a mirror. Not sudden, nor clean, not sparkling bright and of a cutting edge, having no noise but a dim murmur like the swamp, the blunt crack of a bone, the shifting down to dust.

Curio shops are wonderful things. Who would think they lead to graves? Of course they do, like everything else.

One night an astronomer was searching the skies, so high and far beyond Paradys as to bear no relation to the City, when he saw something, beheld something, out in space itself. Naturally, he had been looking for things, for planets, nebulae, after the machines of war had passed, for the machines of war had made the night sky full of other stuff, fire and flesh falling, and metal arrows of death unlike stars.

It was a quiet time, the peace. It was a convalescence. And staring through his extraordinary lenses, the astronomer saw on the tapestry of space a silver man, walking through eternal night.

The immediate reaction of the astronomer, once the initial shock subsided, was to think someone had played a joke on him. Someone had, somehow, interfered with the immaculate telescope, forcing it to produce this sight, some superimposition on the fields of space.

But then he looked again, intrigued, and watched the silver man walk, and the stars show through him, or the nearer ones show *before* him. And a cold clear conviction stole over the astronomer that what he saw was actual, was real. And it meant something, but in God's name, what?

Curiously, he did not think he looked upon God Himself. A god, perhaps. An angel. A giant, who could move about the airless, gaseous regions alight among beautiful poisons, at home stepping across the distant worlds, too large to be seen except like this, suddenly, freakishly, and by accident.

The astronomer stayed at his lens until the great figure finally went from view, vanishing away as if over a hill of galaxies.

The silver man had been only that. He had had nothing very peculiar about him, except that, unclothed, he had neither any hair nor any organs, yet was so manlike he could be nothing but a male. His face was not handsome, but it was perfect. He had no expression. He shone, and the light of suns gleamed upon him like lamps.

After he had gone, the astronomer did not bother to investigate his telescope (although in after days he dismantled it, had other experts in to try it, rebuilt it, and later searched the skies again for his first sighting of the silver man, which was never repeated). He merely sat that night, in his chair, the vague hum and glow of the City beneath him, the cool air of his hilly garden on his face through the open roof.

What he had seen had no significance. It was too monumental to carry any import.

He told no one, making only a brief note in his diary. *I saw tonight a silver man who walked across space*—something like that.

In later years once or twice he referred to the phenomenon in company, without explaining, as if it were a common thing many had witnessed. Perhaps they had.

Once, but once only, he dreamed that as he lay on his bed, the silver man walked through the room and through his, the astronomer's, body. There was no discomfort, not even a warmth or coldness, the feeling of a breeze in the blood. The vast limbs went by like columns, and were gone. Waking, the astronomer felt annoyed, as if he had missed something, but what was the use? He slept again, and in the morning made no note of any sort.

It is a poor little plot, this one. Who is lying there sleeping and dead? Bend down, part the uncut grass, and see.

The Moon Is a Mask

I danced over water, I danced over sea,
And all the birds in the air couldn't catch me.

Traditional

The mask seemed to have alighted on a stand, in the window of a small shop of crooked masonry, wedged between two alleyways—a thoroughfare seldom used by anyone. It was as if the mask, flighting by in darkness, had been drawn to rest there, like a bird at sea that notices the mast of a benighted ship. Somehow it had melted through the glass. The rest of the window was full of secondhand or thirdhand articles, unlikely to draw much attention, a plant pot, a set of fire irons, a rickety table with the feet of a boar. The mask was not like these things. It was a jet and liquid black, black feathers tipped and rimmed by silver sequins in such an aquiline way that it resembled, even alone and eyeless, the visage of a sooty hawk or a black owl.

Although almost no one frequented the alleyways, a very few people did pass there. Sometimes others came to the shop purposely, to sell, and, rarely, to buy.

Twice every seven days Elsa Garba trod up the south alley and turned into the east alley, on her way to clean the house of a rich doctor on the street Mignonette. On other days Elsa Garba took other routes to her other drudgeries about the City, and did not pass the shop at all.

The morning that she walked by, the mask seemed to see her. She stopped, transfixed.

After a moment, she went up the step and pushed at the shop

door. It opened, and a bell rankled loudly. From a strange gloom that comprised boxes, chests, stacks of books, the shopkeeper emerged like a shark from some rock shelf under the sea. He was not surprised to confront Elsa Garba, although he had never seen her before, not even noticed her on her twice-weekly treks back and forth outside his shop. She looked twenty, and was perhaps younger, little and thin and gray. Her hair was scraped into a scarf and her coat tightly belted at a bone of a waist. She was like so very many others. She was nothing.

"I must tell you," said the proprietor at once, in a fruity jovial tone, "that business isn't good. I can't promise you very much, whatever it is you have to offer."

"I don't want to sell," said Elsa Garba. "How much is the mask?"

"The mask? Which mask is that?"

"The mask of black feathers and silver."

"*That* mask? Oh dear me. *That* one." The shark fluttered its fins lugubriously. "I'm afraid I hesitate to tell you. A very beautifully made article, from a festival I believe, worn by royalty—"

"How much?"

The shopkeeper closed his eyes and told her with a look of terrible pain. It was laughable, absurd, that such a creature as this one should even dare to ask.

Elsa Garba said, "Keep the mask for me until this evening. I'll bring you the full amount in cash."

"Oh, my dear young woman. Really."

"I don't suppose," said Elsa Garba, "you'll have many takers. At such a price. But I won't quibble. I expect you to have the mask ready, wrapped and waiting, at seven o'clock this evening."

"I close at seven."

"Then I won't be late."

And so saying, the gray little thing went from the shop, leaving him between annoyance and amusement, definitely unsettled.

That day Elsa Garba stole from the house of the street Mignonette. She had now and then done so in the past, as she had done so from other houses of her various employers. They were all oblivious, having far too much and not keeping proper track of it. In this case it was a bottle, one of many dozens, from the doctor's cellar—she had long ago learned how to pick the lock. She sold it in Barrel Lane, near the church of Our Lady of Sighs. No questions asked. It was a fine brandy. It gave her just enough.

At seven o'clock she returned to the shop at the joint of the two alleys. The proprietor had shut up early, perhaps to spite her, or only to ward her off. Elsa Garba rang the bell on and on, on and on, until a light appeared and next the proprietor. She showed him the money through the window. Then he had to let her in and wrap up the mask—naturally, he had not done so before—and Elsa Garba took her prize away into the night from which it had come.

Elsa Garba had been a drudge all her short life; she was actually sixteen. Her mother had been a prostitute and her father a lout who soon vanished from the stage. At first Elsa had carried the slops, scrubbed the floors, dusted, polished, mopped up vomit and other juices, at the brothel. Then, when her mother perished of overuse, absinthe, and gin, Elsa had been offered work of another sort. She had not wanted it, and besides was thought too poor a specimen to earn much in that line. The madam, however, affronted at Elsa's aversion to the trade, kicked her out. Elsa bore her skills, such as they were, into the wide world of the City.

She could read a little, she was self-taught, and she could write a few words, and add a few numbers together if she must. In this way she was not often shortchanged. She worked in a laundry until she saw how the vapors killed off the laundresses. Then she took herself away and hired herself to anyone who wanted a maid of all rough work. So effective was she at her profession that employers thought her a perfect treasure, and although drab and lifeless she was also clean in her person. She never thieved anything obvious, such as food, and so they loaded her with discarded dainties. Elsa Garba often feasted on the tail ends of salmon, on stale caviar, and exquisite cakes whose cream had ever so slightly turned. Drink of the alcoholic type she disliked, having been given forced sips by her mother and the madam in her formative years.

Soon Elsa acquired an attic room at the top of a gaunt old house near the clockmakers'.

No one was ever admitted to this room.

Elsa had no friends.

At night, when her long day's employments were done, she would climb up the stairs of the old house and come to her door, which she would unlock with two complicated keys in a motion known only to herself. And then she would leave the earth behind, and step into her chamber.

The room was not large, with a ceiling that sloped sharply down to one side, having set in it a skylight. By day, the skylight showed only the skies above the City, their washes and clouds, their dawns and sunsets, and after dark, the skylight showed the stars and the passing of the moon. In itself, therefore, it was valid and beautiful. But additionally around the edges of the light had been fixed on some pieces of stained glass, like a mosaic, which by day threw strange rich colors upon the room. The walls of the room had been covered in an expensive wallpaper of ruched silk, and where here or there a patch of damp or a particularly virulent crack had defaced the paper, some object stood before the blemish, hiding it. In one place was a great urn from which grew a gigantic jungle plant, whose glossy black leaves reached to the skylight and spread across the ceiling. There were pendant paper lamps with tassels and prismed lamps upon stands of silver gilt. The great bed that filled up the higher half of the room had a headboard of ebony and carved posts—how it had been got up the stairs and in the door was a wonder. Embroidered pillows, lace, a feather mattress and quilts covered the bed. In one angle of the room was a tall pier glass. And in the other a gramophone with an orchid of a horn. Upon a silvered rail hung four or five dresses of incredible luster, and from an ivory box left purposely open, spilled jewels which, though made of glass, were nevertheless reminiscent of some trove of the Arabian Nights.

Once Elsa Garba had entered and locked herself in, she put a record on her gramophone. It was a symphony of the composer Cassarnet. Then Elsa stripped off her work clothes and her scarf, and put them neatly away in a chest. She next washed herself from head to toe as, on every third night, she washed also her hair. Revealed, her hair was fine, silken, and inclined to blonde. Next she dressed herself in a dress of sealike satin hung with beads, and delicately powdered and rouged her face, darkened her lashes. Then she sat down at a tiny table to her supper, which tonight was only some sausage, cheese, and grapes from the market, and a crystal goblet of water from the tap in the communal downstairs kitchen.

When she had finished her meal, Elsa rose and went to look at herself in the brightly polished pier glass. Her exotic room was as spotless as any of those to which she attended. Over her shoulder she saw reflected the white china head of a beautiful woman, life size, which she had bought years before and which she called Mélie. By sleight of eye, Elsa was able to transpose upon her own features the exquisite ones of Mélie. And presently, instead of tying it on herself, Elsa took the mask of black feathers from its wrapping and presented it to Mélie. Then she went to the gramophone and re-wound it.

Elsa did not speak to herself, or to any object in the room. She had no need for this solace, which presupposes the desire for a listener, confidante, or bosom friend. Nevertheless, one word did escape the lips of Elsa, as she tied the mask upon Mélie's face by its black satin ribbons. "Oh," said Elsa. It was not a cry of alarm or pleasure, merely a little sound, a little acknowledgment. For the mask, fastened upon Mélie's pure white features, altered her. She became grave, full of flight, *hollow-boned*.

The hour now grew late for music, for like herself the other occupants of the house near the clockmaker's were prone to rise at dawn or earlier. Elsa let the music fade and went to her bed. She always slept fully clothed in one of her beautiful dresses, and such was her instinctive care, that she moved very little in sleep, never harming or crushing them. She slept also in her paint and powder, which she would wash off at sunrise.

Elsa Garba slept, with her hair spread upon the tinsel pillows. And Mélie watched, with the eyes now of an owl.

All was quiet. In the City from far away came once a sound of riot, a smashing of bottles and a drunken scream, but these things woke no one, being not uncommon.

The stars moved over the pane, and dimmed, and the sky began to glow with another light.

Elsa woke as a brushwork of this light fell on her neck.

She rose and washed her face, put off her dress and donned her drudge's rags, bound up her hair, and drank a portion of weak, gray coffee from a china cup.

Then she descended the house, having locked her door upon her chamber, and upon Mélie in the mask.

There were four apartments to clean this next day, and Elsa Garba did not arrive at her attic again until after nine o'clock; she had heard the bell striking from the Clocktower.

The moment that she had opened her door and closed it behind her, she felt an alteration in the air of her chamber. So she did not turn on her electric light but lit instead her candles in their pewter stands. And by this light, then, she came to see Mélie was quite changed. She had become a harpy. The china skin was corruscated

by china feathers, from her head her hair rayed out, tiny claws
seemed to grip the cabinet beneath her. The candles gave to her
eyes within the mask a feral gleam.

Elsa Garba washed and dressed herself in a deep new silence. She
did not bother with the gâteau someone had given to her. She
drank some water, lifted the mask in her hands before the mirror.
Would it be conceivable to risk such a thing?

Mélie sank back into the candle shadow. The tiny claws vanished
from beneath her and her skin was smooth.

Elsa placed the black mask over her own eyes and brow, and the
upper part of her nose, and slowly tied the ribbons.

She felt a tingling. She looked into the mirror. She saw a young
woman, slender as a pencil, in a dress of water drops and cobweb,
and her fair hair flowed down like rain. But she had the face of a
bird, a sort of black-feathered owl, and her eyes were the eyes of an
owl.

"How light I feel," said Elsa, *aloud*. "I feel I would float."

And she lifted her arms. And she rose two or three inches, but
only two or three, from the carpeted floor.

"What shall I do?" Elsa asked. She looked at the skylight. Then,
mundanely climbing on a chair, she opened it a little way. She went
to her bed and lay there. Elsa slept in the mask.

In the morning, Elsa took off the mask and washed her face free
of feathers, and her eyes became human again.

She locked her chamber, leaving the mask lying on her pillows,
where her head had rested.

It took a week of such nights before Elsa Garba turned into a bird.
The metamorphosis was gradual, strange, and sensual. Elsa's sensu-
ality had until now been all to do with *things,* but through the mask
she graduated via an object—the mask itself—into the world of living matter.

At first only her head was altered. She came to see upon her
features not a mask but an integral inky feathered skin, from which
the rest of the face of the owl, its *actual* mask, evolved. Her eyes,
rather than being contained behind the mask, were set into the
mask. It was a curious owl, unlike any she had ever heard tell of, or
seen in any book of pictures her various employers might have
owned.

The feathers spread down her neck, over her shoulders, down
her arms, little by little, with a delightful tickling. Then a vast new

strength came into her thin strong worker's arms. Her hands, that
only makeup and powder could whiten, turned to exquisite claws
like diamond. She had grown smaller, and compact. Her body
bloomed like a bud. Her tiny breasts were feathered and the
beaded dress, now enormous, fell away. Her feet too grew claws.
She raised her arms and, like the spreading of a peacock's fan, she
found herself winged. Armed and armored, weaponed and
flighted.

And so at long last she rose up through her skylight as the bell
from the Clocktower smote for one o'clock in the morning.

The moon was slender and going down, Elsa, or Owlsa, had now
an impulse to soar over it, leaping it like a bow. But instead she
circled the old Clocktower, staring down on the roofs and pylons of
the City, mystic in starlight, weirdly canted, wet-lit, like some painting of an insane yet talented artist.

Here and there in the country of rooftops, she beheld a faint late
light burning. Electricity, even at this hour and from this height,
and behind the proper drapes, had its romance.

Owlsa dropped. She dropped to stare in with her great masked
eyes at the scene of a drunkard sitting over his brandy. She
spurned him, giving off a faint derisive screech, maybe like the cry
of a hunting owl. It startled him; he spilled his drink and staggered
to the window, pale and fearful. Something is always watching us,
especially as we sin against ourselves.

At another window, Owlsa saw the sick, dying, and the priest
bending low, and the incense was so sweet it reminded her again of
the upper air, and she spun away.

She spun like a dart from the City, out over the suburbs, which
the river divided in a cruel and wanton way, its bridges like hoops,
and the lamps upon the banks so wan and treacherous, who could
cross by night without their hearts in their mouths? But there were
people abroad. They moved about.

Far off too, she saw a train, a gust of fire upon the darkness,
springing on its meaningless journey somewhere, clamped to the
earth, without flight.

At last there was a window with an oil lamp, one whose electricity
had failed or been taken from it. The window was ajar on the night
as if to beg a visitor.

This was also an attic room, but dusty and dirty. Tumbled clothes
and books lay about, used plates and glasses.

On a bed too narrow for them lay a young couple. In sleep they had separated as much as they were able. She wore a grubby slip, and he nothing at all, and in the liquid lake-light of the stars, he was naked to the ankles, naked enough that nothing was hidden, but his feet.

Owlsa came on to the windowsill, where by day the girl fed sparrows.

Owlsa looked upon her prey.

She lifted like a ghost and settled like one on the young man's naked breast. Daintily she stepped across him on her diamond claws. She bent her beak to his arched throat, and rent him. He did not struggle, could not wake. He writhed a little, and Owlsa beheld and felt as she stood upon him the mighty thumping of his heart. The blood poured out black, and Owlsa put her beak into his blood. It was good. It was the freshest food and drink she had ever known. She sucked it up, and he trembled and groaned faintly, his smooth body surging under her claws, and she stroked him with her wings to soothe him, until she was done. (His partner did not wake at all.)

Then Owlsa left the lamplit room and soared out again into the night.

She felt filled by lights, by sparks or stars. But she was not satisfied.

She flew away, inward again on the City, and heard the clocks and bells tolling for three o'clock in the morning.

There was a window without a light. It was a window whose frame seemed stuck with platinum and cold, faceted stones. It was not. But it was the window of a rich woman who lived high over the City in a tall tower, in an apartment lined with white furs. And her window stood open, for she thought this healthful.

The rich young woman lay face down in her pillows, having herself drunk a little too much champagne. Over her neck and shoulders streamed long black tresses, heavily curled and shiny from attention.

Owlsa sat upon the young woman's creamy back, above the guipure lace of her night robe. Owlsa parted the long hair with her beak, and fanned softly with her wings: A lullaby. Lulled too by her champagne and her capsules for sleep, the rich young woman did not know Owlsa sucked out her blood from the nape of her neck.

Then Owlsa tore out strands of the young woman's wonderful hair, plucked great clumps, to line her owl's nest. It would be enough to leave the victim partly bald for the rest of her life. With the sheaf of black curls in her beak, Owlsa lifted from the window and flew away. She was satisfied. For now.

Below her the City wheeled. A faint blush was on the edge of the sky. The stars set.

For a moment Owlsa did not know where she should go. Did she not have some nest, high in some ruined belfry of the City? No. It was an attic room near the clockmaker's.

She hurried to outfly the dawn.

As Elsa Garba trudged to and from her work, she saw peculiar tidings on the stands of newspaper sellers. A young woman of great wealth had been set on during the night, wounded, and a third of her hair torn out at the roots. Some gangland vendetta—the money her father had left her being unwholesome—was mooted. Elsewhere, a young man had been taken ill with an injury to his throat, but he was a nobody, and only the smallest paragraph about him worked its way into the journals several days later, following a spate of such attacks.

A plague of bats was suspected. The citizens were warned to keep closed their windows by night.

By night.

How she flew about. She was just. From the poor she drank the life blood, as has always been done. From the rich she took other things. Their glossy hair, their manicured fingernails, small jewels of unbelievable value, silly items they loved and which were worthless. From one, a banker, she took an eye. was only glass, but what terror it caused, and what headlines.

In Elsa's room Owlsa left her trophies. They were cleaned where necessary of blood, and laid out upon velvet pin cushions, the hair wound around silver pins. An eccentric display. Sometimes a name or place she had heard murmured was written down for Owlsa by Elsa. Armand, Cirie, The Steps, The Angel, Klein, Hiboulle.

She did not attack her employers. She discarded them contemptuously. Owlsa did not remember them.

It was a dark wonder in the City, the bat plague. Windows were closed, but always there were some that were not.

There was a tenement that craned toward the moon. Everything below was sordid and unprepossessing. The streets mean, the alleys sinks and quags of filth. Refuse and miserable lives made dustbins of the rooms. But above the skyline of the City, and especially of the tenement, up there, always, something was beautiful. The sky was a source, if not of hope, at least of cleansing. Even the smokes that trailed across it became gracious. The shapes of cloud were wonderful as statuary, the evenings and mornings, the stars and planets. And the moon, which on this night was full.

Alain was a mender of things, and he had been mending some old iron pans, a flowerpot, a doll with a head that had come off, and other articles, for people who could not afford to buy new. By day he worked too, in a graveyard, where he cut the grass with a great scythe, like the Grim Reaper himself, but apart from the scythe Alain did not resemble the Grim Reaper. He was fair-skinned and handsome and his dark curling hair had turned the heads of ladies at funerals.

Alain's room was a cluttered place, of no special attractions. Cracks ran up all the walls, and the lopsided bed would have crippled one unused to it. Everywhere lay the items of his mending, so that it was also like an odd sort of curiosity shop. And in one corner, on a pile of old newspapers, sat a birdcage.

The cage was wonderful. It had belonged to an old lady who had fallen into penury, and once had contained three parrots. It was very large, and its bars were silvered. In shape it was like a great dome with two lesser domes, one at either side. Alain had been mending the bird cage, in which the old lady had perhaps wanted to keep a pair of sparrows, when she had died. Sometimes he thought of selling the cage. But the difficulty of persuading anyone to buy it, or give him what it was worth, daunted Alain. Money of any worthwhile amount was forever out of his reach; to chase smaller coins seemed pointless.

When he had finished his mending of things, Alain would sit long into the night at his narrow window, gazing at the sky. He had become insomniac gradually, although he was so young and worked so hard. He was unhappy with a sadness that can be borne, that does not starve out pleasure, but that never goes nor ever can go away.

And this night, as Alain watched the sky above the tenement, he saw a great black owl fly by, out of a window half a mile off and up over the disk of the full moon.

At once a spark of wild excitement pierced Alain in the side. For he knew (at once) that what he saw was neither natural nor perhaps real. It was as if he had yearned for hallucinations.

Moreover, the owl, as though it knew of his inclination, did not fly away. It circled over and over, and then suddenly came down upon a neighboring ledge only an arm's length from the window.

Alain stared, and quickly saw what was so strange about the owl. Its head was far greater than its body, and was like a beautiful black mask of feathers set with glowing eyes. The owl too had little breasts buried in its feathers, and its claws, of which it had also a pair, batlike, at the ends of its wide wings, were like diamanté.

Alain opened his window, quietly, not to startle the night owl. "Beautiful thing," he called, "beautiful thing." And he poured for it a saucer of some cheap but nourishing wine he had supped on, and put it out onto the sill.

The owl hesitated awhile, but then it came. It landed daintily, and folded its wings. It looked into the saucer and he saw its glowing eyes mirrored there. Then it turned suddenly and flew into his breast. Even as he felt the soft firm feathered warmth of it and his hands went out to hold it to him, there came the needle thrust of its beak as it tore into the side of his neck.

"A vampire," said Alain. "You're a vampire, my love."

And he held the owl gently, supporting it while it drank the wine of him.

The most odd and sensual feelings flowed through Alain, perhaps because he expected them to. As the drinking creature went on, he drew dreamily nearer and nearer to a floating and dissociated orgasm, unfelt since the innocence of childhood. Wild images of a naked woman clad in black feathers, with fair silken hair, pressed to his body, her teeth in his throat, her soft claws milking him another way, tipped him suddenly into ecstasy, and he cried aloud.

The owl, startled after all, went to spring back. Alain seized it strongly. He held it to him, and as the shuddering left his body, he held it still. The diamanté claws—they were hard as diamond—scratched at his breast. But now he was the cruel one. He bore the black-feathered thing to the birdcage on the newspapers and thrust it in. He shut the door on it. "Come live with me and be my love," said Alain, who had shifted back the slabs of storm-tilted stinking graves, and mended toy soldiers. "I shall feed you as you like to be fed. But stay with me. Stay."

In the great cage the owl padded up and down. It found it could spread its wings, and spread them, but there was no room to fly.

"When you're used to me," said Alain, "I will let you go. You'll fly over the City and come back to me."

Then he placed wine and water and some crumbs of bread in the feeding dishes of the cage. The owl tried to peck him with its silver beak. He laughed. The wound in his neck had ceased bleeding. He would wear a scarf tomorrow.

He hung the cage in the window, where his bird might watch the sky, and watched it in turn from his bed until, near dawn, sleep claimed him.

Those who were used to Elsa Garba's punctuality were surprised. "She must be ill," they said. But none of them knew where she had her room, or cared enough about her to inquire. "If this goes on," they said, after the second or third omission of her visit, "we'll have to look elsewhere."

Elsa Garba knew, inside the feathered shell, the mask of Owlsa, that she had another life, but it grew dim and vague as she lived in the cage of Alain.

At first she longed only for freedom. At night, when (the window closed) he let her from her confinement, she beat about the room. She scratched him over the eyes and he laughed at her and slapped her away, and caught her and brought her to his throat. And there Owlsa drank like a child at the breast. Her bad temper faded. When she had been fed, she would allow him to pet her and stroke her feathers. His groans and cries of delight had only the meaning for her of given responses to her own obsessive cue. He was not rich, and so blood was all she asked of him. Soon, when he let her out, she would fly more softly around the room, alighting only to look at things—an unrepaired toy caravan, a pot of dead camellias—then she would spring to his neck and he would receive her. They would lie on the lopsided bed. He would tell her she was a maiden from a dark forest. If he pulled one feather from her wing, she would assume her true shape and he could bind her forever. But he never did this. Perhaps he was afraid her true shape might disappoint him.

Weeks passed, and this was their ritual. But Alain did not yet allow Owlsa free to fly about the City, for fear she would not return to him.

He grew very pale but was not listless. If anything he was stronger than ever, and worked at heaving up the great stones that a winter's storms had toppled. As he scythed the graveyard grass, the young women turned their heads, sometimes even through tears, and saw him.

Alain brought gifts for Owlsa.

He wound the cage bars with bright beads and put mirrors of silver-gilded frames into it. He placed a pot of living camellias in the corner of the cage for Owlsa's convenience, and also to give her a screen, a garden wherein to disport herself. Her cage grew beautiful, as the room was not.

Then came again a night of the full moon, and Alain opened the window, and opened the door of the cage.

"There's the night. Here am I. You must come back to me or I shall pine to death."

Owlsa left her cage slowly. She flew slowly to the windowsill and looked out into the night.

The sky was clear, a lily pond of stars, and the great white face of the moon like a drowned girl floating in hair.

Below lay the city, its slanted roofs, its towers and pinnacles. Here and there a chimney gave a cloud of lighted smoke.

"Remember," said Alain, smoothing her back, her folded wings, "if you leave me I shall die."

But Owlsa lifted up into the sky, up and up, higher and higher until the light of the moon seemed to burn her out.

"Faithless. Lost," said Alain. And he slammed the door of the cage angrily shut upon its riches.

Owlsa flew.

She flew across the tops of churches like palaces and churches like temples. She saw the colored windows and heard the singing to God, which to her was like the sound of cattle lowing in the market, or the rush of the river beneath a boat. The river she saw also, its shining loops and flimsy bridges. It was as if she had forgotten everything. She flew above graveyards and parks. She saw revelry on the streets, where tables crowded the pavements and cold electric lamps were lit, for she was out very early.

She even flew about the Clocktower, and over the gaunt old house where Elsa Garba had had her room. But Owlsa had forgotten Elsa, and Elsa's room was long since raped, the door smashed in, pin cushions thrown out in marveling disgust. A prostitute lived there now, as if in mockery, and her faint complaints could be heard to the music of the gramophone, which now played not Cassarnet but a tune with syncopation and a saxophone.

Owlsa flew and flew. She joyed in her freedom. The night was her tapestry, which she stitched with her wings. The hours were cast off her needles.

The moon turned thinner and gray, as if it might melt and reveal some shadow shape behind it, but it did not. Then toward morning there were only stars.

Owlsa flew toward the tenement that now contained her chamber of bars and beads, mirrors and flowers.

She came to the window of Alain.

She stood upon the sill.

The window was shut.

On the lopsided bed lay Alain in the arms of a young girl like a wilted chrysanthemum. They twined and groaned, and the girl sobbed, and Alain cried out in the way he had cried when Owlsa fed from him. Just the same.

In the cage, the camellias were dying.

Owlsa flew off from the sill like a cinder from a fire. She flew up into the sky, searching for the moon. She felt a frantic need to find the moon again, to follow it down to where it went under the world, and so she rushed with a rapid heartbeating of wings into the deathly west.

And the air tore by her, and the belfries and towers of the pitiless City that cared not even for itself. And as the wind rushed at her, she felt a peculiar loosening, at her face. It was as if a skin came painlessly away, and suddenly winged off from her. She saw it. It was black and feathered, tipped and rimmed with silver. It was the mask. The mask had flown from Elsa, in the sky.

And already and at once she felt herself changing. Her feathers were scoured away and she was only skin and bone. Her slender arms flapped meaninglessly, and her pale small hands. Her legs and feet weighed her to the earth. She fell.

And as she fell, she saw the mask fly on over the hill of heaven into the west, following the sunken moon.

Then she struck the ground. It was stone, and killed her outright.

She lay on a grave, on her back, all smashed. But her face was not damaged, and her face was the face of a beautiful owl-woman, with shining eyes yet open wide, and the long streams of her shining hair running off from her with her blood into the scythe-cut grass.

Those that came on her in the sunrise were amazed. They hid her quickly underground, knowing such things must not be thought of very much, for it was obvious she had fallen from the air.

But in our secret hearts we know: The moon is a mask; it conceals something that hides behind it, passing over the sky and watching us. What can it be?

THE
BOOK
OF THE
MAD

Tired moons ask higher tides.

Zelda Fitzgerald

PROLOGUE

Paradise

The sun shall not smite thee by day,
nor the moon by night.

Psalms

It was early afternoon, but as ever the daytime City was enveloped
in gray mist. The sun had been invisible for years. The architecture
of the City itself—decayed, ruinous, romantic, and depressing by
turns—was visible in shifting patches, or regularly to a distance of
seven meters. So that, as Felion climbed the long stair of a hundred
steps, his world sank away into a sea of fog from which a few ghostly
towers poked. And above, the Terrace of Birds began to form
around a single dot of light—which would be Smara's lamp. That is,
he doubted anyone else would have climbed up here. The unhinged citizens of Paradise were also sluggish and indifferent, obsessed with rituals and trivia.

Felion stepped off onto the terrace. Through the mist, the
strange dim stone figures of bird-headed things perched on the
balustrade, their long beaks moistly shining. In their midst, the
amber lamp floated obediently in the air. Smara stood beneath it.
Slim and blond as Felion, and wrapped in a sleek, pale dress, she
stared at him with essential recognition. They were twins.

"I haven't seen you for a week," he said. "How are you?"

"Sane," said Smara. "And you?"

Felion laughed. "We two," he said.

He went over to her, took her hand, and laid it against his face.
He loved her, but in the wrong way. Brother and sister, they were
expected by their society to be incestuous, it was the custom. But

then the customs of Paradise were wild and sometimes uncouth. The polluted chemical saturation of the atmosphere, which produced the eternal mists of Paradise and eroded the buildings, had influenced the minds that lived there. For some reason, Felion and Smara were not mad, at least not in the accepted manner. They had therefore no friends, no lovers. They had had an uncle, but he was gone. Nevertheless, he was their reason for meeting at this place, for climbing up the hundred steps to his tilted mansion on the City tops.

"Do you remember when he brought us here?" asked Felion of Smara. "These bird statues frightened you."

"That was your fault," said Smara, "and you made it worse."

"So I did. But you were the only one I had power over. We were just children."

"I know why you wanted to come here," she said. "But I'm not really willing. Don't you think, after all, it would be an act of madness?"

"Perhaps. Isn't that good?"

Smara looked away, down across the City. From the denser lower levels of the fog, the decayed towers of the cathedral rose. "Today it's quite easy to see, the Temple-Church."

"Yes. But tomorrow it may be hidden."

"Don't you think," she said, "our uncle might have lied? We were children, as you said. I barely recollect what we saw."

"I've never forgotten. I've dreamed of it for years. That wall of smoking *whiteness*—"

"No," she said. "No, don't."

"You must help me," he said.

"Why? If it *is* a labyrinth, it's simple. One hand always on the left side wall, and it will bring you to the center. And the right side wall to return."

"Then you don't want to come with me to see—"

"Maybe it goes nowhere. Why should it go anywhere? He was mad, too."

Felion gazed up at the bird things. He said slowly, "He named us as his heirs. That was straightforward enough. So we inherit this pile of stone, and we inherit the labyrinth, if it exists—and it does. And then there's that rambling letter he wrote to us. The *rest* of the inheritance."

"Suppose," she said, "you and I are insane, like all of them. But we haven't realized."

He shrugged. She did not look alarmed—even, possibly, hopeful. "We've done our best to act out madness," he said. "What else can we do?" He took her hand again. "Let's go in. Let's see what the house is like, at least."

They went over the terrace to the big door, and Felion spoke to it the numbers written in their uncle's parting letter. The door opened, and a long dark hall stretched out, lined with marble abstracts, ending in a broad stair. High up, a round window let in the sinister light. Mist hung on the air.

They walked in, and for two hours they went over the mansion their uncle had willed to them. It was like everywhere else, no better, no worse, one with the other grand and rotting buildings of the City, bulging with furniture, art objects, defaced books, and technological gadgets, which, usually, had ceased to function.

Finally they came down into the basement, and there they found the narrow door that neither of them, in fact, had forgotten.

"Shall we see if it's still there? Perhaps it's vanished."

He told off the other set of numbers to the door, and when it swung away, he moved down the sloping floor beyond. After a moment, Smara followed him.

At the bottom, in blackness but for the glow of Smara's floating lamp, was the odd little railway track and the carriage that ran along it. But the car refused to work. So then they walked along the track, between the blank walls, and so out into a kind of cavern, which must lie somewhere inside the hill, behind the hundred steps, and under the foundations of deserted houses.

At the far end of the cavern rose a white gleaming wetness.

It was another wall, but it seemed made, of all things, from ice. An arched entry led into it. Inside, only more of the whiteness was to be seen.

"Of course," he said, "it would have scared you. You were afraid of winter, even though there never is a winter anymore."

"It was the picture you showed me on that screen. The snowfields, and the frozen water."

"But this," he said, "how can it be ice?"

"It could be anything," she said quietly. "*He* made it."

Their gnarled uncle had claimed to be a scientist, a physicist and mathematician. That one day in childhood when he had brought them to his house, he had explained to them so many things that they had understood nothing at all. And then he showed them this.

It was a labyrinth, he said, built by him, that formed a connection between two worlds: the world of Paradise and the world of another city, similar but also different. In this other city the atmosphere was clear, a sun and a moon and stars shone down. Technologically, its society was not so advanced, but neither had it atrophied. And while an aspect of madness prevailed there, it was not the rooted insanity of Paradise.

"I believe," said Felion, "that he did what he said. He reached the second city and he lived there. And as he approached death, he decided to offer us, too, the chance of freedom."

"How spiteful of him," she said, "to make us wait so long."

"But time is changeable in the labyrinth, didn't he say so? We could penetrate this world at any point in time, past, future—I don't grasp the ethic of it. It must be random, uncontrollable."

"Or a lie," she said again.

"But he was gone for years," said Felion. "Where did he go?"

"Oh, he concealed himself."

The white wall remained there before them, empty, menacing; unavoidable?

Smara moved away, and began to return along the track in the floor. Presently Felion went after her.

They negotiated the slope and emerged from the door, which shut, back into the basement.

"Did you," she said, "kill this week?"

"Oh, twice," he said. "An old woman on the river bank, and a painter near the cathedral. I saved you his brushes."

"I haven't killed," she said. "So I must. I'll do it tonight."

"Shall I come with you?" he asked, solicitously, gently.

"I prefer to work alone when I can. But thank you. Shall we meet at the bar beside the third broken bridge? I'll kill someone with rings, and bring you one, Felion."

ONE

Paradis

There was a little girl
Who had a little curl
Right in the middle of her forehead;
And when she was good
She was very, very good,
And when she was bad she was horrid.

Longfellow

After the storm the wrecked ship lay on the beach, against the bright broken gray of the sea. From the ship's side spilled her cargo of smashed glass and oranges, like blood from a wound. Her sail hung, a snapped wing. In the sky, great white clouds massed.

Leocadia stepped back from the painting and put down her brush. She rubbed her hands on a rag.

Was the picture finished? Yes. Surely. And yet . . .

Perhaps there should be a figure, hanged, depending from the ruined mast, with long black curling hair.

If she painted that into the picture, it would help them, would it not? Of course, they would say, because she is insane, she paints herself hanged from the ship's mast.

Leocadia shook back her long black curling hair, which fell almost to her waist. Her features were sharply clear as porcelain, and out of her feline face looked two black eyes. She had been admired before, and she had lost count of her lovers, of both sexes, only recalling a few with nostalgia or irritation.

There had always been enough money to do as she wished. To drink and fornicate and paint. She had never envisaged anything else, except perhaps one day a novel she would write, a lover who might truly pleasure or pain her, the possibility that alcohol might undo her. But not yet. She was thirty. Her parents, who had died when she was five, in a car accident on one of the vast new City highways, would normally have lived long. Life expectancy was quite high, and her family, especially its women, survived. There had been the two grandmothers—thin, healthy, wicked old women, vaguely resembling each other—one with hair that, at a hundred and three, was still thick with jet black waves. But the grandmothers were gone now, and the uncle, her guardian, had died in the winter (no one was invited to the funeral) at ninety years of age. He was incredibly, frightfully, frighteningly rich. That had never mattered. Then it turned out that it did.

Leocadia went into the little alcove, and opened the refrigerator. She took out a bottle of white transparent wine and uncorked it. The cold box was full of the things she liked, salads and cheeses, smoked fish, drink. She wanted for nothing. (They saw to that—was it their guilt?) Nothing but that amorphous element, her freedom.

"Imprisoned, poor thing." Leocadia spoke to the wine in the bottle. "Let me set you at liberty."

Her cousin, Nanice, had arrived at ten, on that morning in the past. She had not been alone. The man might have been taken for an escort, a boyfriend. Nanice was ugly, but she too had money. And anyway, the man was ugly also. They stood, uglily, on the steps below the old house which had, nevertheless, been fitted with an automatic door. The door relayed their images to the bedroom, where Leocadia was lying in the sheets with Asra.

Leocadia slept with women more from a wish for power than from lust. She loved their lips and breasts, but mostly she liked their helpless pleasure, and that they would tend to defer to her. Asra, though, was pert.

"Good God, who are those awful creatures?" said Asra.

"I don't know." And Leocadia had touched the intercom. "Who are you?" she asked.

"I am your cousin, Nanice le Vey. And this is Monsieur Saume. May we come in?"

"Lock the doors, load the cannon!" cried Asra.

"It's a little early," said Leocadia. She had felt nothing but mildly annoyed. No premonition.

"It's after ten," Nanice had said with strange smugness. "And we've come such a long way."

"Why?" said Leocadia.

"Do you mean to be uncivil?"

"Probably."

"If we must, we'll wait elsewhere, and return later."

"I repeat, why?"

Nanice preened herself, the redundant gesture of a well-but-ill-dressed, unattractive person.

"It's about Uncle Michelot."

"He's dead."

Nanice frowned. "Yes, I know the poor old gentleman is deceased."

The images from the door were incoming only, and Leocadia rose naked from her bed. Yet Nanice seemed to sense this, and she frowned more heavily.

"I will let you in," said Leocadia. "Wait in the salon downstairs. The service will bring you anything you want."

It came to Leocadia that the salon, which was often quite tidy, dusted by the house service, and the floor polished, accented by fresh flowers, was on that day disheveled. The previous evening she had allowed Asra to have a sort of party, and the service had not yet been summoned to clear up the mess. The ashtrays overflowed with the stubs of cigarishis, the pictures were crooked, bottles and books lay everywhere, the light was still on, and someone, probably Robert, had been sick in a vase.

Leocadia laughed. She visualized the stiff visitors in the midst of chaos as she went to the shower. Asra lay in bed, complaining: She hated people, they had had enough of people the night before. Leocadia, who had been stupid enough to have relatives, must make them go away.

Leocadia went down half an hour later to the salon. She wore a cream silk housedress, her hair was wet, and she was barefoot. In one hand she bore a tangerine, which she was eating, flesh and peel and pips together, and in the other a tall glass of white vodka.

The visitors were perched in the midst of chaos, as anticipated. Monsieur Saume stood, his hat in his hand, and Nanice teetered on a chair as if afraid it must be dirtying her skirt.

The room smelled thickly of smoke and drugs and perfume, thankfully not of vomit.

Leocadia pressed a button and the windows opened.

Outside, the spring day was warm yet brisk, and the gray streets of old Paradis curved and climbed among the ancient plane trees.

"So," said Nanice, "this is how you live."

She looked happy, and quickly smoothed her expression back to one of discomfiture.

Leocadia curled her toes about a black bottle lying on the rug, and picked up the glass with her foot.

"Yes, luckily you came at a quiet time."

"Quiet! My dear Leocadia—what are you doing to yourself!" exclaimed Nanice. Her protestation was so insincere, that even Monsieur Saume seemed embarrassed.

"I am," said Leocadia, "existing."

"And there is," said Nanice to Monsieur Saume, "a young woman in the bedroom, as you heard. And in that glass—don't *think* it's water."

"Would you like a vodka?" asked Leocadia. "I suppose you'd prefer something less pure; tea or coffee, I expect."

"No, nothing, thank you," said Nanice.

"Then perhaps you'd tell me, at last, why you are here."

Nanice lowered her eyes.

Her falseness was so utter, so unflawed, that Leocadia was fascinated.

"You have no guardian, now Uncle Michelot has died. I know," said Nanice, "you haven't seen him, been near him, for years—"

"No one has," said Leocadia. "He was a recluse. He disliked intrusion. One wonders why."

"Oh, I tried to see him," said Nanice. "One *could* try. Cousin Brand and I were constantly making approaches. But as you say, either he was a very private man, or else . . .' Nanice looked momentarily laughably cunning, as if she could hardly credit how clever she was being. "Or else someone put him against us. Against all of us."

Leocadia shrugged. From her uncle and former guardian she had received adequate funds, and once a year, on her name day, she had been sent some gift, always simple, never very expensive, but infallibly strange. The news of his death had jarred Leocadia. She had scanned the letter bordered in black, slightly puzzled by its wording, which seemed to say, euphemistically, that he had gone to better things. The letter told her, too, that Michelot had made provision for her, and she was glad of that. She had never known him, beyond a glimpse or two in childhood. He had chuckled, apparently, when she was expelled from her school, and provided her with private tuition. He seemed to understand her well enough, and did not insult her with feigned affection.

Nanice, of course, would have wanted much more. Family gatherings of hugs and kisses, rich presents, and now, obviously, some remuneration that was, presumably, absent?

"He left you out of his will?" asked Leocadia, pouring more vodka and ice into her glass from the entering service tray, and from a silver pot a cup of delicate, slaty tea.

"His—oh, Leocadia. You know quite well that he left out all of us. This wasn't what I came here to discuss, but if you insist. All twenty-three of his nearest and dearest were discounted. His kindred. All but you, and—well, this is very odd—two other cousins no one has heard of and who cannot be traced. They are mentioned as *your* inheritators. But frankly, we think he *made them up.*"

"Oh dear," said Leocadia. "Is that why Monsieur Saume is with you? In case I've been invented too?"

Nanice looked abruptly flustered.

"Monsieur Saume is—my companion."

"And he has no tongue," said Leocadia. "What a shame. A man's tongue has so many wonderful uses."

Nanice stared. Then she colored. Monsieur Saume did not alter. He had not moved at all, like a skillful lizard on a rock when predators are nearby.

Leocadia took a sip of tea, then a sip of vodka, and let the bottle drop from her toes.

"I still don't see what you want from me. Are you asking me to make you some sort of bequest? I will if you like, but your own lawyers must see to it. Such matters are very boring. I have things I like to do instead."

"Paint horrible nightmarish pictures and sleep with lesbians!" cried Nanice in an explosion of true venom. "And drink your brains to slop. Oh, I know. We've been watching you—"

"Mademoiselle le Vey," said Monsieur Saume.

Leocadia was surprised. At the final response of the silent Saume. And at the idea that someone had been watching her. It was true, Leocadia was used to being stared at: She was both striking and eccentric and did not much care what she did before others. But to be the object of a spy?

"Why have you watched me?"

Nanice compressed her little mouth into a littler line, like a zip.

It was Monsieur Saume who said, "There has been some concern, mademoiselle."

Leocadia raised her eyebrows.

"Well, it can stop now. As you see. Here I am."

"It can hardly stop," said Nanice. The zip wriggled vindictively. Again, Nanice seemed happy.

"But I," said Leocadia, "say it *must* stop."

And as others had done, confronted by Leocadia's anger, Nanice looked alarmed.

"Monsieur Saume," she cried, "you see she's quite unstable, like her paintings we showed you—"

There had been a recent exhibition of Leocadia's work at the First Gallery on Clock Tower Hill. Some pieces had been sold for quite extravagant amounts of cash. Did Nanice resent this, too?

Refilling her glass of white wine now, in the alcove of the refrigerator, Leocadia understood quite well that Nanice had wanted Monsieur Saume and others like him to note the content of the pictures, not their cost. The centaurs with the heads of swordfish, the horses in ballgowns, the women in the arms of women, men in the arms of men, winged cats and burning mansions.

But then, that day in the salon of the old house near the antique City wall, Leocadia had lost patience, and so rendered Nanice invaluable assistance.

"I'm afraid," said Leocadia, "you must get out. You're wasting my time. If I lay eyes on you again, Nanice le Vey, I'll have you thrown, down, off something, into the river. Do I make myself clear?"

Nanice sprang up. And her look now was of real terror mixed with great satisfaction. As she moved toward the door she knocked into the vase Robert had used, which broke on the floor, splattering her with sick and dead ferns.

Monsieur Saume, hat in hand, bowed to Leocadia before he effected his leave. She might have guessed from that, and maybe she partly did, that he had taken an interest in her.

The doctors came at five o'clock (seventeen hours, by the old, unfashionable time scale). Sometimes there were two, sometimes three or four doctors. There were no women among them, and Leocadia had long suspected that this was due to some notion that she would be able to seduce and subvert a woman more easily than a man. Or perhaps because all the men were hideous.

Sometimes even Saume came to see her.

They never stayed long, nor did they arrive every day. She never knew when they would come. Possibly this was meant to disorient, but it only irritated her.

Frequently, she took no notice of them, but now and again they played tricks.

One brought a cat, which Leocadia saw was clockwork. Even so she had liked it, and when they were all, apparently, sure of that, they bore it away and never brought it back. She was not allowed animals. She might "hurt" them. Leocadia explained that it was human things she disliked.

Another time a doctor had left her an orange. When she experimentally peeled it, it bled.

So now she kept an eye on the doctors when they appeared in her apartment.

"Mademoiselle. How are you today?"

"Anxious to leave."

"Ah," playfully, *"mademoiselle."*

They—there were now two of them. Saume and Van Orles—advanced on her painting.

"It's finished." They stared at the wrecked ship.

"Perhaps," she said.

"And what does this represent?"

"What do you think?" said Leocadia.

"A broken heart?" inquired Doctor Van Orles lubriciously, leering at her.

"No," said Leocadia. "Have you considered glasses or lenses for your eyes?"

Van Orles laughed. "Now, now, Leocadia."

"A ship," said Saume.

"Well done," said Leocadia. "A ship run aground."

"Oranges?" asked Van Orles. "Why is that?"

"Why not?" said Leocadia.

"There has been a storm," Van Orles explained to her carefully. "And the cargo has been lost."

"As I have lost my mind? I'm not," said Leocadia, "full of oranges."

"But of broken glass?" asked Saume.

"You're rather ignorant," said Leocadia. "The ancient ships carried smashed glass for recycling."

"Are there monkeys?" pressed Van Orles. "Perhaps the captain kept some." He seemed excited by the painting.

"Give me a model," said Leocadia, "a monkey to pose. I'll add a couple."

"And how much have you drunk today, Leocadia?" asked Van Orles.

Leocadia looked at him. "I don't count."

"But you *should* count, Leocadia. This is so bad for your health."

"All the better, I'd have thought. Maybe I'll die, and then the cousins won't have to pay for my place here. One less annoying little expense."

She had wondered, at first, if they might poison her, and of course they did, but only in subtle ways that would not be disallowed. Beams of light that penetrated the brain, and sounds she could not, or could barely, hear. Some nights, all through the dark, a slender bell chimed far away.

The walls of the room were a pale, soft dove color, restful, but against them, when her eyes were tired, she saw things in the fluid of her sight, disturbing and worrying, which, against a jumble of objects, textures, and colors, would not have been visible.

They destroyed her, inch by inch. Meter by meter. But she would not be destroyed. She must rebuild what was chipped away.

"There are no figures at all in your painting," said Van Orles.

"Alas," said Leocadia.

"Should you care for visitors?"

"Visitors put me here."

"Surely there's someone you would like to see?"

"I'd tell them how you torture me."

"Now, Mademoiselle. You're thinking of terrible crimes of the past. The *old* asylum. You mustn't dwell on that."

"There are drugs in my food. Unseen lights and unheard noises crisscross this room. I'm kept so docile."

"*You?* Mademoiselle, you? *Docile?*"

"You sedate me," said Leocadia, offhand. "How else is it I don't fly at you with my palette knife, my fork, the file for my nails?"

"Because you are civilized," said Saume, "and you don't wish to sully your art, your food, or your person by an artifact used in murder against, merely, us."

She regarded him. He was sometimes quaint and caught her attention.

"I shall need another canvas," said Leocadia.

"Oh, yes," said Van Orles. "It will be arranged. Everything for your happiness."

"Then let me out."

"Oh. Dear mademoiselle."

A week after the advent of Nanice at the house, Leocadia had forgotten her.

Asra, in an effort to energize Leocadia, had taken up with another woman, and Leocadia was quite pleased, getting her house to herself without the effort of making a scene. She intended to remove Asra's code from the automatic door, but she gradually forgot this, too.

One afternoon, Saume called. She would not have let him in, but she had been out walking in the park under the Roman wall, staring at the remains of gravestones left standing in the grass, and the sides of demolished houses up which ivy had been trained. She found Saume on her steps.

"Yes?"

"I am here to see you, mademoiselle."

"I'm afraid you're mistaken."

"I beg your pardon."

"I am going to go in, and you are not."

Saume only smiled—he had dreadful teeth, like something medieval, for generally teeth now were universally excellent.

He held out a slender book.

"You wish me to sign it?" asked Leocadia, for it was her collection, the only one, of short stories.

"I am simply intrigued by the content. Girls who turn into vampire owls. Raccoons who romantically subdue their jailers in prison and tickle ladies with their stripy tails. Where does your inspiration come from?"

"The City," said Leocadia. "These are old stories of Paradis."

"Indeed? I haven't come across them."

"Goodbye," said Leocadia.

She went in and shut the door in his face. He did not attempt to intrude further. Just then.

Summer came, and Leocadia lay under a white sunshade in her overgrown garden, which she had planted to a kind of jungle. Sometimes Asra called her, but Leocadia was noncommittal. She was in a phase when she was more than content to be alone, not realizing that soon this was to become a permanent arrangement.

Her house was supposed to be haunted. Robert said he had seen someone walk out of a wall. Many of the houses near the old wall were reckoned to have a psychic persuasion.

Leocadia painted a ghost standing on a rooftop, looking lost and slightly belligerent.

But when she had finished a painting, generally Leocadia grew a little restless. She had finished one. Now it was a landscape with dancing figures, lit by far high hills in sunset, pumpkin-colored, radiating heat and menace.

Leocadia dressed in a long, pale beaded frock, preparing to go out and dine in the City. And as if on cue, Pir called her. He asked, begged her to come to a dinner at the Surprise Restaurant. "So many people," said Pir. "Lots of champagne."

Leocadia decided she would go, because sometimes, at a painting's end, she liked to move among crowds, experiencing to the full her total difference from them.

Pir was eager and came to collect her in his long car, which moved slowly, as was the City habit now, save on the dangerous fast highways.

The Surprise lay on the lower bank, a block of bright buildings, perhaps (or not) erected on the site of an old tavern. The river glimmered down below, and above the hills lifted from the City with their crowns of new and ancient architecture. The Temple-Church was floodlit, and owls nested in its upper galleries. No bells rang from it now—they had lost their voices—yet sometimes in sleep, Leocadia heard them.

The people of the crowd in the restaurant were stupid and drunken, already stuffing themselves with dishes of quail in jelly and black caviar. On the tables of the private room where the party went on were tall cones of treated meltless ice containing flowers.

Pir led Leocadia to a table. She sat down and drank a champagne which had too much head, like stomach salts.

"All the world says 'never,'" said Leocadia.

"What?" asked Pir.

"An old song. Everybody says 'never,' always 'never.'"

"I don't understand."

"None of them have anything to say, and all of them want to say it."

Pir grimaced.

"You're too clever for me. What will you eat, you beaded monster?"

Leocadia selected a dish from the menu.

Gradually people flooded around her. She found herself the center of an odd type of attention, bantering and fulsome, with undercurrents of insult.

Asra was not there, and presently Jacqueline Degot remarked on it. "She says she's afraid to be where you are, Leocadia. She says you terrify and intimidate her."

"Not noticeably," said Leocadia, who was finding the food rather bland.

"But yes." Jacqueline was insistent. She was clad as a huge blond nymph. "Asra says you have frightened her so much she can't go anywhere near you."

"And yet," added Pir, "one can see she *longs* to do exactly that. Can't you relent, Leocadia?"

Leocadia found this incomprehensible and did not bother to reply. An idea for a short poem was beginning to come into her head. She realized the dinner was ghastly. Inebriated women already lay over the tables, with tiddly men nibbling grapes from their cleavages, and elsewhere. The waiters came and went like well-behaved penguins. Which was foolish, for surely no penguin would ever be so idiotic.

Leocadia considered penguins. She must visit the zoological gardens of Paradis.

"And Asra complains," added Claude Ful, "that you've treated her roughly. That you struck her."

Leocadia took no notice of this either. For some reason the image of penguins had taken hold of her, or rather of one especial penguin, a nun of feathers, upright and perfect on a raft of ice. . . .

She rose to her feet.

"No, no," cried Pir, "you mustn't leave yet."

"But I must."

"Stay—at least until midnight."

"Certainly not."

Pir pushed against Leocadia, trying to refill her glass and grab her arm.

Normally people had learned not to treat her in this way. She thrust him back and he stumbled against a cavorting couple. "Oh! Oh! Don't be so violent, Leocadia."

"Then don't make me so violent."

Pir slipped aside, but others formed a garland around her. She went through them, and their gloved hands broke away, the sliding doors of their bodies slid.

"Stop her!" exclaimed Jacqueline, as if Leocadia were a thief who had snatched something.

Leocadia had never, since childhood—when she had vanquished it—felt fear. But now there was an unease that, in another, might have amounted to fear.

The dinner guests were swarming at her like a herd.

She plucked a silver knife from a table and held it up.

And the wall of flesh crumpled back with tiny sounds of disapproval and drunken laughter. "What's the matter with her? She acts as if we're the enemy."

At the door, three penguins (or waiters) let Leocadia pass without trouble. And she descended the noisy, lighted restaurant and went out.

She was on the street, the river flowing somewhere and the pure lamps of Paradis, which now never failed, shining upon her.

She walked idly, toward a bridge.

But something was happening. What was it? The new and the old areas of the City, rubbing their unliking flanks together; she had seen and moved through this before. Occasionally difficult persons might extrude themselves and attempt a woman on her own, but rarely, for the watching TV eyes of police surveillance were scattered about, and besides, Leocadia did not look a natural victim. Once when she was fifteen a mugger had come at her in an antique lane. She had punched him on the point of the jaw with her slim, steely hand, bruising the joints of her fingers but knocking him out. And now she had forgetfully kept the knife from the restaurant. Doubtless it would be best to throw that in the river, for a woman wandering Paradis by night with a table knife might also be suspect.

She was coming down toward the river, pausing to gaze at the ghost image of the owl-like floodlit Temple-Church aloft. It seemed balanced on a mound of darkness, and the river coiled below, a snake.

The night was warm and clean. Scents of vacuumed rooms and automatically swept squares. And the antiseptic water.

Parked across the road was a large truck, permitted the pavement, as it was in the process of delivery. Some other club or restaurant, for which vast blocks of treated ice were being brought, imbued with flowers.

Leocadia became aware of a noise behind her. It had been cloaked until now in the humming murmurs and squeals of the City.

She looked back.

Leocadia widened her eyes in contemptuous astonishment.

Pir had followed her through the narrow byways, and Jacqueline the obese nymph, and a tirade of others, all squashed and teetering in their polished or satin shoes, tight pants, and fishtail skirts. They bore their glasses of antacid champagne and laughed and called to her.

"Come back, my Leocadia!" howled Pir.

The two men unloading the truck stared at Leocadia. Between them they tilted a block of ice filled with a glowing fan of marigolds.

Leocadia came to the men and hauled the ice, burning, *burning*, from their gloved hands.

"Pardon me."

She flung the heavy chunk across the exit from the thin street, into the shoes and ankles of the approaching herd.

The ice shattered and smoked, and white sparks burst up from the chemicals of the ice treatment, causing Leocadia's pursuers to leap backward, some squawking and falling down.

The deliverymen did not protest, they guffawed.

Leocadia saw marigolds, frozen flawless, the flowers of the eternal deathless soul, glittering in heaps and shoals like flamy fish, and splinters of ice, one of which had torn the fat knee of Jacqueline Dagot so she roared.

And then Leocadia lifted her skirt in her hand and she ran. For the bridge, the upper bank, over the river, into the night, toward the house and her sanctuary. Not knowing why, and not even particularly stung or startled. Instinct. Hunted. But so far, arrogant.

As she entered her street close by the Roman wall, Leocadia saw the darkness of the houses under the flare of the lamps that never failed. Rituals of decorum had come back to the City, and its fashionable quarters rose and bedded early. The manners of a century before, as with clothing, furnishing, but not always thought.

Yet on the street of dark houses, one light burned. It was in the attic room that Leocadia had made her studio.

She did not think for a moment she had left it on. She had shut

the studio door upon the finished painting (removed from the easel) at four—sixteen hours by the abandoned scale. Then the daylight had still been rich and full.

Was the light another challenge?

She walked up the steps and put her finger to the required panel.
Recognizing her, her door let her in.

The hall was in blackness, and only her touch on the proper
switch woke up the hall lamps.

She paused. There was nothing in the air to alert her, only perhaps a faint scent of ozone. And she recalled another tale of Paradis,
where shells from the ocean had been found at the doors of the
Temple-Church, some manifestation of the primeval days when the
City had been covered still by a hot and saline sea—or else a practical joke.

Leocadia climbed the stairs softly. Her hands were empty but
flexed.

On the third landing she sought the smaller, crooked stair that
went to the attic.

There was a faint electricity there, as if something had passed
swiftly, voltage rather than presence.

Leocadia turned a fashionable enamel doorknob.

Her studio opened before her, a cave covered now by a black
glass roof without even the moon. But the work lights shone down
pitilessly, casting out shadow.

Leocadia's eyes went intuitively to her easel, a big bulky frame of
metal that would support her largest canvases.

There was a new canvas there.

It hung by the crooks of its elbows, a sort of parody of a crucifix-
ion. The head was thrown back and the neck arched. The breasts
jutted erotically, but . . .

The nipples of the breasts were a blaring raw orange, and between the hapless female knees, emanating from the secret zone of
sex and life, a curl of orange bled with a menstrual suddenness.

There were orange patterns, too, on the white flesh. Abstractions,
looking like a map of unknown islands.

Leocadia experienced the sharp sour champagne, partially di-
gested, creeping back into her mouth. She swallowed it, and walked
around the canvas to its back.

There, tilted over, was the head and hair of Asra, known as Leocadia had known the naked form.

Something horrible had happened with Asra's head. Its eyes

bulged and showed white. Between the lips was wedged a tube of brilliant orange paint, it had been squeezed to poison and to choke. Orange dribbled from the nostrils and the ears out into the silky fleece of hair.

Leocadia bent double and fire burst from her belly.

Far away, as this happened, she heard a tremendous crash, the roots of the house exploding.

As she stood up, wiping her mouth, and fell again and got up again, holding to the wall, a renewal of the sound of pursuit—the herd—drove up to the house, snorting and thundering on all the stairs.

The attic door bounced open.

It was like a party trick. For there they all were. Pir and Jacqueline and Claude Ful, and behind them Nanice and the peculiar Monsieur Saume. And then four men in white, who moved forward into the room.

Jacqueline began to shriek, as if she had been paid to do so.

Leocadia ignored her. The men in the white coats came right up to Leocadia.

"Now, now," said one fawningly.

"Poor Asra, it's what she feared," said Claude.

And Nanice exclaimed, "I warned you all—she's mad."

They had broken in the door below, and somewhere was the note of a police siren, rushing to contend with the door alarm.

"Oh, no police," said Nanice. "Our family name—"

Leocadia discerned a stinging in her arm, like the pincers of an angry beetle. She looked and saw the needle drawing away. The room wheeled and flew up into the dark.

After Van Orles and Saume had gone, sunset bloomed on the walls of Leocadia's room, deepening the colors of the broken ship that spilled glass and fruit.

On impulse Leocadia had painted a few shells into one corner of the picture, an insulting gesture, as if to overinform the watcher that this was the *sea*.

The room of pale gray was very plain, the furniture comfortable but modern, therefore unsumptuous, a large couch, small tables, a bed with a fearful plastic underlay. In the bathroom the fixtures were white and functional, and the floor was laid with stark black and white tiles, which leapt like rats at her blurred morning eyes.

Leocadia went to the door of the room, which opened. Past eight o'clock, or whenever presumably darkness came, the door did not open.

In the corridor was a hygienic nothingness.

Leocadia stepped to the elevator, which bore her seamlessly down to the garden.

The garden was a long slope of lawn, the grass seared by summer. A birdbath without water mocked the sky. At the bottom of the lawn stood a summerhouse, with curious windows of the shades of cinnamon and milk. Beyond, trees marked a boundary. A gravel walk led away, toward the crumbling biscuit buildings of the old asylum, as unlike the Residence as was possible. Black windows stared from those tall blocks, and copper pipes protruded from the short-bread walls. Between these monoliths and the modern site, an ancient hothouse, broken, held the corpse of an enormous grape-vine, the black and withered grapes mummified upon it.

Huge outer barricades secured the entire complex. Within the labyrinth, you might wander as you wished, unable, ultimately, to get out.

Leocadia walked down to the summerhouse in the brazen glow. On a bench sat Mademoiselle Varc, a madwoman, who always mistook Leocadia for someone from her past.

"Have you brought my fan?" demanded Mademoiselle Varc.

"I'm sorry. It's been mislaid."

"Tssk," said Mademoiselle Varc. She had wispy white hair piled unsuccessfully upon her head, a white shawl. She was a White Queen, and twice as crazy.

"There goes the sun," said Leocadia.

"Goodbye!" cried Mademoiselle Varc, waving.

The sun eased behind the walls of the modern block.

"You're late," said Mademoiselle Varc.

"I'm sorry."

"Soon the police will be here."

As dusk came, wardens stole through the garden, shepherding inmates back to their rooms. Everyone went quietly, for they were always fairly demure. No need for needles, or truncheons.

"The police—yes."

"I miss the sunset," said Mademoiselle Varc. "It used to be so lovely. But now it takes only a moment or two, as in India, you know."

The sun vanished. A bat flew over the compound, exquisite wild thing, ignorant of barriers.

Then a uniformed man came walking up the gravel way. He raised his hand to the two women.

"Time to go in, ladies."

"You know what it is," said Mademoiselle Varc, taking Leocadia's arm and hurrying her back up the lawn.

"No."

"It's that the trees come alive after dark. They stump about the garden and catch anyone who's abroad. They tear them limb from limb, and eat them."

"How terrible," said Leocadia.

"Yes, it is."

She had woken in that bed, that sanitary bed with the plastic underlay, which creaked as she moved, making her think for a moment she lay in a hammock. The room rocked, certainly, but this was the aftereffect of the drug they had injected into her. And as she remembered that, she remembered it all.

A couple of minutes later the door opened, and a friendly dark-clad young woman entered with a tray of breakfast. Rolls and conserves, fruit, coffee, and a little pot of tea.

"I take vodka with my breakfast," said Leocadia, from the bed.

"I'll fetch you some from your refrigerator, mademoiselle."

And sure enough, she went into an alcove and returned with a bottle and a tall glass. "It's nice and cold, mademoiselle. The way you like it. Anything you want can be ordered and kept there. And there's a heater, besides, for making hot drinks."

"This isn't a hotel," said Leocadia. The girl smiled nicely.

Leocadia got out of bed, and the room gradually righted itself. There was the bathroom, black and white and clean as disinfectant.

When she emerged, the attendant was gone.

As she ate a roll and drank her vodka, Leocadia explored the confine. She did not try the door, which she assumed would be locked. (It was not.)

On one wall was a shelf of books, which in turn, at the press of a switch, gave on an alcove also lined with books. These were her own, it seemed, or most of them. She saw at once there were new titles, volumes on art and design, current novels, treatises on animal and human behavior.

At the other end of the room, beyond the bed and the sitting area, was a broad space. An easel leaned against the wall, and three canvases, unprepared, beside it. Leocadia's worktable stood by,

loaded with paints and accessory impedimenta. The light was excellent, windows on both sides of the room, and a light source above
the painting space, nearly as good as the attic.

Leocadia went to both the windows.

The one beyond the bed looked out across the slope of garden to
the summerhouse. Behind that were the trees, and then the vague
shapes in sunshine of colossal block buildings, utterly square in
form, indefinably blind, like a deserted factory—or a prison.

The window at the other end of the room showed only a high
wall, but it was grown with blackish ivies, not unpleasant.

She tried the windows. Each gave easily, admitting light and air
and the song of crickets and birds.

The distance to the ground was three stories. Too far to jump.

She knew at once that Nanice had had her restricted in some
institution, but she was not aware exactly of what kind.

She considered dead Asra. Could Leocadia even be sure that she
had seen such a thing? Was it some obscene jest, or the result of
some tablet slipped into the poor champagne?

No. It must be real. What other excuse for her confinement
here?

She thought of the dead Asra with a combination of revulsion
and rage.

Leocadia was supposed to have killed Asra.

But what had happened, in fact? Who had done it?

Asra had been able to enter the house as she wished, since Leocadia had not blanked out her recognition on the door. But thereafter Asra must have let in whoever it was that attacked her. Was it
some other lover, or only some maniac?

The police had obviously been fobbed, or bought off. There
would have been enough money for that.

Perhaps because of the drug that had been given her, or other
more insidious medicines administered in food sleep, through the
medium of light and sound, Leocardia did not at this point deci-
pher that Asra had been specifically murdered in order to cast
blame upon Leocadia.

Presently, an envelope of plastic paper came through a slit in the
door. She impatiently opened it.

A small printed slip fell into her hand. Someone hoped she had
spent a restful night and enjoyed her breakfast. The music panel
beside her bed, which would bring her whatever music she selected,

would also inform her of the time. At fourteen, some of her doctors would be coming to see her.

This friendly note was not signed.

Leocadia dialed the time on the panel. Thirteen—one o'clock.

In a closet off the bathroom she found some of her own clothes— a selection, but nothing dressy for the evening or dinner.

When she was dressed, had brushed her hair, and had used her makeup—located in a drawer of the dressing table near the window —Leocadia sat on the couch to wait.

Probably, they were punctual.

There were four of them.

They wore smart urbane suits, nothing clinical, and Dr. Van Orles sported a pastel cravat, Dr. Leibiche had a monocle. Dr. Duval wore his hair rather long, with a mustache. Dr. Saume, unfortunately for him, was as she remembered.

They were all ugly, squat men, not obese but having the look of partially inflated balloons. As they dressed in the fashionable pre-century style, just so they had kept old-fashioned unsightlinesses, of teeth in the case of Saume, warts and pimples in the case of Leibiche.

They sat in a semicircle on the three low chairs, with Dr. Duval draped on the other end of the couch.

Then, in a dreadfully personal, insolent gesture, Saume leaned forward and felt Leocadia's pulse.

She allowed this, but when he leaned nearer with some sort of glass to stare into her eyes, she pushed him back.

"Now mademoiselle, we only want to see how you are."

"Angry," said Leocadia. "What else would you expect?"

Perhaps they had expected fright?

"Oh, but there's nothing to be concerned at," said Duval, his hair sliding and slipping about like spilled unguent. "Indeed, you *shouldn't* concern yourself. You must try to be as quiet as you can."

"I was drugged and abducted. Why should I be quiet?"

Saume cleared his throat. He announced, with the gentle gravity of a father who must be stern with a child for its own sake: "Mademoiselle, a fearful thing has been done. A murder has been committed." And then, a phenomenon occurred, a hellish glare seemed to spring up around Saume, a sort of spotlight. A sign of impending ills. . . . "You must understand," he snarled, "only the intervention of your cousins has permitted your enclosure here, at the Residence. Otherwise it would have been the *jail*. Your sentence would have been severe. But under the circumstances, and with the proper evidence we have been able to gather on your critical state of mind, we are able to shelter you here. And here, of course, we may hope to cure you. One day, you may go free."

Leocadia had conquered fear in childhood. But it is a fact with fear that it tends to return in other guises and must be fought off again and again. Eventually, through dint of effort, it may find some means to throw you down into the abyss.

She clenched her hands, but then undid them, seeing all the beady eyes, and the extra eye of the monocle, glinting on her.

They had told her they were doctors, and that she was "sheltered" in the Residence. She had dimly heard of it. A building that rose above Paradis, in the hills, safely out of the environs of the City. The lunatic asylum.

The glare still shone about them. Was it some trick of the sun, or some trick of theirs? Or a warning from her own mind?

She was in the Madhouse, but now it was not even a hospital, but a professed *House*.

She said, "So I killed Asra?"

"You will have blanked the act from your brain, mademoiselle," said Leibiche. "This is common."

"It may be a hopeful sign," added Van Orles. "Indicating that you feel remorse for the deed."

Leocadia, used to saying what she thought, stayed herself. "You said I killed Asra. How did I do it, when I was with so many people at the Surprise?"

The glare fastened on Van Orles and blazed.

"But it was before you left for the restaurant, Leocadia."

"Oh, I see. How sensible."

Leocadia beheld then all the counters of the game lying before her, but it would be a while longer before she set them into their true positions. Before she drew the obvious conclusion.

Hungry for all the spoils of Uncle Michelot's death, Nanice and the cousins, perhaps even those two reckoned to have been made up, had had to prove Leocadia incapable of inheriting. And Asra—stupid, petty, pretty, *living* Asra—had died for their convenience, the stepping stone to topple Leocadia down. They had killed her, had her killed. Orange paint, and cold blood.

Confronted by the four doctors, Leocadia saw at last that she was sunk into deep water. The light glare faded.

She glanced at the easel, the waiting canvases, and said with a deadly compunction, "What am I supposed to do here?"

"Everything you wish, mademoiselle. Don't imagine there are any harsh measures. The old techniques were often crude, but they are long gone." Saume nodded.

"We shall," said Duval kindly, "simply take care of you."

"Talk to you," added Van Orles, "observe your progress."

"You've lived a life that has placed upon you," said Leibiche, "terrible unconscious strains. Once these are eliminated, we shall make headway." His monocle and all his warts and spots flashed like sequins in a smile.

"How dangerous am I reckoned to be?" asked Leocadia. "Since you think me a murderess."

"Ah!" Saume blinked as if startled. Why? "Come now," he said firmly. "With correct supervision, you'll grow calm."

"Things in the food," said Leocadia.

"The most harmless, naturally produced and nourishing—"

"But I'm given a knife for my butter," said Leocadia, "and over there is my palette knife. Also my nail file."

"We trust you," said Doctor Duval.

It flashed upon her, like the fireworks of the warts, that perhaps she was to be left potential weapons in order that she turn them on herself. For this she did know at once, she would never be free.

There would be no "cure." Since she was not ill, not mad, not a murderess, or anything else they said.

All they would want to do, rather than make her better, was to change her into the Leocadia of their invention. Nanice's Leocadia, who killed and was insane.

TWO

Paradys

A trick that everyone abhors
In little girls is slamming doors.

Belloc

Hilde.

Although they had just put her into corsets and long frocks, she was fifteen, and still a child. Pale and perfect. Skin milk white, hair a shining wonderful ginger, now piled up upon her head with tortoiseshell combs.

She did what little girls were meant to do. She was obedient and loving but not importunate. She had a doll who sat on her bed of frills and flounces. She read fine books of which her mother was the guardian. Her father, Monsieur Koster, was a wealthy man, descendant of a merchant family. Now high enough in society, he took care to comport himself with great dignity. Sometimes he chose also a book for Little Hilde to read (she was to them "Little Hilde"). She embroidered too. Her mother had begun to train her in the rituals of wifeship, seeing that the house of polished stairs, lace curtains, and huge ferns in china bowls ran on butter.

And Hilde was happy. It was a safe existence where everything was in its place. God ruled the world. Her father ruled the house. Her mother ruled her. But all three were kind and might be pleaded with prettily for favors. Which they would then grant. God was especially amenable: "Let me not have freckles, like Angeline," and God did not allow Hilde to become freckled. (Her father did not care for freckles.) And her mother would let Hilde buy sweets once a week. Her father permitted Hilde to try a sip of wine at dinner. "It's good for the child's blood."

But Hilde had a secret life. It did not occur to her to share it, let alone confess. It had to do with darkness and her narrow bed, the touch of the linen nightgown on her bareness, and of her hair in a long plait that she might undo, always to the consternation of her maid in the morning: "However did this happen?" And Hilde would be innocent and surprised. For in her heart she knew that her undone hair was not a crime, nor what sometimes happened to her in the dark. They were silly childish things, very pleasant, like playing with the doll, or eating a sweet. Somehow, not so public. A game of childhood out of which, of course, as a woman she would grow, ascending into a cold clever angel, the peerless wife, and adorable admirable mother, in her turn, of other little children.

But the dark . . . The dark was lovely. A special thing she could do. A sort of present. She doubted anyone else in the world was able to.

And strangely, sometimes when she did this marvelous thing, which left her whole body ringing and tingling, beautifully composed for sleep, she had an incoherent image of some weight that pinned her to the bed, and that the hands upon her were not her own. And now and then, she would kiss the pillow, but not as she kissed her mother or papa. She wished the pillow then was more like a fruit, sweeter, and more moist. Once she had dreamed that it was, and in slumber the lovely thing happened on its own. She was amazed and gratified. Truly, it was a gift, and she was sorry she would have to grow out of it.

She had feared slightly, when the corset had been compressed about her and the long dress put on and her hair raised up, that this might be the end of her game.

But it was not. Oddly, in some curious way, it actually heightened her enjoyment. How lucky. How sad for Mama and Papa that they had never known such a thing and never, now, would.

The Koster house was one of a group of elegant mansions high on Clock Tower Hill. Smart carriages drawn by satin horses speeded up and down the street, and trees overhung the pavement. In the mornings, maids might be seen scrubbing the steps, and gardeners toiled over the flowers against the railings.

Two months after the putting up of Hilde's ginger cloud of hair, Madame Koster descended the steps of the house with her daughter. Their carriage stood ready on the street with a man holding

open the door. The lady and her child were going to see a play at
the Goddess of Tragedy. It was an epic from an era before the
Revolution, poetic prose, three hours of it. A stern moral tale, incidentally full of drama, passion, bloodshed, and terror. The afternoon performance had therefore been thought most suitable.

Everyone in Paradys who might be said to be anybody was to
attend at some point. Wishing to go, Madame Koster had assured
monsieur the play was a classic, and should be part of Hilde's education.

Hilde, as a girl, had been tutored at home, and these classical
plays were sometimes gone through by a pie-faced governess with a
high squeaky voice. Something of their power was therefore lost on
Hilde, who accordingly did not look forward to the jaunt, save that
it was the theater. For this, since her earliest pantomimes, she had
cherished a beglamored enthusiasm. She was too, so far, a patient
girl. She had been trained to be. It had also occurred to her that
while the play went on, if it was very boring, there would be the
audience to scan (surreptitiously in the gloom) and thoughts of
other things to be gone over—her doll's new wardrobe, a patch of
garden behind the house that was hers, and so on.

The Goddess of Tragedy towered white and tiered above the
streets. Many mothers and daughters, and some young sons, were
assembled. "Why," said Madame Benoit to Madame Koster, "have
you not heard of the actor who is playing the Roman?"

"No not at all."

"Well, he is quite astonishing. He has brought the part to life.
They say it's frightful, his moment of death."

Soon Hilde was installed in the plush Koster box. Her mother
had not agreed to bonbons or chocolates. It was not that sort of
play.

Hilde sat quietly, and having viewed the fashionable afternoon
gowns, she saw the gas lamps lowered, and the heavy curtain rose.

For twenty minutes it was very dull. So dull that even obedient
Hilde felt a faint jab of rebellion.

But then. Then, *he* came out. Out of the wings onto the plateau
of the stage.

Stage light is always miraculous. It is a magical spell that breathes
on things and changes them, *remakes* them. Besides, the creatures
who people this universe have, very often, a psychic, extraordinary
power. How else can they do what they do?

The man who characterized the Roman wore a costume of black

and silver, the notion of the time as to what the garments of a Roman commander might have been. But he was tall and slender, with wide shoulders. He had a priest's face, and the arrogance of a priest, officiating at his altar. His hair was black as ravens. His eyes, blacker.

From the instant he emerged from nowhere onto the stage, Hilde understood, just as a bird grasps abruptly how to fly, that here was the reason for her instinct and her life. She did not have to question herself, or any other. She did not have the temerity to say to God: *Why?* Let alone, *No, no.*

Her body felt light as cobweb. Her heart was engorged and beat like a gong.

She floated somewhere just above the ledge of the box, and oddly, her mother could not see this. And Hilde knew quite well that the man below, so near, so far, the Roman, she knew that he must also be intensely aware of her. For she blazed like a lamp, and he, being what he was, must see all things exactly. He would sense her, and look up. And so he did. Up to the box, his eyes flaming like stars, over and over. And then Hilde burned, and she must look away. But only, each time, for a moment.

The play, forgotten parts of which the squeaky governess may even have read to her, this time fixed itself into Hilde's mind. She was conscious of every iota of it, every histrionic, profound, and adult emotion. As if a door had been flung open before her, revealing a new world.

When it came time for the Roman to die, Hilde's gonging heart stopped. She felt herself die, too. And thereafter, what could she be save reborn?

She saw him again briefly, the actor-priest, taking his bows at the end of the play. He did this coldly and magnificently, as if to show them he had elevated the Host already, what more could they want? Only one further time did he raise his face toward Hilde's balcony. One ray (like a lighthouse). Then gone.

Hilde went home in the Koster carriage and in a dream, a trance. She had been ensorcelled.

"Hilde, eat your food."

"I'm sorry, Mama, I'm not hungry."

"What is the matter with the child. Are you unwell?"

"No, Mama."

They had not noticed how silent Little Hilde had become because

she was generally a quiet, abstemious daughter, what they preferred.

"It's the weather," pronounced Monsieur Koster, "Eh, Hilde?
Too hot. Take her for a drive, Lysette."

"We had a drive this morning, Solomon."

"Then probably the carriage was too stuffy."

"The carriage was perfect."

They lost interest in the carriage and Little Hilde, and Hilde was
able to leave her unwanted luncheon for the maid to clear away.

As Hilde sat presently, her hands resting on an oval of unseen
embroidery, she heard her mother speaking to a servant in the hall.

"We must have flowers there and there. And I shall want to see
Cook. Some special light dishes that they can peck at like birds."

Hilde's mother was arranging an evening of guests, as she sometimes did. Madame Koster flowed back and forth and so into the
sitting room, where she came to inspect Hilde's work. Hilde
stitched at a rose.

"How listless you are," said Madame Koster. "Is it your time?"
She was referring to Hilde's cycle of menstruation.

"No, Mama."

"I thought not. Well, you must liven up. You're becoming depressing. Tomorrow afternoon you must have a fitting for your new
dress."

"Yes, Mama."

"What do you think?" said Madame Koster, a touch flustered all
of a sudden. "Some of the theater people are coming to my little
evening."

Hilde's hand stayed mute upon the rose.

"Well, you might show some interest, you tiresome girl. All lost in
a world of your own. I don't think you need to meet my guests, but
your father insists. You look so young and charming—why, you
might only be eleven, except for your hair. . . . Perhaps we will
have it dressed down for the night. It's so pretty that way."

Hilde's mother always saw Hilde as very young, and Hilde did
not ever question this, nor why it was an extra delight to her
mother if Hilde should remain very young. At this minute, in any
case, she was not thinking of that.

"Who—will be coming to your party, Mama?"

"Oh, the two leading men of the company, Monsieur Roche and
Monsieur Martin. And a couple of the ladies, I believe. But of
course you've forgotten all about that important play. What a disap-

pointment you were. Everyone else bubbling over and not a word
out of you. I half think you slept right through it."

"Oh no, Mama."

"Well, then, who are Monsieur Roche and Monsieur Johanos
Martin?" demanded Mama, bridling. She was flushed, but exclaimed, "And well you should blush, Hilde. You've quite forgotten."

Hilde lowered her burning face.

"Monsieur Johanos Martin played the Roman."

"One out of two then," snapped Madame Koster.

She was a tallish woman, curvaceous, with fashionable apparent
mounds of hair built up over padding on her skull. Her maid knew
many of her secrets. The coiffeur, the rouge, the manner in which
madame sometimes lost her temper as the corset refused to reduce
her waist below twenty-four inches. Hilde's waist, uncorseted, was
eighteen inches, and in its cage of bones became a flower stalk. Her
hair grew in lush masses, her skin was fresh as if the dew were on it.

Sometimes the maid privately wondered if madame allowed
Hilde so many sweets in hopes of extra girth, or blotches. Hilde had
not wanted sweets this week.

"Your new frock is very lovely and young," said madame. "You'll
grow up too fast. And you're such a baby."

In the dark . . .

Hilde woke. She had been dreaming.

In the dream, the party had begun, and through the crowd of
guests Hilde had found herself moving, not dressed as she should
be, but in her long white nightgown, and her hair loose on her
shoulders. No one had appeared to notice, and after her first terrifying shame, she began to think that perhaps she was dressed quite
properly.

Then, by the open door that led onto the little terrace, he was
standing. He wore black clothes, she could not make them out, not
his costume from the play, certainly, yet neither anything everyday.
A sort of soutane, perhaps, a priestly robe, belted close at the thin
hard waist.

He had looked straight at her, Johanos Martin, the actor. And,
impossibly, she had met his gaze, although her ears roared and her
heart choked her.

Everyone else was gone. It did not matter how or where.

He held out his hand, which was ringless, beautiful, and Hilde went to him at once. He drew her out of the door onto the terrace.

Night had fallen, very black, yet with a sort of silver glow along the tops of the trees, and far away a light was shining that might have been the moon reflected on a window—such detail, in this dream.

"You are mine," Johanos Martin said to Hilde. "I promise I will be with you."

And in that exquisite second, she woke. She woke.

She lay stunned, not knowing, or caring, where she was, out of situation and time. And her body was alive, glowing and spangled by feeling within and without.

She had not, since she had seen him, somehow—she had not dared to touch. But now her hands stole to her body. She laid them on her breasts. And in the dark, eyes shut, she thought of his hands lying on her in this way, firm and cruel, capturing her breasts like birds. And then she thought that she would be afraid, half fainting, and he would hold her up, easily, and crush her mouth with his, as in a book she had once seen, a book of her mother's that perhaps she had not been meant to find, the drawing of a man kissing a woman fiercely in this way, holding her swooning and bent back as if he preyed on her.

Hilde trembled violently. Her stomach churned and sank and melted. Her fingers ran lightly down and touched her there, at last, in the secret place.

"I am yours," she whispered to Johanos Martin, as he bent her back, supporting her, his mouth on hers. And shivers of fire ran upward through her body, familiar and yet unique. Her loins seemed to rock at the impact of deep, rare blows. And the door that had opened in her brain flew open in her womb, showering her with suns and comets, shaking her end to end. She cried out before she could prevent it.

Two minutes later her maid came in with a lamp.

"What is it, Mademoiselle Hilde? You do look hot."

"A dream," muttered Hilde. The first time she had had to practice true deception.

"There, there. Well I must get on if you're better."

"Quite better, thank you."

The maid removed herself. Hilde wept. She did not know why. But she was racked again by tears silenced in the pillow that once, misunderstanding, she had kissed.

The magic art of the night sprang from him, then. He had sent it ahead of him. He too had always known. He and she.

Her innocence was gone, not her naïveté.

She scarcely slept again that night. The doll lay on the floor.

Madame Koster stood in her upstairs sitting room, turning about to regard her dress of ivory satin. From beyond her windows and their cumbersome drapes, the ripe westering light of the late summer evening flattered her with its glow.

A knock, and Little Hilde's maid entered.

"What is the matter with her?"

"She's been sick again, madame."

"Really. Such a stupid child. Well, I can't attend a sickroom now. She must be put to bed."

"Monsieur gave orders that Mademoiselle Hilde be given a glass of white wine."

"Did he indeed? How will that help? It will make her stomache worse."

"No, madame. He said it was very cooling, for the stomache, and that her vomiting was all nerves, so the wine will do her good."

"Nerves! What nerves? I am the one with nerves. She's just a child."

Along the passage in her room, Hilde sat pale as death on a sofa, staring at the glass of wine on the tray as if it were poison.

"Take a sip. It can't hurt."

The maid too was irritated. Madame took it out on her when the daughter did not turn out right.

"But I feel—" Hilde broke off, swallowing rapidly, like a cat before it pukes.

"Well, madame wants me downstairs, so I must go."

Hilde was only relieved to be left alone.

This was the hour of her most awful trial. She had longed for and dreaded this festivity of her mother's, not realizing her emotion would build to such a pitch that she would be made sick by it.

Suddenly she got up, and seizing the wineglass, she put it to her mouth. Like a despairing damsel in a play, she dashed the potion through her lips and swallowed all of it. Then she stood amazed.

Almost instantly her sickness swelled to an orchestral tumult— and perished. It was gone, leaving her light and slightly afloat. A pulse beat in her temples. Hilde laughed. This too was part of the magic. Her dear wise papa had helped her to safety. She had been lifted above the demons and made whole. For him, the one who would soon be with her.

In her turn, freed now, Hilde moved about to regard herself, her clothes and her hair.

Her mother had aimed for a veneer of complete childishness, but the dressmaker had maliciously somehow done something to the frock, so that it was merely very simple, very fresh. And the effect of the loose, slightly coiling amber hair gave, rather than the impression of a little girl, the look of one of the mysterious beauties of current paintings, maidens from legend, standing in bowers, as knights rode by.

Hilde was happy at herself, guessing this, not understanding. Happy to be lovely, not realizing that she was.

He would recognize her. As she had recognized him.

Half an hour later, she descended to the salon.

The event had already begun, and Madame Koster was at its hub. She looked at Hilde askance a moment, as if not knowing who she was. Perhaps sensible: Does one ever know another, or who they are, let alone a "child"?

But monsieur had not yet come in. He was, in fact, rather at odds with the party. It meant he must dress up very stiffly and parade his grandeur to impress them all, and this was onerous on such a hot evening.

There were many people in the salon. They drank from glasses of champagne. And since the servant came also to Hilde—again, was it some sort of conspiracy?—and offered her the drink, Hilde took it wonderingly, and sipped.

Then the crowd parted, and she saw the window that led out to the garden. No one was there. *He* was not.

Hilde sighed, and a fearful intimation of darkness crossed her, like the shadow of a huge, transparent crow.

Would he not come? Why should he come? Never before had actors been invited to these show gatherings. Why had her mother done it?

Oh, but it was all part of the starry plan, of destiny. It must be.

Three women approached Hilde. They were ladies she had met before, acquaintances of her mother's. Her heart slid down as if to hide itself.

"Why look, who's this? Is it Little Hilde? A young lady at last."

"What a becoming dress. How clever of your mother. And the hair's an exact copy of *Ygraine Waiting for Uther*."

"Do you have it brushed every night? One hundred strokes are essential."

A wing lifted off the room. Everything shifted slightly, an earth tremor.

Hilde's mother skated across the chamber. She met in the door the two tall actors from the Goddess of Tragedy. They were unmistakable. And all at once the crowd broke into applause.

Hilde thought: *For him.*

Fanfares of trumpets and showers of petals.

She drank all the champagne in her glass, the magic potion that, rather than make her invisible, would allow her to be seen.

She watched Monsieur Martin enter the salon.

Her mother deferred to him even more than to Monsieur Roche, who, walking behind, looked down the slope of his long face. No, it was Monsieur Martin that Madame Koster drew into the very core of her house, and kept there, so the wine could be rushed to him and the guests flutter up like greedy moths.

How cold he looked. Cruel, but one would not call it cruel, not if one wished for his kindness. Cold and cruel and closed and *set*.

Seen in life away from the stage, his face was pale, and the eyes were not black but a glacial gray. Nor was he handsome, yet there was that in his face which magnetized, some affirmation.

He did glance about him, but saw no one. Then he spoke graciously, and even smiled a little at the ones who clustered around him. He drank the champagne, several glasses of it.

Hilde remained at the edge of the congregation, like the shell in a story, left behind by the ghost of a primordial sea at the foot of the Temple-Church.

He would see her now, or now. And she waited for this finding gaze, this instant of pure acknowledgment, stretched taut as the string of a lyre. But it did not come.

And gradually something gave way a little at the center of her physical and etheric frame. Only a tiny derangement. It should have warned her. But how should she know it?

Presently they went into the supper room. Madame Koster sat at one end of the dainty table, and the actors sat either side of her, Monsieur Martin to her right. Monsieur Koster, who had blustered in after all, too late to be properly noticed, thumped down at the table's opposite end, and in the upheaval, no place had been allotted Hilde. So she sat among some of the men and women who knew her, in the bars of the trap of their patronage.

She could not eat a thing, but she sipped the wine. Some of the ladies noticed and disapproved. "That girl is taking too much. What is her mother thinking of?" "Of Johanos Martin," whispered another lady behind her fan.

Hilde did not hear this. She watched the lord who had given his promise to her in a dream, but carefully. It was not subtlety or care that made her careful. Rather she sensed the fire of herself, so bright, so piercing. She dared not be obvious.

He never looked her way.

Never.

After the supper, Monsieur Roche, a little tipsy, agreed to give a speech from the play. This was second best, but of course Johanos Martin would not perform. He had modestly and arrogantly refused.

Monsieur Roche, though the worse for wine, was very good.

The night had dropped like velvet on the garden. The lamps were lit along the paths, and up against the two small statues Monsieur Koster had had imported.

The guests walked in the soft air.

Madame Koster was arm in arm with Monsieur Martin. However had she achieved it? He looked disdainful, faintly amused. She seemed to take this for his interest.

Monsieur Koster was arguing about business in the salon with three gentlemen from a famous bank.

Hilde walked out between the hedges.

It had taken all her nerve, all the six glasses of wine she had consumed.

Unlike Monsieur Roche, Hilde Koster was not drunk. She was a maenad, given over to the god, and balanced in his hand. But had she mistaken the wrong god for the real one? For the real god of the wine is the god of self-knowing, dark twin of Apollo, black sun of opening and rebirth. Dionysos offers often painful truth with the wine, but he does not actually *lie*. Hilde's god, maybe, was all a lie, and that was what the look of affirmation was, a wonderful, successful sham. Like acting itself.

"Oh—" exclaimed Madame Koster. She was caught in the state known among mothers and daughters. Here was the fruit of her body, which she had loved, and perhaps still did love. Only not now a joy, but an interruption. Worse, a reminder.

And Johanos Martin looked from his height. And noticed Hilde.

She was very beautiful. Better than the poor little mutilated clas-

sical statues. Better by far than the women of the house. He did not
want her, for he had already what he wanted. But still, he looked.
At last, he saw.

"My daughter," said madame. "My little girl. Hilde. This is the
great actor Johanos Martin."

Hilde gazed up, for a while half blinded by his eyes. Then she
glanced down. She held out her hand because she had long ago
been taught to do so. All sense had left her, it was automatic.

"Mademoiselle," said Johanos Martin. And he bowed.

That was all.

"Come," said Hilde's mother, "your glass is empty, monsieur."
And she led him back toward the terrace by the window, where the
servant had appeared with long glinting goblets.

"I'm afraid, madame, I must take my leave," said Monsieur Martin.

"But no—such a lovely night—this garden air is so good for you
after—"

"Ah, madame, you must permit me to know what is good for
me."

Madame Koster was speechless. Unfortunately, she had got used
to people who rarely said what they meant.

And so he slipped from her clutches like the sea.

The two women, one middle-aged and sour, one young and
blighted, stood on the walk and watched the cold priest stride away,
back to his church of Tragedy.

In her room, Hilde became hysterical.

Naturally, she had not meant to. It was a reaction to the wine,
and to grief. (Was Ophelia only drunk?)

She wept in the way one screams.

The maid ran for tired, soured madame.

And madame came like a storm.

"What is the matter with you? Ridiculous noisy child! Be *quiet!*
Here I am with a migraine and all this racket."

Hilde tried to stay her tears, her shrieking sobs, for she was accustomed to obey.

But the grief was new. It ravaged her. She was torn. How, with
her entrails ripped from her body, could she be calm and quiet?

"Well—what is it?"

"Oh, Mama—"

But Hilde did not say what it was. There is a knowledge beyond knowing. Besides, how to speak of the unspeakable? Persuaded to the throne of love, and pushed aside.

"Hurry—three drops of my mixture, quick. Give it her; for God's sake."

The drops were administered. On top of the wine they worked wonders. Hilde was violently sick again, and eventually, exhausted by these humiliations, tumbled into sleep.

Is death this? To wake in a vault and swim slowly upward, and there to meet the blows of memory?

O God—O God—But God had gone deaf.

In her virgin's bed, Hilde wept. Softly now, as after the ecstasy in the dark. Must not be heard. No one must find her. For who would help?

Her maid chided her for not arising. Then for not touching the invalid breakfast.

Madame came, and chided too.

Hilde lay like a wounded snake, spineless, broken.

Then she heard a woman, some gypsy, singing in the street. Servants from the houses chased her off. And Hilde wept again.

But then she thought, *He bowed to me.*

And she recalled how his eyes had, finally, seen her.

But her mother had been by. And all the people. And the lights. Perhaps . . .

Hilde got up and went to her mirror. She was so young, even after the outburst of anguish and tears, still she was what she had been. And somehow her youth infallibly told her she was not yet destroyed.

Of course, there were concerns surrounding him. In the story, the knight must win the notice of the lady. And she, Hilde, she must win his notice.

What could she take to him? Only herself. Surely he must see. Surely, surely, he must know.

She would die for him. That was enough. She must be brave. She must seek him out. Alone. Alone he could not fail to find her, as she, amid a crowd of hundreds, had found him.

Hilde washed and dressed and put up her hair and went down.

Monsieur Koster was at home, and beholding her, he beamed. He had heard she had been naughty, but now she was only his pretty, nice little daughter, his very own, that one day he would sell for a high profit in the marriage market Babylon of Paradys.

"Well, Hilde, got over your sulks?"

"Yes, Papa. I'm sorry, Papa."

"You mustn't be a bad girl. You worry your mother and then she worries your poor papa. A young lady must be demure and gentle. Loving and giving. Docile. Not these unbecoming tantrums and noise."

Hilde drifted past a mirror, and some radiant, true, but deceiving part of her called in her soul: *No one can ignore this. This youth and bloom, this being and nature.*

Loving and giving.

THREE

Paradise

Who put the "art" in heart, the "pain" in paint,
and the ice in Paradise?

John Kaiine

Smara walked through the night mist of the City, under her floating lamp. One hand she kept against the rough and stony, dripping
surfaces of walls. In the other, she carried a long and slender knife.
This was her left hand. She was naturally right-handed but had
trained herself to left-handedness. It had been her first curtsy to
the craziness of her world.

She was on the path beside a canal. A snake, perhaps, glicked and
eddied through the water, but she could not see it, only the blurred
ripples picked up by the lamp.

Then, footsteps.

Smara waited, and a man came from the mist. He wore graceful
gray garments, and a mask like a black bird.

"Beloved—how extraordinary to meet you here," he exclaimed.
And held out his arms to Smara.

She went to him, and plunged the knife slantwise into his throat.
Blood sprayed like thick drops of jet, some hitting the lamp in the
air, but it quickly shook them off.

The man soon fell dead on the towpath, and Smara bent over
him. She removed from his finger a ring of twisted bronze, and
then dragged the bird mask from his face. Beneath he too had the
face of a bird, beaked nose, tiny mouth, protuberant sideways eyes.
Smara held her breath in dismay.

She stood up and hurried away, having only paused to wipe her knife on the bird man's sleeve.

The third bridge had long ago collapsed into the river. It was feasible to go halfway across it, and then to jump into the mercury-colored water and swim for shore. To those who sat in the bar above the strand, the intermittent splashes of these jumps were broadcast spasmodically.

A woman danced naked on a table to the tune of a comb.

Felion sat drinking from a jug of water drawn out of the river. It was highly toxic, more inebriating than any liquor.

Smara went to him and gave him the ring. There was a trace of blood on it. He put it on, and handed her four brushes of wonderful springing hair.

"He was painting shells on the ground in the porch of the church. A shame it was a painter I killed. He was quite talented. But the shells will stay. He didn't smudge them as he convulsed all over the stone."

"Mine wore a bird mask," said Smara.

She drank some water and closed her eyes. She was very pale.

A man came by with a tray of lizard-scaled, fanged fish snared from the river. Felion bought one, and put it into his drink. It revived and swam about. He threw it from an open smashed window, back into the river.

"What are we to do?" said Smara. "Oh, what?"

"Let's go into our uncle's labyrinth."

"No," she said. "No."

"Let me remind you of his will. He had accrued property and funds in the other city—the *sane* city. These riches would come to us. We could live there."

"But to walk through the ice . . ."

"Don't be afraid," he said. His face was beautiful with compassion. "Smara, what can hurt us worse than *here?*"

"I must kill again," she said abruptly.

"All right. Let's finish the jug, and then we'll go together."

Now she nodded. He refilled her glass twice, thrice.

A woman came by selling human eyes set into rings.

"How lovely," said Smara.

"They won't last," said the woman. "I'll sell you one for a kiss."

"Then kiss me."

The woman kissed her, briskly, and gave her one of the rings. The eye in it was pure, a crystal spherical gray.

"How much better than the ring I brought you."

Felion took her hand. "When we go out, you can throw it away."

She nodded. Two silver tears ran suddenly from her eyes. "I try so hard. It's as if I must. Do you remember Mother?"

"She's dead," he answered absently.

"I wish—"

"No, you don't wish that. Let's live. Come on, we'll kill."

They left the bar together and walked along the pebbly strand. From the banks of the City, gleams and glares spilled into the water. Someone leapt off the bridge and drowned.

"This way," he said. He led her up, onto the embankment, and then they turned into the upper City.

Out of the charcoal fog of nighttime Paradise, the open doorways gaped, shining. Here and there processions of citizens passed, chanting and banging gongs, or weeping, or utterly silent.

"Where are we going?" she said.

"To the Clock Tower Hill."

"Dogs run in the streets there," she said.

"Yes," he said, "and when we kill, it will feed them."

So they climbed up the heights of Paradise.

A bell was ringing in the cranium of the cathedral, but when they reached Clock Tower Hill, only the ticking of ancient apparatuses, mimicking clocks, was to be heard, and an occasional snarl.

Felion and Smara found people dancing around a bonfire and lured them off one by one, and sliced them to death in the shadows.

After about an hour of this, only two were left dancing by the fire. Felion and Smara joined them briefly, then stole away.

"Where now?"

"You know where, Smara."

"No, I won't."

"*Please.*"

They stood beneath a street lamp that still burned with a cold luminescence. Smara's personal lamp had faded.

"I won't enter the labyrinth of our uncle."

"Then I must do it by myself."

Smara turned from him.

Lightless, she moved away like a ghost, down a slim alleyway under broken casements, into the fog.

* * *

As he climbed back up the hundred steps to his uncle's mansion, Felion experienced a partly irritated excitement.

When he gained the house, and it had let him in, he went at once to his uncle's study, or workroom, on the second floor. The room was built into a sort of tower and jutted out over the abyss of the steps. In the darkness, anything might have been below, a cliffside, even some sluggish silent sea.

Felion activated the mechanical lights, and then, sitting at the great black worktable, he reread portions of the rambling letter his uncle had left for him. (Smara, of course, had never consulted it.)

All about lay bizarre machines that did not now work, and which perhaps never had, and arrested experiments involving vials of glass and transparent plastic, coils of metal, balances, and fluids that had solidified. Over these the damp dust formed a second skin, in parts thick and vegetable as moss.

". . . I am a scientist who has always longed to be a poet," said the sonorous and self-indulgent letter. "Where, after all, is the difference? Scribbling down on scraps of paper equations and potential formulae, or snatches of mystical words, couplets that rhyme. My labyrinth is also a sonnet. It has its own meter, its own intrinsic meaning. One must reach the heart, and then the farther side, and so new knowledge. This requires concentration, but not necessarily courage. Nothing mechanistic can be taken into the maze. No watch or other timepiece, no devices for measuring. Not even a gun, should you or your sister have come across such a weapon on your karma-collecting activities of murder. No mechanical lamp. You may use one of the torches I have prepared and left for you; each needs only a match to light it. As you pass through the ice of the labyrinth, the torch may melt it a little, but that is to the good. There will then always be a limit on the number of occasions you may go in and out. This isn't a game. You will have to decide whether you want your inheritance, a life in the second city beyond the maze."

Felion glanced about the study. One of the unreliable lamps fluttered, as if winking at him. He turned the page, and read:

"I myself am not in fact approaching death. But I am going away. I won't confuse you by attempting to explain. My first identity I established through a connection—false—to a pair of people in the partially rational City. Metal, which as you know is valueless in Paradise, is almost priceless here. With such a fortune I have done much as I liked but mostly kept to myself. The half-sanity of this second world is in some ways disturbing. I have, obviously, left a will in this place that recognizes such things, and it names you both. I am also the (spurious) uncle or guardian to many persons here, but only one might have proved an obstacle. She is a painter and will find my cash useful. You need not fear she is in your way. Probably she will drink herself to death quite soon. Her madness attracted me to her, although she is not insane in the manner of Paradise, would get no glances there."

The flirtatious lamp went out. Felion shuffled the pages of the letter and held them toward another light.

"The exit from the labyrinth is always subjective. It is controllable only by will. Maybe you won't be strong enough to operate journey's end with any skill. I must warn you, too: The labyrinth, because it is modeled on a brain, and therefore inevitably upon mine, may open randomly to show you one other particular place, or time, where I have gone, or am going. For time slips in the labyrinth, and it is possible to travel into the past. I have never attempted the future, in case the future of the second city should be as dismal as the present of Paradise. You would do best to ignore these latter past excursions. The place involved would not appeal to you, although I have seen its potential and indeed, because I am insane, found it in my destiny to go there. Avoid it yourself, however—it is not for you. Keep your mind on the present parallel world I offer. The woman painter will soon die, and then you can do as you wish. You can even kill in the second city, if you want. I myself have done so, although only once. It was the day that my two introductory people became curious about me, quite suddenly, after a drinking party. On the pretense of playing with their vehicle, I destroyed something in its engine, and an hour later both of them were killed on one of the vast highways that now run over this city. I may add that in the past of the City, I have slain no one. But I believe, even so, there will be death there."

Felion skimmed through the final pages of the letter. They were repetitious and increasingly disordered.

But a little later he found the antique torches in a cupboard, and above on a shelf a box of matches, with some eccentric items, among which were two wooden dolls of Smara's, a necklace, and half a brown glass bottle with a shattered neck.

When Felion had got down to the basement and walked along the track, he reached the cavernous hall that housed the labyrinth, and now he looked at it wryly. That it should truly be the route to another world, and to other planes of time, seemed unlikely. And yet how horrifying it was, this wall of ice, shimmering, and drily wet, in the torchlight.

Like the prince in the legend, he could go in, holding up the torch, and knife in hand. (Smara should have been the priestess who stood to guard the entrance.) And in the maze, at its heart, would be a monster.

Felion listened and heard a faint roaring, like the quake of ocean captured on a screen. But it was only the blood sounding in the shells of his ears.

Suppose he went in, and it was a reality, and he could not get back? He considered Smara, alone in Paradise. In childhood, when they had begun to kill, they had formalized the slaughter, devising a ritual of changing implements. Blades, then cords, then poisons, before blades again. Of these means, Smara found the use of cords, the method of strangling, the most difficult. Generally she needed his help. And if he were not there, she might not manage the act efficiently, and die in turn.

He could burn his uncle's letter—even burn down the mansion, if necessary. Or he could merely leave at once and never come back.

But he was sane, surely, that was the whole trouble, and his sanity insisted he investigate the maze. Smara would not need to begin to kill again for some days. Even if it took him a week to return . . . And then again, would he not anyway reemerge into Paradise at the hour, minute, or moment he had left it? Pieces of the complex wandering letter had seemed to tell him this.

Felion walked across the floor, toward the white wall. It came nearer and nearer. And then he was against it. He touched the surface with his finger, and it was *cold*.

Holding the torch high, the knife in his right hand—he had been left-handed but trained himself otherwise—he entered the arched opening.

At once, everything was altered. Became absolute. Although he could still see the entry point behind him, the wall of ice towered up and up and disappeared into an indescribable nothingness above that was not mist or space—or anything.

The labyrinth was freezing, like a winter, described to Felion in bits of rotten books. The ice breathed out a faint vapor that swirled around the nasturtium tatter of the torch.

There was a smell he recognized, if only from a laboratory. Not chemical. What had it been called?

The ground was like muddied glass. (He was reminded of the shattered bottle.)

Sounds came, rushes, like seas, like . . . blood moving in the ear. And he felt a slight vertigo. But then that would be proper, if the balance of matter had been disturbed.

He moved forward, following the left-hand turnings of the wall.

He believed in the labyrinth now, as he had not done when outside. He believed that it was real, and apt, and led to somewhere. His thoughts of Smara dwindled. The archway had vanished out of sight.

The first specter—hallucination, vision, element of elsewhere—spun suddenly at him, it seemed from the wall. He had not anticipated this, and despite his uncle's warning (*The labyrinth may open randomly to show you one other place or time*) had not understood what the notation might mean.

It was like a surge of the fog that clung about Paradise, but in this fog were lights, shapes, voices. Felion heard a frightful shriek, but he had grown used to shrieking. Then the sight of women was before him, ugly women and one very beautiful in a dark fur cap, or else her hair was fur. Another of the women had been struck down. She lay full-length, and the beautiful one bent abruptly to her, touching gently—and then the mirage was gone.

Felion had stopped. He shouted, "Ah! Uncle!" And then, softly, "O my prophetic soul!" And then he grinned. And saw his grinning shadow reflected from the torch into the ice wall.

Stupid to hesitate. He had had the warning and not heeded it. But the *thing* had done him no harm. No, this was not the Minotaur of the labyrinth.

Felion strode on. He whistled a tune of the bars and dives of Paradise. The walls obligingly caught it up hollowly and it echoed back to him.

The second vision came quite mildly. It was like an aperture, filling the area between the walls, the ice-rink floor, and the illimitable ceiling. He saw a dry, tawny lawn, grass, without mist, rising up to a weird house of glass. And in the glass an enormous vine was growing with bursting black fruit.

He moved toward it, and wondered for an instant, if this was the exact exit point, but certainly he had not come far enough.

And the picture smeared, crumpled, and gave way. And there the labyrinth of ice went on.

"Smara," Felion said.

He looked back. Could he *turn* back now?

Then he cursed his uncle, an awkward obscenity, for Paradise no longer had a God, a religion, or any regularized views of sexuality, to form the substance of oaths.

Felion walked on. He did not whistle.

He came around a turn, and a silver insectile web hung across the labyrinth. In the web a woman sat, her tongue protruding, and snakes for hair.

She was gone in three seconds.

And instead, he found he had reached the heart of the maze.

The heart was empty.

An oval region, with one way in from the convolutions of the ice, and a second way out.

In the floor was a stealthy mark, but it only looked as if something had scratched the surface, without intent. It was not a rune, a message, a cipher.

Felion raised the torch high again.

He recalled the woman who painted and would drink herself to death. He did not think she was one of those he had glimpsed in the hallucinatory visions. But now, standing in the womb of the ice, he credited that other world beyond, which his uncle had named, as if jestingly, *Paradis*.

Felion spent a few minutes at the core of the maze (the empty heart), and then he went on through the outleading arch, and continued, keeping to the left-hand wall.

Felion was primed now for further demons, but nothing occurred.

Nothing occurred until he came around one of the twines of ice and saw in front of him an arch of purest nothing.

It was not like the etheric tapering-off of the ceiling. It was a sort of omission from sight. He did not like to look at it. He looked away.

Here was the end. The *egress*.

Perhaps it was all a joke. A hoax.

Perhaps the labyrinth opened into hell, whatever hell was. Or heaven. Or into colossal snows. Or the sea.

The exit could not be relied on. His will might not be able to control it.

Felion's will was strong. He and Smara had wills of iron and flame.

He glared again at the vacant arch and said aloud, "Her house. The painter who inherited from my uncle. *There.*"

And as he said it he thought, *Maybe, in this other world, there are no houses. Maybe they drift in the air—*

But the archway convulsed. It filled.

He saw a room, in shadow.

And with a howl, Felion ran between the walls, and out into the room. While as he did so, the torch puffed into darkness.

The house of the artist.

He had made it be, at the tunnel's end.

Everything about the room (he deduced it was a room) was totally uncanny to him. It was not that the furnishings and accoutrements were so alien. But no mist hung over it, and above a skylight showed rich, black night.

An easel of metal stood in the room. And elsewhere were stacked canvases, and there, a long table littered with paints, and all an artist's accessories.

He had accomplished his objective.

Felion kept still, and felt after the psyche of the house. The house of the woman who painted and drank. Who was the heir to his uncle's fortune in this other world.

And the house was like a casket, chock-full of nothing. Empty, like the labyrinth's heart.

Felion looked up.

And in the black pane of glass, he could see—*stars.*

Stars.

Felion kneeled on the floor of the studio in the parallel world of Paradis. He prayed to something that had no name.

Later, he investigated the room, but only superficially. He did not move anything from its appointed place.

When he eventually looked around for the way back into the labyrinth—this first time he was quickly satisfied, entirely overwhelmed—he could not see it.

But when he beat his head against the wall, crying, "Smara— Smara—" the wall gave way, and there it was.

As he stepped through, shuddering and hot with fear, the great cold came, and the dead torch—which all this time he had kept in one hand, the knife in the other—mysteriously revived.

He ran through the labyrinth, then. He ran through the heart of it, up against the right-hand wall.

And when he sprang out again into the cavern under the mansion of his uncle, he screamed.

Every stone reiterated his cry. He lay on the ground beside the track, hearing it, and the torch guttered out once more.

The initial killing had been a little like this. But then he had had no additional puzzlement. He had gone to Smara with a severed hand, and shown her, and they had marveled together over the whorls of its fingertips. But now, how, how to tell Smara of *this*?

FOUR

Paradis

Mary, Mary, quite contrary,
How does your garden grow?
With silver bells, and cockle shells,
And pretty maids all in a row.

Nursery Rhyme

Leocadia remained calm.

Like any sentence of death, she did not believe it.

Even after she had taken up her new life, her food and music and drink supplied, books delivered, as she wished, paints and canvas, drawing materials, notebooks, clothes, powder, everything, even then in the hermetic environ of her prison she did not believe in it. Not wholly. Not with her mind.

Was that, after all, a form of madness, then?

Even after she had sorted the pieces, grasped the plot. Accepted that her very calm itself must come from minuscule tasteless particles in her food, and in the air itself, which did not restrain her creative flair or her energy, or ability to concentrate, but which must be controlling her. Not even then.

And as she went to and fro from her room in the daylight summer hours, having found she might, and met in the corridor and garden other inmates of the Residence, who were genteel and well-mannered, sometimes bemused, excitable, but never abusive, loud, or agonized, not then either.

Until in the end even her mind knew, and it was too late, she had accepted it.

For, though powerless, she should have resisted. In some fashion, however oblique or useless.

Her asides to the doctors—*I'm anxious to leave, I'll tell visitors how you torture me*—were not protests or shields, let alone missiles. It was almost a repulsive flirtation, her acid quips, their smirking refutations.

And how did her life differ? She did much as she had always done. She spent a vast amount of time alone. She painted. True, the elegant dinners were gone, but had she ever really enjoyed them? True, she had no lovers, but surely it might be possible, if she were desperate, to seduce some person or other, their bizarre quality or nasty appearance offending her not at all in the onslaught of needy lust. And then again, if she could not be bothered with such unappetizing creatures, this must mean her sexuality burned low, she had had enough.

She missed walking in the City. But then, too, months had sometimes passed without her venturing more than two streets from her house.

Now she did not explore the asylum grounds. A low fence lay across the grass and trees the far side of the gravel walk, beyond the broken hothouse. It was easy to climb the fence, and now and then some inmate might scramblingly do so. But they returned from wandering among the old buildings of the madhouse disconsolate, once or twice crying.

It occurred to Leocadia that she kept the blocks of the madhouse in reserve, making of them something mystical and bad, against the ultimate rainy day of terrifying ennui.

"Oh dear, you're too late, I must go down now," Mademoiselle Varc had said to Leocadia when Leocadia first left her room and found the white woman in the corridor. "If only you had come sooner." And then she scurried to the elevator.

Leocadia then did not see Mademoiselle Varc for several weeks.

Instead she confronted Thomas the Warrior, who might once have been a wealthy old soldier, that in his youth had conceivably seen action in some small foreign war, tanks and carrier planes, and the threat of worse. Now he puffed about a flowerbed he was in charge of, below the summerhouse. It was a wonder of blooms and stone slabs, on top of one of which stood a stone head of Medusa poking out her tongue.

Thomas was elderly, thin and stooped. He paid Leocadia no attention, only speaking to his flowers. Doctor Saume had informed her of his name.

Three or four more went about the garden regularly, and some of the other older ones would bask nervously in the summerhouse. Males and females, they were sad and frequently decrepit, moaning with stiffness that even contemporary medication had not been able to alleviate.

The most immature of those she saw was a young man, possibly twenty-five years old, who crouched along like a dismembered spider. He frowned at unseen things, but meeting humans he usually brightened for a moment, telling them how well and lovely they looked. But of Leocadia he seemed afraid, and ran away and hid behind objects as she approached, even behind Thomas the Warrior and his Medusa, if nothing else were available.

Only Mademoiselle Varc actually greeted Leocadia, now thinking her her maid, her niece, her nurse, and once or twice some kind of empress or queen that she had perhaps been introduced to long ago. On these latter occasions Mademoiselle Varc curtsied, and Leocadia had felt a sudden compulsion, in case Mademoiselle Varc fell over. This was the first compassion Leocadia had ever experienced for a being other than an animal. And so Mademoiselle Varc amused Leocadia, and Leocadia was careful, in her contrary way, always to attempt to be the one she was mistaken for.

Probably the strangest time had been when Mademoiselle Varc had taken Leocadia for an old schoolfriend, and both women had then seemingly become adolescent girls. They had sat under the summerhouse in the shade of the trees, and Mademoiselle Varc had confessed she had no idea what a man and a woman did together. Leocadia had told her a carefully constrained amount, and Mademoiselle Varc had giggled girlishly, even blushed, though Dr. Duval had revealed that Mademoiselle Varc had borne six children.

When she had returned from the sun-fallen garden, kindly driven in with Mademoiselle Varc by the warden in his dark uniform (before the trees could come alive and eat them), Leocadia stepped into the dusk of her room and heard the door shut with its final click, which meant her little freedom was gone until tomorrow.

There was autonomy in the way of lamps, and she switched them on in the sitting area of the room, and going to the refrigerator, she drew out a bottle of white wine and a narrow glass.

Then she moved into the painting area and turned on the working lights.

On its easel, the picture of the ship, the beach, the spillage of oranges.

Leocadia studied it coldly.

Was it some response to the other thing upon an easel? Asra, raped and choked with orange paint, her bare flesh adorned by islands.

The doctors who had oozed charm over this painting had seen it as such; they must have done.

But she, what had she been doing?

The ship was not Asra, and yet the ship was feminine. And the sea had split her, and she . . . bled.

Leocadia drank her wine. A swirl of panic rose deep within her like a beast in a bottomless lake. How long before it would reach her surface?

She tossed the glass against the wall, where it broke. Later the wall would suck up the bits.

But not quite yet.

So interesting, the knives for her food, the glasses that might be smashed.

Leocadia went close to the painting. Yes, it could well be seen as some expression of inner horror at Asra's murder, which murder she had performed, and then forgotten.

Massed sky, the vessel with its snapped wing. And the little shells she had added. And there—what was *that*?

She leaned nearer. She could not make it out. Something white on the sand, a small distance from the shells. But not a shell.

She had not painted it. She did not know what it was.

Then again, it was done in her style, in tiny feathering brushstrokes, half its curve delineated as if cut.

Of course, they could copy her.

Leocadia crossed the room and turned about the two paintings she had previously executed here.

One a scene of a mountain, smoking over a peaceful valley. The other, a road leading into a wood. Both were dark, lowering, sinister. Neither contained a hint of orange, or any image she did not recall putting into them.

Leocadia dreamed not of distant bells but of screaming. It was full-throated and savage. It echoed and swerved through the building of the Residence. On Thomas's stone the Medusa poked out her tongue farther.

Leocadia woke up, and got out of the bed, which squeaked its incontinence plastic at her.

She went to the worktable and picked up a tube of orange paint, which she had employed without thought, as if to prove her innocence.

She uncapped it, and squeezed.

The tube screamed.

It screamed in her hand.

Leocadia kept hold of it. As her fingers relaxed, the scream stopped.

She put it on the table and pressed down on the tube with her whole hand.

Now the scream came vivid and awesome, rocking the room, dizzying her ears.

As it faded, she heard an afternote, like the boom of a massive organ in the Temple-Church twenty miles away.

Not me, Leocadia thought, concisely. It was the drugs in the food and drink, and in the light and sound and air. Or could it even be some other trick, like the orange that bled, the white ball entered in her painting?

"Or is it me?"

She seemed to stand above herself on a height, looking down into her soul, not with brief compassion, as she had gazed at the curtsying Mademoiselle Varc, but despisingly, as if at an expensive, once-reliable machine, which failed.

"Come along, Lucie," cried Mademoiselle Varc. "I've found such an interesting place. It's rather dirty, but you won't mind, will you? You're always braver than me."

Leocadia had been sitting on the hot lawn near the empty birdbath, and now Mademoiselle Varc came up and filled the bath with cold tea from her breakfast pot.

Lucie was the adolescent friend, but she and Mademoiselle Varc seemed to have grown even younger.

Leocadia was not in the mood now for role playing.

"Not today," she said, as if to a fractious infant.

But Mademoiselle Varc took no notice. She put down her alabaster hand and caught Leocadia's arm.

"Come *on.* Before they catch us."

Leocadia guessed correctly from this expression that although it was not in fact barred to them, Mademoiselle Varc wanted to go over the fence to the madhouse.

"No."

"Oh, yes. Oh do. It's really fascinating. There's all sorts of things there. I found it last week, but I didn't tell."

"No one will prevent you, if you go," said Leocadia.

"But they will. They'll spank us. It's an awful place. You know something terrible happened there. You're not scared? I dare you, Lucie."

"Of course, something terrible," said Leocadia. "What else, there?"

The old lunatic asylum. Not like the modern Residence. There had been a story about it, but then was that not the other story about the shells—that the sea had washed in over the building? No, this could never be right.

Leocadia got up as Mademoiselle Varc tugged at her like a ferocious moth.

They hurried by the summerhouse, passing Thomas the Warrior. The young spider man was creeping along and raised his face in delight to Mademoiselle Varc, saw Leocadia and lolloped away.

They rushed across the walk, and over the grass. Oak trees and gray cedar towered above them. Then there was the dilapidated fence.

It was like a boundary in a dream. But Leocadia reasoned she had perhaps already, the previous night, crossed whatever boundary there was.

Mademoiselle Varc tottered over and sat abruptly in the uncut grass the far side, but laughing.

Leocadia followed more easily.

The sun burst on the ruined hothouse and the raisin vine, black, as if mantled with bursting tarantulas.

"We have to go among the old buildings," said Mademoiselle Varc.

"Very well."

Marigolds grew wild in the long grass (and Leocadia thought of the marigolds in ice, which had prevented nothing) and pure white daisies.

Mademoiselle Varc stumbled, but she was a little girl again, only about ten, and she made nothing of it.

"Do you believe in ghosts?" she asked Leocadia. "If you look at the windows you might see them. Even by day. Women in a row."

Leocadia shrugged. She raised her eyes to the foul blank windows, seen closer now than ever before, but they were dead as ever, the optics of corpses.

Pipes thick with rust coiled from the walls of the buildings like flexible bones which had pierced the skin.

They came onto a paved place sprung with weeds. The buildings loomed above.

"This way. Down here."

Mademoiselle Varc led Leocadia toward a sort of alley between the light biscuit walls.

There was no sound. That was, one heard the sizzling chorus of cicadas, and the tweets of passing birds; insects buzzed among the rogue flowers. High, high in the sky, a plane purred almost silently over, a silver cigar with fins. All these ordinary noises. And yet, it was like the loud singing in the ear of utter soundlessness. And everything so still, as if, rather than stunned by heat, the area had been frozen.

The alley was drowned in shade.

Mademoiselle Varc darted along it in quick marsupial spasms.

Above, the ranks of corpse windows, black with grime and weather and time. From the pipes hung cakes of filth.

The alley opened in a square, around which the buildings of the madhouse reared and onto which the windows continued to stare without sight. Three big doorways seemed shut like the gates of hell.

And in the center of the square was a great heap of rubbish, stretching up five meters or more, as if constructed over some more solid base.

"See—see—" Mademoiselle Varc sprang at the garbage mountain eagerly.

Noises were fainter here, and though the sun splashed in between the roofs, it was like being in a new block of bright, thick atmosphere.

Mademoiselle scrabbled at the grisly pile.

"There!"

Leocadia observed.

She saw Mademoiselle Varc was holding up a gleaming rope of syrup, a necklace of amber beads.

How bizarre. How could such a delicacy have been overlooked?

Unless Mademoiselle Varc herself had deposited them here, in order to "find" them.

Leocadia glared into the coalescence of rubble. And as she did so, she felt the eyeless windows watching, as if sudden specters had gathered behind their masks.

A pile of garbage. Old newspapers, a destroyed chair raised high as a throne. And lower down, slabs of tin and wool and corrosion.

"Look!" squeaked Mademoiselle Varc.

She raised a wooden doll with jointed arms and legs and black cotton hair.

How was she finding these things? She must have placed them here, her treasures.

"Here's another," said Mademoiselle Varc, and pointed Leocadia into the heap of debris. A wooden limb poked out, and sure enough another wooden maiden emerged into Leocadia's hands. This one had flax hair and cool glass eyes.

"I wonder what else we shall get?"

It was a festival. It was a barrel of goodies into which you must plunge your fingers.

Something was dislodged from higher up and swiveled down the rubbish with a frantic sound.

It fell at Leocadia's feet.

"Oh just see. It's given you something."

Leocadia bent down and raised the artifact.

It was an old brown bottle, curiously shaped, square, with a four-sided neck and a four-sided mouth. On the front, a label. It showed clearly a weird landscape of ice and glaciers, and before them a black and white penguin with a marigold flash beside its beak. Above, the name. *Penguin Gin.*

Leocadia examined the bottle in a trance. It was very old. It was clean, and bright. The penguin pleased her, for it was realistically portrayed, and into her head came the thought: *I have a model now. I can paint penguins.*

"Yes, I've heard of it," said Mademoiselle Varc, peering over. "There was a slogan for that gin." She held a wooden doll in either hand, the amber beads about her neck, along her whiteness. "Penguin Gin, it eases pain."

"Not in your youth, surely," said Leocadia.

"Oh no. Long before. Long, long ago."

Something shuddered in the pile of rubbish. A thin black smoke uncoiled from it.

"That's enough," cried Mademoiselle Varc. "We must go."

She sprinted back into the alley.

Leocadia turned slowly, watching the deadly walls above. Nothing was in the windows.

But she would take the bottle. She would paint penguins.

Someone knocked on the door to Leocadia's room, the way the female attendant did when she brought a hot meal.

"Yes," said Leocadia.

The door was opened.

It was eleven o'clock in the morning, and the doctors, when they came, arrived at five in the evening. Yet here was Van Orles, all alone.

"What do you want?"

"Why, to see you, mademoiselle."

Leocadia wore her cream housedress, which had so generously been sent to the asylum for her. She had no makeup on. She had been about to don her working smock and prepare a canvas.

Van Orles looked at her insidiously.

"Here I am, as you see," said Leocadia.

"Well, shall we have a little talk."

"If we must."

"Always so bristly!" merrily chided Van Orles, and he came bouncing into the room. He wore another of his pasty cravats. Sitting down on the couch he lit a pipe. Leocadia opened the second window. "You never ask for cigarishis," said Van Orles. "Don't you miss them?"

"I seldom bothered with them. They had no effect on me."

"Yet still you drink."

Leocadia propped up a canvas on her table.

"And you began to drink when you were eleven years old, I understand."

When Leocadia did not reply, Van Orles puffed away at his pipe as if considering her silence an answer.

Leocadia was irritated. She did not like to work with anyone near her, as all her lovers had soon discovered. She went to the dressing table and began to brush her curling hair with harsh strokes.

"What a lovely girl you are," murmured Van Orles. "Don't you miss other things? Companionship? Dalliance?"

A faint livid light was ominously blooming up from nowhere. She tensed. The distasteful man seemed to be making a pass at her.

Leocadia swung slowly around and smiled at him. Van Orles appeared taken aback. Leocadia lifted the brown bottle off the dressing table where it had lain through the afternoon and night.

"Look at this, Where do you think I got it?"

"I've no idea."

"In a junk heap in a yard of the old building."

"Which building is that?" he inquired innocently.

"The madhouse."

"Ah. How quaint. The lunatic hospital. Really, that place should be walled off. The masonry isn't safe."

"Don't you think it's a pretty bottle?" said Leocadia. "Quite old itself, I should say, from its shape."

"Very likely." Van Orles got up carefully and came to stand over Leocadia. "And you are interested in such items?"

"Oh, yes. Why don't you tell me about the madhouse?"

"Now, we shouldn't call it that. They were awful days. The poor sick people weren't treated well. Sometimes they were even displayed to the public, to make others laugh. Immorality and disease ran rife—"

"But what happened?" said Leocadia.

"How do you mean?" Van Orles crouched closer.

Leocadia hit him quite hard on the hand and stood up. She moved away.

Van Orles looked happy. He presumably thought he was being teased, a preliminary.

"I mean," said Leocadia, "something curious took place, didn't it? The madhouse was suddenly closed down."

"Oh, there is some story—a warder was killed, and someone disappeared. Perhaps the inmates attacked the staff for their brutish treatment. But one shouldn't set too much store by tales."

Leocadia held the bottle labeled *Penguin Gin* up to the window. For a moment a screaming and contorted face seemed to writhe inside it, but it was only the action of sunlight and the shadow of ivy on the wall.

"Is that all you know, or all you'll say?" asked Leocadia.

Van Orles chuckled. He seemed to think Leocadia's prurient intriguement was a form of foreplay. Gruesome details of the lunatics might arouse her.

"There was a rumor of a ghost. A great dark thing. Very tall, gliding through the corridors. And something about a bad winter. I can't recall."

"Then," said Leocadia, "I think I'll go out for a walk."

"Now, now, not yet. I must perform a small check on your physical well-being."

Leocadia turned from her worktable, the palette knife in her hand. The glare of light was around him like a halo, the warning phenomenon that had come before.

"But I am violent," she said. "And I might not care for this small check."

"Ah—" Van Orles stepped away. He was still smiling, the smile a daisy left behind by a retreating tide. "Now, Leocadia—"

"If you touch me," said Leocadia, "if you come in here again alone, I will set on you." She was tepid, easy. She had had to threaten others. Generally they accepted her terms. And so did Van Orles.

"You are being most unreasonable, Leocadia. Merely because I can't satisfy your ghoulish curiosity about the lunatics."

"But *I'm* a lunatic," said Leocadia. "How can you trust yourself with me? What would the other doctors say if they knew?"

Leocadia walked to the door ahead of Van Orles and opened it. She went into the corridor. Van Orles stood lost in the middle of the room. Leocadia threw the knife back there, so it whirled past his head. He yelped and ducked low, and his pipe fell on the floor.

"I shall have to report this," said Van Orles.

"And also, of course, that you came to me by yourself, for how else did it happen?"

She did not want to leave him in her room, and sure enough, when she stood right back, he came hurrying out.

"You've turned nasty, Leocadia."

He hastened away.

Probably, she had been ill-advised. She was not free now, and doubtless to make such an enemy was unwise.

Outside, it was hot, the sun going up to the zenith. In the summerhouse the old ones lay like spoilt seals. Thomas was not at his garden. No one was anywhere.

Leocadia looked across the grass and gravel, between the trees to the buildings.

Cries in the night—of course. The sheer misery and abjection of that place had been recorded in its stones. But she, had she now come to the hiatus, the point where she must, even physically, pass over into her new life? The low fence symbolized this.

She could kill herself. They must mean her to, leaving all the handy knives and glasses for her. But first, there was the landscape with the penguin to paint.

Leocadia walked along the fence, not crossing it.

Large chestnut trees arose, and under their canopy she came upon the spider man sitting, looking where she looked, toward the madhouse.

Seeing her, he jumped up.

"Wait," snapped Leocadia.

He gave a wild cry. He ran, not like a spider now but a wounded hare. He rushed at the fence and sprawled across it and charged on toward the madhouse walls.

Leocadia got over the fence also, and holding up her long skirt, she ran after him grimly. Her legs were long and slim and strong; she was soon close.

"Stop," she commanded, but he shrieked and bolted away.

He chased along the paved space under the windows.

Swearing, she caught him in both hands, letting her skirt go.

He hooted, went down, and crawled at her feet.

"I won't," he said. "I won't."

"You will," she said. "Why are you afraid of me?"

"Weasel," said the young man. He touched Leocadia's sandaled foot, tore back his hand as if she burnt.

"I am not a weasel. I wish I were. Or are you supposed to be? You're a spider."

He glimpsed up at her face. He said, experimenting, "You look well today."

"I am. Tell me something about that." And she pointed at the madhouse.

"All gone," said the young man. "They went in a night. All the doors were locked. A great wave." He got up and bowed to Leocadia. "Your highness is so powerful. Do take care," he said. Then he flung himself off again, racing back at the fence, away from the buildings.

Leocadia looked up at the rows of dead windows. They were now familiar. She thought she could hear a bell ringing somewhere, but perhaps this noise was only in her ear.

The crickets were silent, and the birds. The marigolds had scorched in the grass and the daisies withered.

Gone in a night. A great wave.

Shells left behind, but that was the other story.

What had gone on here?

Leocadia turned down an alley between the buildings. It was not the way she had come with Mademoiselle Varc. Yet the alley looked just the same, the deep shade, the walls and pipes.

And sure enough, the alley led into a courtyard. Here there was a stone block. It was featureless and gave no indication of its use. Three doorways (hell gates), as before.

Leocadia crossed the yard, which had no rubbish heap, climbed a short stair, pushed at the black door. It was shut, forever.

The madhouse of Paradis.

Something fluttered on the edge of her eye.

Leocadia turned and stared up. Above, in a window, stood a feminine form with bright marmalade hair.

Leocadia's blood seemed to sink through her. A great wave . . . it hit her feet and vertigo made her drop her face into her hands. Then it was gone, and looking furiously up again, unsteady and sick, she beheld the window empty.

As she came back over the gravel, Leocadia saw Thomas the Warrior sitting under his Medusa, in the flower bed.

"Wait, mademoiselle."

"Everyone talks to me now," she said.

"You have been *there.*"

"There. Where?"

"What did you see?" asked Thomas. He was elderly and gnarled and his voice was cracked.

"What could I see? Some deserted buildings."

"Once full," said Thomas the Warrior.

"Gone in a night," said Leocadia.

Did she imagine it? Was the tongue of the Medusa longer?

"You must understand. In your great-grandfather's time. The doors were all shut. The inmates packed in for the night. But in the morning, all the lunatics had gone."

He stopped He looked like old men from her childhood. This annoyed her. She said, "Aren't we all lunatics?"

"Oh, no, mademoiselle. *You* are only mad."

"What's the difference?"

"One day you'll know. Or perhaps not."

"Tell me anyway," she said, "about the madhouse."

"They vanished," he said, "But not the warders. There were twenty of those. I can see them now—in my mind. All were found

dead. Some were in corners and some pressed up against the ceiling like flies, stuck fast. Can you see it, too?"

"Dead," she said.

"Yes, mademoiselle."

"How?"

"They drowned. And they were drunk to a man. Drunk and
drowned."

"But meanwhile," she said, "these may be lies. Why did you tell
me?"

"You asked."

"That's no reason."

"True. I told you so that you can see all the way around the great
circle, of which you are now a part. My congratulations. Now you're
one of us."

"No," said Leocadia.

"Then," said Thomas, "what are you?"

He rose and came to soldierly attention as she walked away.

The new canvases were gone. That must be the doing of Van Orles,
his repayment.

The rest of her equipment—paints, brushes, knives, and rags—
were still there. Even the easel. Even the brown bottle with the
penguin.

Penguin Gin, it eases pain.

Nothing to paint on.

Her frustration was boiling and immense.

In one of her notebooks—on the surface of which it would be
impossible to apply paint—she wrote down what the spider man
had said to her, and the words of Thomas. But not what she had
seen in the window, the maiden with orange marmalade hair.

Penguin Gin, Penguin Gin, drink it up—

She poured vodka slowly.

The walls of the Residence seemed to be breathing. The gray
screens of them must try to shift, and other barriers pass behind
them, through them . . .

Beyond the window, in the sunset, the madhouse flamed.

Drunk and drowned.

She could hear the screaming, and it was night. And she knew, if
she left the bed and walked to the door, it would be open. An
oversight, an act of malice.

As she went across the cool floor, she was surprised that she heard the screaming still, and yet she thought, *It's not me. I'm not mad. I hear only what is.*

She went into the corridor, belting her night robe as she walked, and got to the elevator. It worked soundlessly. Had someone fixed everything just so? Was Van Orles lying in wait? And if he was, would she kill him?

But the lift went down to the garden and no one was there.

The night was soft and fragrant, without lights except for a few vague glims high up about the Residence. And the stars, sharp as pins and claws, brighter than eyes. No moon. Leocadia could not remember seeing the moon for a long while. Had it gone away from her?

She went down the lawn, the grass crisp on her bare feet, going by the birdbath with the dregs of tea. The summerhouse was ghostly, the hothouse like a fiend, its vampire vine and smashed edges.

Across the grasses the ancient blocks were white now, as if after all a moon shone on them, or within. Yet the windows had stayed blind.

The fence was difficult—perhaps she had chosen a more awkward spot. It tore her robe.

Through the high grass, pleased, like a lion in the park. She got onto the paving and moved toward the alley she had taken last, and so reached the square with the stone block, and the girl phantom in the window.

Nothing now. Nevertheless, she located the particular pane, marked it out. Then she went up the steps, still warm from the summer day, and she thrust at the door.

Which opened.

Leocadia stole into the deserted halls of old madness.

She could see very clearly, a sort of night sight.

She could make out long passages, and rooms that led off them, and stairs ascending.

She did not mean to lose her way.

She chose a left-hand stair and moved up it. These steps were not warm at all. No, they were cold as marble. She shivered. And then she gazed upward.

High over the stair, high on the wall, a mark. A tide mark. Fluid had risen, and stood, and then drawn away. The wave. The wave that drowned. It had been here.

At the stairhead, she turned aside. She was going toward the place where, from the outside, she had seen the girl.

How cold, the building. How silent and—*stopped*. Like a clock that had used up all its time.

Everything was the same. Passages and doors opening into rooms. Bare, polished as bones.

And here was the one, the room that she had looked into from below.

Leocadia crossed the shining floor.

At the window, no one. And yet, the windowpane—She went near and examined it.

Upon the casement, like the play of winter frost, were two fine and narrow shapes, the prints of two hands. Formed in ice. A little moisture trickled from them, but only a very little.

If I'm dreaming, I can wake up now.

But she could not.

The cries and screams had faded. There were only the hand-prints and the print of high tide on the walls, and the freezing stillness out of time.

She left the room quickly. She ran toward the stair and rushed down it. Fear had almost caught her up. Below too she ran, for the doorway, and dashed through it and down the steps.

Too cold.

Up the alley Leocadia flew. It was as if the madhouse might collapse on her, masonry unsafe—

She grazed her feet on the paving, and among the long grasses she fell once but jumped up and ran on.

As she managed the fence, she felt her heart beating pitilessly.

The gravel hurt. It was hot now, after the coldness. She entered the Residence and found the elevator, and it went up with her, up and up, and it took too long, but here was the corridor, so modern and pristine, without the marks of tides. She came to her room, and the door gave without fuss. She closed herself in. She stumbled to her bed, and as she lay down on it, she woke up.

Her eyes opened. She was stretched out full-length. She had been dreaming, then. But she was so cold, so chilled.

She pushed herself off the bed, and stepped over her night robe, which was lying on the floor, with a tear in it. Her feet were sore, yet numb. She got to the door and tried it—fast shut. She had never been out.

Leocadia went into the alcove with the refrigerator. Shivering with cold, she wanted a drink, the revitalizing vodka.

She opened the refrigerator. A gust of delicious warmth poured out on her.

She saw the ice packed in, but like feathers from some glorious bed. She touched it. It was soothing, smooth, like the stone hot-water bottles that had come back into fashion. It gave off heat.

She took out and poured the vodka. Cold, as it was meant to be.

She stood by the refrigerator for warmth. It was wonderful, like a summer meadow.

She turned, to warm her back in its depths, and saw across the room a great shadow. Over two meters in height, like a black column with an aproned core of whiteness. Its elongate and fearful head was moving. Horizontal, elliptical. Daggered.

The glass dropped from Leocadia's hand, and as it broke, she touched the light switch beside the alcove.

The lights roared on. She could not see. And then she did, and the room was empty. The night was warm and the refrigerator cold. Her feet were not sore.

But across the floor, she could still see it, the tear in her night robe the fence had made.

FIVE

Paradys

Georgie Porgie, Pudding and Pie,
Kissed the girls and made them cry.

Nursery Rhyme

"Very well, you may go. Anything to shake you out of this silly mood."

So Madame Koster pronounced, hearing that Hilde was to go over to spend the afternoon with Angeline. Madame did not inquire into this. She was drawn and ill-tempered, had headaches. Normally she would have asked to see the invitation.

Hilde went in the Koster carriage.

Let off at Angeline's house, she loitered until the carriage was gone. Then she found her way, with some difficulty, but with the glow of purpose on her, to the street of the large theater.

She had not thought any of her adventure through. Had not considered that one day, conversing, her mama might mention to Angeline's mama the afternoon the two girls had been together. But then, what did that matter?

Hilde approached the theater diffidently but proudly. She had the pride of youngness, and its abashment, too.

There was an old doorkeeper by the actors' entrance.

"What can I do for you, mademoiselle?"

"Monsieur Martin—" Even to pronounce his name was like a stab of fire to her.

"That's right, mademoiselle. But there's no performance. Not until later tonight."

"I have a packet for Monsieur Martin."

Hilde did not really grasp from where her invention had come. Some novel? But there it was. And, oddly, the doorkeeper responded. Not by asking after the packet (for example where was it?) but by looking at Hilde cunningly and crudely.

"Yes? Well, monsieur never said. Remiss of monsieur."

"I must see him," said Hilde, one minute a flame, and then the white of ice.

"Yes. Well. Monsieur does see a lady now and then. But usually," the doorkeeper rapped his coat.

Hilde did not know why. She, or her actor, should have tipped the old man, this overseer of indiscretions.

"I must—" repeated Hilde.

"Yes, yes. He's there. Go in, then." The overseer spat past Hilde's pretty skirt. "I suppose he'll settle. Later. Or not. But then, mustn't speak ill of *Monsieur*. Oh, no. Up you go. Up all the stairs, then left at the top. Perhaps he'll be waiting."

Hilde did not comprehend any of it, not even that *Monsieur saw ladies*. She did not know, of course, that Martin had come for some adjustment of costume, and that, liking his dressing room for its ambience—the cloister of the cathedral of art—he sometimes lounged about there, looking over his lines and exquisitely twisting them, pacing around and smoking. It was not often that a woman had come there to him, but once, or twice, they had.

Now Hilde climbed the horrible stone stairs, on which lay cigarette corpses, flakes of broken glass, dead flowers, clouded stains— all the evidence of vile prediction. But why should she guess?

As she rose a smell grew more dense. It was of the greasepaints the actors used and the creams whereby they got them off, also of dusty clothes that somehow stank of the history they faked. And there was alcohol and tobacco, and the incense of inner things. It *was* a church, in its way.

Half there, Hilde felt faint and leaned on the wall. But then she braced herself. She too was holy. Possibly it was some emanation of his that had made her into an acolyte. He had not meant it to.

She reached the top of the dark tower.

There had been other corridors, but here was one that was black even in daylight. Had she been older, some intimation of death might have held her back. But she had too recently come the other way. She did not identify.

Hilde walked softly into the corridor and so, as if in some dream, came to a line of doors.

She moved down them, lost. And in that second two men rolled from a corner wheeling a costume hamper between them. They stared at her, and so she said, "Monsieur Martin?" Her password.

One of the men grinned. He directed her. It *was* the helpfulness of the spider in the web: *This way.*

When she had gone, he turned to his mate. "That worm. He gets it all. Nice young bit like that."

"Maybe his sister."

"Oh, for *sure.*"

As Hilde went between the doors and so reached the proper one, the hamper descended to the enormous wings of the stage, where it was left. Here the hollow cutouts of scenery rested like vampirized dinosaurs, and ropes and pulleys, chains and spars were stranded, as if on the decks of a ship.

Cleaners had been sweeping the stage.

"Johan has a girl again," said one of the descended men.

"Poor bitch. What do they see in the bugger?"

"Why, he's an actor," said one of the sweepers, striking a pose with his broom. "Glamour. That means magic."

Storeys up, Hilde knocked on the door.

His beautiful voice (it was beautiful) spoke brusquely. "Yes? What?"

She could not speak, could not, for her life.

But soon, half angry at being disturbed in his meditations, he flung the door open.

So he noticed her again. And she him.

"Yes? What do you want?"

She gazed at him. Speech, strangely, came.

"To find you."

"Oh, very well. What is it?"

But then, but then, he *saw* her once more.

He saw her now as a woman, though young as a new moon. He saw her as lovely—that is, *attracting.* He saw that she was there. Some vague remembrance arrived, too. She was an abject subject of his, a convert. Some well-off sempstress of the streets, probably, who had stitched her fine dress herself and put it on to impress him, for who else would seek him in this way?

And she was charming. Skin like lilies, hair like apricots. Eyes cast down. And trembling.

His art fired him also, Johanos. It aroused him, and he had been viewing his art, here in the cramped room with its piles of stale

clothes, and cluttered screens, and a bottle of brandy, and cigarettes, and manuscript, and *his spirit* crammed in everywhere. The
room that led to the high altar.

Not merely acolyte. Sacrifice.

Down on the stage a mile beneath, the cleaners were mock fighting, being the Roman and his Foe, with brooms. Blobs of dust and
waves of sawdust were stirred, it was like the parting of a sea. And
behind stood the movable walls of the scenes, a hundred countries,
other worlds.

But Johanos Martin said to Hilde, "Yes, I understand. Come in."

And as she entered his cell, the priest took her between his
hands.

Hilde looked up at him. She could not see the error for the
exactitude.

"Johanos—" she said.

"Oh, are we on familiar terms? Perhaps we are."

He did not admit though, that, this being the case, he had forgotten. He bent his head and kissed her lightly and Hilde slid against
him, becoming only soul, dissolving.

So then he kissed her more deeply, this offering. She was fragrant and delicious. Obviously, one must have more.

To Hilde it was the dream come true. It was the truth, reality.

Below on the stage one broomer stabbed the other. Handle jut-
ting out beneath his armpit, this other howled. "Oh! I die! I die!
What cities and what lands fall down with me."

"Bastard," said another, "I'll take my bet he's dying on her now."

He had drawn her to the rickety little couch and there undone
her bodice and slipped in his hands. She cried now with shame and
pleasure. He had never had a girl so young, took her for seventeen,
pulled up her skirt and touched between her melting thighs.

She did not know anything beyond his touch. She had given
herself over to the service of the high altar. She was the sacrifice.
He wanted her and by some extreme telepathy had extended his
need to her innermost mind.

One of the broom men fell "dead." The other straddled him, and
then all looked up into the soaring flies.

They cursed Johanos Martin, whom they hated, for he was stingy
and rude, imperious, mean, and frozen like old winter.

And just then he thrust into Hilde's body, tearing her so she
screamed with shock and hurt and some mad outrage that was not
only of the flesh.

She tried to fight him off. He struck her white face, leaving a lurid mark that faded quickly, for he had not, gentleman that he was, struck very hard.

He finished in twenty seconds. A breach, a ramming motion, the explosion of a passion cold as heat.

"Silly girl," he said, getting up, turning his back, adjusting his male dignity. "I'm sorry I was rough. But you shouldn't entice and then be coy. We've done it before." Even her virginity had gone for nothing. He thought her tight and awkward from inexperience and perversity.

Hilde, too, somehow got to her feet. She stood, drooping, almost bent right forward, like a snapped stem.

Up the stairs a cleaner boy was running. He was bringing Johanos Martin the Hated a gift from the street, but Hilde did not know.

"What have you done?" she said.

"Oh, come now."

"Why have you done this to me—"

"Now, don't be stupid. For God's sake. You'll be asking for money next."

Hilde straightened wearily. She was in pain, as if she had given birth. She had. The birth of terror.

"Please, help me," she said. For in this Ultima Thule of life, still she looked to him, her lover, to offer her hope and help.

But Johanos Martin was disgusted.

"For God's sake, get out. How can I deal with this? Get out, you little whore, or I'll send for the police."

Hilde was numb, and now speechless again. She had entered the world of nightmare, which she would never leave. Or not until another nightmare woke her. Despair had occurred suddenly. As such things do.

She tidied her clothes reflexively, and went to the door, which he was now theatrically holding open for her. As she went forth, the door banged.

So she saw and smelled, outside in the corridor, the shovelful of horse's dung collected for him from the street, and spread out carefully on the ground.

She was beyond fainting, as the starving man is beyond hunger. There were no escapes.

She stepped over the dung and slowly went down through the building.

She would never afterward remember doing so, only the reek of the feces of a grass-eating animal, fed on stuff that was not natural to it.

In a country that has no justice and logic, it is useless to behave normally. Hilde did try. In the nightmare world, she attempted to sleep, to get up, to eat, to dress herself and go about with her mother on the endless trivial errands of their house. But Hilde was passionate. It had been kept closed up in her the way a flower is closed in a bud. Once open it can only bloom and blow, and then the petals fall. The fall had come.

Hilde did not sleep. She wept all night and rent the sheets and bit the pillows from agony. Her maid saw what had happened to the linen and told madame, and madame shouted at Hilde. Was she a wild animal from the zoo?

Hilde did not, and perhaps could not, say what was wrong with her. Neither could she swallow food. She found it impossible to get up from her bed. If forced to do so, she sat in her robe before the mirror, unable to proceed further.

She stared at herself. Who was this?

She had hidden the doll in the wardrobe, that it might not see.

And God—Hilde called to Him but He had not regained His hearing.

The doctor was fetched instead. He said these foolish vapors afflicted young girls, and prescribed a tonic, rest, and exercise. Hilde drank the tonic, which tasted of hot iron. Her mother drove her out, accompanied by the bored and resentful maid, to walk in the parks of Paradys.

Hilde began to suffer from fits of searing rage. She flung a bottle of cologne across her room and it broke. Sometimes she would stand before her mirror and shriek at herself wordlessly.

Her father spoke sternly to Hilde. Hilde sat before him like a dead doll.

Hilde's mother shouted at Hilde and slapped her hands with a narrow silver bookmark. Hilde started to wail and cry.

The truth was expelled from Hilde by the tiny irritant pain of the bookmark on her knuckles, one last straw.

"I can't bear it—I can't! I love him. There's nothing else. He—he killed me."

"What? Who? What are you talking about, you uncontrolled and wretched girl?"

"Johanos—" said Hilde. And at the name, the fissure was soldered shut again. It had let out everything that was necessary.

And now Madame Koster slapped her daughter across the face, as Martin the priest had done.

"What a lying little beast. Are you mad? You've seen him only once, in this house. These idiotic fantasies. Such a man is far beyond you. And besides, unsuitable. A common actor. Don't let your father hear a word of this."

But Hilde turned and ran about the room, up and down, like a dog in a cage. She beat the walls with her fists, and her cries were so loud now they might be heard in the street.

Her mother rushed at her and slapped her hard again, two or three times, until Hilde fell on the floor.

"How can I live?" said Hilde. Her words were unintelligible. "How can I bear it?" She was, of course, too young to know that much of life involves the bearing of what cannot and should not be borne.

And Madame Koster, who did know, being seasoned enough, and who had the passion of a small gnat in her heart, imagined that her self-control was due to her superior type, and that Hilde's lack of it was proof of Hilde's revolting weakness and unworthiness. As Hilde lay there, madame her mother would have kicked her. For being all madame was not. Therefore an insult, a challenge, and a threat.

All love was gone. Dream love, and motherly love.

Hilde was locked into her room, where she lay in a stupor, not caring.

And then madame brooded. And presently she summoned her husband home.

The Koster house was built of respectability, of reasonable sane ambitions, formats and rites. Hilde was a spy of chaos who had got in, masquerading as a daughter.

Two doctors tested Hilde's mind carefully. They conferred with monsieur. Madame shed a few dryish tears.

Only thirteen days had passed since Hilde's return from the Goddess of Tragedy.

"It seems she is the victim of—monsieur, forgive me—a sexual delusion and a frenzy. It affects certain unlucky young women in this way. Such women are feeble, unformed. They are not meant for physical ardor and can't withstand it. The proper female votive of sacrifice and tenderness becomes warped into obsession. She's a danger to herself, and to others."

The Kosters had put it about that their daughter was gravely ill, and when word came that she had abruptly died, there was speculation but no disbelief. Death did descend in this way, and the young were vulnerable. That the parents were secretive and sorrowful was only to be expected. The funeral was very private, indeed, clandestine.

A headstone appeared in the graveyard. Those who discovered and read it were sometimes struck that it was a little odd. "Our dear daughter, Hilde, strayed from our lives . . ."

Massively drugged, insensible, Hilde was taken away in a closed carriage at three in the morning. It was all managed very discreetly. If people saw, they did not understand.

The carriage wheeled sedately through Paradys, along the cobbled lanes and up the wide paved roads, under the churches. Our Lady of Sighs, Our Lady of Smokes. Beneath the Temple-Church. Reflected in the river. It went up into the hills to where the last of the dark trees were, beyond the outlying architecture of the City, and came to a big brick citadel, sometime before dawn.

The walls were high, the gate was straight.

It was the lunatic asylum of Paradys. The madhouse.

The door slammed shut again, on Hilde.

SIX

Paradise

We are outside the Labyrinth now. Searching, only finding.
Staring headlong into a ghost's looking-glass.

John Kaiine

In the garden room of her apartment, Smara had been working the
clockwork cat. The clockwork, however, was wearing out, and the
cat was no longer friendly, as it had been in Felion's and Smara's
youth. It would pad a few meters, and then stop.

The garden room had plants made of black velvet and rubber,
and sometimes Smara dusted them. Their mother had spent many
hours here, before one day she flung herself off a high tower in the
City. Their father was unknown to them.

When Felion arrived, they drank sweet wine and talked about
ordinary things. Smara had killed a woman in a cemetery, manag-
ing to lasso her as she knelt over a grave.

Finally, Smara said, "But you went into the labyrinth, didn't
you?"

"Yes. Shall I tell you?"

"If you want," said Smara. Her face was sharp and anxious.

Felion told her what he had seen in the passages of the ice, the
visions of women, the glass building, the being in the web. He spoke
of the empty heart at the labyrinth's center, and how nothing disturbed him on the farther side, until he emerged into the studio of
the artist their uncle had made his inheritrix.

Smara listened, but she kept moving about. She began to dust the
plants, and the stone head that stood on a plinth against one window.

"And will you go back?" she inquired when he had ended.

"I think I will. There were stars, I saw them, Smara, through a skylight. The sky was a deep black, and there they were. I want you to see them too. And the sun. And the moon."

"Oh, but I've seen that," she said. "In pictures."

Felion began to persuade her, to nag her and wear her down.

She allowed him to talk, but soon she got up and wandered from the room, and so from room to room of the apartment. Felion pursued her, still talking, nagging.

It grew dark, and the opaque gray blanks of the windows changed to ebony. Sometimes a light might shine out there from some height or other, and tonight there was one, quite fierce, and fluctuating. Probably something was on fire.

Felion was hoarse. He left off and only sat looking at Smara. There was nothing to eat in the apartment.

"Shall we go out and find some food?"

But now Smara said, "Why must I come into the labyrinth?"

"To reach the other city."

"Is it so wonderful, then?"

"It must be." He added, "You mustn't be afraid of the ice. It's not like winter." This was a lie. "And I'd be with you."

She did not reply then, but as they walked the wide smoggy streets, she said, "I've been thinking of it, the other city." Then, as they ate burned potatoes in a café, she found a round rock, of course, cooked in with the vegetables. She said, "I asked for bread, and into my hand was put a stone."

Felion flung the rock at the cook, who had appeared in the café. The man shied, laughing, and the rock only broke another window.

"We can go tonight," said Smara. "Yes, I'll try."

He took her right hand at the entrance. In her left he had seen she carried her killing cord. He held up the torch, and the ice wall gleamed.

She looked frightened, but she did not hold back now.

They went in together. They were inside.

Then they walked forward, keeping to the left, not speaking.

The sounds came, the dim roar like oceans. Smara made no comment, asked no questions. Her hand felt as cold as the ice.

Felion waited for the visions, but nothing stirred.

Suddenly Smara said, "Oh, look!"

But Felion could see nothing at all.

"What is it? I don't—"

"That old man in a garden . . . Isn't it our uncle? He's dressed as he was in the photograph, the one taken during the war. And look—oh, *look!* There are flowers—just like the ones the screens show."

Felion could make out nothing, but Smara's white face was alight with interest. Then she blinked. "It's gone."

"I didn't see. But it must be one of the elements he said we'd find here—time slips, images of some other place. He said he went there, as well as to the city. He went there or would be going there . . . And so. Probably you saw him."

"There was a glass building," she said. "It had white and brownish panes."

They went on. Smara moved quickly now.

No images unfolded before Felion, and Smara apparently saw nothing else. Quite swiftly, they reached the center.

Inside this icy oval, Smara hesitated.

She stared about her, and drew her right hand from Felion's grasp.

"This is a terrible spot," she said. *"Something's here."*

"No, nothing at all. It's empty."

"Yes, there is something. Something horrible and dangerous."

"No." Felion put his head on her shoulder.

Smara darted her head upward and pointed, into the height of the ice wall.

And something was there. A kind of hump bulging out in the ice. It had not been present before.

He said, "Smara, you must control yourself. You're making this happen. It's *you*."

She covered her eyes with her hands.

The bulge in the ice did not go away, but it had now a fixed, inert appearance.

"How much further?" Smara whispered.

"I don't know. Not far."

All at once she broke from him and ran off.

He shouted after her, and also ran to catch her up, but although in the City he could have done this easily, here something prevented him. And so she was gone, flying ahead, vanishing. He called that she must keep to the left of the walls. He remembered how he had told her over and over that will had projected him through into the second world, and where they would be going: the studio of the woman artist.

Then, running, he reached the exit point, and saw, with hardly any forethought, the studio outside.

He rushed into it—but Smara was not there.

Again, as before, the house in the second world was vacant.

At first, he barely noticed, searching about in it, uncaring and unthinking, for his sister. Who mattered, what counted, but she?

But Felion did not find Smara.

Instead, he found other things.

The rooms were quaint, some orderly and clean, others jumbled. Dead flowers (flowers!) in a vase, the butts of cigarettes with a scented smell, books—intact—cast about lying on the carpets. There were glasses with the phantoms of alcoholic perfume, but no dregs.

On the walls hung interesting pictures. There were persons in them with the heads of beasts Felion recognized from the screens and portions of books in Paradise.

The furnishings were not so dissimilar to those he knew. That was a chair, and this a table, a cupboard, an ashtray, a cup.

But.

The windows.

It was dawn, he thought, and he saw a sun come up. It was an orb like a lamp, but quickly it became too bright to regard. Then the whole sky flooded with brilliance and color.

Did Smara see this? Where was she?

He hunted through the house of windows, and piece by piece the strangeness, the volume, of what he saw overcame even his concern for Smara.

He did not leave the building. And yet, outside, he beheld streets. There were old trees, growing and real. It was possible to see a long way, because there was no mist.

Felion wondered, if anyone entered the house, what he would do. But no one came to the house, and outside the calmest day went by. Vehicles passed now and then, and sometimes people walked along, in costumes that, as with the furniture, were not so unlike the clothing of Paradise, although he noticed no masks.

He could not find a cooking area, or anywhere to come on a drink; he longed for water. There seemed to be mechanisms that worked for the maintenance of the house, but he could not activate them, for the panels that apparently related to them were incomprehensible.

In the hallway at the bottom of the house there was some evidence of the passage of many people. He noticed that something had been done to the door, externally, which worked to secure it. A spangled woman's shoe lay on the stair.

The day went with the passage of its sun, and bars of light and shadow roamed over the chambers, fascinating him. The whole house was like a clock.

At length, he went back to the upper attic room, the painter's room.

He realized now, something seemed to have happened here, too. He was uncertain what. Some tubes of paint were stuck to the floor. With distaste, he found that someone had vomited in a corner.

As previously, the exit-entry point had disappeared, and in a sudden rage he crashed his fist against the wall.

"Let me through. I want Smara."

It was what they had called *dusk*. He could hardly believe he had spent so much time here, when she—

The wall gave way. It was as much emotion, then, as will that caused the labyrinth to operate.

The tunnel of ice curled before him, and idiotically he glanced at the ground, to see if Smara had left lying there one of her shoes, to guide him. But there was nothing.

He stared around the attic again. He had looked at some of the canvases that were stacked against the wall. One had a blond man standing on a roof, high above a city that was devoid of mist.

Inside the maze, he walked backward, watching the aperture, until it abruptly dissolved.

As he came into the center of the labyrinth, Felion paused.

His heart beat heavily; he was conscious of great fatigue and mental enervation.

It was now incredible to him he had lingered so long in the parallel house of a painter (whose name his uncle had never bothered to tell him) when his sister had vanished inside the maze of ice.

He looked up, and there the bulge still was, in the ice wall. It had changed.

Above, the ice had sunk to a type of darkness, almost like some view of the misty night of Paradise. And in the space thus supplied, the frozen tumor had gone to a blocked and incoherent shape. But it was tall, and had a birdlike head—

In that moment, Felion heard light footsteps on the floor of the ice, tapping toward him. His blood leapt, he looked down, and saw Smara.

She stepped into the heart of the maze nearly indifferently. She was not pale, but nearly luminous, as he had seen her after a particularly fortuitous murder.

She too looked at him, and stopped.

"Here you are," she said.

"You ran away," he said. "Where did you go?"

"Into the painter's studio, where else?"

"But—I was there. I explored the house. I didn't find you."

"Nor I you." She frowned. "Somehow that seemed to be all right. I knew I'd find you *here*."

"We must," he said, "have gone into the studio on different planes of time. Did you see her, then?"

"No, The room was empty."

"What hour of day was it?" he asked. He trembled with relief at discovering her, did not mind what they said, or where they were.

"Day, I think. There was *sunlight*. It fell across the floor from the two windows."

"The window in the roof?"

"No, one in each wall. One gave on a bank of vines. The other window had a view. A lawn and trees, some buildings . . ."

"We weren't in the same place," he said.

Smara scowled, as if he had accused her of some misdemeanor, as had sometimes happened in their childhood. "It was her studio," said Smara. "There was an easel with a painting on it."

"Of what?" he asked darkly.

"A ship," said Smara.

"Do you recognize a ship?"

". . . Yes, from a picture. It had a sail. Things were spilling out of it. I don't know what."

"The bitch must have two studios. What did you do in this room?"

"Very little. I was only there a few minutes. Then I came back to look for you."

"How?"

Smara lowered her eyes. She seemed angry also. "I cried out your name at the wall. I'd got in there."

Felion swept his arm upward.

"What's that?"

Smara glanced. She became pale again and distressed.

"I didn't do it."

"It's your fear. It's some sort of bird of ice. It's formed itself there."

"I won't stay here," she said. She was immobile.

He went to her and took her hand. She still held, limply, her strangler's cord.

"We'll go back, then."

They walked away into the convolutions of the labyrinth. He said, "Don't be afraid of birds."

"You used to flap with the sheet and say—"

"I was horrible. Please forgive me and forget it. We were only seven."

"I saw the picture of a bird once. It was black and white. It had a terrible beak."

"I looked for it in the books," he said, "specially. It was a totem of the peoples of the northern ice waste. A spirit fashioned as a bird, with a black head and a white breast. And it was a good spirit, which they invoked to bring them help. It cured the sick."

"Are you pretending?" she questioned.

No visions came, the ice walls slid curving around them. They did not run.

"It's true," said Felion.

"In her room," Smara said, "I did something."

"What?"

"Will it hurt?" she said.

"I don't know. Damn her, who is she? Who cares?"

"I painted in something white on her picture. I don't know why. A ball of ice."

"How?" he said, again, curious and unnerved. He had done nothing.

"One of the brushes you gave me," she said, "from the man you killed. I had it with me. I used her paint. It was as if I'd always meant to, and—"

"Yes?" he said.

"I hid her spare canvases. The ones she hadn't used."

"Why?"

"I don't know. I hate her. She lives *there*."

In the winds of the ice, he turned his sister toward him and kissed her forehead.

"Forget her," he said. "Then she won't be in our way. Did you like the sun?"

"Yes."

"Wait," he said, "until we see the moon by night."

Smara had shut herself into her apartment. Felion knew that she was there, although she would not answer his signal at the door. She had not been out for days, save for one night when, turning into her street, he saw her gliding up the steps of her home. By the time he had reached it, she was inside.

He too killed desultorily, with the strangler's noose. But he was not interested in the activity now.

The idea of the labyrinth, and the city beyond, had come to obsess him.

He thought about the parallel endlessly, visualizing for himself how it might look, its heights and depths, its river—for surely, like Paradise, it had one.

His own room was in a hovel. He preferred this, he disliked possessions, for they seemed to gain a hold over him. To the clockwork cat, for example, he had had a loyalty, insisting on trying to make it work, to carry out its old antics of play and purring. But the cat was stubborn. It had "died." Smara only used its leftovers for a distraction, it did not disturb her.

In Felion's room, which was in a ruined building near a quay once known as Angel, Felion kept a hammock to sleep in and a steel safe in which lay his weapons, a few fragmented books, and some clothes. Across the door, which was itself off its hinges, stretched an electrical device that kept out intruders. One day, probably, this too would break.

Felion stayed in his room or walked by the river.

Gigantic rats, quite beautiful, but savage, prowled the edges of the water. Sometimes Felion fed them with parts of bodies, but not often. He did not want the rats to become a responsibility.

After two weeks, when Smara was still locked away, he returned to his uncle's labyrinth.

As he walked forward, he counted the turns of the ice wall. He was just inside the fifth turning when the first vision appeared.

Felion stopped, staring.

Like Smara, or as Smara had claimed it, it seemed to him he saw his uncle. But not in a garden. The old man was shambling through an alley, an alley of the elsewhere place, with no mist, and only a light on him that came down from the sky. Felion looked up, and so he saw it, the moon by night.

It was the moon—round as the perfection of all circles, russet as parchment, *bright*—it was the moon, not his uncle, that pulled Felion into the vision.

And the image did not burst or fade. It stayed whole about him.

He was brave, blasé. He thought, *I can get back, in and out as I want. I'm somewhere he told me not to go. So what?*

Felion followed his uncle along the alley in the moonlight, and so up onto higher ground.

It seemed to Felion his uncle was younger, but that might only be an effect of the amazing darkness. Felion heard his uncle's feet on the cobbles and in slicks of mud. Heard his *own* footfalls. . . . But the uncle of Felion did not turn. He seemed, the uncle, immersed in some dream, now and then gazing up at the moon. Just as Felion did.

Smara, you should have seen—you will see.

There was a bar or drinking shop up the slope beyond the alley, and Felion's uncle went in there. Felion stalled. Then he, too, made to go in. There was a sign hung over the door: A half-transparent figure hurried over a hill, under which was a rim of light; a ghost fleeing the dawn, as in Paradise, maybe, it would not have to? On a wall in the picture curled something with the black head of a bird. Felion did not understand this sign, nor the writing beneath. The letters of it were like those of Paradise, but not the language. His uncle had not warned him that in Parad*is* they would have to learn to speak a foreign tongue.

Inside the bar, under the beams, Felion's uncle sat drinking and writing on a tablet of paper.

The clothing of the people here was not quite like the garments Felion had glimpsed from the artist's house. It was, evidently, a different time.

From another table, a gang of evil-looking humans raised their glasses to Felion's uncle.

"Here's health to you, poet!"

Felion withdrew, back into the street.

In the alley a woman was selling herself to a man. As Felion went by, she smiled at him, over her customer's bowed skull. "Only wait a moment."

It came to him that after all he understood their speech, only their writing was incomprehensible.

Felion reached the end of the alley, and walked back, as he meant to, into the labyrinth of ice.

How easy. He must assure Smara again of how straightforward the adventure was.

No other visions come.

He reached the heart.

He made himself look up, and there that bird thing was, still shaped out of the ice.

Across the murky floor had been scattered some scraps of brown sugar, or glass.

Felion turned around. He did not want to go on without his sister. He would have to bully her again. He wanted her to see the moon.

He walked back out of the maze, and nothing happened. It was as if he had cheated or mocked it, and he expected trouble, but there was none.

Below the hundred steps leading to his uncle's house, Felion found a woman and, with a kind word, strangled her abruptly. He took her earrings of pearl for his sister and put them through the receptor of her door, impatiently, when still she would not let him in.

A day after, they met by accident in the nave of the cathedral. No one else was there but for a corpse lying in a side chapel, unknown by sight to either of them.

"Come back into the other city."

"I went there," she said, "in a dream."

"That isn't the same," he said.

Smara shook her head sternly. "How can we know? I saw *her* studio again, by night. I was outside and I opened the door. Someone was sleeping there, but I didn't go in. I stayed outside. There was an elevator. . . . Downstairs there were lawns and tall trees. In a lighted window was a man peering out at me. I ran back again. There was," she added, "a house of glass with a vine of fruit in it. But the vine was dead and the glass had broken."

"Was the glass brown?" he said.

"I don't think it was."

"Come with me," he said.

Smara said, "Not today. Not yet."

SEVEN

Paradis

The north wind doth blow,
And we shall have snow.

Nursery Rhyme

Hot summer light: The room seemed arid, and larger than before, and Leocadia sat with her robe across her lap, examining the tear at its hem. She must have got out of the bed and wandered around the chamber, and caught the silk on something. On what? Some shred of broken glass the mechanical device had not cleared? (During the night the second broken glass had also been cleared up, the glass she had dropped when she saw a black pillar with a beaked dagger of head standing there across the room.)

The panel that supplied music and told the time had also a small button to summon the attendant.

Summoned, the girl in the dark uniform now knocked and entered. It was always the same girl. Or could it be that they simply employed a number of girls who closely resembled each other, sisters perhaps?

"Yes, mademoiselle? Would you like a cooked breakfast? There are some excellent rolls, just made—"

"No, I don't want breakfast. I want to see one of the doctors."

"I understand, mademoiselle. Are you feeling worse?"

"Worse. You mean, I'm always ill, so now I must be worse. I'm neither. Duval will do. Or Leibiche. Even Saume, probably. *Not* Van Orles."

The maid—one thought of her as a maid, rather than a jailor—

smiled. "Very well, mademoiselle. I'll take your message. But I can't promise anything. The doctors are always very busy."

When she was gone, Leocadia went to her refrigerator. She opened it quickly. Chill air smoked out, winter in little.

Last night the refrigerator had been warm and she had basked against it.

Now she poured out vodka, and drew forth a long sliver of white cheese.

If the temperature of the refrigerator had failed, the food would be spoiled, and it was not.

Had she still been dreaming? The warmth, the apparition? No, for another of the glasses was missing, the one she had dropped in startlement.

Leocadia glanced aside. Nothing was disturbed, no shards of glass on the floor. Her canvases, removed by Van Orles when she was out, were still missing.

He must be amused, gratified. All her painting materials left to her, and no means for their use. Of course, even such a fool would know what this would do to her.

If one of the other doctors came, doubtless he would have been told Leocadia herself had demanded the subtraction of the canvases, or made some threat having to do with them. It would be unwise to accuse Van Orles of anything, let alone report his graceless lechery.

How many, trapped here, had submitted, to him or to some other? And would she have to prostitute herself to get her canvases back? After all, anything could be taken away from her, a reason could always be found, since she was insane.

All afternoon, no one had visited. Nor at five o'clock, the usual time.

Leocadia went down into the garden.

No one was there, either.

The summerhouse and flower bed, empty. A pigeon flew away from the Medusa's head at Leocadia's approach.

The lawns and walk were vacant, and across the grass, through the trees, the buildings of the madhouse were like old rocks in a desert.

Penguin Gin, Leocadia thought, *Penguin Gin. Drink it up, it will—*

Leocadia could not recall, out in the garden, where she had left the antique bottle with its square neck and top, its label of ice floes and bird.

She felt almost afrighted, a kind of pang.

Leocadia made herself move slowly back toward the Residence—someone might be watching.

When she gained her room, the bottle was standing on her work-table. Had she put it there? Had it been there all the time?

Leocadia picked up the bottle and examined it, an archaeologist with a flask of Egyptian pottery, some tiny god incised upon it.

Drink it up, it will—

Maddening, a rhyme that did not conclude.

Maddening.

Of course, possibly they watched her in her room, in the same way that unseen sounds and unheard lights threaded through it. But then again, if they had decided to keep clear of her—some campaign of theirs, or else some ploy of *his*—probably they would monitor her response but not interfere.

She felt a consoling violence as she prepared the wall beyond the book alcove.

The best of the light fell here, almost as good as the spot where the easel balanced.

There would be difficulties, but they must be met in the nature of challenges rather than of barriers.

The walls had always annoyed her. The pale gray surfaces without texture, against which she saw the motes in her eyes.

To change the wall, smother it in shadows and densities, illusions and images, that was a fair return.

And whatever else, unlike canvas and oiled paper, the plaster, the bricks and mortar, could not be taken away from her.

She covered a large area, larger than any canvas she had ever attempted.

Then, leaving it to dry, she took the gin bottle to the ivy window and studied it again.

The next day, Leocadia walked around the asylum grounds and across to the old buildings.

She patrolled their alleys and looked up at their windows. She paused in their courtyards, listening.

She did not come on the great teetering rubbish tip—either it had vanished, or she had chosen the wrong entry.

Leocadia saw and heard nothing.

There was no one else about, as on the previous day, except that, coming back, she beheld Thomas the Warrior in his flower bed.

She spoke to him.

He took no notice.

"The silence is broken," said Leocadia. "You talked to me, at some length."

Thomas paid no attention.

In the summerhouse, Mademoiselle Varc lay sleeping, and Leocadia did not try to wake her.

Returned to her room, Leocadia drew across the white expanse of the prepared wall the guideline of a horizon. Here the snow would end against the silver of the glaciers. And here, below, a penguin would stand, comic and baroque, like one note of music played too loud. She began to sketch it in. It was tall.

Van Orles had not thought to remove the finished canvases, although she might have painted over these. How had he known she would not? Was he clever after all?

She stared at the ship that spilled fruit, and on the sand beside the shells the white thing lay, which now she recognized. It was a snowball.

The hot light made the snow of the wall very rich and enticing. And in the same way the brown glass showing through the label of the bottle made that snowscape also alluring and warm. Warm as the refrigerator.

White snow gentle as a young summer.

Leocadia drank wine, and let fly a tuft of darkness on the drawn penguin's daggered head.

EIGHT

Paradys

But had I wist, before I kissed,
That love had been sae ill to win,
I had locked my heart in a case o'gowd,
And pinned it wi' a siller pin.

Ballard

Everyday about noon, Dr. Volpe toured his kingdom, the lunatic asylum. This gave him a feeling of uneasy and strange power, which he confirmed for himself as the sense of duty. He always hoped that nothing had gone wrong, that none of them had become violent or terribly ill. He liked them to be docile, sitting or wandering about in the straw of the large white rooms. Some nodded or rocked or swatted invisible insects, some sang quietly. These aberrations were normal and he found them almost soothing. The bad smell of confined bodies or those who had messed themselves he was accustomed to. Snuff taking had dulled his nose; he brought with him a scented handkerchief. Now and then there would be an upset. One would not eat, or had set on another, or banged his or her head against a wall. These inmates were restrained, and the sight of their tethers, and the mad-shirts confining their arms, calmed Dr. Volpe.

Sometimes more drastic treatment was required, the Swing or the Waterfall. Doctor Volpe disliked these measures, as he disliked shutting his patients in the upright coffins that permitted only their faces to be seen. He preferred where possible to administer huge doses of opium. As the raving creature sank into oblivion, Dr. Volpe felt an iron clutch slacken on his own muscles.

After his noon perambulation, he would return to his apartment in the adjacent block. Here, when the door was shut, he might, aside from the occasional interruption, have been in some luxurious flat of the City, a gentleman of leisure. There were his shelves of books, his piano, his plants, his various collections—of birds' eggs, butterflies on pins, and so forth. He could potter about all day, and in the evening, the housekeeper brought him his dinner, after which he would drink a bottle of fine brandy.

It was another concern of Dr. Volpe's that some of his warders drank inferior liquor. Although it was, of course, reasonable to drink large amounts of a decent vintage. Amid his brandy Dr. Volpe played scherzos at his piano. His thoughts ranged. Finally he slept well, indeed late into each following day. But to drink all one could afford of a cheap and dreadful gin, which, it was said, was actually poisonous . . . He did not berate the warders. They were curious men and women, bound to their profession by ties Dr. Volpe did not always care to consider. One must not cross them, or one could not exact service. But nevertheless, he had once or twice glimpsed the terrible gin bottles, brown and queerly shaped, with a peculiar label.

Dr. Volpe let out his inner excellence at his piano, and every six months it was carefully tuned.

Playing, he knew a faint loss, for he could have been a great pianist. Misfortune and the pressure of his bourgeoise upbringing had led him where he was.

In fact he did not play very well, fumbling and bluffing works he should not have attempted, firing off like explosions or farts cascades of horrible wrong notes. Besides, and worse, he lacked expression. There was no tenderness, let alone the delicate neurasthenia so often called for. At his most fiery he was at his most appalling. This he did not know.

He was dreamily thinking of his music now as he passed along the galleries above the pens of white rooms.

The women and men were to have been kept separate, but ultimately it was easier to enclose them together. They were scarcely human after all. One woman warder and two men kept watch today, or rather were playing cards at a table.

Dr. Volpe moved over the room like a visiting meteor. All was well. A couple were tethered, the rest moved freely about, or sat in arrested attitudes on the ground. One of the females kissed her hand to the doctor up in the air. He had always liked her gesture, and saluted her gaily. He did not know who she was. Only the troublemakers became, temporarily, known to him.

"Judit is frisky again," said one of the doctor's attendants.

"Judit?"

"The bitch who kissed her hand to you. Better be careful, monsieur doctor."

"Oh, now, now," said Dr. Volpe.

"There is the new female patient," said the woman attendant somberly.

"Ah. Yes."

"She's in the cells."

The "cells" were the place to which newcomers or desperates were assigned. Until their especial malady had been glanced at, they were not herded out with the rest of the prisoners of the asylum.

"Then, I must interview her. Is she lucid?"

"Not very. She's young. About fourteen."

"How tragic," said Dr. Volpe, who was wishing that the cells were unoccupied. He had begun a Russian novel of vast import the night before and longed to get back to it. "What cause is known?"

They shrugged.

"She's crazy. A girl of good family. Suddenly afflicted with *melancholia* and *hysteria*." (The words he would approve of were stressed.) "Her parents were vague."

Dr. Volpe pursed his lips. This kind of mania particularly offended him. Perhaps the woman attendant knew it. Her face was like a wooden box with a nose, and twinkling eyes. She drank the perfidious gin, he knew.

"Well, shall we go along now? I'll see her."

They crossed the last of the gallery and were gone from the rooms. (None of the beings below now seemed aware of them.) They descended stairs and went through a door, and so across a yard where sometimes the mad people were pushed out for exercise. There was a stone block in the middle of the yard. It had been put there for a statue. The statue had been going to represent Madness, with snakes for hair, but in the end this had been thought too strong, and also a waste, for mostly only the mad would see it, and not understand its significance.

The doctor and his warders entered another block, went up a stairway and along other corridors. Below were rooms of treatment, containing the Swing and the Waterfall, and a sample of other apparatus. Above was a set of offices, and near these were the cells.

The wardress unlocked a door. They went in.

Beyond a lattice was a place with a bed, a sort of pallet having one pillow and one blanket. Here someone lay.

Her eyes were open, but they might have been closed. Long bright hair rayed over the pillow. She was dressed in ordinary garments of the City, for she had not yet reached the level of an inhabitant.

"I'll wake her up," said the male warder. His name was Desel. Dr. Volpe believed that he was cruel, but efficient, perhaps necessary.

Desel strolled over, and came into the shut-off portion of the cell. He stood over the bed, and then he slapped the feet of the girl with his stick.

She was still wearing shoes, which had not yet been removed. Nevertheless, the shock boiled through her, and she sat up like a jack-in-the-box. She did not cry out.

"Sleeping Beauty wakes. Doctor's here," said Desel, smiling.

The girl looked at him with utter disbelief. As if he, the warder, were entirely mad.

"Get up, you. Get up and be respectful."

And the girl got off the bed and stood, looking around her, the way a doll would if someone unwisely brought it to life.

"What is your name?" called Dr. Volpe through the lattice. "Do you know?"

"Hilde."

"Good, good. You know your name."

"What is this place?" she asked faintly. "Is it hell?"

"Oh, hell." The doctor laughed. "No, it is to be your heaven."

"I was thrown down. I was held! They struck me," said Hilde. But she seemed bewildered.

"It was for your own good. No doubt you were irrational."

"What is this place?" repeated the girl.

"A hospital. You'll soon be better."

The girl began to cry. This was like a demon coming on her.

A second demon: The warder Desel, started to chuckle with enormous amusement. And the girl, looking up at him, screamed until her throat cracked.

"Go in, comfort her," said Dr. Volpe.

"I? She's dangerous. She tears things," said the woman, Marie Tante.

"Well, then. What do you think?"

"The Waterfall," said Marie Tante. She added mildly, "That will sedate her."

Dr. Volpe grimaced. The Waterfall did not, he had long reasoned, half-kill. It softened, eased.

"She's so young."

"A savage case. Look at that hair. A tricky color. She was vicious with her own mother."

The girl with orange hair had gone on screaming, and they had been forced to shout.

Desel stood by, waiting only for the girl to rush at him. But she did not. She fell suddenly down and lay on the floor. Silence.

"There, the fit's passed."

"Better be sure," said Marie Tante.

"Prepare her," said Dr. Volpe. These people were indispensable. He must follow their advice.

They led Hilde Koster to a large white room that was somehow like a giant's bathtub turned upside down. There was another partition, this time of glass, and beyond it a terrible little black chair, the highchair of a malign child, with bars.

In this chair they put Hilde, Desel and Marie Tante, who, now the girl was to be "subdued" did not seem to fear handling her. The bars of the chair were fastened, across the throat and lap and ankles.

Hilde put out her hands, and Marie Tante slapped them back.

"What are you doing?" Hilde asked.

"Ask no questions," said Marie Tante cheerfully.

"A little wash," said Desel, and grinned.

Hilde seemed embarrassed, confused. All violence had deserted her, run away and left her at their mercy.

The two warders came out of the area with the chair and joined Doctor Volpe behind the glass.

From the ceiling of the room, above the chair, hung a black tube, large and coiled, a sort of serpent.

Dr. Volpe peered through the glass.

"Is she quite ready?"

"Of course. She can't get away."

The doctor stretched out his hand to a lever, then hesitated.

"You shall do it, Desel."

Dr. Volpe had an air of conferring a favor. And Desel was

pleased, Marie Tante almost jealous. In fact, Dr. Volpe did not like to perform the action. He would have preferred not to watch.

The warders, though, were avid, and Desel, taking hold of the lever, plunged it down.

In the ceiling the serpent suddenly snapped straight, and out of its headless mouth there rushed an avalanche of water. Its weight was unimaginable, although it had been precisely gauged. It crashed upon Hilde in the little black monster chair and she vanished. Her first shriek of terror was cut off in a frightful choking. Then all audible sound was crushed under the gush of the Waterfall.

Desel's face was now a picture of content, and Marie Tante's was pale with some sort of oblique arousal, pinched and pointing. They stared through the glass, and Dr. Volpe stared too, but with his hand up to his face, shielding his eyes.

For ten minutes the onslaught of the water raged.

"That will be enough," said Dr. Volpe.

"Surely," said Marie Tante, "a few minutes more."

"Oh, yes, then."

"To be sure," said Desel, helping him.

Dr. Volpe thought of his Russian novel. This would soon be over now.

It was over. Marie Tante pushed up the lever, and the incredible Waterfall slackened to a pulse, a flickering tail, a few harsh drops.

The girl sat still in the chair, impossibly not smashed and flushed away. Yet she was colorless, her clothes like rain, her skin like white paper. Even her vibrant hair, though darkened, seemed diluted out.

Marie Tante now managed Hilde alone. She undid the bars of the chair and dragged the drowned creature out of it. Hilde's eyes rolled, yet she was still conscious. Water ran from her mouth. Marie Tante thrust the girl along before her, holding her up by the back of her sodden dress.

Dr. Volpe was more sunny. He shook Desel by the hand before hurrying away to his sanctuary. He had done all he could.

In another cell, Marie Tante and the woman Moule stripped Hilde of her soaked clothing. When she was naked, they prodded at her, saying she was too soft. Marie Tante tweaked Hilde's nipples and asked if she had been a bad girl. "Push your finger in and see," said Moule, but neither she nor Marie Tante did this. The girl, unable to stand, lay on a pallet. They hauled her up. "We should cut her hair," said Moule. Marie Tante scraped back Hilde's wet and deadened tresses and, holding them in her fist, hacked them through with a pair of scissors. Hilde gave a faint cracked cry, the first since the treatment, but she did not seem to realize what had happened, even so. "Shorter," said Moule. "That will do," said Marie Tante. "Look at it," said Moule, "all that hair, at least a meter of it." "It can be sold," said Marie Tante, "but not for much. If it had been black, now. But some ginger cat will buy it in the slums." "Don't forget I helped you cut it," said Moule.

They dressed Hilde, then, in the uniform of her prison. A coarse seamless petticoat and over that the death-white dress of the asylum, tied at the waist with a black cord. On her legs were gartered woolen stockings, and her feet were shoved into heelless cloth shoes.

Hilde was ready now, for the ball.

She was just able to walk, though not to speak, and probably not properly to see or hear.

They conducted her from the building and out across the yard with the stone block. In the shadow away from the sunlight, Moule drew a glinting brown bottle from her pocket. She gulped some liquid down and smacked her lips, then reluctantly passed the gin to Marie Tante.

"They say the vats are all corroded," said Marie Tante. "The rats die that drink the dregs."

"And someone has poured acid in it, too," chortled Moule. "Penguin Gin takes away your pain."

It was almost autumn, and as they crossed the last stretch of yard between the black doors and window-eyed walls of the madhouse, an intimation of fall sweetness drifted from the air—the low sun, the smolder of the trees outside. But the two wardresses did not heed, and the girl was past knowing what it was.

Beyond the asylum, an apron of untended garden ran off into a wood, the trees of which were sometimes cut down. There, over the barricade of an outer wall, lay the countryside, impossible as a foreign land. Even the warders took no notice of it. They too lived in hell, going out rarely, and then in a sort of disdain.

Back inside the first building, Marie Tante and Moule bore Hilde through into the succession of white rooms, where the mad people were.

They moved her out into the middle of the floor, over which the ill-smelling straw extended, giving the space a peculiar farmyard touch. They left her there, like a landmark, and drew back, the two women, to see how the indigenous population received her.

But nothing happened. No one went near.

The mad continued at their insanity quietly, not bothering with the new mad one.

"Here, here," Moule took hold of a man who kneeled on the ground, swaying, "there's a new girl, go and give her a kiss."

The man who swayed began to cry. He curled up on the floor and Moule kicked him with her booted foot.

"Useless," said Marie Tante. "No spirit. Slugs."

One of the male warders had come in, and seeing them, walked up.

"A new lovely for you," said Marie Tante.

"None lovelier than you," said the warder. "Do you have a drink on you?"

"No," said Marie Tante. Moule twitched her pocket uneasily.

Hilde stood alone in the middle of the room. She looked down into the straw, and presently crumpled and slipped over.

"No trouble with her," said the man.

"She's been swimming in the Waterfall."

All around the white forms with cropped or shorn heads bobbed slowly at their antics, like leaves on a pool.

"They make you sick," said the man, "this filth."

They went on into another room, where there were one or two tied up who could sometimes be tormented into noise.

Hilde lay on the straw, and a roach with transparent copper wings crawled over her wrist but did not hurt her.

A woman sat on the straw by Hilde.

Although her hair had been cropped, her head shaved, a dark shadow downed over her skull, which was exquisitely shaped, so that it did not mar her beauty. She was very beautiful, a face of bones and eyes and lips, the thin body of a damask lizard having breasts. Some kind of sphinx?

As Hilde raised her fluttering lids, the woman spoke. "I'm Judit, Queen Judit. I come from a distant country, where I rule. Barges of metal with silk sails go about on my river, and palaces of marble rise. But here I am."

Hilde gazed, her sight returning, into the face of a mother, for the mother to the tiny helpless child is a goddess, infinite and gorgeous, inexorable, yet kind. And all this Judit was. Queen Judit, the mad, who had been a whore in the alleys of Paradys.

"Help me," said helpless Hilde.

"Of course," said Judit. "You mustn't be afraid. This is a great trial. We queens are born to it, and grasp its syntax. But you are only a little angel fallen into the beastliness. Don't be frightened. I'm here."

"Oh," said Hilde.

Judit held her wrist, over which the bracelet of the roach's running had gone. Judit kissed Hilde on the eyebrow.

"Now you're my handmaiden," said Judit, "all will be well."

"But," said Hilde.

"Forget the past, my dear," said Judit. "This is like death. Of course, it will end and we shall go back, in victory. But would you rather come with me to my own country? The mountains embrace the sky. Hawks feed from my hands. I've had a hundred thousand lovers, great kings and lords. Each brought me a fabulous gift, and my house is seventeen stories high."

"How do you reach the top?" asked Hilde, stirring a little, like a wounded bird.

"A flying carpet," said Judit. "How else?"

Pleased, for she had an answer to every question, and liked to display her skill, Judit laughed.

Her teeth were flawless, but for one eyetooth that had been struck from her mouth by a warder (Desel) long ago. She did not recall this. She knew she had lost the tooth in a fight, when she had defended a king who had lain with her, a long dagger in her hand. Judit's beauty had grown with her delusions of beauty, and her strength too. Never, as a starveling harlot, had she had this excellence.

"How did you come here?" asked Hilde.

"A trial. Didn't I say?"

"But why?" Hilde, only half in the world, at once revealed her sense of the truth of Judit, for how should a queen, of Sheba, Egypt, or Andromeda, be *here?*

"There was a face of bronze," said Judit, "which I killed." She was satisfied. "That is why. And how. But I'll triumph over all ruin. One passes every day to whom I blow a kiss. He doesn't know that each kiss is my power; he'll fall under the spell of it."

"Will you help me?" said Hilde, sleepily. The fortitude of Judit had lulled her.

"Poor child. You are mine now. Fear nothing."

And Judit drew Hilde into her lap and held her, stroking the crinkled apricot hair, all that was left of it.

In a hovel Judit had slain a man who had tried to mutilate her for his pleasure. And Judit had gone mad. Mad with anger and justice, to escape the foulness of her world. Now she dwelled among shining thoughts, remembering always she was a queen.

Her fingers were like honey after the horror before. Judit was fire to heal the blows of water. She smelled unclean, but not impure.

The man who had cried had also crept to her, and Judit had not thrust him off. He lay with his mouth against her skirt, asleep.

Judit sang softly of her palaces, of the lions that drank from the river, and the curtains of spun light, and the flowers of her garden, which were fed dead murderers. Her song sounded like gibberish, but this did not matter.

After a time, Hilde told Judit what had happened to her, and Judit listened carefully, her perfect head turned a little to one side. Judit wept, her tears were flames. Hilde saw this, but she was not afraid.

Twice a day, the inmates were fed. In the morning a gruel was brought, and in the evening a type of stew without meat. Both these meals were slops. Bread was served with them that had, as often as not, gone a little moldy.

The cauldrons of food were brought through the rooms on a contraption like a four-legged stretcher with wheels. Certain of the patients were recruited to dole out rations, overseen by the warders with their sticks. To every patient, rounded up and herded to the cauldron, was given a small bowl. There was no cutlery, as even a spoon might be put to dangerous use. They ate with the bread and with their fingers and mouths.

Those who would not eat were watched, and after the third day taken to a room the warders had nicknamed the Banquet Hall. Here a tube was thrust down their throats and they were force-fed on a kind of ant food or sugar water. Sometimes a patient had died from these feasts, from mere shock, or because of the carelessness of the operative, who had inserted the feeding tube into the air vent rather than the esophagus, and so flooded the lungs and drowned them. (These poor patients were always found to have choked while eating too greedily.)

Of such things Judit warned Hilde as she drew her gently to the cauldron.

While they waited their turn, a male warder came to Judit and was familiar with her, putting his hands on her buttocks. Judit laughed in his face. Her body had no scruples and no modesty, and she was, besides, a queen. But when the warder turned to Hilde, as if to extend the treatment to her, Judit came between them, smiling. "Get off, you old whore," said the warder, and backed away, menacing Judit with his stick.

In the bottom of the cauldron, under the soggy vegetables, something glittered.

"There are spikes there," said Judit.

Once a small man, a dwarf, had hidden in the tureen and so got to the kitchens, where he took a knife and attacked some of the warders. Now the spikes were in the pot to prevent another such attempt.

Hilde did not want to eat, but Judit urged her to take a little, especially the disgusting bread. The warders had not realized, it seemed, that the fungus on the bread helped keep off infections. Judit's grandmother in the alleys had taught her this, but she had forgotten, and now explained a great physician had exposed the fact to her.

After the cauldron was removed, most of the warders went off to their own dinner of meat and potatoes in another building. Only four were left on duty, two playing cards in a central room and two patrolling.

"What is it they drink?" asked Hilde.

"A venom," said Judit. "I, too, have tasted it. Unlike the wines of my own country."

Judit took Hilde by the hand through the many large mirror-like white rooms, on which now late afternoon was gathering from the high barred windows that showed nothing but the closing sky.

Hilde stared at the mad people in still wonder. She was so shocked, so wrecked, that now her capacity for fear was virtually gone. She had entered a translucent state, as human things sometimes do when they lose their personalities. Everything that had happened to her seemed to have happened to another. All the world was alien and illogical and this piece of it no more so than the rest. She wanted nothing, except perhaps eventually to sleep. She was glad of Judit's company and seemed to have known her countless years.

Several of the mad acknowledged Judit, and some even bowed or curtseyed to her. But others were too busy. One was an insect and waited in her web for flies and another was talking to spirits or invisible people. One crawled in a circle around and around.

In perhaps the third room a man had been tied to the wall by a thong about his throat. He wept ceaselessly and his neck was raw from trying to pull free. Judit went to him and wiped up his tears with her long hair, which no more existed. A second man was in a mad-shirt, and he rolled along the floor, biting at the straw and making strange hoarse barks. The warders had beaten his legs on their patrol.

In a fifth room there was an arrangement of old broken furniture that rose in a hill higher than the gallery that ran along the wall. The hill was some distance from this, and from all the windows. At its top sat a skinny man, looking out like a gull from a roof.

"There's Maque," said Judit.

She began to climb the structure, her firm legs, bare of stockings, revealed up to the white knees. Hilde did not follow, for though she was no longer able to be afraid, some physical nervousness remained. But then Judit turned and beckoned her, and Hilde did go up the stair of furniture, which was actually quite solid, its uneven places simple to avoid.

Aloft, on a table, sat Maque, and here they joined him.

The glory of the height was its view through a window. Although about six meters away, unreachable, it showed sections of burning sky and the crowns of burning trees. The sun was setting there, as if it had never before done so, and meant to make the world pay attention.

They stared at it, their faces lit like potter's clay.

Maque was extraordinarily thin, and in his ears were tears from which the rings had been torn years ago, on his arrival at the asylum. Elsewhere now, in the City, his ill-omened earrings were worn; they had got free.

"I've sailed the sea," said Maque presently. "I had a pet monkey that died of old age when he was twenty-three. I've seen Eastern ports where women dance naked but their faces are veiled in black. I've smoked hemp under the shelter of an elephant and eaten powdered pearl for the pox, which cured me." His conversation, or rather monologue, was somewhat like Judit's. He said, "Ten men gone overboard in a tempest. We came to an island. There were unicorns there, but our mate said they were only a kind of goat. A virgin may capture a unicorn."

The sun went under the window, and the bars stood on thick burnished sky. Shadows spread among them. Below the hill of furniture some of the mad people made small sounds.

"This child can never," said Judit, "capture a unicorn. She's been violated."

Hilde was not shamed. She nodded, distantly.

"Yes," she said, as of another, "that happened to me."

"She went to him in love," said Judit.

"Look," said Maque. And he got up on one knee and pulled from under his right thigh a brown glass bottle. "Empty, of course," he said, "Thrown away near the latrine."

"A gin bottle," said Judit. She took it and gave it to Hilde. Hilde had never seen such a thing. On the label was a great black and white bird with a flush of amber next to its head. Behind was whiteness.

"I never saw a land such as that," said Maque the sailor. "A cold country with mountains of snow. But I heard of them. The freeze forms vast cliffs of ice that float into the sea, and when they meet they clash like glass. These birds live there. Penguins, they're called. They can't fly, but stalk about like kings."

"Are they little birds?" asked Hilde childishly, for this was her protection now, between Judit and Maque.

"Some, maybe," said Maque. He pointed at the bottle. "But not this fellow. Look at him. He could be seven feet high. And his beak's a knife."

Below the furniture, many of the inmates had gathered close, and looked up at Maque. Maque rose, and taking back the bottle, he raised it. One last spark of sunlight came in at its top and shot a ray from sky to ground.

"And they said," said Maque, "the snow is warm, there. So warm you can lie down and sleep in it like a feather bed. And flowers grow when the sun shines on the ice. The sun never sets but hangs low, so it's always dawn or sunset. That is Penguin Land."

"I'd do without my country, to see that," said Judit.

"But," said Hilde, some dim rationality struggling deep within her. Yet she had no use for it anymore, and abruptly let it go. "You could play at snowballs in Penguin Land," she said, "and never burn your hands on the snow."

"You would never be hungry or thirsty," said Judit. "Fruit and sweets grow on the trees and wine runs down the ice."

The light ray melted from the bottle and went out.

The room was very dark.

And through the doorway stamped three wardresses, jingling their keys.

"Get down, you bitches," shouted one at Judit and Hilde.

"What is it now?" asked Hilde.

"Now they lock us into our dormitories," said Judit. She smiled. "After dark, we're sinful, so they must separate the women from the men."

When they were near the bottom of the furniture, Marie Tante seized Hilde and pulled her off, bruising her. "Not quiet yet? Perhaps you'll need more subduing."

The women were marched away by women, and men came in a crowd, toting their sticks, to get charge of the male inmates.

Darkness was full now in the asylum. One of the female warders carried a lamp, and the outer corridors had been sparsely lighted.

They passed up a stair, and a door was unlocked. Into the women's dormitory they went.

The beds lay along the floor. They were straw pallets covered by thin blankets and having each a soiled and impoverished pillow. Every place was foul, and a worse smell came from buckets of necessity set at intervals and doubtless not frequently emptied. On a wall facing the beds and buckets was a wooden cross. This was ignored by one and all.

The women went where they wished, or where they felt they must, and sat or lay down.

Marie Tante drove Hilde the length of the room to a pallet apparently unclaimed.

"Here, my lady. Your couch."

Hilde got onto the bed and crouched there. After all, fear remained of this woman who seemed grown to a preposterous size. (Why not then a giant penguin?)

"You'll have lice by tomorrow," said Marie Tante. "What a stink in here. We must hose these beasts down."

"That one's been wetted already," said Moule.

The third wardress giggled and swung up her lamp, to make the room career and spin. The madwomen gazed at this phenomenon silently.

The wardresses left them, locking the door.

The room was black, and in the black the women rustled and whispered. One moaned over and over.

Hilde sat in dull dismay, for Judit was far off. The awful smell oppressed her, but then she sensed a current of cleaner air. Some tiny panes of glass were missing from the window above, and now a night breeze blew. It would be cold in winter, not warm as the snows of the Penguin Land.

An hour later, the moon entered the window. And so the room.

On the space of black floor below the powerless crucifix, the milk-white squares of the barred window appeared.

One by one, two by two, the madwomen left their verminous beds and came down to the pool of light.

Here they moonbathed. Some washed in the moonlight, rubbing their arms and faces, or lifting up the whiteness between their legs. Others lay down and swam among the squares. The woman who moaned tried to prize the shadow bars away and could not, and crept back, made dumb, to her bed.

Judit stood up in the center of the reflection, her face raised into the light, which tinted her like snow.

But the moon passed over, and total darkness returned. And in this dark, the door was unlocked, not brashly now, but with stealth.

The male warder who had come after the moon sought Judit the whore among the women, and mounted her. They heard her say, in a voice of velvet, "What, are you here again, oh my king? What an honor." And then they heard the man strike her. It was Tiraud, who would drink to capacity and then seek out the queen of harlots. Soon finished. He called her filthy names and exclaimed now over the fetor of the dormitory.

At the door another chuckled. And away along the corridors there started a wild whooping and screaming.

Hilde sprang up, and Judit was by her, for even so soon she knew Judit's touch.

"They do things to the men they don't dare try with us."

The awful crying went on, and the women huddled off their beds. They congregated around Judit, as they had gone to the moon pool. Her skirt was sticky, but she was yet a queen.

When the cries stopped, there came instead a crazy clatter in the air, and at the door the jailors laughed raucously.

Something flew against Hilde, leather and fur, and she shrieked in turn. No, fear was not all gone.

All about, the women gurned in panic. Into the dark it was not possible truly to see, only to hear, as they burrowed and howled and ran at the walls. The other thing also did that, swooping from side to side.

Judit had stood up again, and she raised her arm, and mysteriously she was half visible as if faintly luminous from within.

So, by Judit's shine, Hilde saw the bat the warders had let go in the room. It whirled overhead and dipped suddenly down, settling on Judit's fingers as the hawks did in her dream country.

A demon with a fairy face, the bat folded its wings.

Judit carried it to the wall, and put it there, and the bat detached itself and crawled upward, into the high embrasure of the window. Here it found a broken pane and slipped through.

"Very good, very good," said the men at the door. "She's clever, is Judit."

As they locked the door behind them, the cries began again across the building. Dr. Volpe, two blocks away in brandy sleep, would not hear them. And if he did? Lunatics were noisy.

Hilde lay back. She pushed the crying from her and thought of the bat in the cool sky, and of the warm snow.

The mandarin leaves fell slowly and sparingly from the trees on the lawn and in the wood. Gray geese passed over.

An extravagant hothouse built for Dr. Volpe on the lawn outside the asylum blocks began to burgeon with harvest, black grapes on a vine, apricots, toasted roses.

The mad people were never allowed as far as the lawn, and never beheld it from the windows.

There had been plans for a summerhouse too, maybe a small lake. But these things had never come to be.

One evening an agent brought Dr. Volpe a wonderful new prisoner, a dead butterfly with huge bright wings.

Hilde did not cause any trouble, and Marie Tante had lost interest in her. One of the men had taken to shrieking, and was conducted to the Swing, where, in a sort of box, they rotated and reeled him until he vomited and swooned. Thereafter he sat quietly in his mad-shirt on the straw.

Hilde came to recognize her fellows, though usually not by any name.

Judit showed her the poet Citalbo, who had gone insane from reading drama and writing verses. Citalbo walked solemnly from room to room, sometimes scribbling on small pieces of paper that the warders allowed him, as Dr. Volpe had decreed. The warders often stole the papers, however. This did not appear to matter. What Citalbo wrote now was nonsense, frequently illegible. He never seemed to miss his former works, or anything that was stolen, as if, once he had put down an idea, God had it in safekeeping.

During the days of straw, Judit occasionally told stories, histories perhaps, of her queendom. At night also, now and then, for they would not always sleep at night in the dormitory, as by day sometimes they would. Maque sat upon his hill. They did not speak or approach him again. The brown bottle had vanished—confiscated? No one mentioned the Penguin Land.

One morning the warders beat a man in front of all the others. He had been running to and fro and the warders caught him suddenly and threw him down, kicking him with their boots and striking him with their sticks. The noise rose in the madhouse then like a storm in a cage of parakeets. The screams and cries of the mad did not quite overcome the oaths and grunts of the male warders or the shrill giggles of the three wardresses who were present.

The beaten man was left lying, and somehow recovered, or at least did not die.

When Dr. Volpe went along the galleries at noon, the lunatics were generally very still. Some tried to hold their breath. Most did not know who Dr. Volpe was, only that he appeared rather like a clockwork toy, at a certain time, also that he presided over the worst tortures.

There were other incidents: The shaving of a woman's head, the force-feeding of another, a drunken song the warders indulged in without warning. The afternoon that something was added to the slops which gave the inmates pains in their bellies, and how Judit raved about the healing tinctures of her land, and between calmly told Hilde this had occurred before, and would soon pass. By night, intermittently, Tiraud, or others, came into the women's dormitory, to use Judit's body. She did not resist these rapes. Once or twice some other woman was violated as well or instead. In particular darknesses, outcry resounded from the men's cloister.

The moon came often to the women's barred window, at different hours, and laid its light along the floor. The women did not always go down to it. And one night Hilde stood alone in the midst of the pool, staring up at the window, its source, above. She had lost all comprehension of the place she was in, she did not look for rescue, if she ever had. The image of Johanos Martin had long

since withered from her, as had her night game, the sweet mastur-
bation of her innocence. In a manner, the asylum had done what it
had promised, driving out the devils that had brought her here, but
only to replace them with others.

Judit, who had been preyed on three times that night, lay sleeping. Hilde went to her and curled up by Judit's feet. It was cold.
Hilde thought of the Penguin Land.

Dr. Volpe dusted the leaves of a palm, and standing back, surveyed
its effect against the autumnal window. He could see down toward
the hothouse, and the chestnuts and oaks of the wood. This was a
pleasing view and might be that of any country retreat.

A knock on the outer door alerted him and he pulled a child's
sulky face.

His housekeeper entered.

"The gentleman from the theater, Dr. Volpe."

Dr. Volpe had forgotten.

His face of distaste became harder and more adult.

"Very well, you may send him in."

Dr. Volpe paused beside the case with the new butterfly in it. He
would linger just long enough to show the visitor what was important, and proper.

But the visitor, the blustering gentleman from the Goddess of
Tragedy, launched at once into a speech, not waiting to be asked.

"We are delighted that you'll do as we desired, Dr. Volpe. This
will render my actors a great service. And in the course of art—"

"It is a disgrace," said Volpe, his face swollen now. "To bring
sightseers here. As if into a zoological garden. These people are my
patients."

"Quite, quite." The visitor brushed Volpe's words and stance
aside. "But as you're aware, the minister has overridden your objection. I'm sure you don't set yourself above him, doctor."

Volpe was ruffled. He was at the mercy of upperlings and under-
lings.

"If he thinks so. I'm not certain the minister was correctly informed."

"Oh, *quite* correctly."

"To have your troupe here, staring at these poor deranged
souls."

"What harm can it do?" said the agent from the theater. "And so
much good. The lunatics won't notice, I expect. And for my actors,

an invaluable help in the preparation of the mad scene for our next production."

"I dissociate myself from the proceeding," said Dr. Volpe.

"Of course. I suppose your warders are capable of overseeing the affair."

Dr. Volpe imagined his warders poking the mad people with sticks, forcing them to caper and wail to interest the actors. But they would do it, too, if he was present, and then there would be the shame of it. The warders would expect to receive large tips.

He did not offer the agent refreshment, and when he was gone, Dr. Volpe walked among his birds' eggs, caressing their smoothness (each a tiny coffin, but he did not consider that).

Soon after dawn, the dormitory was unlocked and the women were hustled out again, down to the common rooms. Today it was not the same.

Marie Tante, and the wardress Bettile, stood at the doorway. They took hold of Judit at once. "This one," they said, "she's much admired."

The other women, thinking Judit had been singled out for some therapy (punishment), shied away, all but Hilde.

Marie Tante reached and gripped Hilde's arm.

"This is a pretty one. Look how quickly her hair's grown back. You'll have to be shorn again, my lady."

Hilde hung speechless in her grasp. But now Bettile grabbed two other girls from among the women.

"These will do. For the *pretty* ones."

"Hah! They'll pass."

The four chosen women and the one other Bettile hauled out, who whimpered and then sobbed, they led away along the corridor to a big tiled area.

Hilde felt again the invasion of terror. This was like the white room in which she had been tortured. She could recall very little of it, but she had thought that she died there, and came back very changed.

"Don't be afraid," Judit said sternly.

The warders told them to take off their garments. Judit removed hers almost blithely. Despite her captivity, she was still very beautiful, and though her breasts were not those of a girl, they were full as two blown roses.

Marie Tante jeered at Judit: "Not bad for an old whore."

But Judit laughed, and Marie Tante turned her attention to the other women.

These were malformed and undernourished, or oddly fatty, their bodies blemished by moles and pimples, inner subsidences of the flesh.

Hilde was ashamed to bare herself, and Bettile charged at her and ripped the clothes off her body.

"Too proud, eh? What have you got to be proud of, ugly little runt?"

When all the women were naked, hoses were turned on them. The water was icy cold but not extremely violent. Some fell down. Hilde dropped to her knees. Yet, since the water only occasionally covered her head, it did not completely recall the former horror. Almost, she missed the landmark of it.

When the sluicing was over, rough sheets were flung to the women, and those that could dried themselves. Two could not, and these Marie Tante saw to with harsh buffeting swipes.

They were given new tunics, and white sashes, bundled into them.

The warders mocked the women. "Just need a spot of powder." "Some flowers for the hair."

They were removed next to a narrow chamber, and awarded some of the breakfast gruel. One of the women spilled the fluid on her new robe, and Bettile cuffed her. "Dirty sow. Do you think you'll get another washing? You'll have to go as you are."

"What will they do to us?" Hilde whispered.

Judit said, "Sometimes ladies and gentlemen pay to look at us."

Hilde relapsed in apathy, but when they were presently taken out again, she stayed close to Judit.

The women were then put into a long room that faced onto the yard with the stone block, and here they were left some hours, with Bettile to watch them, but Bettile drank her gin, set out her cards, and fell asleep.

Two of the women sat down on the floor, where one wept until the snores of Bettile, perhaps taken for a reprimand and threat, silenced her. Judit and Hilde and the fifth woman went each to one of the three windows that looked onto the courtyard. There they stood in a row.

Outside it was a fine, still fall day, the misty sunshine soft as gauze. At the center of the court, about the stone, was a curious structure, in fact a makeshift stage Tiraud and some of the warders had put up. It was only a foot or so high, and composed of trestles, over which some sheeting had been draped.

On the far side of the court was something even more incongruous. An awning had been erected and armchairs put under it. And there was a table with a white cloth on which now began to be laid plates of food under napkins, dishes of fruit from the hothouse, coppery pomegranates, oranges and apricots, and black grapes. Into buckets went slabs of ice. Judit said, "That will be for the champagne. Someone has looked after them. Perhaps they're princes," and she spat abruptly on the floor.

"Ice from Penguin Land," said Hilde, to please her.

"No," said Judit, "the ice from there would never melt. The ice there is warm."

And Hilde was humbled by her mistake. She put her hand on the warm glass of the window.

Her back had begun to ache from standing immobile so long. But the draw of the courtyard, a view it was possible to gaze at, kept her there. Besides, she waited nervously to see who had come. She had forgotten people—she and the inmates of the asylum were not people—and so in turn human things from the outer world had become like wild beasts. What would they do, or require? Would they sniff and paw, or rend? She dreaded that she would have to show herself to them, but not because of the state to which she had been reduced, only because they were so alien.

Now she said, to please Judit again, for Judit was real, "What is the name of the Penguin Land?"

"Maque will know," said Judit. She added, "They'll display Maque. He's a model patient, controlled and articulate. And Citalbo, perhaps. Because he speaks poetry."

There were sounds below. One of the black doors opened, and Desel came forth. He was taking on the role of guide that Dr. Volpe might have assumed, and Desel had dressed up in suit of clothes and a high collar. He looked fearsome and terrible, like some species of poisonous insect that has adopted the gaudy wings of something it has recently killed. The fifth woman at the window groaned, and going sadly away, sat down on the floor with the other two.

Out of the doorway after Desel came the beasts who were people, the beasts who had come to visit the zoo.

There were a couple of ladies in flowered dresses, with hats and parasols, and a group of men, two rather tall, each smartly dressed.

Hilde drew back from the window.

Hilde pointed.

Her fingertip touched the glass. Now it was cold.

And Bettile awoke.

"Oh, are the bastards here? I expect Desel will give you bitches autumn crocuses to hand to those fine, jumped-up ladies, to show how well we've trained you."

Judit turned her shaven head on her white neck, like a snake, looking at Hilde, then turned back and looked down again into the yard.

Hilde moved even farther back, her arm still outstretched, as if frozen.

"What's up?" said Bettile. She rose, taking as she did so a swig of gin.

"Johanos Martin," said Hilde. Her face suffused with an appalling embarrassment.

"Oh, the great Martin," said Bettile. "Fancy, you know the name. When were you at the theater?" She elbowed Hilde's shrinking body aside and peered out. "Well, so that's the bugger. The tallest one, I've heard he's tall."

The gray eyes of Johanos Martin passed smoothly over the windows, seeing nothing. He was accustomed to looking up, from a stage, blind to those who hung above.

Hilde ran into a corner and curled herself together. Bettile swung round and marched toward her.

"Get up, slut. Get up, I say."

She pulled Hilde to her feet and Hilde screamed. She forgot who Bettile was, and fought with her, and Bettile felled Hilde with a single blow.

In the gilded day, ten lunatics were let out on the platform.

In the awning shade, drinking freely the wine their theater had sent them, picking at segments of chicken and orange, the actors watched. It made a change for them, someone else putting on a show. They did not completely like it, you could see. And they stared acutely to tell how much better they would be able to do it, to act the insane.

Desel did not have his stick now but a cheap florid cane he had bought in the City. With this he poked at the madmen, making them whine or snort or shy. Sometimes they did not respond at all.

Some crawled, others walked in a curious apelike way. The more interesting specimens were directed to the front of the trestles.

The ladies made disapproving sounds over the one who drooled from his permanently grinning, tooth-barricaded mouth. His smile was a rictus that never went away, his lips dark and his teeth long and sallow. His eyes were thick with pain he no longer considered.

"The man who grins," said Desel, as if he had invented all ten lunatics, carefully, in a laboratory. "He never speaks, and forces food between his fangs only when we make him. His grin goes on while he sleeps. What a happy sight to keep before you. Imagine this one in your sitting room." He was a touch impertinent, Desel, for now he was dressed up as gentleman, and they were only actors.

After the grinning man, a man came who seemed to think he was a dog. He moved on all fours, panting, and now and then he licked his own hands.

And after this one came the one on a tether, led by Tiraud. When Tiraud jabbed the tethered man with his stick, the madman began to sing in a shrill voice songs that were just recognizable as old ballads of love.

Presently they drove forward the man who was surrounded by a swarm of invisible wasps, at which he beat wildly. Tiraud struck this man's ankle, and the man fell upon it, biting and snapping at his own flesh, trying to pull something not there away from him.

Others were left standing in the background, where they drooped or padded about in small circles.

After these first men, some women were brought, shaven-headed and in matted gowns. The wardresses, notably Marie Tante, shouted at them, and the women moved about with a hobbled gait, like lost cows that do not understand but know the smiting of sticks.

Desel stepped into the middle of the stage. He commenced giving a lecture on the types and attributes of madness. He sensed the actors had become bored and saw that they grew restless. He did not like them. Nobodies risen to fame by dint of luck, and whoring. Look at the actresses—strumpets. And the men, doubtless lax of morals, perhaps given to unnatural vices.

The tallest man, the one called Martin, looked at Desel with icy and expressionless eyes. These eyes flustered Desel. He wished for a moment Martin had been in his power.

But it was the other man, Roche, who called out, "Ah, come on, come on."

Desel concluded his address hurriedly. Turning, he struck one of his charges so the man squeaked and leapt over the stage, making the trestles creak ominously.

The crowd of male and female lunatics was herded aside, and some, the most troublesome, were removed from the court. (A couple had soiled themselves from fear or need.)

Now the women came who were supposed attractive, and fairly docile. Desel had thought the ginger girl, Hilde, would be among them, but she was missing.

Bettile led the women forward.

"Curtsey to the gentlemen and ladies," said Bettile, and swung her rod at the backs of legs. Two women curtsied, and one tumbled to her knees. Judit stood. "This one won't," said Bettile. "Tell the people why you won't."

Judit glanced at Bettile, then she gazed at Roche. Her dark eyes passed through him, and Judit murmured, audible and sorrowfully, "A queen does not obeise herself."

Roche stood up and doffed his hat. He bowed.

His eyes were not at all full of mockery. He said, "I believe she is."

But Judit only smiled forgivingly, and raised her eyes to the sky above the buildings.

Soon three or four more men were brought to be shown off. Among them was Maque.

"This man was a sailor," said Tiraud. "It was the sea sent him crazy. Now he invents lands that don't exist."

"All lands exist," said Maque.

"How true," said Roche. "In the world and out of it."

Roche was drunk perhaps. Most of the champagne bottles were empty. The actresses were flushed. Even Martin had a slight trace of color in his face.

"Tell the gentlemen about your travels, Maque," said Tiraud.

Maque said, "My last voyage was to this place. Here they tore the metal rings out of my ears. I was locked in a room no bigger than a hutch, and later in an upright box. I could not move my hands. I was fed on rotted bread and stale water."

"He attacked a warder," Desel explained carefully.

Tiraud said grimly, "Speak of your sea trips, sailor."

Maque closed one eye. "I forget."

"The Swing for you," whispered Tiraud in Maque's mutilated ear.

Maque said, "I saw a land once, covered with snow. And on the trees grew bottles of gin."

Tiraud hit Maque across the spine.

Maque did not turn. He stared away, as Judit had done.

All the champagne was gone; the actors had become instead the receptacles.

And the warders were full of spirits.

They brought Citalbo, the poet who had gone mad.

He stood on the stage, and spoke to Johanos Martin in a sonorous voice of leaden silver.

"Why," said Roche, startled, "he's saying your lines from the play —the Roman—"

"He speaks very well," said Martin, and gazed up the short distance at Citalbo.

"Empires shall go down like suns," Citalbo said. "And ships beach in the bays as locusts do, on the firm corn."

He inclined his head, and waited courteously.

Johanos Martin laughed. He got up, and said, ringingly and perfectly, "So it was, and so it shall be always," and paused like a coquette.

And Citalbo went on: "Until the earth is a dry husk and the sky falls, and in never any house—"

"A girl sits," Martin said, "to braid her hair. Or a warrior stands—"

"To buckle on the brass of war. But then," Citalbo said, "we shall be dust, and thus—"

"Who cares for those that do not think of us?" Martin finished.

Roche applauded. The other actors and actresses were caught up, and put their gloved and bead-garlanded paws together.

"Monsieur," said Martin, for Citalbo had dared to speak his lines with great beauty and skill, "as I am, you are: an actor."

"Then you, sir," replied Citalbo, softly, carryingly, "must be as I am. Mad."

Martin's face closed. His eyes were steel. He drained his glass, and turned away as Maque and the others had not been able to.

"Let's leave. We've seen enough."

"Oh," said one of the actresses, with whom once Martin had made unsatisfactory love, "his lordship is suddenly squeamish."

"Not at all. I consider you. The sun can be harsh on the complexion at your age, Susine."

* * *

Dismayed, Dr. Volpe had stepped about his room. His books gleamed and he read their titles, remembering *I have this, and this.* He examined eggs and ornaments (*and this*). Across the blocks of the asylum things went on, but he might pretend they did not. This was his apartment, his country retreat. The palm in the window, the autumn woods.

He went to the case where the new butterfly was displayed, and stopped—in revulsion, distress.

The pinned specimen, which had been like flame and night, was crumbling. Its wings were showering off in soot and embers. Its body had twisted as if tortured, into a corkscrew.

When they brought Hilde from the tiny box where they had locked her, the "coffin," her head was shaven like a bronze ball. She was shut now into a straitjacket, a mad-shirt, her arms secured across her body. One of her shoes had been subtracted.

They put her in the straw. She could barely move.

The women came.

As animals softly nose at each other in the winter fields, just so they approached, not actually touching, but mute, reserved, at one. They knew her. She was themselves.

And then Judit was there, and sat by Hilde.

Judit spoke of the land of snow, where the lovely fruit grew and the dawn-and-sunset sun poured out its jasper radiance. Birds sang and far off the sea glistened, waters that were not cold and into which the wine streams cascaded.

Hilde listened.

When Judit ceased, she said, "Judit, I'm dying."

"No, poor child. You must simply endure."

"But I am. You see, my blood's turned to water."

Judit stroked Hilde's face. "Why do you think so?"

"Because my time hasn't come. Not for weeks."

"Your time? Oh. The female cycle . . . Once, I too." Judit frowned. "My womb's burned out. Yours also? Be thankful. They shame us here, when we bleed."

Hilde bowed her head. "Then this is good?"

"Oh, yes," said Judit strongly. "Be glad, dear."

NINE

Paradise

Love that moves the sun and the other stars.

Dante Alighieri

Months had passed, but Paradise had no seasons, as it had no sun, no moon.

They had killed with cords, but then came poisons. This often called for a particularly intimate attack—besides, they tried to find new types of bane. It taxed their ingenuity, and this time Felion and Smara put off the task. They did not poison anyone. They told each other, when they met, of their oppression at shirking the labor. Both had come close to it. Smara had even lured a man to her apartment, meaning to put some of the acid from the clockwork cat's leaking panel into a glass of wine. But then she had not done it. The man had left resentfully; obviously he had expected something. "He may only have anticipated sex," Felion told her.

They did not talk about the labyrinth, or the City beyond.

The mystery was like an ache that never went away.

Smara dreamed that she was moving through a pale warm building. An elderly woman in white was hurrying down a corridor, and when she passed Smara, the woman said, "Go away, Lucie. Go to your nurse."

There was a long room that gave on a flagged patio, and here some men sat at ease, drinking tea. They did not seem to see Smara, who prowled about them, half wondering if she might drop poison in their cups. One man smoked a pipe and another toyed with an eye glass. They were elegant, and one very handsome, with longish silken hair. Smara took a fruit or vegetable from a bowl on a table. She threw it past them, out onto the lawn. There it rolled like an orange snowball, away and away, until it hit a low fence in the distance.

Smara did not tell Felion about this dream, in which there had been clarity, daylight, and no mist.

Felion did not dream about the other City, or its environs.

They walked the broad fogbound boulevards, that sometimes echoed at their voices or rang with unknown laughter.

One afternoon, they came, seemingly by chance, to the foot of the hundred steps.

They stood for some time, as if awaiting another person.

Then, in fits and starts, frequently stopping to stare away across the blank of Paradise (the cathedral tower was invisible today), they climbed the steps.

On the Bird Terrace they did not pause. Felion opened the door with the chant of numbers. They went into the house, through, and down.

In the basement a small machine had woken and was bustling about, moving little metal boxes, cogs, and bunches of wire from one place to another, apparently without logic.

As they walked along the track, it skittered after them, then veered away, twittering angrily.

"It believes we're intruders," he said.

"Are we?"

"Yes, but we were meant to be."

Then the ice wall was ahead of them.

Felion picked up the torch he had left lying, and lit it.

"We can run through," he said. "Keep hold of my hand or we may be separated again."

"I'm not afraid," she said. "And that seems wrong."

"They've done something to the door of the artist's house," he said. "That may make it difficult to leave the premises. We must break through *outside* the house. You must *will* that, too."

"I don't know how."

"Demand it then, aloud, of the labyrinth. How else did you get in and out before?"

"It seemed . . . easy," she said.

"It is easy. Yes," he added, "of course, it must all be wrong. The heat of the torch will finally spoil the ice—what then? We have to decide, Smara, where we want to be."

In the labyrinth they did not run, but walked briskly, she striding and he slightly checking his pace, to stay in step with each other.

A glowing thing bloomed in the wall.

"Look!" she said.

He saw it too, presumably the same vision. A child watching a tiger in a cage. It was a horrible child, sneering at the incredible and flawless animal, which, if the bars had not been there, would have destroyed the child fastidiously and at once.

Then the image dispersed.

They had come suddenly into the oval heart of the labyrinth.

On the floor was a fruit, an orange fruit.

Felion let go of Smara's hand, bent down, and picked the fruit up. But Smara was gazing at the bird-headed thing that had risen above out of the ice. If anything it was now more clear, more like the statues on her uncle's terrace.

Felion tossed the orange fruit up at the ice statue. The fruit struck it a weightless blow and sailed on, and over into nothing, whence, surely, it had come.

"I'm not afraid of that now, either," said Smara. "It's only a shape."

Felion took her by her hand again quickly.

"Let's go on."

A sound rose, the oceanic breathing roar of the labyrinth.

Smara moved reluctantly. "I thought it would crumble a little, when I said it didn't frighten me."

Beyond the heart, keeping to the left, they strode forward.

"Remember," he said, "the *outside* of the woman's house. The street there."

"Are you still holding my hand?" she asked.

Felion hesitated, and as he did so, the torch flickered as if a wind rushed through the maze. And Smara slid away from him.

It was as though she were moved away on runners. She did not seem to notice. When he called out in alarm, she only nodded. *"Outside* the house," she repeated.

And then she was furled aside into the ice wall.

Perhaps Felion had been pulled aside in this way as he followed his uncle, or the man who resembled his uncle, those months before when he had come back here alone.

Felion was appalled nevertheless. He tried to approach the wall, but it was solid, ungiving, and Smara had gone.

He had no choice, it seemed to him, but to proceed to the labyrinth's extremity. Maybe, anyway, he would find her there.

When he reached the end of the tunnels, the torch was fluttering sickly. Ahead, in the opening, lay a cloudy void.

Felion spoke aloud to it, telling it harshly what he expected it to become, the street outside the artist's house. But even when he walked right up to it, the exit from the labyrinth showed nothing but formless clouds, save far away, he seemed to glimpse a shape like a mountain.

"But it's easy," he said. He dropped the torch by the exit point, and plunged his hand and arm out into the cloudy aberration.

Perhaps the tiger's cage was there, and his hand had gone in through the bars.

Felion drew his arm back. It was whole.

Then he shut his eyes, lowered his blond head, and jumped through the gap straight into the cloud.

Smara stood on the golden bank of a malt-dark river. She was not distressed. She had not been so before, when she had lost Felion and arrived in another world. Not to be distressed was possibly distressing.

And this was not the other City. Assuredly not.

The air had an exceptional brightness and lucidity. Distant mountains embraced the sky.

Below, on the honey strand, tigers and lions were feeding on something among the onyx boulders.

Above, a city did line the bank. High, white, pillared buildings, glistening with metal. Huge trees which might have been palms, but their fronds curved to the ground.

Around Smara was a garden, and everywhere in it girls in white were watering the flowers. Probably Smara had not been noticed for this reason, for in her hand was a bronze dipper filled by water. Smara went quietly up the slope of the turf and came out on a walk. On the horizon was a marble palace of extreme tallness. Nearby, a queen or empress was seated under a white sunshade. She was beautiful, more beautiful even than Smara's mother. Around her throat was a rope made of twenty or so chains of enormous pearls. Her black hair fell from a starry coronet to her feet.

A man sat at her feet.

He was tanned almost to leather, and in his ears winked diamonds. He was telling the beautiful queen boldly about a voyage he had made in a timber ship. He showed her on a map that was stretched over the grass.

"But she ran aground, Majesty. We lost the strange fruit and the priceless glass vessels. I was there ten days, with my men, before the king of the land heard what had befallen us and sent his chariots to our assistance."

"I have never known luck like yours," said the queen. "Maque, you know you're worth more to me than any cargo. But who," she added, "is that girl, listening?"

"Your favorite handmaiden, surely."

"No, she has hair like ginger spice. This one has hair like cream. Who are you, young girl?"

"Smara," Smara said, and she bowed. But then the dipper spilled all over her skirt.

"She's in search of some other country," said the queen. "Be careful," she added, "not all of them are good."

"Madame," said the sailor, who had been called Maque, "in a way, it's true of us all—that we search for other countries. Of the mind, the heart, and the soul. And sometimes even we search for hell on earth."

The queen smiled. She laid her hand on his arm. "Where are you going?" the queen asked Smara.

"To Felion, my brother."

"Do you love him?" asked the queen.

"Yes."

"Love can do anything," said the queen.

Smara turned, and a cloud was there behind her. She dropped the dipper on the grass, and then—

And then it seemed she was her mother, falling, falling from the whirling tower, into the stony mist.

The sun was beginning to set, and for a while he forgot even his sister.

Felion was high up, above the City, the wonderful City that had not been corrupted by mist. He could see all of it. The scales of its million roofs, like plates of a crocodile's back, its towers and domes, and far off the loops of its river, tiger's-eye, catching the rays of the extraordinary sun.

But then he wanted her to see this, this fabulous City, beautiful beyond any dream or wish. Oh, he wanted Smara to be here with him. He wanted to live with her, here.

A flight of pigeons passed over the disk of the sun.

Tears streamed down Felion's face, and dried. He had never before, not once, known such joy.

And then Smara came walking toward him, out of a brick wall just down the street, which was not the street outside the artist's house. She looked about shyly, but when she saw him, her face lit with more than the glory of the sun.

He took her hand again, and not speaking they stood together on the height, and watched day move down below the curve of the earth.

Every architecture rose black against its shining. And then the disk was drawn away, and a wonderful softness closed the air, and a magical nocturne of dark, and stars burned up as if nowhere, not in a thousand worlds, had there ever been stars before, or eyes to see them.

"Smara—where did you go?"

"A garden. Not here."

"And I came out miles from that house. Who cares? What does she matter, our mad uncle's artist?"

Hand in hand, they walked the streets as the night filled them. Lamps lit on poles. A breeze blew, sweet with the smell of blossoms from a spring that maybe had not yet begun.

Higher up, they reached the cathedral. The great door was carved with saints and devils, and stood open. An owl flew over their heads.

They entered, and the church was like the stomach of a cliff, it went up for miles. Some service (they had heard or read of such things) must have taken place, for hundreds of candles had been left alight. In the aisle, paper flowers had been scattered.

Felion and Smara separated and went about the body of the cathedral, where no one else was.

Above the altar, a book lay spread on a stand, but when she approached it, Smara could not read the prayer.

Felion, however, found another book in an alcove over a granite tomb. And somehow he read this: *"And the names of the three, who are jointly this demon, are OBLATIC, SAMOHT, and TOLEHCIM."* Which for some reason made him laugh. And after that the words blurred over and became nonsense, he could not make any phrases out of them.

He and she kneeled under the altar.

"What shall we pray for?" he whispered.

"What is 'pray'?"

He could not answer. He said, "I love you. I always have. If we stay here, we can be lovers."

She turned to him with a look of wonder and happiness. "Could we? Oh Felion, how I'd like that."

They got to their feet and left the cathedral.

Outside, the night was as black as ink now, and the stars had paled before the street lamps, but the big white moon was up, horned, asking only a sky to find its way.

"Where shall we go?" she asked.

"We can go where we like," he said.

So they walked the City.

Paradis has been many things, but seldom heaven on earth. No, Paradys is a venue of shadows, its own books tell us so. But not now, not for these hours. That is the madness of Paradys. It can be also holy, benign, bountiful, and tender.

Outside a café lit by lanterns, Felion and Smara are randomly but charmingly summoned to join in a bridal feast. Delicious food and drink are given them, gratis, food without stones in it or serpents— and wine, not hemlock.

Later they stray up into a park, and here there is a masquerade. Beings with the heads of beasts and birds, deities, and imps. Smara is given a mask of black feathers tipped with nacre, and Felion a sun mask ruffed with gold. They discover that though they cannot read as yet the writing of Paradis, they know its dances, as if taught in childhood.

All night they drink and dance, and later, under a panther black cedar tree, they kiss like the lovers they wish to become, timidly, sensually, carelessly, caressing each others hearts in surprise.

"We can stay here now," he says.

But Smara is abruptly startled. Perhaps the nightingale singing in the tree has interrupted her thoughts.

"But—not yet."

"Why not? What do we leave behind?"

"We must go back, one last time."

"Why?" he says. "Why?"

"I don't know. But don't you feel we must?"

"Yes. I feel it."

"How can we live there?" she says.

"This City takes care of us."

"Tonight it has," she says. "But will it, afterwards?"

They stare across the park, from whose grassy floor one or two absorbing graves rear up their slabs. (Those of whom Paradis has not taken care?)

"Our uncle," Felion says, "trusted himself to this City. I think, in more than one time. He gave himself to it. Let it be cruel, and kind to him. As it wanted."

Smara sat up. She shivered. "I want to go back."

"To what?"

"We were born there."

"All right. Yes. We must."

They left their masks lying, the bird and the sun. There on the grass among the graves.

It was cold before the dawn, the stars were going out.

"Look," he said, "down there, there's the bitch's street after all. Do you see?"

Smara frowned.

They did not, now, touch at all.

On the grass a cloud had formed, showing them, like a temptation, the way back into hell. But they knew hell. They had got used to hell. They went into the cloud.

The labyrinth was freezing and both of them ran through it.

It took a long time, it seemed like hours, to reach the oval heart. And there, panting and dismayed, they halted.

"Has it gone?"

"The ice bird? No, still there."

"I don't mind. It's nothing."

They stood on the glacial floor and he let the guttering torch droop.

"I know how we can be safe in the other City," he said. "We're the heirs of our uncle. And so is she, this artist. We must kill her, Smara. Then we'll have her place."

"Yes," Smara said. It had seemed to her they would never kill again. But she had been in error. "We'll poison her," Smara said, deciding.

Through the labyrinth something roared, and sighed.

They went slowly now, Smara walking just behind Felion. Not careful, not afraid. They were exhausted. The banquet, after starvation, had been too much, for there are those who have died from something like that.

TEN

Paradis

What's the use of worrying?
It never was worthwhile,
So, pack up your troubles in your old kit-bag,
And smile, smile, smile.

George Asaf

Brassy chrysanthemums were bursting from the flower bed. Black
ivy had climbed the pedestal of the Medusa, but not reached, or
had avoided, the neck and straining mouth, the protruding tongue
of stone, and the petrified snakes.

Thomas the Warrior was tying up flowers to sticks.

Leocadia stood over him. Suddenly, intrusively, he reminded her
of her infantile memory of her Uncle Michelot.

"On your feet," she said briskly. "Soldier."

And Thomas rose, and stood to a stooped, cramped attention, his
chin raised, hands quivering.

"Madame."

"I want a report, Thomas."

"Yes, madame. The chemical attack is over. The losses were
slight. The suits held up."

Leocadia raised her brows. Chemical weapons were illegal.
Where had they been used and what was he recalling? But it was
not this past that mattered. Perhaps he was trying to sidetrack her.

"That's good. Now tell me about the asylum."

Thomas relaxed a little, and looked down at her.

"When I was very young," said Thomas, "a child was eaten alive
in the zoo, by a tiger. No one knew how the tiger escaped. Its bars,

they said, seemed to melt. It was supposedly destroyed, but not in fact. Someone took it away, it lived in a private house. God knows what meat they fed it. Children, perhaps."

"That's marvelous, but not what I asked you, soldier."

"I am," said Thomas, "a voluntary patient. This is my cage, but I don't mind it. I need a cage. I went mad in the service of my country."

(Oh! Uncle!)

"But *are* you mad?"

"Yes. I have a paper to prove it."

"And I'm mad too, am I?"

"Don't you have a paper?" asked Thomas. "You should ask for one. Then you know where you are."

"I know where I am. In the madhouse."

"Not at all. And anyway, that doesn't make you, madame, a correct candidate. Although you may be," Thomas amended, respectfully.

"I believed you thought I was."

"Well, madame, my opinions alter. Part of my condition, of course. Everything does change, here."

"Yes?" Leocadia scented some element of interest, tart as the tang of citrus zest.

"The buildings, for example," said Thomas the Warrior, "move. As the continents do. Slowly. But now in one direction, now another. The hothouse, for example. I recall it was farther off." He indicated the elder asylum. "Gradually, it crept this way. Perhaps to evade capture."

"Capture by what?"

"Who knows?" asked Thomas.

She saw suddenly through him, how he had been young once. And had he ever been a tiger of a man?

"Tell me about," said Leocadia, "the gin bottles. The brown glass ones with the penguin on the label."

Thomas smiled. His teeth were good.

"Penguin Gin," said Thomas. "It's an old rhyme. A corruption of the original slogan of advertising."

"And how does it go?"

"Penguin Gin, Penguin Gin, drink it up, it'll do you in."

"Ah," said Leocadia softly. "And did it?"

"I expect so. Poisonous, apparently. Lead and copper in the

pipes, if such there are in the making of gin. Modern gin is completely wholesome and without additives."

Leocadia said, at her sweetest, "So it poisoned them."

"Oh, there was a story I read once," said Thomas, untying a flower from a stick. The stick but not the flower fell down. "An actor, quite famous, from the era of the gin. His name—Martin. He visited the asylum and charmed the patients with recitals from the plays of the great. But later his brain was curdled from the experience. He began to drink gin in low dives of the slums over the river. One evening he died, in a shocking way." Thomas did not look shocked. Nor did he elaborate. He retied the flower to another stick, and breaking the stick that had fallen, he tossed it over the lawn. Then checked. "I always forget. My dog grew old. Have you ever kept pets, madame?"

"Animals are too good for me," said Leocadia.

Thomas seemed pleased by her reply.

He said, "Johanos Martin was killed by Penguin Gin."

Leocadia said, "You're a mine of information today, Thomas. Tell me some more."

"Today I am," said Thomas the Warrior. He pointed at the Medusa's head. "That was a statue of Madness, once. It crawled or hopped here from the old asylum. I found it in the flower bed one morning. The dew was on it."

"Oh, the dew," said Leocadia. "I've not seen it often. And the leaves are falling now. Will there be snow?"

Thomas stared at her, and through her, and away to his chemical battleground which ought never to have been.

"I remember black snow," said Thomas. "Go away. Our conversation is over."

Leocadia said, "Just one further thing. What do you know about the doctors? What can you say about them?"

"Enemies," said Thomas, "who are friends."

"Van Orles," said Leocadia, with distaste.

Thomas turned and walked off along the lawn. The spider man was coming from the other direction, and pawed at Thomas, murmuring he had a good color.

She felt a momentary great loss.

Why had she not thought to paint Thomas, or the head of the Medusa which was not. It was too late now.

*   *   *

She returned uneasily to her room, but her paint had not been removed, her brushes lay where she had left them, and the dangerous bottle, now associated properly with death. The wall of nascent images had not been touched either, yet she was dissatisfied with it and might wish to make changes. (Suitable to the changeable asylum?)

Then again, it was a risk to attempt anything, until she had dealt with her enemy-friend, Van Orles.

Leocadia went to the refrigerator and opened it. Cold.

Leocadia used the button to summon the attendant.

The girl—or one of the girls who all looked the same—arrived.

"I said, I must see the doctors."

"They are so *busy,* mademoiselle."

"I must have Van Orles. It's urgent. It must be Van Orles."

The maid considered her, then went out.

Leocadia drank the pure, cold vodka.

Then she took off her clothes and donned the cream silk housedress.

If parts of the old asylum moved, then too the Residence would move, sliding bits of itself surreptitiously in among the ancient buildings. And the old asylum slunk up over the new, covering it like a rampant animal.

Leocadia left the neck of the dress loose. She brushed her hair viciously. But then there was a noise at the door. She laid down the brush. Her face was smooth as an egg.

Van Orles came in, shut the door. He was all alone, as before, pale and puffy and agitated, trying to be bold and lofty. The warning light around him was like a dry white neon.

"Now, now," he greeted her. He sounded more silly than she had ever heard, like a caricature of himself. He did not light his pipe. He glared, and Leocadia laughed. At that, he backed away. "No violence!" he squawked. "I have warned them, you may be out of control. Someone will come with an injection."

"And spoil our fun?" asked Leocadia.

Van Orles' silly face became a pudding of startlement.

"At least," she said, "you came back alone. I expected you days ago. What a man. What a tease."

Van Orles looked uncertain. He blinked.

"You were unhelpful," he said, "contrasuggestive, previously. You misunderstood my intention and became hysterical."

"I understood everything," said Leocadia. "It was you who made the mistake. Letting me chase you off, when all it required was a little strength. A little manly firmness."

"Your meaning?" demanded Van Orles. His voice was indeed stronger. He sat down on the couch, took out the pipe, and began to toy with it.

"Why should I explain? Are you simple?"

"Be more respectful, Leocadia. In my position—"

"Oh, hush. Such nonsense. Your position is, you're a man, and I am a woman. Do you agree?"

Van Orles assented.

"I was—playful," said Leocadia, sadly, "and you took fright and ran away. He will return, I thought, sweeping all before him. What did you do? You stole my canvases."

"I—"

"Naughty man."

Leocadia offered the unsuspecting Van Orles a grin she had seen displayed in the painting of a famous whore of bygone times. To her irritated unsurprise, Van Orles mellowed immediately, and smiled upon her. What a fool, there in his orb of almost blinding, radioactive light, the light that showed her where the danger was, brighter by the second.

I shall try to see him, she thought, *as a pie with legs and a head.* Just so she would have painted him, if she had been forced to paint him.

"I meant to make a miniature of you," she said. "I meant to paint it on my thumbnail."

Van Orles sniggered.

"What a woman you are, Leocadia."

"Instead I have to paint penguins on the walls. Will it be allowed?"

"Whatever you want, dear Leocadia." Van Orles patted the couch. He slipped the pipe lasciviously into his pocket. "Let me take your pulse."

"Once you brought me a clockwork cat," said Leocadia. "And a fruit that bled."

"Did I, dear Leocadia?"

"Then you won't tell me why."

"Oh, Saume," said Van Orles, "his little experiments. But truly. I don't recall a fruit that—bled, you say?"

Leocadia allowed a button of her cream silk bodice to come undone. Van Orles was riveted.

"My pulse as yours," said Leocadia, "keeps temperate time."

Another button.

"My pulse," said Van Orles, grinning now like the whore, "is quite fast, Leocadia."

And another button. Van Orles puffed, without aid from the pipe. His small eyes bulged.

Leocadia let slip the silk, inch by inch, along the contour of her breast. She waited, and Van Orles made a tiny sound. Then the silk slid over and the globe of whiteness appeared entire, round and pointed too, with its tawny nipple like a sweet or nut.

Leocadia cupped her breast in one hand.

"Do you think," she asked, "I'm losing my looks?"

"Oh—Leocadia—"

Van Orles got up like a stuffed chair on two legs and blundered toward her.

She allowed him to catch her, to rub his face into her naked breast and rub at the other with his hand. In her turn she caught deftly at the fuming doctor. Through the material of his clothes, the familiar bulge amused her experienced fingers.

Van Orles writhed in her grasp. "Ah—no, Leocadia—"

"And here is the other breast, not a stitch on it. And what is here. Look. My legs are long, don't you think? I've been told they are. And white. But all this bad black hair . . ."

"Ah—Leocadia—I can't—"

"I can feel you moving. What a strong man. You can't resist me, can you?"

Van Orles struggled now, but Leocadia held him firmly in her clever hand, caressing, goading. He stared down between them at her loins, screwed up his eyes, and made a spluttering noise.

"Alas," said Leocadia.

In horror now, Van Orles peered down at the wetness spread upon his upholstery.

"Such is your effect—er—this is—I—" Gravely embarrassed, annoyed, cheated, and overheated, he limped toward her bathroom. "Excuse me."

Leocadia wiped her hands with turpentine and did up her dress.

When Van Orles emerged he was in a worse state, the wet patch now a soaking extravagant monument to vast incontinence of apparently every sort.

"Hurry and hide, before anyone sees," said Leocadia. "If you were noted in your present state—"

"But I—"

"I'm afraid," said Leocadia, "you do look such a sight."

Van Orles' face was now florid. He perambulated about the room in total confusion, staring at things wildly as if they might assist him. Reaching the door he flung himself on it and bolted out.

Leocadia glanced at the wall of ice crags, the dark glimmer of the penguin.

Had she shamed Van Orles sufficiently to safeguard her work?

She walked to the wall, and taking up her brush, loaded it with whiteness whiter than a breast. She was exhilarated. She smiled in a painful rictus, and created mountains.

During the night, Leocadia dreamed that Asra, her hair full of bleeding orange paint, stepped out of the refrigerator. Nothing else happened in the dream, but the next morning, a visitor was shown into Leocadia's room. It was Nanice, her ugly cousin, the inheritrix who had ousted her, put her into the madhouse, *cunning* ugly Nanice, who had had Asra murdered.

Nanice was a picture.

Not that she had grown beautiful, but someone had dressed her as though she might be. Her lusterless hair had been permitted to grow and it had been curled. She had put on a long "artistic" frock, patterned stockings, and unusual shoes. From her left ear dangled a second ear, made of silver, from which, in turn, hung a single polished diamond. Nanice spread her hands in a theatrical way. On her fingers were silver rings shaped like fingers wearing rings.

"How are you?" asked Nanice, beaming.

"Not dead yet. My apologies."

"Always so tragic," said Nanice. "I can't stay long. It was my duty to see you. I've tried before, but they said you were violent. But here I am. Though my friend is below. *She* hates to wait."

Leocadia deduced that Nanice was implying her friend was a female of the intimate sort.

"Art," said Nanice, savoring, "is very freeing. I understand you now so much better." And she removed from her bag a flask, and drained it. Nanice hiccuped.

"And what do you want?"

"To show you how well I am," said Nanice promptly, like a precocious child—and with such a true and perfect malice that it was both naïve and blameless.

"Yes, you're well. But who runs the firm of assassins you hired to dispose of Asra?"

Nanice blushed. She said, "How can you speak so lightly of that terrible crime?" She added, "Artistic license can only go so far."

"It was clever of you," said Leocadia, "in a filthy, muddled way. And then, did you wait in the street until Pir and Jacqueline and the others had broken down the door? How much were *they* paid?"

Nanice flounced and the silver earring danced. "Your horrible uncouth friends burst in your door for their own edification. Pir was howling that you ruined his dinner, and that woman Jacqueline said you had run out with a knife in your hand and must be stopped. They hated you, and were impossibly drunk—drunk in the wrong way. They're vandals. But yes, we were on the street, Monsieur Saume and I. I told you, you were being watched. I too was afraid for you." For a moment, Nanice looked her old pious self. Then she smiled, kindly.

Leocadia cackled.

Nanice said, with the air of a canny child changing the subject tactfully, "Robert has been sick in your studio. Robert is always sick, isn't he?"

Leocadia felt a dim rush of fury, but she held herself against it and it sank.

"I have an urge," she said, "to pull off your ear."

"Isn't it wonderful? This jewelry is very fashionable." Nanice was not ruffled. She said, determinedly, "It was such a pity Robert was sick in the studio. I've begun to paint there."

Leocadia now felt wooden, almost lifeless. She had never fainted, but perhaps this was what the sufferer experienced in the instants before awareness went out. Hollow, adrift yet fixed, immutable and flowing. She could not explain this. She said, stiffly, "I suppose you paint little images of pretty ladies you think are yourself."

"Oh no. Not at all. I'm painting a woman with the head of an elk, riding on a horse on wheels."

Nanice did not, as she had vowed, stay long. Her visit had been improbable, as if maybe the friend-enemy doctors had requested her to come: one more test. Or—and for a minute or so after the visit, Leocadia seriously considered this—had she hallucinated Nanice? But would a mad woman conjure something so trite?

Yet the creature who was Nanice was no longer precisely trite. Nanice had taken over the role that Leocadia had played so well and so diligently for thirty years, in the City of Paradis: The bad woman, the eccentric, drinking artist.

Leocadia sat on her couch, turning her brushes in her fingers.

On the wall the penguin stood amid the snow, large and three-dimensional.

Leocadia thought about Van Orles coming stupidly outside her body, and the warning light, which had faded as he rushed out of the door. She thought of Thomas, who had begun to look so like Michelot, her uncle, who had been kind to her. And of Asra, of course of Asra, whom she had never really liked.

But Nanice had taken Leocadia's life from her, her persona, her obligations of thought and deed. Her memories? And if Nanice had done that, was Leocadia relieved of Leocadia? No more duties to Leocadia. Leocadia, like a bundle of heavy clothes, rolled up and packed away.

Who am I?

She, whoever she was, rose and went to the refrigerator and took out the tall bottle of vodka. Then, with a sigh, she put it back. She did not really want it. She did not have to drink it.

Who *was* she now?

Strange, she must still paint. The painting on the wall drew her like a window full of light and air. Perhaps, then, like Mademoiselle Varc, and Thomas, she was now a conduit for the madhouse. Whoever she was, she smiled at that. And anointed her brush.

ELEVEN

Paradys

Penguin Gin, Penguin Gin,
Drink it up, it'll do you in.

Popular corruption
of an advertising slogan

At the Cockcrow Inn, the blackish scum of the alleys had risen to
the surface. Outside, the hovels of Paradys clung and clustered to
the rainy bank, dark mounds with slitted, small, dull eyes. The
interior of the tavern was raucously alight with oil lamps and thick
with the smoke of pipes and the foulest cigars. When the tall man
entered, heads lifted up into the avaricious glow. They knew him,
he had come in before, several nights now. They knew him also as a
confidence trickster, a deceiver like themselves, but honored in his
profession, as they were not. An actor.

He had not spoken to any of them. Those few who had recognized him had informed the rest. This did not make them like him,
or his silence.

When the bar girl had initially told him, pertly, there was no
brandy, but only the popular drink, raw gin and sugar, he had
taken that. He drank a great deal, and when he was drunk, sitting
in his corner, he had muttered things from plays.

Citalbo the poet had once drunk at this inn. It was an old inn,
and had had other names.

Perhaps Johanos Martin had been curious about the madman
who had given line for line to him. Perhaps he had meant to visit
the inn only to see if some essence of Citalbo, or of Citalbo's ultimate fate, had lingered there. Or maybe Citalbo had put a spell of

magic upon Martin that had driven the actor down into the inn as another might be sent into Tartarus.

On this sixth night of Johanos Martin's appearance, two of the other deceivers got up from their places and went and sat with him.

"You're the great actor, aren't you? Martin, of the Tragedy."

They spoke of it as if it were a sort of jest, something he might laugh at. But Johanos the priest looked down upon them from the high altar of lamplight and gin and said calmly, "I am Martin."

"Well met," said the bigger of the deceivers, a robber who had once slit throats as regularly as two a night. "Allow us to buy you another drink, monsieur."

"Very well," said Martin. "But what do you want?"

"Oh, the pleasure of your company, monsieur, before we go off on our evening's labors." And with a whistle the cutthroat summoned the bar girl, and bought from her a brown bottle with a penguin on its label. "The best drink in Paradys. This will add fire to your turns on the boards."

"He doesn't lack fire," said the other man, who was only a runner for the squadrons of robbers, capable enough with a club, but mostly good at racing the alleys and climbing up to roofs. "No, it'll cool him, this will. Mixed with snow, this beverage is, and hence the label of ice and freeze."

But Martin was not interested in the bottle. Not yet—he would come to be. Now only the contents had his attention.

They saw to the drink for him themselves, and the runner stirred in sugar.

Then all three drank.

The eyes of Johanos Martin were as ever cold and clear and far away, yet he did betray now a slight nervousness. He said, presently, "You gentlemen are generous. But I hope you don't believe you can rob me. I'm not such a fool I brought any valuables into these slums."

"Rob you? Why, monsieur, what do you take us for?"

Martin smiled faintly.

"This inn," added the big man, "is a kind of fellowship. You're safe enough here. Although, I might say, your greatcoat would be worth a little trouble to one or two, if they were to catch you before you reached the bridge."

"Are you threatening me?"

"Indeed not, monsieur. In fact, since you're seen drinking with us, I think you can be easy on your way."

"*He* is the important man," said the runner, indicating the cutthroat. "Like yourself, monsieur. A star in the dark."

"Oh, yes," said Martin, so disdainfully his companions laughed.

And then Martin made a slight move, as if to get up, and a third man who had come into the corner from another table slapped him on the shoulder.

"We like you, monsieur," said the cutthroat. "Don't go. Have some more gin, and then do us a recitation from one of your plays."

Johanos Martin had already been fairly drunk when they first approached him. (And afterward it was speculated upon that he might have been insane, that the jaunt to the asylum had sent him so, or why else had he risked his person in this sink?)

Martin said, "If you wish."

And possibly he was willing to perform, unfed, for a table of creatures such as these, where he would not for the supper tables of the upper City.

But it did not come to reciting. For something in the gin thickened Martin's tongue, as his other tipples had not. Thickened his tongue, and paved his brain with luminous crystal thought that told him he was not in jeopardy, just as all men know they can never die.

Near midnight, they led him out, the cutthroat and the runner and the robber, and two or three others, and together they went along the worm trails of the low bank, through places very old, built over again and again, like some terrible painting that could never be finished.

It was winter, and cold. Above, only occasionally hindered by lamps, the stars were pocks of snow in the sky, the footprints of something, going somewhere. But Johanos Martin did not look at these. He was a great actor but he had no true spirit. Besides, he could not, after all the gin, properly see.

They led him into a house above a coil of the river.

It had not been planned, at least, not in their conscious brains. They let him lie down on a bed, and then they ripped off his precious coat, and then they tied him to the iron bed frame.

When they took from him other clothes, they found his body was pale and hard, in better condition than their own, from his exertions on the stage.

Although drunk, he cried out when, one by one, they invaded him.

In prisons, orphanages, aboard ships, in gloomy watches of the soul, they had found out this means of sodomy, which now they brought and worked out upon Johanos Martin. They raped him many times. Without a single kiss.

And finally it was the runner who thrust into Martin's body the empty gin bottle. Who worked with that upon him.

Inside the anus of the helpless man the four-sided glass neck shattered. (Normally, only orgasm would be sufficiently strong to break such glass.)

Much later, after the deceivers had left him, he was found. And thus, later still, five days later, in a paupers' hospital, Johanos Martin died of a bottle of Penguin Gin. The death was disgraceful, and hushed up.

No last words, or quotations, remained, for in a delirium of agony, such things did not arise.

No one mourned him in particular, yet the spectators of the City did so, for he had held many in thrall that he had not met. The love of strangers.

All that escaped was the rumor he had died of drink.

They did not mind that. It was romantic, tragic: usual.

Hilde woke, weeping in the darkness. Hearing her, some of the others began to cry, and the woman who made sounds made them, over and over, like a bell.

Judit came to Hilde across the moonless black.

"You must be brave. One day, we'll be free. We will go to my country. Or into the heaven of snow, Penguinia. For that is the land's name. Yes, I asked Maque. Don't you recall?"

It was winter, and the room was icy. Hearing Judit's voice, the women whispered and were mute.

"Think of the warm snow," said Judit, "warm as feathers. And the sweet wine."

"I'll never see it," said Hilde.

Judit touched her gently, her head, her neck, her shoulders and hands, Hilde's stomach. There, Judit hesitated.

Like all the beings of the madhouse, Hilde was ferociously undernourished, and she had become very thin. Her hair they had let grow, but it was not as strong as it had been, not springing or bright. The woman Moule had said she doubted it would be worth trying to sell Hilde's second crop of hair. Hilde's belly, where Judit's hands had paused, was hard and round, like the gut of a terrible hunger.

The warders had not noticed, for they did not investigate their charges once novelty wore off, and Hilde, so slight, looked only swollen in the way of malnutrition. But to Judit's fingers, the fact of this pathetic taut belly now became apparent.

Judit, who had been a whore, sat back in queenly stillness. Within the black, Judit closed her beautiful eyes.

"We must prepare."

She bowed her head in a gesture of acceptance and mourning.

Hilde said again, "I'll never see the Penguin Land. The Penguinia. Never. It isn't real."

"Yes. And you will see it, child. Before I do. Penguinia is the country of joy that lies behind this place of pain."

Far off, from the men's dormitory, came the lonely hyena calling of despair.

It was not true that Maque had named the Penguin Land. Judit had done that. After the day the actors came to look at them, Maque had been punished in various ways, and he had grown silent. He did not climb on top of the hill of furniture, and one morning the warders dismantled it. They threw the old chairs out into a yard of the asylum.

Citalbo had become quiescent too, and no longer wrote his snatches of verse. The noise from the male dormitory reminded Judit of these silences.

While inside Hilde, a bud had formed, even as the hair grew from her shaven skull. After a few weeks, Marie Tante and Bettile had ceased fastening Hilde into the mad-shirt. As well, for otherwise, they might, even they, have seen.

But the child in Hilde's womb was without quickness. Judit had felt such things before, in her previous existence.

So she prepared, not for the arrival of life, but the advent of death.

Hilde Koster, in the madhouse, carried the dead child of dead Johanos Martin for a little more than five months. Any symptoms of her pregnancy she mistook easily for the constant malaise due to ill treatment, and the minor poisonings to which the inmates of hell were subjected, the lack of any care. And Hilde, who had once been "Little Hilde," was ignorant of biological fact.

So she walked about in the straw of the white chambers, and sometimes in the stone court of exercise, and she slept in the room of the moon, stunned by the horrible cold, a dummy of flesh closed tight around this small lump of mortality.

At the beginning of the sixth month, about fifty days after Martin's death in the paupers' hospital, an incredible quiet sank on the asylum.

The warders prowled the rooms, sometimes slashing at the mad people with their sticks.

"What are they up to?"

Even the ones who crawled in circles or beat at flies did so in utter noiselessness.

Into the yard had been shunted a few of the men and most of the women, among them Judit and Hilde.

The day was frigid, like gray quartz, and up into it the biscuity walls rose, gray also in the stasis of the light. Hilde's ruined hair was like a beacon, the only brilliant thing visible, a drop of autumn sun, the splash of a summer fruit. But under the trails of this hair Hilde was a white shivering Madonna of death, who suddenly dropped down, her mouth shaping into the grimace of a mask, a shock too vast for sound.

Figures of ice, the other women stood about, a chorus in a play without words, and without motion.

"Damn the pigs, why don't they make a noise?" demanded Bettile. "Go over, Marie, and hit one of the bitches. Pull that fat one's hair."

The air was stony and silence hurt their ears.

Bettile took a step toward the group of women. And at this instant Hilde screamed in agony.

"Ah, there goes one. Again, again, you slut. Let's hear you!" cried Moule.

And as all the women began to shriek, and inside the block the men yowled like dogs, the warders shook themselves and passed back and forth the brown bottle that only a shameful convulsion could shatter.

Like a hedge, the mad women solidified around Hilde on the ground, and unseen, Judit kneeled by her.

There was no time for Hilde to question or protest. Death broke from her in a shattering spasm of water, and of blood.

Hilde screamed, and the women, her chorus, screamed.

The wardresses congratulated them. They smote one or two across the legs. These women skipped and grunted, and then resumed their outcry.

"Old Volpe will hear," said Moule, with satisfaction.

They were tickled.

If Volpe heard, up in his apartment on his country estate, he pretended to himself that these were the cries of winter geese blown inland from the river miles away.

Something tiny and dreadful was squeezed from Hilde's broken body, and lay on the stone ground, linked to her by a silvered cord.

It was if her soul had been squashed out in the shape of a monster.

The warders had gone in, it was too cold for them in the yard. The women stared down on the death that had been born of Hilde.

It was a child, a child in parenthesis, not wholly formed. In color —in color it was like the skin of a pumpkin. An orange child, the product of wronged blood or a damaged liver, the product of a flame that had burned out.

Judit took Hilde's hands.

"It's over," said Judit, as in the back streets of her past she had said it to this one or that, silken girls murdered by reproduction, the task devised of a male god, or demon.

Hilde could not speak. Behind her eyes the sea was drawing away. She lay aground upon the beach. Hollow, adrift yet fixed, immutable and flowing.

"Don't be afraid," said Judit. "You ask me where you are going to? Now you'll see Penguinia."

For a second a light lit in the tidal windows of the eyes. Was it so? After this interval of the impossible, the redemption most human things hope for? Then the light flickered and faded. So swiftly, so clumsily and unbelievably, we must leave.

They were all dead now, the father, the mother, and the child of a cursory act one had wrought on the other.

Only the force and sorcery of the appalling event remained, and hovered there like the smolder of the blood, and was breathed in, through lips, through stones.

The women drew away. There was no more they could do. The ghastly orange gnome of the stillborn must be left for the warders to discover and remove, as the corpse of Hilde, the last door of all slammed on her, must be come on and tidied, roughly and with oaths. A piece of earth somewhere on the premises was kept for such debris. Dead lunatics were cast into sacks and so into quicklime, that there should always be space for the next one.

* * *

Outside the walls, about one hundred and thirty meters along the road, and among some desolate somber trees, Tiraud and Desel stood in the dusk before dawn.

Tiraud was grumbling that he had hurt his back, lugging "that bitch." Desel was sullen, in the grip of a sort of agoraphobia, that often came on him when he had to go beyond the asylum precincts.

The burial of the dead female lunatic and her stillborn infant had been gone through on the previous evening. Dr. Volpe had not attended, and it was Desel who spoke the prayer over the dead—which consisted of a drunken burp. The warder had botched up some evidence of the correct event, and then laid the two corpses together in a stout sack. It had been more difficult in earlier years, when Volpe had nerved himself to oversee all obsequies. Frequently then there had been nothing to salvage for the sinister carts that came up the road, with the morning star.

"Here it is now," said Tiraud, as he gave over the gin bottle to Desel, the Penguin of Joy. "Are they going to haggle again? He's lucky to get it. Such a fresh one, and only a girl. And the abortion's grand for study. Some doctor will delight in it."

Such was the security of the house of madness that they had easily been able to carry out the pitiable sack between them. Those that saw knew and approved their errand.

The cart came rolling up the road, a bundle of shadow, the lean horse pulling it, like some medieval image of Death.

But it was a cheery, leering individual who craned down.

"What have you got for me, eh? Something nice?"

"A young girl of fifteen, only a day old. And a premature child of unnatural coloring," said Desel. "Do you want to see?"

"No, I trust you, *gentlemen*. You know there'd be trouble if you lied."

One bag was hoisted up into the cart. Another, lighter, plopped down.

"It's not enough," said Tiraud. "You promised more."

"Ah, but there, you see," said the carter, "you think this is a rare treat for me, this young lady and her calf. But they're harder to dispose of, these oddities. More questions are asked. And some of my clients turn shy. They'll take a strapping great man without a qualm. But a maiden and a monster baby—who can tell? Why, I may have to tip the lot in the river."

"You bloody liar," said Tiraud.

"Don't waste your breath," said Desel. He took the money bag and began to walk up the road toward the loom of the asylum, which, from this juncture, looked like a weird mansion or fortress, probably romantic, in the half-light and mist.

Tiraud made after him, as if afraid to be left alone and standing in the world.

The carter eyed their retreat.

"Mad things," he said to his horse. "Madder than their charges."

As he turned the cart, the sack rattled under the cover. It lay amid sacks of potatoes and swart cabbage, and once he would have taken more care to ensure it was jumbled, the unvegetable death, among his other goods. But this did not matter much now, for the way he went by, into Paradys, was watched by those with whom he was on friendly terms.

It was a winter morning, and the dawn star was very radiant, sending fine shadows away from the standing things of the landscape. A bleak scene, the road and the black trees that periodically flanked it. Here and there a shorn field. Presently there would come gaps where the earth swept down, and the City might be glimpsed, curled around its river and smoking as if deadly on fire. The morning fog preempted the sense of smoke. A silence pushed in against the cart.

"Mad people," said the carter of cabbage and death. "The world's mad. Take me. I could be snoring in bed. Take you, horse, letting me fasten you to this cart."

Something moved in the cart's interior. It might be potatoes tumbling through a sack.

The carter cocked an ear. He knew the noise of potatoes.

"What's that, eh?" He did not look back. In his particular trade, he had heard the stories, the corpse that sat up, perhaps wearing the face of a loved one. But the carter had no loved ones. "Better keep still," he wheedled. "I'm taking you somewhere lovely. I am. To help in the pursuance of knowledge."

There was a sound now like a knife slitting a sack.

The carter mused.

"Just stay quiet," he said.

Then something rose up in the cart, and dislodged the cover. Because the dawn star was behind it, its shadow fell across the carter and his lean horse.

"Christ, now," said the carter.

He turned slowly, and looked back.

As he did so, a darkness fell through the air, and then a pallor, and something stung his cheek. It was a snowflake. And in the cart, on top of the sacks, was a huge rock of a bird, black-caped like a nun, with a breast of ice, and an amber blaze against the blade of its beak, which resembled—or might have been—obsidian.

The carter did not know what this creature was, although he had seen it represented somewhere.

In the silence it towered over him. A smell came from it, the odor of spirits, killingly sweet.

During those moments, before the carter could in any way respond, the reins jerked in his hands—the horse began to run.

As the carter clung to the reins and shouted, the darkness seemed to swirl about his head, and the only picture that was with him was of that stone beak like a dagger plunged between his shoulders. Yet he had no choice but to strive with the running horse.

Snow dashed in his face like pieces of a broken moon, a moon made of dead white flesh.

The horse grew tired suddenly and stopped still, the cart juddering and slewing to a halt behind it. With a loud cry, the carter turned again then, and saw the fearful bird thing had vanished from the cart. There instead strewn on the sacks, were the corpses of the dead girl and a little swathed thing that might have been anything small and once alive.

"Now," said the carter, "now, now, now."

He glanced over from the cart, through the flurry of the snow, and saw a hollow place into which they had almost fallen; the horse had stopped on the very brink. Below was a black pool not much larger than a well.

Touching the dead did not bother him, but now he would rather have not. Even so, it must be seen to. The money was lost, but he had cheated them anyway.

He hauled the girl and her fruit off the cart and flung them over into the hole of water. They went without a note, the water closed, and they might never have been.

When he was a mile farther off, the snow ceased. He gazed back and saw it falling still among the uplands and the raped fields. The trees had the shapes of birds waiting motionless, but for what?

Marie Tante moved with her lamp along a night corridor. She was searching for Moule, who always had gin upon her person. Sometimes Moule would slouch up to the room beside the chamber of the Waterfall, and sit behind the glass partition. Marie Tante had often come this way to find her. There beside the lever they would stare into the dim inverted bathtub, with its hanging serpent and the horror chair beneath.

At the unlighted corridor's end, Marie Tante found that she had lost her way. She was not where she had believed she would be. For years she had come in this direction and by this route. She checked in surprise. Here she was on the other corridor, which led to the little cells where newcomers were confined. How could this have happened?

Marie Tante had no imagination. Cruel things stirred her obscurely, but most of the nooks of her brain were closed up, or vacant. It might have been said she was a being who should never have been allowed to live but rather sent back at once to be refashioned, for her life had never gained anything for her, and to others, often, it had been the cause of atrocious evil, misery, and pain.

Lacking intuition, Marie Tante did not consider that something bizarre had occurred, although she knew she should not be where she was. She did not think anything had misled her, let alone that sections of her plane of existence had *shifted*. No, she merely retraced her steps, and got again onto the path toward the Waterfall.

Then however, as she was turning the corner, her lamp cast up a gigantic shadow on the wall high above her head.

Even Marie Tante was arrested.

She stopped, holding the lamp, and looking.

Then she looked back, over her shoulder.

Far off, at the passage's other end, something moved. How its shadow had come forward, and so through her lamp, was a mystery. No other lights burned in these corridors when they were not in use.

Marie Tante could not be sure what she had seen. She took it for another warder, a tall man, and called. But the shape was gone now and the shadow also.

She went on and opened the door into the room that overlooked the Waterfall.

Something black rose up in a lump from the floor.

Moule balanced in Marie Tante's lamplight, hugging herself, pulling faces. On the ground was a smashed bottle. So much for the gin.

"What's up, you fool?" said Marie Tante.

"Something's out there."

"Yes, old Big Feet wandering about, or that other one, Bettile's fancy."

"Oh yes," said Moule, "oh yes."

"What did you think it was?" demanded Marie Tante, irritated by the lack of drink. She toed the shards. In a pool of liquid, the label floated, sodden.

"Do you remember," said Moule, "when we cut off that girl's hair?"

"What girl?"

"The one who died."

"The ginger slut? What of it? You got your share of the money."

"That baby. It was a strange color. Like her hair, the color."

"Tiraud and Desel will have seen to that."

Moule mumbled. She glanced into the chamber of the Waterfall, and squeaked. "Look, Marie."

Marie Tante looked through the glass, where her lamp vaguely shone, and saw that fluid was running from the hose above the chair.

"You dolt. Why work the lever now?"

"I didn't. See, it's in place."

"Some fault in the apparatus," said Marie Tante. "I'll report it." The smell of the spilled gin was very intense.

"Let's go away," said Moule, spinning about like an unwieldy top. She clutched at the lamp, but Marie Tante kept a firm hold on it.

"It's the drink," said Marie Tante, "it's addled you."

"Oh, it could be. Let's go back, where the others are."

"Yes, they may have some gin."

Moule followed Marie Tante closely as a scared child, along the dubious, quiet, and unlit passageways.

Down in the courtyard, they passed a pile of furniture, wrecked chairs and parts of tables. Marie Tante seemed to remember it had been stacked up elsewhere, but she did not dwell on this, for obviously the pile had been moved.

The night was bitter cold.

"It'll snow," said Moule, staring up at the bright black hardness of the sky.

"So what? We'll keep warm."

The lunatics had been propelled, for the period of the dark, to their segregated dormitories. In one of the annexes off the vacated rooms of straw, the warders had a fire going. Into this area Moule darted and went shivering up to the hearth.

Desel and Tiraud sat among the men, smoking their pipes and gambling with the cards. Some of the wardresses too had a game, but Bettile was making a shawl, working the smoky wool cleverly, with harsh sharp twists. The hands of Bettile, which had inflicted so many blows, so much hurt, which had struck down Hilde when she would not parade before the actors, and later held her while another shaved the girl's scalp, now forced into the shawl some awful psychometry. Only she, on a holiday, could have borne to wear it.

Tiraud got up abruptly. He had been uneasy since this morning's transaction over the sack.

"Ah, he's off to his harlot," said one of the men. "Give Judit my kiss. Tell her I'll be by."

Tiraud spat. "Judit? That vermin. I'm only going to stretch my limbs."

"Don't take cold. The women's pen has ice hung from the windows."

Tiraud was away, removing in turn the lamp Marie Tante had brought in with her.

The room was sunny with firelight, a merry picture, dear friends gathered at a hearth.

There was the drink also. They portioned it out, starving predators with a kill, who must protect each other for the strength of the pack.

The fire described them, their faces and their hands, the angles of their bodies.

And one by one, it described how they flinched and touched at their cheeks or necks, and then gazed up.

A faint whiteness . . . fell softly through the room.

"Snow," said Bettile, shaking it from her shawl. "The roof's leaking. A fine thing."

"How can it leak? There are the rooms above."

The snow fell. It fell thickly now and swiftly. They got up. It sizzled in their fire and in the lamps, which flickered.

Then the snow stopped, and only the wet spots were on them, like the marks of God.

"Volpe must be told. Some crack in the wall—"

Marie Tante took a swig from her mug. The gin was hot and laced with sugar from the can on the table.

Moule crouched over the fire. She was thinking of a sister she hated, who lived north of the City, and how she might go calling on her very soon.

* * *

"Judit, you filthy cow. Open your legs."

The queen of lands beyond Sheba and Babylon lay under Tiraud. Her face of a damask sphinx was exposed to the ceiling of the women's dormitory, and so she saw the snow begin to fall at once. Judit smiled.

"Like it, do you?" said Tiraud. "Dirty whore."

Judit raised her slim hands into the snow, and Tiraud finished in her with a series of unmusical grunts. As he left her, he stood up into the snowstorm.

On all sides the women were sitting up or getting on their feet. They made little noises like birds greeting the morning sun.

"What is it?" said Tiraud. His eyes were wide. He knew perfectly that the snow was falling in the room, out of the ceiling itself.

"Penguinia," said Judit calmly, also getting up, her unclean skirt dropping to hide the vulnerable wound of her body. "The country of ice is coming."

The women were romping now, in the snow, holding out their hands to catch it, rubbing it on their cheeks and eyes. The snow gleamed with its own light, defining the room with a beautiful silver deception, so that the meanness and foulness disappeared, the perspective of pallets and buckets and walls went on forever, becoming hills and distant tumuli. And the women looked young and fresh, lovely, tender.

Tiraud tried to flail the snow away from him like a swarm of wasps. He heard Judit say, "It's warm as roses." He rushed toward the door, grabbing up the lamp, flinging himself outside.

"What is it? It's some trick. Some insane trick of theirs—"

And he heard, from the men's dormitory, a sudden ululation, not the howls of distress or terror that generally went up there, but a full-throated, gladsome baying.

"Desel—" said Tiraud. He ran down the building, down a flight of stairs. A few lamps burned below, and he raced toward the light, for the darkness was not safe.

The snow had not been warm, not to him. He shuddered and sucked his frozen fingers as he ran. Of course, it had only blown in through the broken windows. What was the matter with him? Crazy as the stinking mad people.

He stopped at the bottom of the stairway, amazed at himself. And from the shadow just beyond the lamps, came a statue, walking.

Tiraud identified the creature at once. Laughable and absurd.

And yet. It carried with it the soul of the darkness, and all the fearful majesty of some god of the Egyptian underworld. It was the spirit of the gin bottle, and only through that could Tiraud, ignorant of all things but self, have identified it: The Penguin.

It moved as a penguin moves, in a lurching waddle, but very slowly, ponderously, like a juggernaut of the East, a mechanism that had the power of ambulation. It was seven feet in height, perhaps taller. On its white breast the smudge of foxy color. Its head black as stone, black-eyed, and its beak was made to be a weapon of death.

From the dark it came, bringing the dark with it, and went across the space, not heeding the man who watched it, paralyzed, and away again into shadow.

Tiraud's legs gave way and deposited him on the lowest step. Here he flopped, not able for some while to recollect motion.

Then at last he rose, cuddling the stair rail, and next shot himself staggeringly off into the passage *It* had left alone.

And as he wove and sped, Tiraud screamed. The scream burst from him uncontrollably, like steam from a kettle.

He reached the dayrooms of Madness, screaming like this, and screaming he thrust back among his brothers and sisters, the warders. So, being used to it, and to a particular reply, they took him, beat him, knocked him to the earth.

"What now? Are you cracked like the rubbish upstairs?"

"I saw—" said Tiraud, lying at their feet.

"Saw what?"

They did not seem skeptical, but as if they had anticipated this messenger out of the web of the building.

Yet even now he did not dare to tell the truth. He sat and nursed his knees. "Give me a bloody drink." And then he thought of the image on the bottle and pushed the liquor aside. "Someone's out," said Tiraud. "One of them's escaped. Wandering in the corridors." That was all he could say, to them, and to himself, to justify what he had seen. For what he had seen was not real. Then for a moment, he thought of the dead body in the sack. So he reached for the drink after all.

The warders became ferocious, accusing one another. How had one of the lunatics evaded the nightly shutting-up? (And Tiraud, drinking, realized he had not relocked the women's dormitory. He had left them scampering about there and the door had only to be tried—)

And all at once, miles high it seemed, the bacchante cries of women flew through the upper air of the building and unravelled away.

"The beasts are out—all of them," exclaimed Marie Tante, Her eyes lit, and Bettile put down her shawl.

There, in their cave of firelight, they listened. The vision seemed conjured in the room, the mad people in their white rags, flying along the upper corridors, down the steps, across the yards, and up into the other blocks, figures painted by a strange white light, like the moon, with streaming hair and outstretched arms.

Desel strutted forward.

"Idiots! Some of you—you and you, you three there—go to the men's place and see to them. Use your sticks. And you women, you go after those bitches. You'll be sorry, Tiraud, screwing your brains out on that trollop and forgetting the door. I know. Go and alert Volpe now. Why should *he* sleep, the bastard?"

In his downy bed, within his luxurious flat, Dr. Volpe, full of dinner and brandy, was dreaming.

He performed on the piano to a vast audience, up on a great white stage. He felt his genius flood from him.

But it was very cold. His fingers were losing feeling. They stuck to the keys, burning. It came to him, the piano was made of ice, and the stage also was ice. In horror he stared about him, and found he was adrift on the ice floe in the midst of a coal-black sea by night. And from the sky rang hammering blows.

These blows woke him. He lay huddled, the warmth slipping back into his body, gradually understanding that someone smote on the door. His housekeeper had gone to the City on some errand. He would have to attend to the door himself. And what could it mean, this nocturnal racket, but only trouble?

Still shivering, he lit his lamp, and fumbling himself into his dressing gown, he sought the door.

The warder Desel and some other man stood there.

"The lunatics have escaped, doctor, and are running all over the buildings, perhaps the grounds."

"What?" said Dr. Volpe.

Desel repeated his cryptic news. Volpe sensed, correctly, that even in agitation, Desel drew enjoyment from Volpe's fright.

"They must be caught," said Volpe superfluously. "They may damage things—they may harm themselves."

"The others are going about, doctor, trying to capture the wretches. They will, of course, be as gentle as they can, but restraint or blows are probable."

"No, no," feebly said Volpe.

Desel glowered with authority.

"They're violent. Suppose they get out on the road?"

"Ah . . . yes."

Volpe drew back into the room. He strained his ears but heard nothing at all, not the faintest cry.

Desel said, "We'll inform you, doctor, of events."

"Yes," said Volpe. "Good, trustworthy men. I can leave this—in your hands."

When he had shut them out, Volpe bolted and locked the door. He hurried to the window.

Something pallid flitted among the chestnut trees—or did he imagine it? He was sensitive and now his nerves were bad. He could no longer see anything moving there.

A loud crack caused him to jump. He gazed transfixed at the hothouse. Some panes of glass had given way, he could not see them, yet he felt the hiss of coldness coming in upon the winter fruit.

Because he had been woken, the brandy he had drunk was affecting him uncomfortably. His heart beat in a rattling way in the midst of his frame.

There was an impure and acid smell in the room.

Dr. Volpe turned, tracing the smell at once to the ewer of water standing beside his plants. He went to the ewer, sniffed at it. He recoiled. One of those men must have played a joke on him. It was in bad taste, and besides he could not think how it had been done, since neither of them had entered the room. The ewer, however, was full of their disgusting gin.

Volpe wanted to open the window and pour the muck out but was afraid to. Perhaps the mad people were on the roof and might, somehow, reach down—

And perhaps one of the mad people had got into his apartment as he slept, and contaminated the water.

Volpe was immobilized by terror for some minutes.

Finally, trembling, he lit the other lamps in the room, and then in the bedroom, and armed with the poker from the dead fire, he stole around, parting curtains and peeking into closets.

No one was there, and nothing but the ewer had been disturbed.

A dreadful compulsion made him go at last to the ewer, dip in one finger, and lick it. The flavor was like venom; it made him gag, as he had known it would. He raised the jug and bore it into the bath chamber, pouring it away through the drain of the bath. Then he employed the tap, and from its nozzle ran a stream of stuff that stank just like the gin, that surely *was* gin, although how could it be?

Volpe shut off the tap and panted back into his sitting room.

In the lamplight, the birds' eggs and the growing plants glistened oddly, as if they had been coated with moisture or frost. And on their pins the butterflies flamed, and the remains of the butterfly that had crumbled were like metallic dust.

Reaching the male dormitory, the three men found the door was shut and locked. The calling of the women had faded, and they had seen none of them. Marie Tante and her crew would take care of this.

There was no longer any noise, either, from the male dormitory.

Armed with their sticks, and certain other implements, iron hooks, and so on, the warders decided to go in and effect a lesson on the madmen who had howled of their own volition.

The door was undone.

The long room, substantially exactly the same as that which housed the women of the asylum, was undisturbed. But by their pallets the men stood, every one of them, voiceless and intent, as if ready. Even the worst cases, who seldom kept still even asleep, were poised and altered. The man worried by insects did not hit out at them, the swaying man scarcely moved. On the grinning face of the man who grinned, the pain had been mitigated by a curious attention.

"What's this row, then?" asked one of the warders, irrationally, of the silence, and a couple of others hefted their sticks and hooks.

Thin as the thinnest rope, the mad sailor, Maque, walked forward from his bed place.

"I've sailed the seas," said Maque, "but I never saw the cold country of the snow."

"Shut up, you," said the foremost warder. "Or do you want a bit of this?"

Maque leapt up in the air, straight at the warder. Maque's bony hands and nails like claws tore furrows in the flesh of throat and face. And as the warder raised his stick, shrieking, his fellows roiled forward. But in that moment a colossal sound passed through the building, through atmosphere, through stone, and through every atom in between. It was the resonance of an enormous organ, or perhaps the music of the arctic wind that threaded some hollow pipe of ice floating in eternity.

After the sound, the wind itself rushed across the room. It blasted against the warders and threw them back, and they careered about with their eyes starting, yelling at the cold savagery of it, the sticks and iron ripped from their frozen hands.

Where they fell, the lunatics sprinted by and over them. As if at this signal, the prisoners darted out to freedom.

Of the felled warders, the two that could got up and pursued the madmen, shouting and cursing. One man, whose leg had been snapped, pulled himself along the corridor, begging his comrades not to leave him, but when he reached the turn of the passage a huge shadow went by and the warder buried his head in his arms, gibbering.

Marie Tante, Bettile, and their sisters could not find the madwomen. In small groups, they spread out through the buildings, searching. They too carried lamps and sticks, and a few had brought mad-shirts, in preparation.

From outside the blocks of the asylum, it was possible to see these lamplights passing up and down the windows of the buildings, and now and then over the yards, which gave the bizarre impression that parts of the masonry were shifting about, going from spot to spot, crossing over one another.

Sometimes a shout would echo down the night, but it carried no meaning except alarm or rage.

No snow had fallen on the outer ground, or if it had, it was invisible. Only the great cold was there, and the moonless shine of stars.

In the last block, Dr. Volpe's apartment burned with frantic light. Once or twice he appeared at the window. He had heard a peculiar sound but now believed it was only his overwrought nerves that had caused it, inside his own head.

Small pieces of glass from the hothouse lay on the grass like fragments shed from the duller stars.

* * *

The captives of the asylum strayed down, maybe from force of habit, to the rooms of straw to which they were herded by day. They had never been there in the dark.

Citalbo met Judit, and Maque appeared with blood under his nails. The rest followed them.

Uncoerced, they went into the annex where the warders had been sitting at their fire. This room was warm and magical, and the people called lunatic wandered about in it, examining the things their jailors had left lying, the cards and pipes, and the hideous shawl, which Judit cast suddenly into the flames of the hearth.

They sipped, too, at the abandoned mugs of gin. But their systems had been denied alcohol so long they did not like it, indeed some wept and spat the gin onto the floor.

All about them, the madhouse was rife with searchers and destroyers, but here in this firelit heart they were in sanctuary. Had their warders returned here, they would have found these freed slaves easily. But they did not return. Only darkness and whiteness, with a flash of amber, came and filled the entry.

Then the people were afraid.

But Citalbo said, "No. This is the hour."

And Maque said, "They're mild birds. They don't do harm."

And Judit said, "He's like a king, a great monarch. We must go with him."

And so, as the Penguin moved from the entrance way, they went out, all of them. And in their path, right across the rooms of straw, there was a wall. And on the wall was a painting. It was of ice floes and sheets of ice, and beyond the ice were mountains. A marigold glow hung over it, and there before its face the Penguin was, as if it had been painted too, onto the wall.

"Penguinia," said Judit. "I'll give up my land, to be there."

There are instants of immeasurable beauty. They evolve and are and cannot be argued with.

Out of Penguinia came the organ note that shook the asylum to its roots, and next came the wind of the snow. But it was not cold. It was warm as the fire on the hearth and much, much sweeter. And as this happened, as Penguinia breathed upon them, the wall of the painting opened, and became actual, like the gateway into a garden.

So they saw the soft, warm snows, and the trees blooming up from them with their apricot and orange fruit, and the sun purred on the ice, and a stream bubbled like champagne. Flowers grew in Penguinia, and beyond the slopes of white, a golden sea sparkled.

Some broke away at once and ran and ran through and ran out into the landscape of this country of heaven.

"I dare," said Citalbo. "Let's go there."

And Maque and Judit and Citalbo walked up to the edge of the snow and stepped over among the flowers.

Then the others came after, all of them, the ones who slouched like sad apes, and the ones who shook and the ones who had cried alone in the night for years. And as the soft ground of Penguinia received them, they looked up in wonderment.

Judit bowed to the spirit, the great Penguin, and then alone hastened over the snow toward the sunlit sea, where the seals were diving and descending like mink ribbons.

"Worlds set like suns," Citalbo said, "and rise like suns. That's mathematics."

"There'll be huge white bears," Maque said, "and little white foxes."

"But kind," Citalbo said, "here."

Behind them the rooms of straw had become only a hole of darkness, which was dissolving.

Maque looked back.

Through the aperture, some of the warders appeared. They had blundered into the lower building from the yard. Marie Tante was there, and Tiraud. They gaped at Penguinia.

"Close the gate, quick," said Maque.

On the platelike faces of the warders was a look that had nothing to do with reason or duty. It was a gaze of fury and jealousy, of wicked, blind human bestiality, which had been cheated.

But then the hole back into hell went out, like a momentary flaw in sight. It was gone, and the world was gone, and there was simply *here*, which would be kind.

Only Tiraud ran at the empty space and smashed at it with his stick. Only Tiraud roared.

Marie Tante had already dismissed the mirage. As what? She did not have the wit to specify.

Moule sniveled, thinking she had gone mad.

While all across the buildings of hell, the others bounded up and down, with their lights and instruments of hurt, seeking, stumbling, and in his flat, the collector of murdered birds and butterflies, Dr.

Volpe, tapped at his piano in objectless fear. And the walls and planes, the walks and yards and lawns, slid and shifted this way, that way, and abruptly froze to stillness.

"What's that noise?" said Desel, pausing on a stair.

"I smell gin," said Bettile suspiciously.

Dr. Volpe stared inside the piano lid.

There was a trickling, and then a flow, like a thousand taps. That was all. And then there gushed from every pipe and drain, from every cup and bottle, out of every crevice and pore and tiniest crack, the Wave.

It reeked. It reeked of gin. It was gin.

Iridescent and limitless, it crashed through all the lower chambers, and up all the stairs. It plowed across the rooms like a liquid wind of steel. The lamps sizzled out.

They heard and saw it come, and *smelled* it come. This climax of poisonous despoilment.

There was a handful of seconds, during which not one moved, but everything in them lunged and boiled in an attempt to keep its life. But the very smell of the jolly fluid, on which they had sustained themselves, was vilely overpowering. Tears ruptured from their eyes and nostrils and dribbled, salivating helplessly at the onset of death. For death came, it swept in on them like the tsunami, the tidal breaker of an ocean. The putter-out of light.

Then they screeched. Each and all of them. They had been made one.

Drooling and retching, tears and snot running down their faces, they tried to get away before it, but the Wave caught them, effortless, and swallowed them. They were lifted off their feet, turned over, bobbed up to the very ceilings and peaks and slammed there.

Full. They were filled. Bellies, sinuses, lungs, arteries, blood. Brains. Spasms uncontrollable and useless convulsed bodies, drowning in liquid fires, everyone trying to heave inside out and so expel the invasion. Mindless, soundless sneezing, spewing, acrobatic in the wet globe of rushing spirit. *Drowning*. Gin skins.

They gave up their ghosts through their mouths, and there came then the last squeezed fistful of seconds, during which hallucinations settled on them, devils and nightmares, the beasts of the labyrinth of an alcohol-drenched mind, the children of the Minotaur.

And so Marie Tante was skinned in slices by bald, taloned things, and Moule was choked with skeins of hair, and Bettile beheld swimming toward her the net of her shawl, which tore off her breasts and reached in for her heart, and Tiraud lay on a dissecting table, conscious, while his organs were prized out of him, and Desel was stretched on a rack until he broke. . . . And in his apartment, Dr. Volpe was trying now to burst open his window, and it bit at his hands, and so he witnessed his plants had hold of him like things of the sea, and as they held him the eggs hatched, and out erupted prehistoric birds to peck his eyes and liver, while the butterflies flew in the flood of gin and scratched him with their pins.

When the twenty-one overseers of hell were dead, the Wave sank swiftly down, leaving only its tidemarks on the walls, and here and there a body, stuck against the plaster, or on the stairs, or the floor.

The Wave melted and only the night replaced the Wave. And presently the moon rose over the pristine buildings, and the lawns and the hothouse, which had grown cold. The moon was round, and white as snow.

The penguins waddled and preened on the flowery ice. The people played.

The man who was tormented by insects held out his hands, and the butterflies that now flighted around him sat like fiery papers on his fingers. The man who swayed was dancing. The woman who mourned, sang. The man who grinned was solemn, not a trace of a smile, as he paced beside a small pale fox. Citalbo walked with bears. Maque sailed the golden sea.

On Judit's head was a starry crown.

It was dawn forever. And a day.

TWELVE

Paradise

See, the Minotaur has two daughters; call them
"Left" and "Right." Sometimes.

John Kaüne

"Do you remember our uncle's dog?" Felion asked Smara.

"No," she said. "He can't have had a dog."

"Yes, a feral dog from Clock Tower Hill. It lived with him to a
very old age and died in its sleep."

Smara laughed. "I do remember now. He said it could purr."

They sat facing each other, over the woven carpet they had
brought to sit on. They were at the heart of the ice labyrinth, had
been there most of a day, picnicking on bottles of river water, fried
lentils, and dry bread soaked in wine.

Above, the shadow of the ice bird hung as if against a starry
night. Both of them had noted this. The torch burned steadily. It
did not seem the ice had melted at all.

"When we were born," said Smara, "we were energy. But it became flesh. It became *us*. If we'd died at birth, where would it have
gone?"

"Back into our mother."

"But she might have died too."

"Why do you ask?" he said. "We didn't die."

"I dreamed someone dropped our mother into a well," said
Smara softly.

"She threw herself off a tower."

They drank the water of Lethe, and stared at the patterns in the
carpet.

Each of them recalled the hours in the other City, the amber light, the sun and moon and stars. But all this seemed far off. And what they had to do—that was farther still, perhaps unreachable. Both had killed so often, it was nearly a commonplace, a piece of work that required cleverness, quickness, application, and toil. But simple. Now, eventually, they had arrived at a killing that would be momentous: the murder of their uncle's heir, which would cement their chance in the world beyond the maze.

Sometimes Felion, or Smara, would have got up, but some laxness or nervous gesture of the other's put them back again.

At last he said, "Shall we do it now?" Smara said, "Suppose she isn't there?"

"We must want her to be there. We must want to meet with her. And if she isn't, we must wait in the house, for however long it takes her to come back."

They rose.

Smara wore the earrings Felion had recently brought her, and he the ring she had awarded him.

They had agreed. They would use, since it was the term of poison, the means they found to hand in the artist's studio, for these would surely be unique, unlike anything they had employed ever before.

They left their carpet and their picnic lying, and walked out along the left-hand way, into the labyrinth.

"If we're separated," he said, "we must each try to find the other. By thinking of the other. That seems to be the way. We always do find each other again."

"And we're always parted."

They did not touch, they did not hold hands. They carried nothing with them save the torch.

The labyrinth seemed, now, very silent. No visions had assaulted them when they first came in, and none flowered out on them now. They might have been in an ordinary cold, weird corridor, some vein of their uncle's house, going nowhere very special.

And then they turned a turn and found the exit point before them.

"Can you see anything out there?" Felion asked Smara.

"No," she said, "just darkness."

"Yes, only darkness. No moon. No stars. We'll have to trust it. It seems to demand that. Don't be afraid."

"I'm not," she said. "Only cold."

He put down the torch. They went forward, without faltering, side by side. And side by side they passed through the exit of the labyrinth. And were parted from each other as day from night.

The woman was there. Before him. In the studio. She had her back to him, and she was naked.

Felion kept entirely still.

Overhead was the skylight. Black, moonless. And the lights in the studio were so bright he could not see the stars.

But the woman was clear. Her white body and long fleecy hair.

And as he watched she turned about. She saw him at once, but in a misty way, amused rather than amazed. She was drunk or drugged. In her hand was a tube of orange paint, with which she had been daubing her slim, smooth body, shapes like islands.

"Well, hallo, hallo," she said to Felion. "Have you been hiding here long? Have you enjoyed the show? My, I thought the door was only set to recognize *me*. And all the while she's had another secret lover." The girl paused. "I'm glad I told them all those lies now, about her. About her violence. What a cat. She deserves it." She shook her hair. "But you're a real beauty. Oh, yes. Who are you?"

"Felion," he said.

"Felion. What a pretty sound. And I'm Asra."

"So that's your name," he said.

She wiggled the tube of paint down her skin, leaving a glowing trail like a snake of alien blood.

"Do you like my canvas? It's a new gimmick, edible paint. It tastes of *oranges*—yum. I thought she might like to lick it off. But now that I've seen you, perhaps you'd like to? Just think, if she comes back and finds us together. You know what a beast Leocadia can be." Asra, Felion's uncle's heir, the artist in her studio, dipped the edible paint against, between, her loins, and squeezed. "Won't you try a little?"

Felion moved toward her, and reached on the way the table with its paraphernalia of materials.

Another tube of the orange paint was there.

"And is this edible," he asked, "or toxic?"

"Oh that's the real stuff. No, leave that alone. Look, there's plenty here. Why don't you let me put a little on you?"

Felion left the table, the other tube of toxic paint in his hand. He came up against Asra, against her satin body, smearing it slightly, and then stepped around her, behind her. He slid his left hand about her silky throat and up over her lower face. In a second he had blocked off all her air, and she was kicking and writhing, her feet off the floor. He let her drunkenly struggle for half a minute, not exerting enough force to choke but only enough to stifle.

Then he slapped away his hand from her and pushed instead the opened tube of toxic paint between her lips. As her mouth gaped wide to gasp the air, he compressed the tube strongly.

The finesse of many murders had made him more than competent.

He held her as she convulsed, as he had never held a woman in the death throes of love.

When Asra, his uncle's heir, was dead, he raised her and hung her over the easel in the middle of the room.

He stood a moment, taking in the picture that she made.

Then he walked over against the wall.

"Smara!" he called.

The wall opened, and there, simplistically, was the way back into the ice. Smara must be there. Or she would meet him there, as before.

He glanced behind him, but the studio was already reeling away, swaying and bucking, on a chain of light. He seemed to have lost hold of it, all connection to it. He had a sense of panic—but then he only stepped over into the labyrinth; he had done what he came for. He must find Smara. Then they must return at once, outside the house. They must go back to this City for good, the City of the sun and moon, and nothing would stop it. They could never be separated again.

Even as he emerged into the heart of the ice (so quickly he got to it), Smara ran into the space after him, as if she had only been concealed somewhere in the wall, and it was a game. She was giggling.

"I did it!" she cried. "Without you."

"What did you do?"

"I killed her," said Smara, happily. "And then I came here, to look for you."

Felion said, "Wait. You killed her?"

"I went straight into the studio. The room you described, with the skylight. I think it was afternoon. She was blind drunk, going about in front of a canvas smothered in daubs of paint. There was a bottle of white spirit I knew was poison. I ran at her and tipped half of it down her throat before she realized what was happening."

"But Smara," he said, "*I* killed her."

"You?"

They stood as if frozen in the heart of ice, in the silence, and in the shadow, for neither he nor anything had bothered with the torch, which had gone out. They stood and stared at each other.

"If we both," he said, "killed a woman in that room, which of us killed *her*"?

Smara said quietly, "Or did neither of us kill her?"

"We must go back," he said. But they started together as if magnetized.

And from above came a huge crack of noise, like the thawing of a frozen sky. Stars rained over them, but they were stars of ice.

Felion and Smara looked upward, and framed by a smothered darkness, like Paradise, they saw the bird of ice, a column with a great beaked head, leaning over on them as if it meant to speak. Neither of them uttered a sound. They flung their arms about each other, and through their skulls swirled the images of their lives, bright as sparks, and over these a closing curtain thundered like a wave.

The ice statue crashed directly onto them, crushing their bodies together, so that the bones of each broke through the other's skin and mingled, and next mashing them down deep into the ground surface of muddy glass, from which their picnic had vanished. The bird beak of white obsidian went through their hearts, and pinned them one to the other, and pinned them to the earth. The bulk of the bird thing cracked on them like a boulder, covering them, stoppering them beneath into the floor of the labyrinth.

When the silence came again, it was imperfectly. For it was full of a faint tiny sound, like dripping water. The shadow and the cold wavered and dulled, and a sort of rain began to fall, but there was no one to see or hear it. No one to wonder what it might be. If it was anything at all.

EPILOGUE

Paradis

Boys and girls come out to play,
The moon doth shine as bright as day.

Nursery Rhyme

Between waking and sleeping, twilight illusions would come to her, not really dreams. As she grew older, she liked these times, and sought them out. From them she had garnered much of the material that now she painted, but always the backdrop of these pictures was the same. She had come to love and want to paint the same vision, over and over, only subtly altering it here and there, adding, as years passed, the diamonté trees and glimmering fruit and bonbons, the animals, the ship on the sea, and the dancers on the shore.

There had not been an exhibition of her work for two decades, and *then* they had said, "Leocadia's senile. Does that still happen? Look, how repetitive and trifling."

Nanice's one great masterpiece was still at the academy near the Observatory, the modern building with the dragon of bronze on its roof, and antique graves paving the garden at its foot.

Leocadia would cackle when she thought of Nanice. After all, Leocadia was now ninety years of age, and to cackle, finally, was quite becoming. Her gray hair was still thick, and still kept its obstreperous curl. She wore it loose to her waist. The rest had gone the way of all flesh, shrunken and fallen. And yet a young photographer who had come to visit in the autumn had obviously found her beautiful, not sexually, but spiritually, in her second youth before the coming of age of death.

Leocadia did not miss sex, she had had so much of it—precisely enough, in fact—in her earlier years. Only during her sojourn at the Residence had she been celibate, and that omission had only lasted nine months, the length of a pregnancy.

The scales had dropped from her eyes. And what scales! After she had painted the penguin and the ice floes on the wall. A day, two days, ten, went by, and gradually, softly, it came to her that everything had been a delusion. She discovered her canvases then, stacked up among the books in the alcove library, where she must have placed them, hidden them from herself, pretending that Van Orles had done it as a punishment. Indeed, it was Van Orles who congratulated her on the wall painting. He had followed her work for years, and this, he said, was an honor for them, and a great pleasure, to have an original landscape by Leocadia le Vey to enhance the room. It would be therapeutic for whoever was lucky enough to be put in here.

Van Orles was not ugly. Nor were any of the other doctors. Saume's teeth were even and white, Leibiche did not have pimples, only one coy beauty spot beside his mouth. Duval was extremely, nearly stupidly handsome. What had she been seeing? She asked them.

"Ah, we were your enemies, posing as friends. Beware of Greeks bearing gifts. Your line of defense, mademoiselle, was to remake us as monsters."

When she told Duval she had found him ugly (which she could not resist doing), he blushed, like a plain woman complimented on loveliness. Obviously, no one could ever have said this to him before.

When Leocadia had not drunk anything alcoholic for seventeen days, they urged her to take a little wine. Her system was not ready for such drastic deprivation after the influx that had gone before. So then she had a glass of wine with her dinner, and a little gin in the afternoon. She fancied gin. It was totally pure, colorless, not like the liquid that had been in the mysterious brown bottle.

They were intrigued by the bottle. Sometimes, they said, the Residence guests did find things of historic interest. Did she wish to keep the bottle? Leocadia kept it.

They began to let her go for walks in the countryside, and presently to journey by car to the City. A doctor always went with her. When she could, she chose Van Orles. She had begun to find him very attractive, better than Duval, who was like a classical god, a sweet too pretty to eat. Van Orles was muscular and brawny, with thick dark hair. He did not speak in the peculiar threatening way she had believed, and when they talked, answered her freely, offering his past among a family of cooks, and how he had made his way with difficulty into his profession. No white neon, like a rampant moon, shone around him now, nor did it with the others. She did not know what the light had been, save it was a warning—of her own misjudgment, presumably. She could not be sure how much she had only imagined, although evidently many scenes had not occurred at all. She thought this entertaining rather than unnerving. Perhaps things had taken place on some other plane, in some parallel world. There Van Orles had harassed her, and there she had made a fool of him. But not, certainly, here. Now Leocadia did try to seduce Van Orles. And she began by telling him of the delusion, what she thought she had done, baring her breast and forcing him into a premature ejaculation that had spoilt his trousers. Van Orles lowered his eyes. "Naughty Leocadia," he said. And then, when she kissed him, gently, "You're a wonderful woman, and I'll admit I've had a crush on you for years, before even we met. But how can I now? You've been, and still are, my patient. I'm selfish. I'd lose everything. And you'd only laugh." He did kiss her back. She never forgot his kiss. It was strong, courteous, amorous, frightened. "Of course I'm afraid," he said, "Look what could happen, out in this field." For she had made the car stop on the way to Paradis. She did not do so again.

She briefly hated the City. It looked unfamiliar, as if it had been up to something while she was away.

"For a long while," he said, "you've been out of touch with yourself, and everything."

She insisted she had not killed Asra. But recalling the episodes of accusation swathed in light, she did not think he would say that she had. And he said, "No. Unfortunately the murderer has never been found. But it wasn't ever thought to be you. You seemed to think so, from time to time. But even your cousin, Nanice le Vey, was quite belligerent on the matter of your innocence."

The pastel cravats suited him, mild on his tanned, bold shyness.

She had misinterpreted everything, but something in the painting of the penguin and the snow had released her. Why and how? They spoke to her of projection, of unknown country being the cipher for death and so of rebirth. She knew the moment she had begun to be reborn—or at least the moment of death. Nanice had done that for her, by taking Leocadia's role. They would not admit they had tried to use Nanice as a catalyst, only that she had been an insistent visitor they had at last allowed to call.

Leocadia herself experimented with the others, the bizarre people of the Residence. Mademoiselle Varc had reached the end of her treatment, which she had been receiving for a premature senility. She was now quite sane. Soon she would travel far away. She sat in the summerhouse with the white and cinnamon windows, and held Leocadia's hand. "You were so patient with me. Do you know, I'm a journalist? It's almost a surprise to me, I can tell you. I can't wait to get back, I've missed so much. Thank God, they've made me myself again. And did I call you Lucie? She was a dear child. No, not my friend—my daughter, who died. But yes, there are five others. Each has a different father, and all are fascinating. But there, the proud mother."

Leocadia mentioned the wooden dolls and the amber necklace Mademoiselle Varc had drawn from the rubbish tip in the yards of the old asylum.

"But I believed *you* put them there—for *me*!"

Leocadia said, "Oh. You've found me out."

It was then that truly she began to slot together all the pieces. Having no guide, she did not know for sixty years what they formed.

She only said to Van Orles, then, "The asylum itself is mad."

"What else?" he said.

Thomas the Warrior would no longer speak to her, and perhaps never had. Van Orles explained that Thomas was a war hero from a campaign seldom spoken of, erased from government files. He was almost unreachable, but he feared dogs. He would never reveal why. He also feared high towers, apparently.

The spider man, too, was not as Leocadia had thought him. His odd way of moving was due to a spinal injury that had proved incurable. He was afraid of anyone who walked upright—almost everyone—and Leocadia found that if she sat down immediately he appeared, he would come and talk to her. He was a poet, and the most exquisite phrases poured from his lips. One evening, before the sun had quite gone and they were expected to go back to their rooms, Leocadia lay in his arms under a cedar tree, out of sight of everything but the biscuit blocks of the old madhouse. Nothing happened, but she knew she had made him glad. She knew, greedily, he would put her into a poem.

For by now she was greedy. She ate roast chicken and potatoes with cream, mandarin tarts, orange caviar.

They let her go in the very early spring, before anything but bark was on the trees.

She had by then heard about Nanice.

Leocadia's cousin, who had taken on Leocadia's life, living in Leocadia's house, adorning herself as an artist, painting in the studio, drinking in Leocadia's style. She had been infected, as if the house were full of a plague called Leocadia. Poor Nanice, she had led such an exemplary and careful existence until then, incarcerating Leocadia from moral concern, or was it moral jealousy and wild hunger?

Nanice, in her Leocadia role, was painting in the attic one day, dead drunk. Her works were a disaster, she had no talent, but Nanice had not noticed this. Nor did she notice in her inebriated confusion that the bottle she gripped contained white spirit and not vodka. She had drained it. There was no hint she had intended suicide. Her lover, a young woman of slight mind, had told how Nanice was full of life. By which it was thought she meant full of money.

In the death seizure, however, Nanice fell headlong onto her current canvas, and the resultant chaos, when it was peeled from beneath the corpse, had become a sensation of the City.

It was exhibited at the academy, and popular acclaim kept it there. In its queer and ragged runnels, its smears and gobs of color, Paradis read impassioned and macabre secrets. Dead, Nanice became one of the most famous artists of her era, far eclipsing Leocadia le Vey.

Even so, the house near to the old wall was left vacant, and Leocadia moved back into it, and her inheritance returned to her without hindrance. There had been no plot. Asra's death had driven her out of doors from an already wavering mind. Though why was in some ways a dilemma. Again, sixty years would need to elapse before it would seem that possibly she had had to go mad, had been needed to go mad, in order that she enter the Residence, and there perform the magical spell upon the wall.

Emerging from the asylum was far worse, more uncomfortable than emerging from insanity. Now she must leave her true friends who were not her enemies. She did so. She shut them all out.

She scoured all trace of others from the house. She made it white, with sofas and drapes of snow, carpets of simulated polar bear fur, mirrors like glaciers. Her studio she filled with treated ice sculptures that did not melt, holding ivory daisies, marigolds, lilies, ivy.

It was said in Paradis she was still mad, had got worse.

Although she took lovers and ate dinners and strolled in the City, she closed herself in, every month more and more. She painted huge canvases of a land of ice, with mountains of ice. And as she picked her way across this snowy id, she reached the sea, and there she painted the meeting of a black-haired queen with a young girl who carried in her arms a child. And Leocadia painted also ships with carrot sails, and seals, and dancers, and butterflies. And still, she did not know why.

The photographer who came to Leocadia in what she supposed must be her old age was in love with her painting (like Van Orles— now, alas, long dead) and with a little novel she had published, about a land she called *Penguin*.

They sat in Leocadia's white salon, drinking orange-flower tea and tiny goblets of crystalline gin.

She showed him the brown bottle with the four-sided throat and the label.

"Is it awfully old?" he asked.

"Older than I am."

"Oh," he said, "but you're young."

"It was the time I went mad," she said. "I found it in the grounds of the lunatic asylum."

He said, "You're one of the truly sane."

She showed him the pictures, all the views of *Penguin*, some with proper penguins stamping humorously about the ice. And sometimes there was a tiger-colored moon, very bright.

"Have you heard about the penguin spirit, Koodjanuk?" he said. "I think you must have. The ice peoples invoke him to heal the sick."

"Yes, I must have," said Leocadia. Something clicked loudly inside her skull. One of her elderly bones shifting, perhaps. "Also a vengeful spirit," she said vaguely.

"Maybe all spirits are, if you go against them." He smiled at the penguins, which were small and playful. "And who is this girl—may I ask?—with ginger hair?"

"I saw her once," said Leocadia firmly. "She must have died, because she was a ghost."

And Leocadia thought, *How wise and elegant I've become, with ninety years*. And again, click.

"But here she is too," said the young photographer, "and here, dancing with a young child—it's charming."

"God knows who she is," said Leocadia. She thought, *But I know her really. She's the young virgin at the Sabbat, before the cocks crow. Through her the power comes, to remake things.*

She thought, *And through me. Something I did. I made a world. I gave it life. And the sun and the moon.*

Leocadia dreamed that one day she would be painting among her solid statues of ice and flowers that did not die, and a touch would come on her shoulder, or something harmless would be thrown at her neck. And she would turn to find the path into *Penguin*, which she had earned, and which was, presumably, only the afterlife.

When the photographer went away, bubbling with fizzy youth, to write a whole book about her, Leocadia went up to her studio, unhaunted by the deaths of Nanice and Asra.

She stood among the canvases and considered. Possibly death did not matter. Possibly stupidity and cruelty, banality, and rheumatism (which even the best drugs could not quite dispel) did not count.

What counted, then?

Why, what we want. What we truly desire.

"Write," said Leocadia, "in the great fat tome of time. Real desire, of any sort, is what counts."

And when she was one hundred and five and a half, Leocadia was painting the Penguin Land in her studio, slowly, because her hand was stiff. When in the ice sculpture before her, beyond the picture, she caught an image.

It was of a girl—two girls, but one not long ago a child. And both had marmalade hair.

She heard their laughter like distant bells.

Leocadia imagined that behind her the wall had opened, and there lay heaven, with snow and flowers, a sea of golden wine, a penguin king and a queen in a crown of ice.

If she means it, the minx, she'll throw a snowball at me. Then I'll look round and it will be there, and I can go in.

And Leocadia would be young. And though it might not be forever, it would be, at least, for one long, shining day.

And then the snowball, which was warm as toast, struck her shoulder.